DEAD GUILTY

Michelle Davies

PAN BOOKS

First published 2019 by Pan Books
an imprint of Pan Macmillan
20 New Wharf Road, London N1 9RR
Associated companies throughout the world
www.panmacmillan.com

ISBN 978-1-5098-5687-9

1 3 5 7 9 8 6 4 2

A CIP catalogue record for this book is available from the British Library.

Typeset in Janson Text LT Std 11/14.5pt by
Palimpsest Book Production Ltd, Falkirk, Stirlingshire
Printed and bound by CPI Group (UK) Ltd, Croydon, CR0 4YY

Visit www.panmacmillan.com to read more about all our books
and to buy them. You will also find features, author interviews and
news of any author events, and you can sign up for e-newsletters
so that you're always first to hear about our new releases.

DEAD GUILTY

Michelle Davies has been writing professionally for eighteen years as a journalist for magazines, including on the production desk at *ELLE*, and as Features Editor of *Heat*. Her last staff position before going freelance was Editor-at-Large at *Grazia* magazine and she currently writes for a number of women's magazines and newspaper supplements. She lives in London and juggles writing crime fiction with her freelance journalism and motherhood. *Dead Guilty* is the fourth novel featuring DC Maggie Neville, following *Gone Astray*, *Wrong Place* and *False Witness*.

Also by Michelle Davies

Gone Astray
Wrong Place
False Witness

For Lyndsey and Ruth

1

Tuesday

Philip Pope stood at the end of the bed and surveyed the chaos. A week's worth of his wife's knickers lay strewn across a mound of T-shirts that had slipped from their folds on the journey from drawer to bed, and on top of them was a flip-flop that had lost its mate. Then, jumbled alongside, he counted three dresses in prints his wife loved but were too lurid for his taste, a pair of shorts similarly bright and two pairs of sunglasses minus their cases.

Laid neatly upon his pillow was his own packing: two pairs of cream shorts, both knee-length, two pairs of light-weight stone-coloured trousers, five polo shirts for the daytime, all white, three short-sleeved shirts for evenings, striped, and enough underpants to last the trip.

Missing from both piles were his trunks and his wife's swimsuit. Patricia was insisting there should be no swimming or sunbathing; it would be improper, she argued, no matter how inviting the pool was, or how much they longed to warm themselves beneath the sun's glorious rays. They had an image to project in the coming week and 'carefree tourist' was not it. Philip gazed down at the bed and wondered how the brightly coloured dresses and shorts fitted in with her vision.

The bedroom door swung open and Patricia entered carrying two folded beach towels. He winced as his wife threw them down on the bed with the rest of her stuff. For someone who had spent her entire professional life being orderly and demanding the highest of standards from those she managed, she had all too willingly embraced chaos in retirement. It drove him mad.

'Why haven't you got the suitcases out of the loft yet?' Patricia queried. 'I asked you ages ago.'

Impatience nipped at her words, making them sound brittle and unfriendly. Philip mentally counted to ten as his counsellor had taught him, and his irritation at being nagged had ebbed by the time he reached the end. It's the stress of the occasion making her like this, he told himself. Don't rise to it.

'I'll get them now,' he said. 'I was sorting my clothes out.'

Patricia eyed the neat stack on his pillow.

'Is that all you're taking?'

'What else do I need?'

'You don't want to be photographed wearing the same thing every day.'

'I don't want to be photographed at all, I told you.'

'Oh please, don't start that again,' said Patricia, sweeping across the bedroom to her glass-topped dressing table and picking through the bottles of scents and creams lining the top. Philip resumed his counting as she lobbed her selection onto the bed.

'You know how important it is that we make ourselves

as accessible as possible to the media throughout the holiday.'

'I thought this wasn't a holiday,' said Philip. 'What was it you said? "A holiday implies relaxation and fun and time to gather one's thoughts away from the demands of daily life. This trip will provide none of those things."' He quoted her primly, like the art curator he had once been.

She turned on him, her blue eyes flashing with anger. Forty-five years ago those eyes had stopped Philip's seventeen-year-old self in his tracks outside a Soho coffee bar: Patricia was sitting with her friends, had looked up as he'd passed and had smiled at him – and that was it, he was smitten. Age might've dulled their colour, but his wife's eyes could still pin him to the spot all these years later.

Their daughter's had been the exact same shade.

'You're twisting my words. I know we're not off on our jollies, but you could at least act as though what we're doing out there isn't the worst thing imaginable.'

But in his mind it was.

On the back of the bedroom door, snuggled together on the same hanger for convenience, was a knee-length black dress Patricia had purchased especially for the trip and Philip's most formal suit, dusted free of mothballs. Binding them together at the neck was a loosely knotted black tie. These clothes would go in last, carefully laid out over the shorts and the flip-flops and the bottles of suncream Patricia had bought in bulk from Boots. They were to be worn only once, as they honoured their daughter's memory at the place where her remains were recovered.

'This week is about reminding people that Katy's killer is still at large,' said Patricia.

Philip was suddenly assailed by a memory of the four of them sitting at a table at that lovely Italian restaurant on the sea-front, faces tinged pink from too much sun. It was their first evening in Saros and Katy's boyfriend, Declan, had treated them to champagne and they'd laughed and chatted and marvelled at the view across the bay as the sun languidly melted below the horizon and stars that shimmered like diamonds filled the sky.

It had been the most idyllic holiday destination, until it wasn't.

'I don't think I can go,' he stuttered.

Patricia looked across at him and for a fleeting moment he saw in her expression the sorrow she'd held at bay for the past ten years by focusing every ounce of her energy on finding whoever had murdered their daughter. The campaign had distracted her from her grief and gave her purpose, but privately Philip wished she would, just occasionally, give in to tears and in doing so let him comfort her. Perhaps then she might do the same to him.

His wife gathered herself, pushing her desolation back down from wherever it had sprung.

'Don't be silly, it's all arranged,' she said briskly. 'We can't cancel now. What would the police think after all the fuss we made?'

She had a point. Once they – well, Patricia – had decided to go ahead with the trip and memorial service, she'd begun pressuring the Met to send officers to join them. Katy's case was still open, under the name Operation Pivot, and Patricia had argued that a British police presence was needed on the island for the anniversary to remind everyone, particularly the Majorcan police, that the search for the murderer was still ongoing. The Met had eventually conceded – possibly, Philip suspected, to shut Patricia up and avoid any more negative press.

Indeed, Philip was quite certain Operation Pivot only continued *because* of Patricia and her previous standing as one of the highest-ranking female officers in the Met. She had been a chief superintendent in line to be made a borough commander when Katy was murdered on their family holiday in June 2009. Returning after an extended period of compassionate leave, she found she couldn't pretend to care about solving other crimes while their daughter's death remained a mystery, and had accepted early retirement.

Since then she'd devoted all her time to keeping Katy in the public consciousness with endless appeals, headline-grabbing speculative claims about who might be responsible and fierce, relentless criticism of the joint investigation by British and Majorcan police for failing to meet her exacting investigative standards.

However, in spite of her exhaustive efforts, the ranks of Operation Pivot had dwindled from the dozens of officers deployed at the start. Now the team was down to a detective chief inspector, two lower-ranking detectives and a family liaison officer, the most recent of whom had been redeployed elsewhere two weeks ago because Patricia had objected to how overfamiliar she'd become. A new one had yet to be appointed and it was looking unlikely that would happen before the trip, much to her annoyance.

'Have you dug your passport out?' she asked, the change in subject signalling that, for her, the matter of Philip not going to Majorca was now resolved. 'Put it on the bed with mine.'

With a resigned sigh, he began rooting around in his bedside table for it. The landline phone on Patricia's side started to ring and she snatched up the receiver.

'The Pope residence,' she said officiously.

Philip paid no attention to the conversation until his wife remarked, 'This is rather out of the blue. Why now, Declan?'

'Declan Morris?' he hissed at her, seeking confirmation it was indeed Katy's former boyfriend, whom they hadn't spoken to in eight years. The same man who had, at one point, been the police's prime suspect in their daughter's murder.

Patricia nodded vehemently.

She listened for a few moments then replied in a faltering voice, 'Are you sure? Could it be someone playing a prank?'

Another pause.

'Fine. Yes, we shall both be here. See you shortly.'

She hung up and turned to her husband, her shock palpable.

'He's coming round now.'

'Whatever for?'

'He read about the memorial on my blog and wants to come to Majorca for it. But that's not all.' Patricia sank down on the bed, clearly too stunned to stay standing. 'He's received an anonymous email from someone saying they know why Katy was murdered – because they were the person responsible.'

2

The boy bucked and thrashed in the pushchair as the woman hurried to fasten the billowing rain cover to its frame. Maggie was instantly reminded of her niece, Mae, who at the same age would have a similarly violent reaction to being sealed behind hers, however protective its intention. Now almost school age, Mae walked everywhere and had a prized umbrella covered in cartoon cats and dogs to shield her from sudden deluges like this one.

'What are you grinning at?'

Maggie looked away from the window, but not before she saw the woman secure the last loop of the rain cover with a triumphant flourish. She then grabbed the pushchair's handlebar and turned sharply in the direction of Upper Street.

'Nothing,' Maggie answered.

DS Andrew Mealing stared down at her with a look of ill-concealed contempt.

'Really? Because it looked to me like you were daydreaming . . . *again*.'

Maggie bristled at his tone but said nothing. She had learned from experience that answering Mealing back only served to stoke his nastiness, like squirting lighter fuel on a barbecue.

'Is there something you wanted?' she asked instead, trying to appear impervious to the sneer on his face.

Mealing hadn't always hated her. In fact, when she'd arrived at Islington six months ago from Mansell he couldn't have been more reasonable, offering to show her the ropes and help her settle in. But she was never entirely comfortable in his presence and the constant monitoring soon planted the suspicion that he was trying to catch her out – a suspicion that was proved the day she unfortunately did make a mistake. It was a minor administrative infraction, easily corrected, but from that moment forward DS Mealing had taken every opportunity to question Maggie's suitability for the Met.

He was subtle enough that his remarks went unnoticed by their colleagues, but she was under no illusion that he wanted rid of her from their squad. He would make digs about where she'd transferred from ('Mansell's in the back arse of beyond, isn't it?'), her specialism as a family liaison officer ('It's a known fact women want to be FLOs because it's a cushy job sitting on people's sofas'), to questioning why their boss hadn't trusted her with a bigger role in any investigation she'd worked on so far ('He clearly thinks you're not up to it').

The last one rankled the most because Maggie was beginning to fear there was some truth in it. The Detective Superintendent said he wanted to be sure she was ready for the responsibility, because working on a Murder Investigation Team in London was very different to what she was used to, working with CID in the more rural Buckinghamshire, where Mansell was situated. But that sounded like an excuse and Maggie fretted that the real reason she was being held back was because the one time she had stepped up on a case, to the rank of Acting DS, there had been a terrible incident in which her colleague was killed. She had been exonerated of blame by an internal inquiry, but maybe that wasn't enough to quash all doubt about her ability.

Mealing ignored her question and posed one of his own.

'What are you working on?'

'The Curtis statement.'

He leaned over Maggie's shoulder to scan the witness statement from a stabbing in Highbury she'd been typing up.

'Hmm. Well, you'll have to leave that for a minute. You're wanted downstairs.'

'By who?'

'Desk sarge says a woman's come in wanting to report a historic crime. The boss said to give it to you, because everyone else is busy on more important stuff.'

Another dig that she ignored like all the others. At some point she had to hope Mealing would tire of picking on her.

'No problem, I'll head down there now.'

Before she had time to realize what he was doing and stop him, Mealing reached for her computer mouse and closed the statement with one click.

'I hadn't saved that last bit,' she reacted angrily.

'Whoops. I guess you'll have to stay late tonight to redo it.' Then he walked away, a malicious smirk spread wide across his face.

3

Maggie was still angry as she took a seat in the witness interview room next to reception, but did her best to hide it for the sake of the woman sitting opposite her. Lara Steadman had never been inside a police station before, a fact she revealed twice inside a minute of them meeting and once again as they sat down. Her nerves manifested in the jiggle of her left leg beneath the table and the tight clutch of her fingers around the strap of her handbag as it rested on her lap.

Forcing from her mind all thoughts of the revenge she'd like to exact on DS Mealing, Maggie rested her arms on the table, notebook open and pen poised.

'You told the desk sergeant you wanted to report a crime that happened some years ago. Why don't you give me the basic facts, then we can run through it in more detail?'

Lara bit down hard on her bottom lip as she nodded. She was immaculately made up, her make-up verging on professional, but a trace of red lipstick lined the bottom of her front teeth as she opened her mouth to speak.

'I was drugged and held captive in someone's flat while on holiday in Majorca ten years ago.'

Outwardly Maggie stayed impassive but inwardly she was frowning. However serious the crime sounded, the fact it had occurred abroad posed the biggest problem, as it was beyond the Met's jurisdiction and technically a matter for the police there.

Lara watched Maggie warily as she twisted the bag strap even tighter. Her impressive diamond engagement ring and matching wedding band hung loose on her finger and she had the haunted look of someone who hadn't slept well, if at all.

'Okay, that does sound serious,' she said. 'Let's start from the beginning. When was this exactly?'

'It was April 2009, not long after Easter, and I was on holiday with a bunch of friends – just us girls, no partners. On our third night there we went to a club. I'll admit I drank a lot, we all did, but I know I wasn't out of control. Then I had one more drink and the next thing I remember is waking up the next evening in a strange apartment. My friends assumed I'd gone off with some guy,' she added, before Maggie could ask why her friends hadn't noticed her leaving. 'It was something I'd done in the past, on other holidays, even when I had a boyfriend waiting for me at home. But not that time, I swear. I wouldn't have done that to Mike. We were getting married and I wouldn't have cheated on him.'

Maggie inwardly flinched: she'd once slept with someone who was in a relationship and it had almost cost her dear.

'When you're with the right person, you don't think about it,' Lara continued. 'Or I didn't. Mike and I are still married,' she said with a smile, her first since she'd sat down.

'Did your friends see you talking to another man, and that's why they thought you'd gone off with someone?'

'No, they just assumed it, but I hadn't spoken to anyone other than them in the club; I was on the dance floor for the most part.'

'You don't remember leaving?'

'I do have a vague recollection of going to the toilet and feeling like I was going to be sick, and one of my friends checking on me, but then, after that, nothing.'

Lara gave a little shrug as though it was no big deal, but the unshed tears glossing her eyes told otherwise.

'What do you remember from when you woke up?' asked Maggie.

'I came to on a sofa. My back was so stiff from the position I was in that I must've been lying there for ages.' She dropped her gaze and her voice lowered too, as though she didn't want to be overheard. 'I'd accidentally wet myself. I must've been too out of it to get up and use the toilet.'

'Were you alone when you woke up?'

Lara nodded. 'I was terrified someone else was there, but the place was empty. My bag was missing so I didn't have my phone on me to call anyone. When I went to leave, the door to the flat was locked and I couldn't force it open.' The first tear fell. 'I was so scared that whoever had taken me there would come back. All the windows were locked too.'

'How did you get out?'

'There was a door off the kitchen that led to an outside balcony, where I think there was a washing machine and a clothes dryer. The door had a big glass pane in it, so I smashed it with a chair. I didn't care about the damage – I just wanted to get out of there. Then I climbed over the balcony railing and escaped. The apartment was on the ground floor, so I was lucky.'

'Your recollection is good, considering it was ten years ago.'

'I've never been able to forget it,' said Lara morosely. 'I have a daughter myself now. She's only four, but when I think about something like that happening to her when she grows up, it terrifies me.'

'I understand. So whereabouts was this in Majorca?'

'Saros, a town in the north.'

Maggie had holidayed on the Balearic island once with her parents when she was younger but hadn't heard of Saros.

'It's a small place, pretty quiet,' Lara explained. 'The club we went to was the only one there.'

'Can you remember what it was called?'

'Salvador's. It's still open. I looked it up before I came here.'

'I appreciate this may be difficult for you to answer, but do you think you were sexually assaulted?'

Lara's face flushed. 'I don't think so. Nowhere hurt, let's put it that way. I just felt really groggy.'

Maggie thought for a moment. Whoever had taken Lara to the apartment had left her unconscious on the sofa for the duration, so did that mean there was no intent to harm? She cleared her throat.

'I'm not saying this is necessarily the case, but have you considered someone might've seen how drunk you were in the club and took you home to keep you safe, because you were unable to tell them where you were staying? Maybe they left you on the sofa to sleep it off while they went to work?'

'I have thought that, but why lock me in? Why not leave a note explaining where they'd gone and leave a key for me to get out?' Lara shuddered. 'I know I'm not explaining it very well, but it didn't *feel* like that. When I woke up, it was like straight away I knew I was in danger and I had to get out of there or else. I dread to think what would've happened if whoever it was had come back.'

'If you're reporting this now, does that mean you never went to the police in Saros?'

Lara's eyes widened as though horrified by the thought.

'God, no. I didn't tell anyone, not even the friends I was with.'

Maggie was surprised. 'Why not?'

'I was so ashamed of being so out of it and I didn't want Mike to find out. He'd have been furious with me for putting myself in harm's way. We used to argue a lot about me drinking too much and I knew it would be the final straw. I was scared he'd call off the wedding.'

'So why come forward now, ten years on?'

Lara grew fearful and the strap twisting became more pronounced.

'He's tracked me down.'

'Who has?'

'The man who locked me in the apartment.'

Maggie took a moment to process what she was saying.

'But I thought you didn't know whose apartment it was?'

'I didn't. But two days ago I received an email from him.'

Maggie shook her head. 'I'm sorry but you're not making sense. You didn't know who it was but now all of a sudden he's emailing you? How do you know it's him and how did he get your email address?'

'I know it's him because he said so in his message and he must've got my details off my phone,' said Lara hotly. 'I told you my bag was missing when I woke up – he's kept it this entire time.'

Maggie was about to ask if it might be someone mucking around to scare her, but then remembered Lara said she hadn't told another soul about the incident.

'What did the message say?'

'Here, see for yourself.' Lara took her smartphone from her bag, swiped her thumb across the screen a few times then slid it across the table to Maggie, the email open and ready to read.

Hello Lara, remember me?

We were having a wonderful time together in Saros until you smashed up my back door! I often wondered if you would return one day, so I kept your belongings just in case, although I admit the wrap of coke you had in your bag is long gone. Sorry! Call it payment for having to clear up the mess you made of my door and my sofa.

I was very, very upset you ran away before we truly got to know each other. We could have had something beautiful. But it taught me a valuable lesson – always question a woman's true intentions. The one who came after you learned that the hard way, which is why I will be celebrating a very special occasion in her honour in Saros very soon! Can you guess what it is?

It would be wonderful if you could join me. I wouldn't let you get away so easily this time.

X

The address the message was sent from struck Maggie as odd: me@threedates.com.

'Well, what do you think?' Lara pressed.

Maggie chose her next words very carefully as she slid the phone back across the table. The last thing she wanted was for Lara to think she was victim-blaming her, but asking difficult questions was part of the job in establishing whether indeed any crime had been committed. 'He sounds like the worst kind of smarmy git. Are you sure you don't remember meeting him in the club?'

'No, I don't. And even if I had, I would never have gone off with someone like that.' Lara suddenly burst into tears. 'I think he stole my engagement ring. When I woke up, it was gone. I had to tell Mike I'd lost it swimming in the sea. He was so lovely about it and bought me another one to replace it.'

While Lara wiped her eyes on a tissue she plucked from the depths of her bag, Maggie surreptitiously checked the time on her watch, a men's chunky Seiko that was on its last legs. They'd been talking for twenty minutes and even though she believed Lara's version of events that she had been taken to the apartment after being drugged, it wasn't a matter for the Met. It was down to the police in Saros to deal with any alleged abduction and the theft of the ring. That was the advice she must give Lara so she could wrap this up and get back to her desk to finish the Curtis statement.

She opened her mouth to speak but was silenced by Lara placing a copy of the *Evening Standard* on the desk in front of her. A quick glance at the date on the front page told her it was yesterday's edition.

'Turn to page five,' Lara instructed.

Maggie did as she requested. Her eye was drawn immediately to the photograph dominating the page, a smiling young woman posing on a rock next to a beach with her arms outstretched. Lithe and tanned in shorts and a vest, she had wavy dark-brown hair that rippled over her shoulders. Further down the page was a smaller image of a man and woman, in their fifties or older. The woman looked familiar.

Maggie read the headline: KATY'S PARENTS TO FLY OUT FOR ANNIVERSARY SERVICE.

'I don't understand why you're showing me this,' she said.

'The girl is Katy Pope, the police officer's daughter who was murdered in Majorca ten years ago.'

Ah, so that's why Maggie recognized the woman: she was a former Met officer and a very senior one at that.

Lara noisily sucked in her next breath then exhaled.

'I think the man who took me might be the same person who killed Katy.'

Maggie stared at her. 'What?'

'Katy was killed in Saros two months after I was there. She was missing for a week before her body was found. The police believed she'd been held captive before she was murdered.' Lara scrabbled for her phone again: '"The one who came after you learned that the hard way, which is why I will be celebrating a very special occasion in her honour in Saros very soon",' she quoted from the email, before slapping her palm down on the newspaper, making Maggie jump. 'What if Katy was the one after me, that the same man drugged her and took her back to the apartment, then killed her? Katy's family are going back to Saros next week for a memorial service to mark the tenth anniversary of her murder. This interview is them talking about it. The special occasion he mentions could be the service.'

Maggie struggled to formulate a reply. It sounded too implausible, but Lara wasn't swayed.

'I think this email is from her killer,' she breathed. 'He wanted me to know he's back.'

4

The number of times Declan Morris had sat in their living room must've run into the hundreds, first as the shy best friend their son George brought home from university one weekend, then as Katy's boyfriend. Yet how jarring it was to see him now, settled on the cream sofa, a cup of tea in one hand and a biscuit in the other. Philip eyed him charily over the brim of his own cup, taking in the changes in Declan's appearance since their last meeting. His light-brown hair, which he'd previously worn long and wavy to his jawline, was now cropped close and he had gained weight, his student wiriness presumably fleshed out by fat-cat lunches with clients of the bank he was working for.

Philip contemplated the face Katy might've pulled on seeing Declan now. His daughter had possessed a sensitivity that made her desperate not to hurt other people's feelings, even though it meant hers were regularly trampled on. She took after Philip in that regard, which is why he could always read the little looks she gave instead – expressions that gave away her true sentiments. Declan now would've surely raised an eyebrow.

Polite pleasantries dispensed with, an awkward silence

had settled over the three of them. Even Patricia, who could usually be relied upon to start a conversation in an empty room, seemed stumped for something to say. Philip had expected her to raise the subject of the email immediately, but it was as though she'd decided the bad news could wait until she was ready to hear it.

Declan took another sip of tea then cleared his throat nervously.

'Tamara sends her regards.'

Philip saw his wife's features pinch sharply, before she hastily rearranged them into a smile.

'That's kind of her. Is she well?'

Philip knew how difficult it was for Patricia to enquire after Declan's fiancée, how the words must've stuck in her throat like a piece of gristly steak before she'd politely uttered them. The point of contention wasn't that Declan was in a relationship – neither of them had expected him to stay single for the rest of his life – but rather who it was with.

Tamara had been Katy's best friend. They had met on their first day at senior school aged eleven and, apart from the occasional spat, had been inseparable. They had even been planning to go to the same university, such was their despair at the thought of being parted. But while Tamara did head off to Durham as they'd planned, Katy's future was abruptly and horrifically extinguished by her murder that summer.

Tamara was as devastated as the rest of them, but it was only nine months later that she and Declan began their relationship. It was driven, they said, out of a desperate need for solace, but Patricia could forgive neither of them for the perceived betrayal. As far as she was concerned,

Tamara should never have laid claim to the life Katy was robbed of having and nor should Declan have offered it to her.

'She's well, thanks,' he replied to Patricia. 'Actually, she's pregnant.'

Declan at least had the grace to look sheepish as Patricia's plastered-on smile stretched even wider.

'Gosh, that's a surprise. Will you be bringing forward the wedding?' she asked, her voice noticeably tight.

'No, we're delaying it until after the baby comes.'

He glanced at the mantelpiece where, in the centre, was a large framed photograph of Katy and her brother, George, who was older than her by three years. George and Declan had been close friends after meeting at Oxford but now they hardly saw one another, as was proved by Declan's next question.

'How's George doing?'

'He's qualified as a barrister now,' said Patricia. 'He has a big trial coming up at the Old Bailey.'

Declan looked impressed. 'He's done well for himself. Is he married?'

On seeing his wife's face fall again, Philip decided to spare her the torment of having to answer that particular question by posing one of his own.

'We are rather surprised you want to come with us to Saros. We haven't heard from you for years, so why now?'

'Obviously I'm aware the anniversary is coming up and then the other evening I saw on your website that you were planning a memorial service and, well, I thought I should be there. It'll be a nice way to remember Katy, and ten years is significant.'

'Five years was significant too, but I don't recall you rushing over to honour her memory then,' said Philip.

Declan set his cup down with a clatter on the saucer Patricia had provided.

'If *my* memory serves me correctly, you made it very clear when I got together with Tamara that I was no longer welcome in your home, and that, as far as you were concerned, my part in Katy's life was forgotten. And you know what? I understand why you said that. I do, I really do. I know my being with Tamara must've been confusing for you both. But me being with Tam doesn't change how I felt about Katy, and she knows that too. I loved your daughter very much,' he said, his voice thickening. 'I know we were young, but I used to think about what it would have been like to have settled down, bought our own place once she'd graduated. Even now I think about her a lot, about how things might've turned out if that sick bastard hadn't taken her from us.' Philip felt a pang of sympathy for Declan's obvious distress, but Patricia's face was set like stone. 'I hate that he's still walking free. That's another reason why I want to come to Majorca with you – I want to do whatever I can to help with the new appeal if it means we catch him at last.'

Patricia stood up and moved to the fireplace, grasping the mantel with one hand while keeping her back to the room. Philip knew she was taking a moment to compose herself. He set down his own teacup, wondering if she would object to what he was about to say, but thinking that her allowing Declan to come to the house in the first place today already signalled a suspension of previous hostilities.

'That's very kind of you, and we will welcome your

support at the memorial,' he said. 'But as for Tamara—'

'She won't be coming,' said Declan hastily. 'It'll just be me.'

Patricia swung round. 'Good.'

Philip understood the sentiment behind her abruptness: it would be hard enough to have Declan accompanying them, his first trip with them back to the island since Katy's murder. Tamara coming as well would be too much to cope with on top of everything else.

'Now tell me about the email you mentioned on the phone,' she ordered.

Philip wanted to interject with 'tell us' but thought better of it. Patricia was in no mood to be needled by him. Her fuse had always been short but these days there was barely the stub of a wick to keep it in check.

'At first I thought it was spam, because of the random address it was sent from and because over the years I've had a few people get in touch claiming to know stuff about Katy's death who have turned out to be trolls or fantasists. That includes a couple of crazies saying they were her killer.'

Philip frowned. 'We didn't know that.'

'I did tell the police at the time,' said Declan. 'I would've told you too, but we weren't talking.'

'What makes you think this message is genuine?' asked Patricia.

'The detail involved. Not about her actual death, but about her.'

Patricia paled and Philip's fingers clenched the arms of the chair.

'What kind of detail?' his wife asked.

Declan shifted uncomfortably on the sofa. 'I'd rather not say.'

'Sexual details?'

Declan squirmed under Patricia's cross-examination and Philip squirmed with him. Her old interrogation habits were hard to shake and it was excruciating when she badgered people over the smallest thing if their first response didn't satisfy her. His personal coping mechanism, again suggested by the counsellor he had been seeing for the past six years since the breakdown, was to leave the room while she was mid-flow, so she would take the hint to stop.

'Well?' Patricia pressed.

'No, it wasn't that. Not exactly.'

'What does that mean?'

'Sorry, this is hard. Katy was so private that even though she's not here and it doesn't matter what I say, all I can think is that she would hate me for telling you.'

Philip nodded. Their daughter had been private and modest and shied away from salacious talk. She used to find it mortifying if a sex scene came on the television while she was watching with the family and would often bolt from the room on the pretext of making a cup of tea.

Both he and Patricia remained silent as Declan wrestled with how best to frame the information he was about to share. He took a deep breath, then the sentence tumbled out so quickly that it took Philip a moment to work out what he'd said.

'Katy had a termination.'

Philip was speechless, while his wife retorted, 'No she jolly well did not.'

'Yes, she did. Four months before we went on that holiday.' Declan looked at them beseechingly, his cheeks beginning to colour. 'I am so, so sorry. We thought we were being careful. I was up for keeping the baby, but Katy thought it would stop her going to uni and ruin her prospects, so she decided it was best to deal with it. I had to support what she wanted.'

Patricia sank back down into her seat.

'I don't believe it.'

'It's true.'

'But it never showed up, when her body – the post-mortem . . .'

Philip stared at his wife, surprised at how her shock was rendering her inarticulate. She returned his gaze. Both of them were stunned their daughter could've gone through something so monumental without them realizing.

'Well, we know the Spanish weren't thorough with their investigation,' said Declan. 'They obviously didn't pick up on the fact she'd previously been pregnant. It was early days when she had the termination, just seven weeks.'

Patricia turned to him. 'That's what was mentioned in the email?'

He nodded. 'But here's the thing: we didn't tell anyone. Not you, not my parents, not George or Tamara, not a soul. So when I got this email repeating details only Katy and I had been privy to, I knew it had to be genuine. Because the only way the sender could've found out was from her.'

'I think you're romanticizing my daughter's reluctance to gossip,' said Patricia and the snippiness of her tone made Philip's heart constrict. Knowing about the pregnancy would tarnish his wife's memory of her now. She'd put Katy on a pedestal from the moment she was born and to know she wasn't perfect would be a damning blow. 'She could easily have told a friend other than Tamara,' Patricia finished.

'We made a pact not to say anything. You know how loyal Katy was – she wouldn't have told anyone once we'd decided not to.'

Philip had to agree with that: his sweet, trustworthy daughter probably took many secrets to her grave.

'It doesn't explain why, even knowing what they did, you think the person who sent you the email is her killer,' said Patricia.

'He pretty much said so, like he was boasting. Then he said something along the lines of they could've had something beautiful together, but that she had disappointed him and he had to teach her a lesson.'

Philip coughed loudly as bile rose up and scorched the lining of his throat. Patricia shot him a look of distaste.

'Was there anything about where she was in the week she was missing?' she asked Declan. 'Any clues as to where he kept her?'

There had been many days since Katy died that Philip would rank as the worst of his life – the day her remains were flown back to Britain, the day of her funeral, the day he should've been toasting her eighteenth birthday but instead laid flowers on her grave – but those seven days between her going missing and her body being found were by far the cruellest. Each day saw their emotions see-sawing as reported sightings of Katy raised their hopes of her being found, only to have them dashed hours later when the police had ruled them out as false. The not knowing was excruciating and still gave him nightmares now. Was Katy kept alive in that week, did she suffer before she was killed . . . did she call for him, her dad, asking him to save her, and cry when he never came?

'No, there's no mention of where she was.' Declan paused, then looked solemnly at the parents who might've been his in-laws eventually but were now strangers to him. 'But he said she died on their third date.'

The bile rose to Philip's mouth this time and Patricia was equally ashen.

'You need to pass the email to the police. DCI Walker, I can call him,' she said.

Declan nodded. 'I think we should, because I'm worried about what might happen if we don't take it seriously.'

Philip was suddenly gripped by fear.

'What do you mean?' he croaked.

Declan looked directly at Patricia. 'The last line of it . . . it was a promise to save you a sun lounger on the beach when you're back in Saros next week.'

'Me?' Patricia repeated slowly.

'Yes,' said Declan. 'I think her killer is planning to be there for the memorial too.'

5

It was agreed Declan would travel separately to Saros, for reasons of practicality more than anything else. The only flight he was able to book at such short notice was one leaving at 5.25 a.m. from Stansted on Monday, whereas the Popes were flying out on Friday afternoon from Gatwick, the closest airport to their home in Crystal Palace in South London.

The issue of accommodation had been less easily addressed. Declan had recoiled in shock when Patricia breezily informed him they were staying in an apartment at Orquídea, a luxury complex a couple of minutes' walk from the expansive golden beach of Saros – and also the place where Katy's dismembered remains were recovered, after they'd been dumped in the huge ornamental ponds in the grounds.

'Why on earth would you stay there? Of all the places,' he'd said, aghast at the idea.

Patricia had dodged the question while Philip mumbled something about availability. Declan left saying he would arrange his own accommodation.

'I don't know how you can set foot in that place, let alone

eat and sleep there,' he'd hissed at Philip as he was shown out to the front door.

'It's what Patricia wants,' Philip had replied, embarrassingly aware of the hollowness of the statement. 'You do know the memorial service is to be held in the grounds, by one of the ponds?'

Declan was even more horrified.

'I thought it would be on the beach, where she went missing. Not where her torso, head or whatever was found!'

There were eight blocks in the Orquídea complex, hosting six apartments within. Each block had its own private swimming pool for guests, and interspersing each of them were landscaped lawns and gardens and a series of ornamental ponds. It was across six of the ponds that the killer had deposited Katy's remains, weighted down by chains beneath the lilies. An unlucky child called Luke discovered them: he'd been using a stick to poke the lilies to scare the carp that swam under them and in doing so had dislodged her left leg.

Philip shared Declan's revulsion at them staying there but his loyalty to Patricia would not allow him to admit it.

'It's all arranged now,' he'd said lamely. 'Does that mean you won't come?'

Declan had thought for a moment, clearly conflicted by the prospect.

'No, I'll come,' he'd said, but grudgingly. 'I still want to be there for the service.'

Philip could hear Patricia ranting even from the garden. He'd gone outside to escape her latest tirade and now her poor sister Nell was getting it in the neck, albeit over the phone. The source of his wife's ire was, once again, DCI Walker, and his refusal to drop everything and come to the house to discuss the email Declan had been sent. She could not understand why the officer in charge of Operation Pivot did not share her urgency at investigating it.

'I do appreciate he is busy preparing for the trip,' she said, which had made Philip smile to himself because in reality Patricia seemed to appreciate nothing about Walker. 'But how can I take him seriously if he won't do his job properly?'

Philip nodded as though to affirm her complaint, but secretly he thought Walker was doing a marvellous job. It certainly wasn't an easy one, with the weight of Patricia's expectations on his shoulders and the limitations in budget and manpower he faced. But he'd been diligent in re-examining every lead in the case when he'd been appointed to Operation Pivot two years ago and had even made a breakthrough with the amethyst and silver ring Katy wore on her right hand, something none of his predecessors had. The ring was a present from them for her sixteenth birthday, but was missing when her body was recovered. Walker had managed to track down a jeweller in the city of Palma, the island's capital, who remembered a man coming into his store a few weeks after she was murdered and asking how much he could get if he sold one matching the description.

Unfortunately, because of the time that had elapsed, the jeweller couldn't remember what the man looked like, but knowing when he'd gone into the shop was useful. Assuming it was the killer, it meant he must've stayed on Majorca as the original police investigation got underway, an audacious move. The jeweller said he hadn't come forward previously because it hadn't been published anywhere that Katy's ring was missing.

Patricia had been withering in her response to the jeweller's admission: had the Majorcan police had been more vocal in searching for the ring in the first place he might've heeded the appeals for information and come forward sooner. But the local detective in charge at the outset, Chief Inspector Galen Martos, had withheld the information from public knowledge, believing it might one day prove instrumental in nailing the killer.

Philip moved further away from the house and the sound of Patricia's braying. To distract himself, he set about pulling up the weeds threatening to choke the bed of buddleias at the foot of the garden. This was his sanctuary, a place of shelter where he could almost satisfy his craving for silence. Almost, because their road was a thoroughfare between the Crystal Palace triangle and neighbouring Gipsy Hill and could be busy at times.

Patricia never understood why he hankered for quiet so much, why working in the hushed great rooms of the National Gallery had been the dream job he'd never wanted to leave until she insisted he retire, like her. Katy had, because she was exactly like him: much happier with her nose stuck in a book than listening to music at top volume. Her brother, George, took after Patricia: so loud you always heard his presence long before you saw it.

Philip smiled with affection as he thought of his rambunctious son. He had often said to Patricia that as a family unit they worked a treat, two yangs versus two yins, the quiet versus the loud. Now, without Katy, the unit felt painfully lopsided, with him the odd one out. Yet despite their differences, George had been Philip's rescuer when his initial grief threatened to pull him under; when the breakdown finally did, George had taken charge of family matters so his father didn't have to. As the years passed Philip had secretly hoped George might settle down with a young woman who was reserved like his sister, to even out the family unit again, but his son was only thirty, consumed by his job and, unlike his old friend Declan, content to play the field for now.

Philip couldn't get his head round what Declan had told them about Katy getting pregnant. It was distressing to think of his little girl in that way. He didn't want to believe it, and the fact that her post-mortem never revealed signs of her ever conceiving meant he simply couldn't believe it. Declan was lying, he had to be.

Patricia stuck her head out of an upstairs window.

'Nell said I should've demanded Walker came round,' she hollered down to him.

Philip raised a hand in acknowledgement and smiled to himself. Of course Nell had. She'd said what Patricia wanted to hear, because that's what they all did for the sake of a quiet life. But he was glad DCI Walker had dug his heels in, because the thought of discussing the email right now made his blood run cold. He couldn't believe it was true – any of it.

6

It was nearing seven when Maggie left the station, the journey home taking her one stop on the Northern Line from Angel to King's Cross, then six stops on the Piccadilly to Turnpike Lane, the closest stop to her flat. She'd finished the Curtis statement then briefed her boss about Lara Steadman. He agreed it was a matter for the police in Saros but ordered her to contact DCI Walker at Operation Pivot, the special investigation team still looking into the Pope murder, outlining what Lara had said. Maggie offered to write up the statement in full but her boss said no: if Walker wanted to take it further, he should re-interview Lara himself. So Maggie wrote a detailed email to Walker then called it a day.

She hurried from the main Tube exit at Turnpike Lane and turned left, scooting alongside the green expanse of Ducketts Common which, despite evening descending, was still thrumming with activity, the basketball courts packed with groups of young men playing and the outdoor gym equipment being put to good use by a few pensioners. Less welcoming was the sight of a passed-out drunk in the middle of the grass, empty vodka bottle resting on his tummy.

Her new neighbourhood was known as Harringay, which had confused her at first because the borough itself was Haringey. Living there had taken some getting used to after the relative calm of her old town, Mansell; the level of deprivation in some parts of the borough was eye-opening, particularly as it sat shoulder-to-jowl alongside the multimillion-pound houses of Crouch End and Muswell Hill. The street where she lived straddled both sides of the divide: expensively renovated family homes terraced next to council-run flats that had seen better days. The rent she received from letting out her own two-bedroom flat in Mansell was short of what she needed to cover the monthly cost of a one-bedroom flat in Harringay, but her salary saw to the rest.

Tonight she wasn't going straight home, though. Her boyfriend, Will Umpire, had been in London for the day on a training course and they'd arranged to meet at a bar near her flat. She relished the chance to see him after months of sustaining their relationship at weekends either in London or in Trenton, a town in the north of Buckinghamshire where Umpire served as a DCI with her old force. Conducting their relationship long distance was tough at times, but what kept them going was the fact that, eighteen months on from when they first got together, they both agreed it was worth the effort. Maggie saw her long-term future with Umpire, he with her.

The bar where they'd arranged to meet was a short walk from her flat and, like her, a relatively new addition to the neighbourhood. Loved by hipsters, it stood out like a sore thumb amongst Green Lane's infamous Turkish restaurants, jewellers, hardware shops and the imposing Salisbury pub, but she liked it because the atmosphere was laid-back and it served great burgers.

Reaching the entrance, she wished there was time to nip home and freshen up – or at the very least brush her hair and teeth. She didn't want Umpire to think she couldn't be bothered to make an effort.

A blast of music hit her as she dragged open the heavy glass door. Her eyes needed a moment to focus on the room, so low was the ambient lighting, and when her gaze fell upon Umpire sitting in the corner, nursing a pint, the corners of her mouth lifted and her weariness began to seep away. Then she saw he wasn't alone and her face fell. Next to him, staring at her murderously, were his kids.

7

Maggie fought to keep her expression neutral as she picked her way across the room to reach their table. Why hadn't Umpire warned her the children would be with him? More to the point, *why* were they? He didn't normally have them on a Tuesday evening.

Flora and Jack lived with their mother, Sarah, Umpire's ex-wife, in North Finchley, which was about a twenty-minute drive away. Yet Maggie had only met the children a handful of times in the eighteen months she and their father had been together. Flora, who was fourteen, had taken an instant dislike to her and demonstrated it by being surly and unresponsive in her company, so meetings were now kept to a minimum. Jack, two years younger, was initially receptive but now aped his sister's behaviour rather than end up on the receiving end of Flora's temper, which exploded whenever she thought he was being too nice to their dad's girlfriend.

Maggie hesitated as she reached the table. Kissing Umpire hello would unleash a spiteful response she felt too tired to handle right now, but fortunately he had no such compunction and rose to his feet to greet her. As their lips met, Maggie saw Flora out of the corner of her eye pretending to retch so she tried to pull away, but Umpire held her close so he could whisper in her ear.

'I'm sorry. The kids found out that I was in London today and asked to see me. I couldn't say no to them tagging along. I'll have to take them home later, so I can't stay tonight.'

'It's okay,' Maggie murmured back, even though it wasn't. She lowered herself into the seat next to Jack.

'This is a nice surprise,' she lied.

Jack flashed her a wary smile. 'Dad says the burgers here are brilliant.'

'They are,' said Maggie, shrugging off her jacket. 'They also do great milkshakes.'

'If you don't mind getting fat,' said Flora, giving Maggie a pointed look.

Here we go, Maggie sighed to herself. She understood it must be difficult for the children to see Umpire with someone other than their mum, but she had no idea why Flora was quite so resentful as her parents had split up long before she came on the scene. Whenever Umpire raised it with his daughter, Flora claimed the reverse, saying Maggie was cold towards her and she must obviously hate children.

Luckily Umpire knew that wasn't true, because he'd seen at first-hand Maggie's close relationship with her two nephews, Scotty and Jude, and her niece, Mae, who were her sister Lou's children. From the moment they were born – aside from a period of estrangement last year – Maggie had been a de facto guardian to the kids and doted on them. These days the children lived near Portsmouth with Lou, but Maggie saw them often.

Thinking Flora might be fearful of what she represented, Maggie had followed the textbook advice and made it clear she wasn't trying to take their mum's place, but even that assertion had fallen on deaf ears. She'd also addressed the age gap between her and their dad – Umpire was forty-four to her thirty-one – but Flora had pulled a face like the very mention had disgusted her, so Maggie let it drop.

'I'm going to have a chocolate one,' said Jack, ignoring his sister for once. 'What will you have, Dad?'

'I'm sticking to this,' he said, raising his pint. 'What do you want, darling?' he asked Maggie. 'Beer, wine, cocktail?'

Automatically she glanced at Flora, expecting another reaction to him calling her 'darling', but the girl was absorbed in reading a message on her phone.

'Glass of dry white wine, please.' She shot him a look. 'Make it a large one.'

Umpire took their food orders as well and went to the bar to pay. Maggie felt awkward left alone with the children and scrabbled for something benign to talk about.

'How's football going?' she asked Jack.

'Good. I scored two goals on Saturday.'

'Well done you.'

'Then I got a yellow card for a dangerous tackle,' he added impishly, as though that was the greater achievement.

'Football's so boring,' Flora butted in. 'You should play basketball like Jude.'

Maggie thought she'd misheard her, and asked her to repeat it.

'I said, he should play basketball like Jude,' she repeated, her tone suggesting Maggie was being thick for asking.

'My Jude?'

Flora frowned. 'He's not yours – he's your nephew. He's just made his school team.'

'How do you know that?'

Flora waggled her phone at her. 'Snapchat.'

Maggie couldn't have been more surprised if the girl had thrown a drink over her. Since when had she and Jude been messaging? They'd only met once, in the Easter holidays, when the boys had stayed with her for a few days. Maggie had organized tickets for the London Eye and suggested Umpire bring his two along in the hope it might elicit a thaw in Flora's behaviour. From what she remembered, Jude and Flora had barely exchanged a word all day, both teens glued to their smartphones the entire time. Jack and Scotty, on the other hand, were instant friends, nattering non-stop about their shared passion for football.

Flora smirked. 'What's the problem?'

Maggie wished she could say *you are*, but the nuclear fallout wasn't worth it. Instead she smiled.

'It's nice you and Jude get on.'

Flora pulled a face as though she'd just vomited in her mouth. 'Why is everything always nice with you? It's such a blah word.'

Maggie regarded her for a moment. 'Don't worry, I shan't use it about you.'

Flora's expression tweaked as her brain raced to catch up with the comment. It didn't sound like an insult, but it was, wasn't it? Before the girl could make her mind up, Maggie announced that if Flora and Jude were friends now, maybe they could have another day out when he next visited.

Flora shrugged non-committally, but Maggie saw her

eyes spark with excitement and she had to suppress a smile. Oh to be fourteen and experiencing your first crush.

'I'll mention it next time I speak to him,' she added, an idea forming in her mind. 'We talk a lot, Jude and me. He's a great kid, really respectful of grown-ups.'

Flora stared at her.

'He's so protective of me too,' said Maggie airily. 'He hates it when anyone upsets me.'

She stopped then, fearing she was ramming home the point too obviously and not wanting to stoop quite to Flora's level, the pettiness unbecoming for someone her age. But as Umpire rejoined them, she glanced across at the teen and, to her amusement, received a weak smile.

The penny had dropped.

8

Flora was so preoccupied as they ate their burgers that, in spite of their many run-ins, Maggie began to regret toying with the girl. *She must really like Jude if she's this worried I might say something,* she thought, and it occurred to her that she might be able to use the girl's crush to her own benefit. She waited until Flora and Jack had finished eating and were both immersed in their devices, her on her phone again, him on his Nintendo Switch, both oblivious to the world, then moved round the table to sit closer to Umpire.

'It seems my nephew and your daughter are now friends. Did you know they were in touch?' she said in a low voice.

'Flora did mention last week that they've messaged a few times,' said Umpire, frowning. 'It didn't sound like a big deal.'

'Well, it is. It's been more than a few times. I'd say it's pretty constant, in fact.' Maggie grinned and tilted her head towards Flora, who was ferociously typing out a message on her phone.

'Are you saying they're an item?'

There was something in his voice that pulled her up.

'Would it bother you if they were?' she asked.

'I suppose, well . . . look, Jude's a nice enough lad but I

don't want it getting out of hand. We both know what kids get up to online these days and the stuff they send each other. Flora's not as mature as she likes to think she is.'

Maggie bristled with indignation.

'I hope you're not saying you think Jude's going to force her into sending him explicit pictures. He isn't like that.'

'That's not what I'm saying,' said Umpire, his voice dropping to a whisper as Jack shot them a look. 'Don't twist my words. I like Jude a lot, he's a responsible kid, but I think they're both too young for a long-distance romance.'

'I've got an idea about that. Why don't I call Lou and arrange for them to come up for the weekend? It might take the heat out of things a bit. Show them the reality versus the online fantasy.'

'You want to call your sister?'

'I know it's still early days, but we're getting on better every time we speak.'

'That's because you mainly text.'

Maggie grinned. 'We talk too. It's a step up, anyway.'

The previous year she had become estranged from Lou and the children for seven long, painful months, after Lou discovered a secret Maggie had been keeping from her and was furious. Now they were talking again and while they hadn't quite reclaimed the closeness they shared before their falling-out, their relationship was finally back on track.

'So it's a good idea,' she badgered her boyfriend, 'getting them to come up for the weekend? We can all do something together and at the same time you and Lou can have a talk with Flora and Jude about boundaries and being appropriate when messaging each other.'

Umpire rolled his eyes, knowing he was beaten.

'Okay, give your sister a call and arrange it.' He took another sip of beer. 'They'll have to stay at mine though, you don't have the room.'

'Is that okay?'

He eyed his daughter, who was still typing away.

'I think I'd prefer it.'

'You've got to let her grow up,' said Maggie astutely.

'I know, but she's still a little girl to me. Go on, call Lou now. I know you want to.'

Smiling at the way he'd read her mind, Maggie took her phone outside to escape the bar noise.

'Hey, what's up?' asked Lou, answering on the third ring.

Maggie felt a flood of gratitude that her sister had found it in herself to forgive her. It hadn't been easy: the secret was that Maggie had slept with Lou's fiancé, Jerome, when she was pregnant with Jude. Jerome then died in a traffic accident while the affair was ongoing, so Maggie chose to keep it a secret all those years. When Lou did find out last year, by chance, it had felt to her like a double betrayal.

'Are you free the weekend after next?' she asked.

'Apart from the boys doing their usual sports stuff, yeah, we are. Why?'

'I think Jude might be happy to give basketball a miss for once,' Maggie grinned. Quickly, she filled Lou in about him and Flora.

'That's why I can't get him to put that bloody phone down,' said Lou. Maggie could tell her from her voice that she was amused, not concerned.

'Will suggested that we all stay at his, because there's more room.'

'That sounds good.'

They were discussing the best way for Lou and the kids to get from Portsmouth to Trenton when a beep on the line indicated Maggie had a call incoming. She didn't recognize the number but knew she should take the call, in case it was related to work. With Mealing breathing down her neck, she couldn't afford to be blasé.

'I'm sorry, I have to take this. I think it's work.'

'No problem, I need to get Mae down anyway.'

Maggie hurriedly rang off and picked up the other call.

'Hello, DC Neville speaking,' she answered.

'Ah good, this is the right number,' said a male voice. 'Sorry to call this late. DCI Gavin Walker here, Operation Pivot. I got your email. You did a good job with Lara Steadman and we shall be following it up with her.'

'Oh. Right, thank you,' she said.

'But that's not why I'm ringing. Is your passport up to date?'

'Sorry?'

'I've got a vacancy on my team. I've just spent the past half an hour reading up on you and I think you'd be a good fit. That Kinnock girl case, it was high profile and you handled the pressure by all accounts.'

'You mean join Operation Pivot? Sir, I don't think I can,' she spluttered. 'I mean, my team, the boss—'

'I've already cleared it with him. If you're up for it, he'll approve the temporary transfer.'

Maggie wasn't sure she liked how quickly the wheels were spinning on her career without her say-so.

'What's the role, sir?'

'I need a FLO,' he said, pronouncing it the correct way as 'flow'. 'Or rather Katy Pope's parents need one. It will mean you coming out to Majorca with us on Friday for the anniversary. We're staging a press conference after the memorial. I need someone with experience of those, and you've got that.'

Now Maggie's head was spinning to match the wheels. Joining Operation Pivot could be a great opportunity and the thought of working on an investigation overseas was exciting, but time away from the squad at Islington might make it even harder for her to integrate when she got back. Mealing was hardly going to welcome her back with open arms, that's for sure.

'Well?'

'Can I have some time to think about it, sir?' she asked.

'No. I need an answer now. I've got to get everything and everyone in place before we leave.'

Maggie glanced through the vast window of the bar to where Umpire was sitting. He smiled and raised his glass at her. She knew he'd tell her to accept the offer, but then she hadn't told him about the problems she'd been having with Mealing and what the secondment might whip up on her return. Then she checked herself: was she really going to let an arsehole like Mealing sabotage her doing something that could be good for her CV?

'Yes, sir, I'm in.'

'Good. Now, I need you here first thing for a briefing.' He rattled off the address for New Scotland Yard.

'Doesn't my boss want to see me at Islington first for a handover?' she asked.

'It doesn't sound like there was anything urgent he needed from you, so no. You're part of Operation Pivot now. See you in the morning, DC Neville.'

9

Wednesday

The middle-aged commuter sandwiched next to Maggie on the Tube platform was wearing headphones that appeared expensive but had a sound quality that fell far short of their aesthetic. The loud tinny noise escaping the black-and-silver cans made her want to stick her fingers in her own ears and the man had cranked the volume up loud enough that she could make out every word of Chris Martin singing 'Paradise'.

She shot the man a pained look in the hope he would catch its meaning and reduce the volume, but he stared straight ahead at the posters lining the Tube wall opposite the platform and moments later she could've sworn the sound increased. It was Ed Sheeran now, which she minded less. She had his first album on CD, although right now she had no idea where it was. Either in one of the boxes she still hadn't unpacked or still in Mansell, in a box gathering dust in a storage facility on the outskirts of town with the rest of the belongings she hadn't the space for.

Another commuter walking past caught her shoulder with theirs and Maggie reared backward, mindful of how precariously close her feet were to crossing the yellow line at the platform edge. The eastbound District Line platform at Victoria was packed and her chest began to tighten in response to being in a confined space surrounded by lots of people. Being claustrophobic, she should've given more thought to what living in London and commuting on the Tube would involve, but her eagerness to start her new job with the Met meant she'd overlooked the impact it might have on her. Most mornings it was a struggle to stay calm until she'd disembarked at her journey's end.

A collective groan suddenly rippled along the platform and Maggie looked up to see the words THERE IS A DELAY ON THIS LINE DUE TO SIGNAL FAILURE scroll along the bottom of the announcement board. The time until the next train's arrival spiked to ten minutes.

'Shit,' she muttered under her breath. Someone nearby in the crowd echoed her sentiment with a stronger expletive.

Her face flushed as she debated whether she should wait for the train. She didn't want to get off on the wrong foot with Walker by being late for his briefing.

To say his request for her to be liaison to Philip and Patricia Pope had been a surprise was an understatement. For one thing, she hadn't been the FLO on a single case since joining the Met. This was partly because there hadn't been any investigations where it was felt she was the best choice to serve the family's needs, and partly because she hadn't been brave enough to put herself forward for any. Mealing's constant undermining really had chipped away at her confidence.

Now, after a night sleeping on it, she was excited – and not just because her secondment meant a break from seeing Mealing for the next week at least. Katy Pope's murder was part of Britain's grim history of unsolved crimes, her name almost as recognizable to the public as Madeleine McCann's was, and it was going to be fascinating to work on an investigation so long in the running.

Katy Pope was seventeen when she went missing from a beach in Majorca while on holiday with her parents and her boyfriend, who was a university friend of her brother, George. It created headlines from day one, partly because Katy's mother was a senior Met police officer and partly because of the horrific way in which the girl's body had been disposed. Although interest in the case had dipped over the years, the anniversary trip was going to attract media attention and Maggie was ready for it: she'd had experience of what it was like being in the eye of the storm when she was the FLO to Lesley and Mack Kinnock, EuroMillions lottery winners whose daughter, Rosie, was abducted in 2016.

Another groan went along the platform as two more minutes were added to the time until the next train. Knowing she couldn't wait any longer, Maggie turned towards the exit and saw the platform was four deep already. Clutching her bag in front of her, she pushed her way through the crowd, issuing apologies as she stepped on toes and grazed bodies with her elbows.

By the time she reached outside she was perspiring from the effort of climbing the escalator two steps at a time but there was no chance to think about the sweat soaking her armpits or that her dark-blonde ponytail was plastered to the back of her neck because she had precisely nineteen minutes to sprint the twenty-four-minute route past the bus terminus, round the side of the Apollo Theatre and along Victoria Street until she hit Parliament Square, where she would then bypass Big Ben to reach the Embankment where New Scotland Yard was. Flagging down a cab was pointless because the roads around Parliament Square were usually gridlocked at this hour.

Grateful she'd had the sense to pick out her flattest shoes to wear that morning, Maggie hitched her bag back on her shoulder and broke into a run.

10

Her pace slowed as she crossed the short distance from Westminster Bridge to New Scotland Yard. She'd run fast enough that she now had a few minutes to spare.

Outside the impressive curved glass entrance, she faltered as she passed the eternal flame dedicated to fallen officers. Set within a tranquil pool and encircled by a dome of light beamed from inside the building's reception, it immediately brought to mind the colleague who had died in the line of duty last year in Mansell. They weren't what she would've described as close friends, but they had been growing closer in the preceding months. Maggie had been in charge of the op as Acting DS and many times since she had rewound the fatal moment in her mind and examined it from every angle to see if she could have done something differently to prevent it happening. She didn't think she could have, but she carried a heavy burden of guilt regardless.

Pulling herself together, she hurried inside the building, a frisson of excitement zipping through her as she crossed the threshold. In her six months with the Met she'd only been to the Yard a couple of times and it never failed to impress. It wasn't where Operation Pivot was based, however

– that was Belgravia police station, on the opposite side of Victoria Station from where she'd just come. But according to the email DCI Walker had sent her overnight to get her up to speed, today's briefing was important enough to be upgraded to the Yard because the Assistant Commissioner for Specialist Crime and Operations was going to be sitting in. With all eyes on their trip, he wanted to be sure the team was leaving nothing to chance.

Maggie reported to reception and was directed to the conference room where the briefing was to take place. Walker wasn't there yet, but her new colleagues DC Vince Paulson and DS Amit Shah were. Feeling like the new girl at school, Maggie said a tentative hello. Both greeted her warmly and Paulson pointed her towards the pots of tea and coffee laid out on a table at the side of the room.

'Only rubbish biscuits though,' said Shah. 'Blame cutbacks.'

Maggie smiled. 'I think I'll live. No sign of DCI Walker yet?'

'He's running late. Had to take an important phone call apparently.'

'Probably Mrs Pope telling him what he should and shouldn't be doing again,' said Paulson sardonically.

Maggie was surprised to detect an Australian accent.

'Oh, you're—'

'Ten years since I transferred,' he said, obviously used to explaining his provenance. 'Hot, sunny, laid-back Sydney just can't compete with this place.' He chuckled at Maggie's raised eyebrow. 'Met a British girl when she was back-packing, got her pregnant, decided I didn't want to miss seeing my son grow up, so I followed her back to the UK.

We're not together any more, in case you're wondering. Or hoping,' he smirked.

Maggie didn't react.

'Now Amit here is happily married, so don't go getting any ideas,' said Paulson, nodding to his colleague, who looked embarrassed. 'But he's the man for you as far as this investigation goes. You can ask him any question about the Katy Pope case and he knows the answer because he's absorbed every document connected to the case and committed them to memory.'

'Really?'

Shah looked sheepish as he nodded. 'I just have a very good memory. Always have had.'

Paulson palmed two digestives off the plate and was still chewing the last one when he asked Maggie what she'd heard about former Chief Superintendent Patricia Pope. She tried to ignore the crumbs he sprayed in her direction as he spoke.

'The same as you, I imagine.'

Maggie didn't want to admit she had stayed up late reading everything Google had to say about her.

The two officers exchanged knowing looks.

'Have you talked to Katinka yet?'

'No, but the boss has filled me in.'

In his email, Walker had explained that the previous FLO, DC Katinka Kasia, had been redeployed at Patricia's request but would be happy to do a handover with Maggie. But, Walker wrote,

I can tell you now what Katinka will say: Patricia Pope functions more from the viewpoint of a former chief superintendent than she does a grieving mother and she expects the Operation Pivot team and especially her FLO to respond accordingly. The problem you'll have, which Katinka also had, is that she doesn't rate family liaison – she thinks it's a superficial specialism. So, be warned, she can be a bloody nuisance. Then again, ten years is a long time to not know why your daughter was brutally murdered and by whom. The husband's lovely though. I get on well with him and Katinka did too.

'It sounds like Mrs Pope is determined to find out who killed Katy and can be pretty strident about it,' Maggie added.

Paulson gave a throaty chuckle. 'Strident is definitely one way of putting it.'

'A fucking pain in the arse is another,' said a voice from the doorway.

Maggie spun round to see a shambolic-looking middle-aged man enter the room. His wiry grey hair needed a cut, a comb *and* a wash by the looks of it and the elbows, knees and thighs of his navy suit were shiny from over wear. His paisley-patterned tie was so wide it pretty much hid the shirt he was wearing, which was probably as well because Maggie could just make out a stain on the placket.

He came across and shook her hand.

'DCI Walker, pleased to meet you,' he said. 'I hope these reprobates have been making you feel welcome.'

'They have, sir.'

'Forget that "sir" nonsense, Maggie. "Boss" will do fine.'

He looked over to the refreshments, clearly harried.

'Where are the chocolate biscuits?'

'There aren't any, boss,' said Paulson.

'For fuck's sake.'

The three of them exchanged bemused glances as he slopped coffee into a cup then stirred in four spoonfuls of sugar. Maggie wondered if he was always like this. Not the swearing, but the anxiety that was coming off him in waves. He was as taut as a violin string.

'Sit down, sit down,' he ordered them as he took a big slurp of his coffee then winced as it scalded the inside of his mouth.

Maggie took a seat next to Shah, with Paulson on the other side, as Walker paced in front of them.

'Is the Commissioner not joining us?' asked Shah.

'No, something more important came up. Which is bloody annoying because we've had a development I need to tell her about, which has come via Declan Morris of all people. He went round to see the Popes yesterday.'

'Still trying to clear his name, I see,' said Paulson with a wry grin. He turned to Maggie. 'For a time our boy Declan was the local police's *primer sospechoso* – prime suspect. This was despite Katy's parents providing his alibi that he was on the beach with them when their daughter vanished. The inspector in charge of the investigation latched on to the theory that Declan had offed Katy to get his hands on some savings she had.'

'Which was ridiculous, because for Declan to have got the money after her death, he would have had to be a beneficiary in her will,' Walker interjected. 'She was seventeen; there was no will.'

Shah leaned forward in his chair. 'I thought he and the Popes were estranged, boss?'

'They were until yesterday. The reason ma'am has been on the phone making my ears bleed *again* is because Declan's been sent an email by someone he thinks could be Katy's killer.'

Paulson swore and Shah's jaw dropped.

'Are you serious?' asked Shah.

'I'm serious that she made my bloody ears bleed. Ma'am wanted us straight round there to discuss a strategy –' Walker pulled a face as he made quote marks in the air with his fingers – 'but I said we're busy preparing for the appeal and asked her to get Morris to forward the message on.' He paused, pulled his phone out and checked his emails. 'Nope, still not got it. I told her I didn't need to read it in person with her watching.'

'Why don't I go round to see them after this briefing?' suggested Maggie. 'I should meet them before we fly out to Palma and this way she'll feel like we're taking it seriously.'

Paulson chuckled as he side-eyed Shah. 'Ma'am won't be happy if the boss sends an underling.'

'No, she won't. But she's never happy anyway, so where's the harm in one more incidence of pissing her off?' said Walker. He let out a long sigh. 'The way she's carrying on, we're all going to need a bloody holiday after this trip.'

11

Crystal Palace was one of many areas of her new city that Maggie hadn't yet got round to visiting, but she immediately warmed to the place as she walked along its neat high street lined with independent restaurants and shops. There was something village-like about it, not to mention it offered the most spectacular view. Maggie stood for a moment at the top of the sloping street where the Popes lived and marvelled at the sight before her. She could see almost the entire city, but her eye was drawn to the business district where the skyline was dominated by the shimmering Shard and supported either side by buildings she'd now come to recognize, including her personal favourite, 122 Leadenhall Street, known colloquially as the Cheesegrater.

She walked down the street, searching door signs, until she found number thirty-one.

The Victorian terrace house owned by the Popes rose impressively over three floors. Maggie was nervous as she walked up the chequered tile path to the doorway – Walker and Paulson's comments about Patricia had left an impression and now she was worried she might not pass muster.

It took ten seconds of meeting Patricia for Maggie's fears

to be founded. The woman took one look at her and went to shut the door.

'I don't like being pestered on my doorstep for donations. Go away.'

'I'm not collecting for charity,' said Maggie, cursing herself for not having her warrant card ready. 'I'm DC Maggie Neville, your new family liaison officer. DCI Walker sent me. He thought we should meet before I join you in Saros and because of the email sent to Mr Morris. I'm here to see that you're okay.'

'Oh.'

Maggie never knew one small word could convey so much disdain. Already it felt as though she'd got off on the wrong foot and it was going to take all her professional skills to avoid being kicked off the case in DC Kasia's wake.

'We're still waiting for Mr Morris to forward the email to us, but perhaps you and I could discuss the content based on what he told you?'

'I thought you were our FLO,' said Patricia. 'Why are *you* looking into the email?'

Maggie had lost track of the number of times she'd had to explain to people that even though she was their family liaison, she was a detective first and foremost and expected to investigate, but she was surprised to have to explain that to a former high-ranking officer and wasn't sure how to frame it without making it sound as though she was being critical. Fortunately for her, Patricia didn't have the patience to wait for her response and said, 'I suppose you'll have to do. You'd better come in.'

Maggie followed Patricia into a bright, airy hallway lined with the same tile pattern as the pathway. There was no time to take in more of her surroundings though as Patricia walked briskly through a doorway into the reception room and Maggie hurried to follow. Once inside, she only just managed to resist blurting out *whoa* in response to the décor: all four walls were painted the most vivid, headache-inducing shade of crimson she'd ever seen. This was not a room to relax in.

'I shan't offer you anything to drink because the sooner you get back to look into this email the better,' said Patricia, although she did at least invite Maggie to sit down.

In the flesh, Patricia resembled only a little of the stern-faced officer she was in her official Met photos, which Maggie had found online last night. The white-blonde hair severely scraped back into a chignon was now worn long and loose to the shoulders and there were far more grey streaks than highlights. But one thing hadn't changed: her granite-like expression.

Maggie got out her notebook and went straight to questioning her about the email. Patricia began describing the message in a perfunctory manner then stopped.

'What is it, Mrs Pope?'

'The second part of the email detailed a private medical matter of my daughter's that I would rather not discuss with you. Suffice to say, Declan confirmed it as being true.'

A few scenarios came to mind but Maggie decided not to push Patricia to pick one – she'd know soon enough when the email was forwarded to them. A good FLO knew when to back off if a relative was getting distressed during an interview; Patricia might be doing a stellar job of containing her upset, but it still filled the room.

'How did the email finish?' she asked.

'He said he planned to return to Saros for the anniversary, which suggests he doesn't live there. Make sure you tell Walker that,' said Patricia, as if they were too stupid to deduce it themselves.

'Did Mr Morris happen to mention the email address it was sent from?'

For the first time Maggie saw Patricia's veneer slip. Only by a fraction, but enough to make her think the woman was human after all.

'I – I didn't ask. I should've done, but I didn't.' High spots of colour appeared on Patricia's cheeks.

'That's fine.'

'I know it is,' snapped the woman, the haughtiness quickly returning. 'I can't be expected to do your entire job for you.'

Maggie ignored the dig and cleared her throat.

'I know you are well aware of what a FLO does, so I won't insult you by explaining what my role will be when we get to Saros. But if there's anything you would specifically like me to do on your behalf, please ask.'

'I'd like you to do your job and to know your place,' said Patricia evenly. 'The last girl managed neither. I am not your friend and neither is my husband or my son.'

Bloody hell, she really is a prize bitch.

'I understand. I would like to introduce myself though. Are either of them here?'

'George, our son, left home years ago and even if he hadn't he would be at work now. He's a barrister,' she said, with obvious pride. Then, less so: 'My husband is in the garden.'

Maggie waited for Patricia to get up but the woman sat impassively.

'Is it okay for me to go out and say hello?'

'You'll meet him soon enough. He doesn't like to be disturbed when he's gardening.'

Maggie didn't buy it for a second. Patricia didn't want her to meet Philip because she was establishing her ground rules: she called the shots and Maggie was to deal with her, not her husband or anyone else.

'Is that all?' Patricia got to her feet.

Maggie rose too. She steadied her nerves with a deep intake of breath. If she didn't say this now, she would forever be on the back foot with Patricia and it would make her job impossible. She had to make her position clear, even though her heart was thumping wildly in her chest as she spoke.

'Mrs Pope, I take my job as your FLO very seriously. I want to do what I can to support you and your family during the trip and the memorial service and to assist DCI Walker in making sure the press conference achieves its aim of bringing forward new witnesses and fresh evidence in your daughter's case. To do that, I need to have a good working relationship with you and your husband so we can discuss what needs to be done.'

Patricia stared at her but said nothing, which Maggie took as a sign to continue.

'I don't know what your feelings are about family liaison but I am as focused on the investigation as I am the relatives I'm assigned to. Please don't mistake me for someone who simply doles out tea and sympathy.'

The final line was in reference to the out-dated reputation family liaison used to have.

She held her breath as she waited for Patricia to respond.

After what was only seconds but felt like hours, she finally did.

'Every officer should be passionate about the job they do,' she said.

Well, it wasn't exactly an endorsement but it wasn't censure either, thought Maggie, as she followed Patricia back into the hallway to the front door.

'Thank you for your time,' she said politely, shaking Patricia's hand.

'Indeed,' said Patricia. Then she shut the door without another word.

12

Friday

Philip quailed in the blast of his wife's anger, which she was articulating loudly enough that people were turning to stare at them.

'I simply don't understand it,' Patricia was saying. 'Why are there so few of them here?'

'I don't know, darling. Perhaps something more important has come up. You know how the news cycle works these days, it changes so quickly.'

Instantly he knew he'd said the wrong thing.

'What do you know about the press?' She couldn't have been more dismissive if she'd tried.

'Dad's right though,' George chipped in. 'You did all you could to get as many journalists as possible here, but something else must've got their attention so let's make the most of the ones who are, eh?'

With a wink at Philip, George steered his mum towards the small group of reporters waiting by the entrance to Gatwick's North Terminal. The group was made up of a lone reporter from the Press Association, who said he'd be sending his copy to all the nationals and snapped pictures of the family on his phone, a stringer for the *Evening*

Standard and a crew from ITV's *London Tonight* news programme who couldn't say for certain that the footage would run.

Philip was grateful to his son for the intervention. If anyone could placate Patricia, it was George. He was as unflappable as she was, but had a natural charm his mother sorely lacked. While she rubbed everyone up the wrong way, George would having them eating out of his palm.

He gripped the handle of the luggage trolley bearing their cases as he watched the two people he loved more than anything in the world tell the press why they wouldn't rest until Katy's killer was found. A curly blond forelock flopped across George's forehead as he spoke and not for the first time Philip's mind registered how dissimilar they were in looks as well as temperament: his son was as golden as he was dark. As though sensing his father watching him, George glanced over his shoulder and flashed Philip a smile of reassurance. *We'll get through this, Dad, I promise.* It was the same promise he'd been making for the past ten years.

'Mr Pope?'

The unexpected interruption made him jump. He looked round to see a smartly dressed young woman standing beside him. She had dark-blonde hair and striking green-blue eyes, and she was holding a warrant card.

'I'm sorry to startle you. I wanted to introduce myself: I'm DC Maggie Neville, your new family liaison officer.' She offered him a handshake to go with her smile. 'It's nice to meet you.'

This must be Katinka's replacement, thought Philip. He had been sorry to see her go and certainly didn't think her 'crime' warranted it, although he had yet to confess to

Patricia that it was he who suggested she take her shoes and socks off while they were sitting in the garden chatting. He'd read somewhere that you absorb Vitamin D best through your feet because the skin is thinner there, and thought the officer could probably do with a top-up after being cooped up in an office all day. If he'd known Patricia would take such umbrage at seeing the young woman's toes he'd never have suggested it.

He returned Maggie's handshake.

'It's nice to make your acquaintance. I was very sorry to have missed you when you came round the other day.'

'Likewise. Hopefully there will be more opportunity to chat while we're in Saros.'

Philip felt his mood plunge at the mention of their destination. His hatred of the place had worsened the closer their departure. It was like this every year, but still Patricia insisted they make the pilgrimage. She said she felt closer to Katy in Saros, which Philip found baffling. For him it was at home, in the rooms she'd eaten, slept and sat in, in the hallway she'd walked through, on the stairs she'd climbed every day. He didn't understand how his wife could most keenly feel Katy's presence in the place where she was murdered.

His anguish must've shown in his expression, because Maggie asked if he was okay, her own face a picture of concern. He nodded and tried to brighten his tone.

'Philip, please. We ought to be on first-name terms, don't you think?'

'That's entirely up to you. I think your wife would prefer a more formal address though,' said Maggie.

She had a twinkle in her eye that Philip liked.

'Call her whatever she wants, but I'm Philip,' he said firmly.

'I'm sure you're already familiar with what my job involves because of DC Kasia, but if you have any questions, please do ask.'

'I have one,' a voice suddenly boomed behind them.

It was George, his interview wrapped. Philip glanced over to see that Patricia was still going. Onlookers surrounded her and the journalists now, clucking sympathetically as it dawned on them who she was and why she was at the airport. He looked away, unable to bear the sorrow their faces were projecting. He carried too much inside him to dwell on theirs.

'If you're coming to Majorca for a week,' George continued, his gaze fixed on Maggie, 'where's your suitcase?'

13

'I mean, you must have your toothbrush stashed somewhere,' George added, slowly looking Maggie up and down. 'I can't begin to imagine where though.'

It wasn't the first time in all her years as a FLO that a relative had made an inappropriately suggestive comment to Maggie, but it was the most blatant. But instead of putting George Pope in his place, she was lost for words and could feel herself blushing to her roots as he grinned at her.

'You must be Maggie,' he said, offering his hand. 'Not as in Thatcher, I hope.'

She was tempted to refuse the cheeky bastard's greeting but thought it would appear rude to his dad. So she offered her hand but then had to pretend-cough to cover the noise she nearly uttered when the touch of his palm against hers sent a jolt right to her groin. She snatched her hand away, mortified.

George threw her a bemused look.

'You haven't answered my question.'

'I've already checked in,' she said, squaring her shoulders to get things back onto a professional footing.

'That's a shame. We could've asked to be seated together.'

Before she could react, George swung his attention to his father.

'We should check in too, Dad.'

'I already have our boarding passes, we just need to go to the bag drop.'

As Philip and George checked the computer printouts that were their passage onto the plane, Maggie stood uncomfortably beside them, unsure what to do or say. Every now and then George stole a look in her direction that made her feel even more flustered.

'I probably should go and check where DCI Walker and the others are. If I don't see you again here, we'll catch up at the departure gate.'

As she moved to leave, George shot her a smile that made her stomach curl then Philip put out a hand to stop her.

'Before you go, has there been any progress on the email Declan was sent?'

Maggie channelled Patricia and set her face into the most inscrutable expression she could manage.

'No, not yet.'

'That's a pity. We were hoping something might come of it.'

Maggie had to walk away then, knowing her front would slip in the face of Philip's disappointment if she stayed any longer.

Walker had ordered her not to say anything to the Popes until further investigation had been carried out. The email Declan forwarded on to them *had* given them a breakthrough, and a significant one at that. The sender was me@threedates.com – the same address used to email Lara Steadman.

14

Saturday

Saros ranked as one of the nicest places Maggie had ever visited. It was early morning still, before eight, and she was ambling along the seafront to drink in the fresh sea air and the view before meeting Walker, Shah and Paulson for breakfast back at their hotel. The entire stretch of seafront, from the marina to the peninsula in the distance where the whitewashed blocks of Orquídea loomed imposingly over the sea, was entirely paved over and the absence of vehicles only added to the resort's charm. The place was teeming with families – the children were almost entirely preschool age, as there was still a month to go before the end of term back home – and Maggie could see the attraction: with no cars to worry about, weary parents could watch their children play in the sand in their eye-line while they took respite under the awning of a nearby cafe or restaurant.

Saros felt like the safest place imaginable, but Katy's murder had shown everyone otherwise. Walking along now, feeling the already hot sun on her face – when they landed yesterday it had been thirty-one degrees and today was predicted to be even hotter – and seeing families begin to stake out their places on the very same beach from where

Katy vanished, Maggie struggled to equate such a beautiful setting with such a horrendous crime.

Realizing it was nearly time for her to meet the others, she doubled back. The hotel where the Operation Pivot team was staying had been chosen for its no-frills reputation: the entrance was via a door sandwiched between a Spar supermarket and a cafe. There was no pool, no exclusive section of beach for patrons as provided by other hotels along the front, and only a tiny courtyard bar tucked away at the rear of the hotel. That at least meant they could avoid prying eyes if there was time for a drink at the end of the day. The team, Walker included, was under strict orders not to be seen enjoying themselves: the last thing the Met needed was the public thinking they were sunning themselves on a taxpayer-funded freebie instead of working.

By the time she reached her room – her claustrophobia made her walk the stairs rather than take the lift – Maggie was hot and sweaty. But there was no time to nip inside and change her shirt because on hearing her fiddling with the key card in the slot, Walker stuck his head out of his next-door room.

'Ah, you're up. Good. Change of plan – it's a working breakfast on my balcony now.'

Maggie followed him into his room, noting the reams of files and paperwork strewn across his double bed. He'd obviously been up early too, but hard at work.

Shah and Paulson were already on the balcony, helping themselves to croissants from a plate piled high with them.

'Morning,' said Paulson, raising his croissant at her as though it was a wine glass. 'Sleep well?'

'Yes, thanks.'

She didn't return the question. A few days in Paulson's company had taught her that he could insert innuendos into any conversation on any topic. Walker found it hilarious, but it really grated on her – and Shah too, judging by the way he spent most of his time in Paulson's company rolling his eyes – so she now took care not to say anything that he could spin into a line. Which meant she hardly said anything to him at all.

Walker offered her a glass of orange juice poured from the jug on the table, which she gratefully accepted.

'I thought we should have breakfast here and not in the restaurant downstairs because I want to get cracking on revisiting some of the witnesses who were interviewed first time round and obviously we need to be discreet. I don't want Babs from Blackpool overhearing us and plastering it all over Twitter,' Walker said.

He sat down in the vacant seat.

'First up, the emails to Lara Steadman and Declan Morris are untraceable as the sender used a proxy server to scramble the IP address. But a forensic linguistics expert has confirmed it's the same writer. Apparently they can tell by the phrasing. Given the detail about Lara's abduction and Katy's termination, it's safe to say the person who wrote them was either the killer or an accomplice in the murder.'

Maggie immediately thought of Lara and the lucky escape she'd had.

'Are you going to tell the Popes?'

Walker shook his head. 'No, not yet. I don't trust what ma'am will do with the information. She's blabbed too many times to the press. I want to sit on it, in case we need it as leverage further down the line.'

'Boss, I did an internet search for the phrase "three dates" to see what came up, and it widely refers to the ideal number of dates a woman should go on before she has sex with a man if she wants their relationship to amount to anything,' said Shah. 'Apparently it was on an episode of *Sex and the City* and then became a thing.'

Paulson turned to Maggie. 'Why didn't you know that?'

She gave him a withering look and he had the decency to look embarrassed.

'I didn't find any organizations that go by the name "three dates" and the only company I found was a Libyan date producer based in Tripoli who's got a page on Facebook,' Shah continued. 'So unless our sender has a taste for dried fruit, we can assume he thought up the address for himself. It's the why I can't work out.'

'Let's do a PNC and Interpol check to see if there are any other cases where the phrase "three dates" has cropped up,' said Walker to Shah, who nodded.

The DCI lifted a piece of paper from the tabletop with notes scribbled all over it in his handwriting. Then he peered over the top of it at Maggie.

'I know you've done well to get up to date on the case file in the short time you've been with us, but I'll just run through the details of these witnesses to make sure you're up to speed. I need you to muck in with these two on interviews so we can cover as much ground as possible between now and our flight home on Friday.'

'Of course, boss,' she said.

'Right, the first one I want us to review is an ex-pat named Terry Evans, who ten years ago owned a garden apartment in block three at Orquídea,' said Walker. 'The local police had him in for questioning pretty swiftly because they'd received numerous complaints against him over the years. Evans hated the revolving door of tourists staying at Orquídea, even though most of the apartments were already holiday lets when he bought his, so he got into the habit of nicking any kids' inflatables left by the pool overnight and puncturing them with a knife. He'd also dump any rubbish left in the poolside bins outside apartment doors for guests to trip over in the morning, and would scream abuse at anyone he felt was making too much noise late at night.'

'He sounds pleasant,' said Maggie grimly.

'It was Evans's fondness for knives that made him a suspect, but like Declan Morris he also had an alibi for when Katy vanished from the beach – he was at a business meeting in Palma. The police did stick a tail on him during the week she was missing, just in case, but he stayed indoors the entire time and was alone apart from his solicitor coming and going.'

Maggie was confused.

'You mean Evans had a tail on him at his apartment and the killer still managed to waltz inside Orquídea with the body parts?'

'Ah, that's the thing,' said Walker, wagging his finger at her. 'Evans complained his privacy had been violated when his apartment was searched, so he booked himself into a hotel in Palma and instructed his solicitor to push for damages so his apartment could be deep cleaned. He was more bothered about it being messy than he was about being questioned.'

'The man was a neat freak,' Paulson chipped in. 'Couldn't

abide people touching his stuff. Afterwards it was assumed the killer chose Orquídea to dump the body because Evans had kindly ensured the police's focus was elsewhere.'

'Evans could have been an accomplice and planned it that way with the killer to distract the police,' Maggie pointed out.

'Every possible angle was checked with Evans – phone records, emails, *everything*,' said Shah. 'There was nothing to suggest he'd been plotting to murder Katy or anyone else. There wasn't even the tiniest coincidence linking him to her.'

'It's crazy no one saw her body being dumped,' said Maggie. 'I know June isn't high season, but Orquídea still must've had a lot of guests staying.'

'That's the irony of Evans not being there when it happened,' said Paulson. 'He was such a busybody that had he been at home he might well have spotted something.'

'The pond areas are also secluded from the apartment blocks by dense bushes and trees. It wouldn't have been as difficult as you'd imagine to do it undetected,' Walker added. 'The killer could've driven a car through the gate with Katy in the boot and dumped her in minutes. There was no CCTV in the complex back then either.'

'Did Evans move after his apartment was defiled?' asked Maggie.

'Actually, he stayed,' said Walker. 'The pond nearest his apartment is the one where they found her head.'

15

Walker let his comment settle uneasily over the team then consulted his list again.

'Next on my list is Julien Ruiz, a Madrid-born postgrad who had strong family ties to Saros,' said Walker. 'In June 2009 he was here working as a waiter at a bar on the town square, which is where he met Katy. She and Patricia had gone out for dinner alone one evening at the end of their first week and stopped off for a final drink. Julien was their waiter. Patricia went back to the villa after one drink, but Katy stayed on because she'd got chatting to a young couple at the next table and discovered they lived in Penge, which is down the road from where the Popes lived in Crystal Palace. Katy told her mum she'd finish her drink with them then follow her home. Because she was only a couple of weeks away from turning eighteen, Patricia thought she was old enough to travel back alone in a taxi. She'd only had one alcoholic drink all evening, a cocktail her mum permitted her as a nightcap.'

Maggie recalled reading the Penge couple's statement when she'd gone through the case file back in London in the two days she had to prepare before flying out. 'Are they the ones who flogged their story to a tabloid?'

'Yes, that's them,' said Walker. 'They claimed Katy had been coming on hot and heavy to Ruiz, that he'd reciprocated and that Katy said she planned to go home with him when his shift ended. The couple left the bar at one a.m., forty-five minutes after Patricia left, and said Katy's last words to them were to ask if Spanish condoms were as safe as British ones.'

Paulson chipped in again.

'Ruiz said it was bollocks and that the couple had made it up to get a big fat cheque from a tabloid. He said Katy left ten minutes after they did, but he couldn't prove it. Neither Philip, Patricia nor Declan heard her return because they were asleep.'

'Surely Declan noticed she wasn't in bed?'

'Your parents must've been more liberal than Patricia Pope was,' grinned Paulson. 'Katy and Declan weren't allowed to share a room. She and her mum used to have blazing rows about the relationship. The day before she disappeared, Katy was seen sobbing her heart out on the seafront because she and her mum had rowed again about Declan.'

'The witness who comforted her is on the list of people I want us to revisit, but I'll come back to them in a minute,' said Walker. 'So, Ruiz had a reputation for sleeping with anything in a skirt, but the police in Saros decided this was the one time he'd sent an attractive girl packing without so much as giving her a peck on the cheek and ruled him out.'

'He did have an alibi though, boss,' said Shah, who Maggie now recognized was the team's voice of reason. 'Ruiz was ruled out as a suspect in the murder because he boarded in a hostel with dozens of other restaurant and bar workers and his movements could be accounted for the entire time Katy was missing – he was either at work or at the hostel. One of those friends also said he remembered Ruiz coming back to the hostel, alone, not long after the bar shut.'

'However,' said Walker, shooting Shah a look, 'there was a back room in the bar that he admitted to using with other conquests where he easily could've shagged Katy and then killed her. The place wasn't checked for forensics and, had it been, traces of her might've been found there.'

'He swore blind he never slept with her,' said Shah in an aside to Maggie. 'He said Katy had told him she was going to come back another evening with her boyfriend so he could try the cocktails too.'

'The Spanish police might've cleared him of any involvement but as far as the public was concerned, it was his word against the couple from Penge and everyone believed them that he'd slept with Katy,' said Paulson. 'Then lots of other stories came out about him. Where's that front page, boss? Maggie should see it.'

'It's on the bed.'

Paulson disappeared inside the room.

'Is he still in Saros, then?' asked Maggie.

Walker nodded. 'He owns an apartment in the old town.'

Paulson returned to the balcony holding a print. 'Well, he was hardly going to return to the bosom of his family in Madrid after gems like this.' He held up a photocopy of a tabloid front page from 2009 that was dominated by a picture of an attractive young man with his arms round two beaming women, one in her twenties, the other a couple of decades older, and the headline KATY'S ISLAND LOVER SLEPT WITH ME – AND MY MUM!

He and Walker broke into laughter.

'Ruiz's family disowned him and told him he wasn't welcome back in Madrid after this story and others came out,' Shah addressed Maggie. 'His parents were devout Catholics and were horrified by the media image of their son as a promiscuous philanderer.'

'What do you hope to gain from re-interviewing him now, boss?' she asked.

'It won't hurt to rattle his tree and see if he's ready to confess to sleeping with Katy.'

'Why does it matter now, boss? His alibi for the murder is solid,' said Shah.

Walker looked peeved for a moment.

'I know it is, but we need to go back to London with something, otherwise the stopper is going back in the money box for Operation Pivot. The Met doesn't have an infinite budget and what it has given us we've pretty much bled dry. So getting Ruiz to admit he did shag Katy and lied about it could be useful. The one thing Patricia Pope and I agree on is that the original investigation by the local police here was atrocious – clues were missed, evidence lost, forensics not carried out, witness statements not written up. You name it, they ballsed it up. It was a bloody shambles. So if we get Ruiz to change his statement, it strengthens the argument to keep Operation Pivot going to undo the mess the Spanish made in the first place.'

Walker's cheeks were flushed pink by the time he finished and it suddenly hit Maggie that this wasn't just a professional endeavour for him – he cared deeply about keeping

Operation Pivot going so they could finally nail Katy's killer.

'We hear you, boss,' said Paulson. Maggie and Shah quickly nodded their support.

Walker cleared his throat and composed himself.

'Third and fourth on the list are two known sex offenders who both lived within two kilometres of Saros when Katy was abducted. Both had alibis that ruled them out of further involvement but, again, let's assume the Spanish police weren't that thorough in their checks. Neither man lives in the area still, but the people who provided the alibis do and I've got their current addresses, so I want you two,' he nodded at Paulson and Shah, 'to pay them a visit.'

He looked serious again for a moment. 'We have to remember to tread carefully. We're only here at the invitation of Majorca's Director General of Police and he's made it crystal clear that the local coppers in Saros aren't happy about it. That, coupled with the fact Brexit has made us pariahs in Europe, means one toe out of line and we're on the next flight home. So don't forget that when you're dealing with these people. We've got to play nice.'

'That's going to be tough with the next one on your list, boss,' said Shah, looking troubled.

'Who is it?' asked Maggie.

'A taxi driver whose brother happened to be Saros's Chief of Police.'

16

An hour later Maggie found herself walking back along the seafront towards Orquídea, her pace far brisker than it had been before breakfast. She was on her way to speak to a witness called Annika Lindstrøm, who had lived in Saros for two decades and now owned a restaurant that was part of the Orquídea complex. The reason Walker was keen for them to revisit the woman's statement was that she claimed to have seen Katy crying on the seafront the day before she went missing. The girl had been so distressed that Annika was compelled to go over and check that she was okay and Katy apparently told her she'd had a row with her mother about her relationship with Declan – something Patricia vehemently denied when questioned.

As she hurried to her destination, Maggie reflected on how many people Walker wanted them to re-interview in the few days they were in Saros. As well as Evans, Ruiz, the taxi driver – who had a previous conviction for spiking the drink of a girl similar in age to Katy so he could assault her in his cab – the two other known sex offenders and Annika, there were six other locals on his list. The statements of those six had been less helpful to the inquiry – one was from a woman who worked in a swimwear shop near the marina who thought she saw Katy leave the beach the day she went missing, but was only eighty per cent sure – but Walker wanted them checked again. He wanted to light a fire under Saros during the anniversary to flush out the killer if, as he'd threatened in his emails, he did return.

With so much to accomplish, Maggie had to hope she could still be the FLO the Popes needed her to be. Patricia had summoned her to her own briefing at eleven – she didn't quite label their meeting like that, but it was obvious that's what she meant when she said she had an itinerary of tasks she wanted to discuss. It was nine thirty now, so Maggie should have enough time to talk to Annika, provided she was free, and get to the Popes' apartment in time for eleven. Maggie hated to think what Patricia's reaction would be if she didn't.

Fortunately for her, Annika was available to chat when she arrived at the restaurant, which was barnacled to the side of Orquídea but separated from the inner sanctum of the complex by a security gate. In the five minutes Maggie sat waiting for Annika to join her she watched four guests struggle to remember the code to pass through it. One waited until someone walked out in the opposite direction so they could hold the gate open, and the other three waited until a person who did know the code let them in after them. As security gates went, it wasn't the most secure.

Eventually she saw Annika approaching, carrying two tall glasses filled with water and ice.

'I thought you might want this,' she said, handing Maggie the glass.

She was a striking-looking woman, with silver-grey hair

that trailed down to her waist and green, cat-like eyes framed by dark, thick brows. Despite the grey hair, she was only in her early forties, maybe younger, and she had the kind of slim, firm body that suggested a devotion to yoga or Pilates.

'Your hair colour is amazing,' Maggie blurted out. 'Is it dyed?'

Annika laughed. 'No, it's all mine. I started going grey at fifteen. By twenty-two I decided there was no point fighting what you cannot help. So I stopped dyeing it.' She wound a thick strand round her finger and examined it. 'I'm lucky it went silver and not witchy-white.'

Twenty years of living on Majorca had done nothing to eradicate Annika's Swedish accent.

'So, how can I help you, officer?'

'Myself and three colleagues are in Saros for the tenth anniversary of Katy—'

Annika cut her off with a smile.

'The entire town knows you're here. It's all anyone's been talking about for days. It's caused quite the stir.'

'I take it not in a good way?'

'You guess correctly. People are frightened by the presence of the British police. It has taken Saros a long time to recover from what happened,' she said solemnly. 'The murder of a tourist was very, very bad for business. The summer afterwards, bookings were down by two-thirds and not just amongst the British. The Germans, French and Dutch stopped coming too. Bars and restaurants that had been in families for generations closed down and people were forced to move to other towns for work.'

'We don't mean to upset anyone by being here,' said

Maggie. 'But the killer is still out there and he needs to be caught.'

Annika nodded. 'The people of Saros would like nothing more. We see the Popes here every year and our hearts break for them. But don't expect people to welcome you and your colleagues with open arms is all I'm saying.'

'Well, I'm pleased you're a friendly face at least,' said Maggie. She pulled some stapled-together pages from her bag. 'I have your statement here from ten years ago. Can I ask you some questions about it?'

'Of course.'

Back at the hotel, Maggie had highlighted some sections. 'Had you come across Katy before you saw her crying on the seafront the day before she went missing?'

Annika's eyes narrowed.

'Did I know her already? No.'

'So you went over purely because she was crying?'

'That's what I said.'

'Actually, your statement implies you recognized her.'

'What?'

Maggie read from the paper: '*I could see she was crying, so I went over and said, "Katy, what's wrong?"*'

Annika shook her head.

'I didn't know her name when I went over. They've got that wrong.'

'It's my understanding that your original statement was recorded in Spanish and translated into Swedish so you could sign it,' said Maggie, remembering what Shah had told her. Paulson hadn't been joking when he said Shah really did know everything about the investigation. 'This is a copy of the one you signed and this here,' she held up three more sheets, 'is the same statement translated into English.'

'I think I would've noticed an error like that. Can I see it?'

Maggie handed her the Swedish version. Annika lifted the first two sheets to check the third.

'That's not my signature.'

Now it was Maggie's turn to exclaim. 'What?'

'It's not even close to what mine looks like.' Annika took the pen tucked in the waistband of her denim cut-offs and signed her name in the notebook she used for taking orders. She held both notebook and statement up to Maggie: she was right, the signatures didn't match by any stretch. Then she laid the notebook on the table and turned back to the first page of the statement. 'I think I should read the rest,' she said.

'Please do.'

Three times Annika muttered 'I didn't say that' under her breath as she read. When she reached the end and looked up, her green eyes flashed with anger. 'It's not an entire work of fiction, but details have been added that I most definitely did not say.' She turned to page two and stabbed a paragraph with her finger. 'Here, when I talk about Katy telling me she'd argued with her parents, I never said it was about her boyfriend, Declan. She never mentioned Declan's name. I didn't know what it was until I read it in the paper.'

'But she did say there had been a row?'

'Yes, about a boy her parents didn't want her hanging around with. But she never said the words *boyfriend* or *Declan*.'

'So it could've been anyone?'

'Yes. Please, tell me, how is it possible the police I spoke to got this wrong?'

'I don't know,' said Maggie, careful not to make any comments or judgements about the local police's handling of the investigation that might end up being gossiped around town. 'Were you given a copy of your statement to sign and read?'

'Yes, but it wasn't this one.'

It was a sobering accusation and one Maggie couldn't wait to feed back to Walker. If the version of Annika's statement that had been passed to Operation Pivot by the Spanish police was at best incorrect and at worst had been doctored, it might not be the only one.

'What else is wrong with it?' she asked.

'It's missing what Katy told me about her mother: she was frightened of her. Katy said she had a secret that if her mother found out she would be very angry, but she didn't say what it was and I certainly didn't push it. But she was very upset. It took me ages to get the poor girl to stop crying.'

Maggie suspected the secret might've been the termination they now knew Katy had undergone four months before her death. Declan had confirmed it to them in a conversation he'd had with Walker after forwarding the DCI the email from me@threedates.com.

'Katy's mum denied any row took place the day before she went missing.'

'I had a mother who was also a narcissist and that's what she would do – deny, deny, deny. Nothing was ever her fault.' Annika suddenly appeared downcast. 'I told Katy she needed to learn to stand up to her mother, because she was nearly an adult and would soon be free to make her own choices, so she should get used to saying no to her. As I say, my mother was the same, so I recognized how Katy was feeling. That's why I ended up here, thousands of miles away from my homeland.'

She picked at the edge of the table. 'I thought I was helping the girl's self-esteem, but then I heard it was because they'd had another row that Katy had stormed off the beach the day she went missing. If I hadn't told her to stand up for herself, she might not have left and then she'd have been safe.'

'You can't torture yourself wondering. Katy could easily have found another reason to leave the beach. She might—' Maggie stopped as an idea exploded in her mind. 'The boy she rowed with her mum about: did she say anything else about him to you?'

Annika thought for a moment. 'Nothing specific. I only recall her saying her mum thought he looked like trouble.'

'Did it sound like he was someone Katy already knew, back home in England?'

Annika's features shifted, a spark of realization lifting them. 'You know what, no, it didn't. The way Katy spoke it sounded like someone she'd met in Saros.'

Maggie fought to hide her elation. This could be significant: Katy had met someone on the holiday her mother disapproved of who wasn't Declan – what if that boy, whoever he was, was the person who killed her?

But the question that really needed answering was why Patricia had never once mentioned him.

17

Maggie made it to the Popes' apartment with only a minute to spare, so there wasn't time to call Walker and brief him on her conversation with Annika. Patricia needed to be tackled again on that row in the light of Annika claiming it was about an unknown male and not Declan, but because she had already denied it ever happening Maggie wasn't sure she should be the one to broach it. As she pressed the buzzer outside the apartment door, she decided she would hold off raising it until she'd spoken to Walker first. Being FLO to the Popes was, she was coming to realize, unlike any other case she'd worked as family liaison: dealing with a highly experienced ex-senior officer was a minefield.

Patricia opened the door with more enthusiasm than she had the first day they'd met in Crystal Palace.

'Come in,' she said. 'Would you like a coffee?'

'That would be great, thank you.'

This was promising: Patricia appeared to be in a good mood.

Maggie followed her into a long room that housed both the lounge and the dining area. The first thing she noticed was that the air con was on an arctic setting and the second was the presence of George Pope. He was on the sofa in shorts and a T-shirt and, as Patricia ushered her closer, Maggie could see that the thick golden hairs on his legs were standing to attention from the chill.

'Nice to see you again, Maggie,' he said, smiling widely.

'You too,' she said awkwardly.

They hadn't spoken since Gatwick, although she had seen him since arriving in Saros. She'd sidestepped getting into a conversation with him, feeling unsettled in his company and not wanting to think about why.

'How's your hotel?' he asked.

The unobjectionable question relaxed her a little.

'It's fine, actually. How's everything here?' She glanced across to the door that led to the kitchen, where Patricia was now preparing a fresh pot of coffee. 'How are your parents coping?'

'Mum like the Trojan she always is. As you can see, she's been busy.' George nodded at the coffee table in front of him. It was covered in flyers with his sister's face on them; some of the wording was Spanish, the rest English.

'I can help her put those up,' said Maggie.

'She'd appreciate that. We want to cover as much ground as possible.' He moved a pile of flyers off the seat next to him. 'Here, sit down.'

Maggie lowered herself onto the sofa but stayed perched on the edge.

'I don't bite,' he grinned. 'Well, only at a full moon and on Bank Holidays.'

Maggie ignored the comment. 'How's your dad?'

'Wishing he was anywhere but here, but he's being stoic about it for Mum's sake.'

'What about you? Do you find it as hard coming back?' His face fell.

'Fuck, yes. I hate it as much as Dad does. Being here makes me absolutely loathe summer and Katy wouldn't have wanted that. It was our favourite time of year as kids. Do you have any siblings?'

'Yes, a sister.'

'Make the most of having her,' he said softly. 'I took mine for granted like all siblings do; now I'd give anything for just five minutes again with her.'

He turned his head away swiftly to hide his tears. 'Sorry,' he said, wiping them away with the backs of his hands. 'Normally I'm fine talking about her, but everything is amplified being here.'

'That's understandable,' said Maggie. 'It's a tough week for you.'

George reached across and squeezed her hand. 'Thank you.'

Blushing scarlet, Maggie pulled away as Patricia came in with a tray of cups and a full coffee pot. She sprang to her feet. 'Here, let me take that.'

'I'll just clear these away and you can set it down on the table,' Patricia said.

As his mum gathered up the flyers, Maggie could sense George was staring at her. She glanced over at him and he smiled. Two of the cups clacked together as the tray wobbled in her grasp.

A few minutes later the three of them were sat discussing the memorial service as they sipped their coffee. When Maggie enquired after Philip, Patricia told her he'd gone for a walk. It struck Maggie that he appeared to have little say in what went on in his daughter's name – or perhaps he preferred it that way.

'So, how are matters progressing your end?' asked Patricia, once they'd covered the topic of who locally had been invited. The British Consul in Palma had confirmed a representative would be present but it sounded as though Patricia was pinning her hopes on the mayor of Saros being there.

'We've been busy,' said Maggie, fearing it was a trick question and whatever she said would be the wrong answer.

'Doing what?'

'DCI Walker has drawn up a list of witnesses from ten years ago he wants us to re-interview. People who still live in the area.'

Patricia looked pleased. 'Good. Who is on the list?'

'It's probably best if DCI Walker briefs you,' said Maggie politely. 'You may have questions for him that I'm unable to answer right now.'

Patricia steadied her gaze.

'A FLO is meant to be the conduit between the Senior Investigating Officer and the family of the deceased. It is the job of the FLO to make sure information sought by the relatives is addressed quickly and answered to their satisfaction,' she said in a slow, measured tone.

Maggie couldn't believe it. The woman was actually quoting from the Met's family liaison guidelines. She decided to fight fire with fire; she might not remember the section verbatim, but she remembered enough to make it sound as convincing.

'There may be times when a FLO is unable to share information with the family because it may jeopardize future criminal proceedings, but they should always make it clear when that is the case,' she replied evenly.

Unless she was mistaken, Patricia's mouth almost twitched into a smile. George, on the other hand, showed no such restraint.

'Touché,' he laughed. 'So, does that mean there might be something, but you can't tell us yet?'

As openings went, it was a good one: George had given Maggie the opportunity to jump straight in and tell them what Annika had said. But she held back, knowing Walker should be briefed first. There was a reason that nowhere in the case file did it mention that Patricia and Katy had rowed about another boy and not Declan Morris the day before her disappearance. Patricia would've known that was a crucial fact, so if she was withholding on them that needed looking into as much as the row itself. Maggie also wondered what Philip Pope might have to say about it now.

'It means we've only just started re-interviewing, but we will share the information we gather when we can. The point I was trying to make is that if you,' she addressed this directly to Patricia, 'want to know who is on the list, it really should come directly from DCI Walker.'

To her relief, Patricia nodded then changed the subject.

'Tomorrow is Sunday. My husband and I will be going to Palma to attend a service at the cathedral and shall be gone for the day.'

'Leaving me here on my lonesome,' said George with an exaggerated sigh. 'Unless you want to come and hang out?' he asked Maggie, who blushed again.

'You have work to do, for your trial,' Patricia told her son firmly, 'and so does Maggie. She'll be busy with all those interviews. It's not her job to be at your beck and call.'

George released a sigh even more drawn out than the last.

'More's the pity.'

18

Monday

Philip watched as Maggie furtively plucked a small compact from her handbag and reapplied another layer of powder to her already matte nose.

'I'm not sure that is going to suffice,' he said, kindly. 'I'm afraid your nose is rather too sunburnt to be disguised.'

Smiling, Maggie snapped the compact shut and dropped it back into her bag.

'Serves me right for not buying suncream with the highest SPF,' she said.

'Oh, I don't think any of us imagined it would be quite this hot.' As though to illustrate the point, Philip removed the white cotton trilby-style sunhat he'd purchased at Palma airport when they'd arrived on Friday evening and fanned them both with it. 'It's nearly thirty-four degrees today, much hotter than the last time we were here.'

They were sitting beneath a sun canopy outside Annika's restaurant that was next door to Orquídea. It was nine thirty but neither of them had had breakfast yet, and the piquant smell of omelettes being cooked was making Philip hungry. But he felt they should wait until Patricia had joined them before ordering. She had risen early to deliver flyers to the restaurants and cafes on the beachfront: she wanted to make sure word was spreading about the renewed appeal for information ahead of the memorial service tomorrow.

'How was Palma?' asked Maggie.

'We had a lovely day, thank you. Have you been into the city yet? No? You must visit the cathedral if you have the chance. It is simply stunning, one of the most beautiful examples in the world.'

'I imagine it was nice to get away from Saros for a bit.'

Philip nodded. 'It's not my favourite place, with obvious reason. How are the preparations for the press conference?'

'Good. The mayor of Saros has agreed we can have it on the beachfront and he's also confirmed he'll attend the service.'

'Patricia will be pleased when you tell her. I don't know how much press interest there will be, though,' said Philip fretfully. 'She was disappointed by the turnout at the airport.'

'She shouldn't be. Our press office is saying the interviews she and George gave sparked a lot of interest. I think some of the bigger papers are now sending reporters out for the press conference and the service.'

Philip cringed. He felt the memorial should be private, just them, George and now Declan, who was flying in from London later, but Patricia was insisting anyone could attend.

'It will still be the special occasion you want it to be,' said Maggie gently.

He appreciated her perceptiveness and kindness. In fact, Philip found he was rather taken with her and any fears she might not be as nice as Katinka had vanished. Maggie was professional without being sycophantic, warm and friendly but not presumptuous. He could tell Patricia was thawing towards her too: after their meeting at the apartment on Saturday his wife had remarked that Maggie was straightforward to deal with, which for her was high praise indeed.

This morning he was finding Maggie delightful company and the heavy sorrow that had entombed his heart the moment he saw the first road sign for Saros on the drive from the airport was easing a fraction.

'It must be difficult coming back,' said Maggie.

Philip nodded gravely. 'I understand why my wife wants us to be here, but if I had my way, we would be marking the anniversary privately at home.'

He fiddled with the red band that trimmed his hat for a moment then placed it back on his head. 'Do you think we'll ever find out who did it? I'm sorry, I can see you weren't expecting such a direct question,' he said, catching her look of surprise.

'I wasn't, but since you've asked I shall try to answer as best I can.' She paused, as though collecting her thoughts. 'Sometimes all it takes to crack a case is one tiny piece of evidence. It could be something that's been overlooked so far, or something new that suddenly presents itself. If we can get a breakthrough like that in Katy's case then I do believe it could lead to us apprehending the killer.'

'Truly?'

Maggie nodded. 'It's not unheard of even in cases that have remained unsolved for decades. I don't want to give you false hope though. We need to find that evidence first and there have been a few case reviews that haven't thrown up anything new.'

'Until DCI Walker took over – he found the jeweller.'

'It was a good lead,' she agreed. The email to Lara Steadman was another, but still Walker didn't want the family to know about it.

Maggie shifted her chair closer to Philip's; the sun had crept round while they were talking and a shard was hitting her directly in her already rosy face.

'Your wife might've mentioned that we're re-interviewing witnesses.'

'She did.'

'One of them is Annika, who runs this place.'

'Oh, I had no idea.'

'Annika was the witness who found Katy crying on the seafront the day before she went missing. Apparently she and your wife had had a bit of a row.'

Philip shifted awkwardly in his seat.

'My wife already told the police there was no row.'

'Annika's adamant there was. In her initial statement she said Katy told her the argument was about Declan, but Annika's now saying it was about another male Katy had met in Saros who Patricia didn't like.'

'That's preposterous,' said Philip. 'Katy couldn't possibly have met anyone else because she was always with Declan. In fact, that's why she and Patricia rowed on the beach the day of her disappearance. Katy and Declan wanted to do something on their own in the afternoon and Patricia wanted her to spend more time with us.'

'Oh. I see.'

'We were honest from day one about the row on the beach, as uncomfortable as it was to admit. Had there been a row the day before we would have said so,' Philip went on, upset that Maggie didn't appear convinced. 'I'm sorry to disappoint you, I really am. I would love for you and DCI Walker to have a new lead to follow up.'

They sat in silence for a few moments.

'Where is DCI Walker anyway?'

'He's gone to Palma to meet the Director General of Police. It's a courtesy visit to thank him for allowing us to come to Majorca for the memorial and to hold the press conference.'

Philip winced.

'I'm afraid we've ruffled a few feathers along the way with the local police,' he said. 'My wife has been – how can I put this delicately – rather robust in her critique of their handling of the case.'

'I think I'd probably be the same in her shoes,' said Maggie generously. 'It goes with the territory, thinking you could do it better if you were in charge.'

Philip chuckled. 'Patricia certainly wishes she was.' He drained the last of his coffee. 'Shall we order another?'

'Can I please have a glass of water this time, lots of ice? I need something to cool me down.'

Philip peered over his shoulder to see if service was close by. A man was already walking in the direction of their table so he raised his hand to beckon him closer. But as the person came into sharper focus, he gasped.

'Johnnie?'

'It certainly is,' said the man, grinning.

Philip rose to his feet.

'My dear boy, what a glorious surprise.'

Gestures of intimacy didn't always come easy to Philip but he hugged Johnnie as though his life depended on it. As they parted, he saw Maggie was staring at them curiously.

'Maggie, allow me to introduce Johnnie Hickman-Ferguson, our godson. His father is one of my oldest, dearest friends. Johnnie, this is DC Maggie Neville, our new family liaison.'

They shook hands politely.

'What are you doing here?' Philip asked Johnnie. 'The last time I spoke to your father he said you were in Brazil.'

'I've been back a month or so. I was in London for a week then I've been staying at our place in Ibiza ever since. When Dad said you were all coming over to commemorate Katy, I didn't want to miss it, so I sailed over yesterday.'

Then, to Philip's utter surprise, Johnnie burst into tears.

19

Maggie felt awkward being witness to the exchange between the two men. It was clear Philip had no idea how to console Johnnie, who was now sitting at the table weeping into his hands. He delicately patted him on the shoulder and said 'there, there' in a manner that was more uneasy than reassuring. Maggie thought about saying something herself but didn't want to undermine Philip's efforts, however ineffectual they were.

In the end Johnnie did them both a favour by releasing a big sigh and drying his eyes and cheeks on a paper serviette plucked from the chrome dispenser in the middle of the table.

'Sorry about that,' he said gruffly. 'Don't know what came over me.'

Compared to Philip, who was as neat in appearance as he was in deportment, Johnnie looked like he'd emerged from a skip. He had dirty blond hair almost as long as Maggie's and the weathered face of someone who spent a lot of time outdoors – telltale white creases fanned out from his eyes from being screwed up against the sun. She guessed his age was early thirties and he was scantily dressed but weather appropriate in a singlet vest and scruffy shorts. She couldn't see his feet under the table but would put money on him wearing battered Birkenstocks or Havaianas.

'It's perfectly understandable,' said Philip kindly, then turned to Maggie. 'Johnnie is the son of my best friend, Howard. Patricia and I are his godparents and Howard and his wife, Lydia, are George's. Our children grew up together and Johnnie and Katy were always tremendously close.'

Maggie's gaze flickered towards Johnnie. He was about to say something when Annika glided over to ask if they wanted to order food yet. They all declined anything to eat, but Philip asked for coffee for him and Johnnie, while Maggie requested a glass of water.

After Annika went, Johnnie began to talk.

'My parents owned the villa where these guys were staying when Katy was murdered,' he said to Maggie. 'We were all devastated, and still are. That's what set me off – being back here and seeing Philip and being reminded again how awful it was to lose her. She was an amazing girl.'

'Is your father here too?'

'No, just me. He's not well enough to travel. Heart problems. And no, I don't have any siblings, before you ask.'

For someone whose physical appearance suggested a relaxed attitude, Johnnie Hickman-Ferguson was coming across as uptight and prickly. Maybe he resented Maggie, a stranger, seeing him cry and intruding on his reunion with Philip, or maybe he was simply distrustful of the police. He wouldn't be the first.

'Well, I am grateful you've made the effort,' said Philip, 'and I know Patricia will be too.'

'Where are you staying?' asked Maggie.

'I'll crash on my boat. I'm moored in the marina.' He turned to Philip. 'You're not really staying there are you? Dad told me.' He tilted his head towards the security gate that led from the restaurant into the Orquídea complex. Philip clasped his hands tightly as he answered the question, as though clinging onto himself for support.

'Patricia thought it would be helpful if we were close to where the memorial service will be, for reasons of practicality. We did look at alternative accommodation, but ultimately Orquídea was the most convenient.'

Johnnie arched an eyebrow.

'Bit morbid, isn't it?'

Philip struggled to answer and Maggie felt sorry for him, because however he argued otherwise, it *was* morbid staying in an apartment that directly overlooked the dumping ground where his daughter's body parts had been scattered.

'It's what Patricia wanted,' said Philip feebly.

Thankfully, Johnnie chose not to labour the point.

'Where's George?' he asked.

'He was asleep when I left to meet Maggie, but I imagine he's working now. He has a big trial next week to prepare for. Declan will be arriving shortly. I think his plane touched down around eight a.m., but don't quote me on that.'

Johnnie reared back and bared his teeth, like a dog seconds before it unleashes a volley of barks.

'You're letting that fucker come?'

'Johnnie, please,' implored Philip. 'There's no need for that kind of language.'

'There is where he's concerned.'

'You two were friends once, don't forget.'

'Yeah, I hadn't forgotten,' said Johnnie grimly.

'Whatever is causing this anger, you need to let it go,' Philip replied warily. He hated any kind of confrontation and his hand shook as he removed his hat to wipe the sweat that had accumulated under the rim.

Maggie shifted in her seat.

'I think I'll go inside to hurry up our drinks.'

'No, let me,' said Philip, scrabbling to his feet, patently grateful for the opportunity to escape his godson's ire.

Watching him walk away from the table, Maggie noticed – not for the first time – that he had the gait of someone much older than sixty-one: his back was stooped and his stride uncertain.

'I take it you're no fan of Declan's,' she remarked to Johnnie, once Philip was beyond earshot.

'No, I can't stand him. Never could.'

'Can I ask why?'

Johnnie gazed at her, as though weighing up whether to trust her or not. After a few moments he evidently decided he could.

'He was too controlling. He wanted to know where Katy was twenty-four seven. She was sick of him and wanted to call it off.'

That stopped Maggie in her tracks. Aside from the claims that Katy had slept with the waiter Julien Ruiz, which he denied, nowhere was it documented that Katy had been anything but happy with Declan.

'How come you're so sure she wanted to call it off?'

'She told me and I believed her. She wasn't happy.'

'Why?'

Johnnie shifted in his chair.

'She was only seventeen and he treated her like they'd

been married for thirty years. His behaviour was suffocating. She was going to tell him before the holiday that it was over, because he was starting to guess something was up. I was surprised when the holiday still went ahead.'

'She must've changed her mind.'

Johnnie shook his head.

'The last time I saw her she was fired up about dumping him. She couldn't wait to go to uni and leave him behind.'

'If Katy was the one planning to end the relationship, why all the hatred for Declan?'

Johnnie raked a grubby hand through his stringy hair. 'This is starting to feel like an interrogation,' he grumbled.

'I'm sorry, but this is significant. It's never been suggested before that Katy was unhappy with Declan. If she wanted to end their relationship as you claim . . . well, that raises questions.' Maggie paused. 'Did you ever suspect he was involved in her murder, like the police did?'

Perhaps it was the sun canopy throwing shadows, but as Johnnie glared at Maggie his light-brown eyes seemed to darken until they were almost black. He was disconcertingly intense and she quelled the urge to lean away from him.

'You guys accepted his alibi. Case closed.'

'That's not what I asked.'

His eyes bored deeper into hers.

'Did I think Declan was capable of killing her? Yes, I did.'

'But, as you say, he had an alibi. Katy's mum and dad.'

'I know,' said Johnnie unhappily.

'I don't remember seeing anything from you among the witness statements I've read.'

'You wouldn't do. The police never interviewed me

because I wasn't on the island when it happened. My parents owned a few properties in the Balearics back then, so while the Popes were staying in our villa here I went to our apartment on Ibiza with Camila, my girlfriend at the time, in a place called Es Cana. It's where I've been staying since coming back from Brazil. We don't own the villa here any more; my parents sold it after Katy died.'

'When exactly did Katy tell you she wasn't happy?' Maggie hoped he'd answer quickly: she could see Philip starting to head back towards their table.

'A few weeks before the holiday. I was passing through London for a couple of days and we met for a coffee.'

'Why didn't you come forward afterwards with that information?'

'I didn't want to upset her parents by telling the police. They were devastated enough.'

'Surely they'd have wanted the police to know? It's pretty crucial, their daughter being so unhappy with the boyfriend who was later accused of killing her,' said Maggie hurriedly. Philip was almost upon them.

Johnnie shook his head.

'It would've meant them admitting they knew how she was feeling – and that they were the ones refusing to let her dump him.'

20

Philip's arrival back at the table cut the conversation dead. Maggie waited a few minutes then made an excuse about needing to fetch something from her hotel room. Philip was happy to let her go and leave him and Johnnie to their reminiscing. As she got up from the table to leave, she made a point of asking Johnnie how long he'd be on the island.

'At least a week, so plenty of time to catch up with everyone I need to talk to. My boat's called *La Novio*,' he added.

Maggie made a note of the name as she walked away. DCI Walker would definitely want to pay Johnnie a visit on his boat to quiz him further about Katy's plan to dump Declan Morris. If what he was saying was the true, the big question was whether Declan really had guessed Katy wanted to end their relationship. The police in Majorca and those drafted in from the Spanish mainland had at one time suspected him of arranging her murder because he was after her savings – what if Johnnie had just given them the more plausible motive of a rejected lover seeking revenge?

She found Shah and Paulson in the room they were sharing poring over documents spread across the twin beds.

Thankful for air conditioning, she flopped down onto the room's only hard-backed chair and told them about Johnnie and his proclamation that Katy had been planning to give Declan the elbow.

Shah made a sweeping gesture with his hand over the files on his bed, which was the one nearest to the sliding balcony doors.

'There's not a single statement in here that backs that up,' he said.

'I know, that's what I said to him. He claims he never came forward because he didn't want to upset her parents,' said Maggie. 'According to him, they were the ones refusing to let her end the relationship. Quite how they could force her not to, he didn't say.'

'What's his name again?' asked Shah, reaching for a pen.

'Johnnie Hickman-Ferguson. He was in Ibiza with his girlfriend when Katy was murdered.'

'Hickman-Ferguson? That's the same surname as the people who owned the villa where she and her parents and Declan were staying.'

Maggie nodded. 'His dad, Howard Hickman-Ferguson, is Philip's best friend from years back and Johnnie is Philip and Patricia's godson.'

'We should take a statement from Johnnie,' Shah said. 'Where's he staying?'

'On his boat, moored in the harbour.' She read out the name.

'Why come forward with this now?' mused Paulson. 'He's never said a word for ten years and all of a sudden he's grown a conscience?'

'I think it was triggered by Philip telling him that Declan's coming here for the memorial service. He clearly loathes him,' said Maggie. 'He's always believed Declan was capable of murdering Katy.'

'He wasn't the only one to think that,' said Shah broodingly. 'We'll have to ask the parents about it and whether it's true they were pressuring her. Ma'am's always said Katy was happy with him.'

Paulson turned to Maggie, a sly grin spreading across his features. 'That's one for you, DC FLO.'

Maggie pulled a face back, but she was smiling too.

'I've dealt with trickier relatives than Patricia Pope, trust me. I've been working my magic on her and she's even calling me Maggie instead of "you, here". I think she likes me.'

Her colleagues exchanged amused looks.

'If you say so,' said Paulson.

'Wait until Walker gives you the okay with that line of questioning though,' Shah cautioned. 'He won't want ma'am upset unless it's absolutely necessary.'

'I will, don't worry.' Maggie eyed the paperwork on the bed. 'What are you up to, anyway?'

'We're about to pick short straws on who goes to interview Terry Evans and who gets Julien Ruiz,' said Paulson.

'You literally are picking straws,' said Maggie, eyeing the two clutched in his hand.

'Great,' said Shah as he picked the shortest one. 'I get the arsy ex-pat with a fondness for knives.'

'Want to come with me to interview Ruiz?' Paulson asked Maggie. 'He might appreciate you questioning him more than me.'

'Why's that, exactly?' she replied, guessing what his

response was likely to be, but wanting to see if he'd show even a modicum of embarrassment as he said it.

He didn't.

'The man clearly likes attractive women and I think he'll respond well to you.' On seeing Maggie's annoyed expression, he shrugged. 'Where's the harm in admitting that?'

'The harm is you sounding like you don't take me seriously as a detective.'

'Of course I do, but I'm also not going to look a gift horse in the mouth when I see one. If the boss was here, he'd be saying the same.'

'Only because he objectifies women as much as you do,' said Shah crossly. 'You know what, it's coming out with outdated bollocks like this which explains why you're still single, mate.'

He was rewarded with an eye roll from Paulson. 'I do all right, trust me.'

Shah caught Maggie's eye and smirked. 'He last had a date in 2013.'

She didn't respond, already tired of the banter. It was making her wistful for her CID department back in Mansell, which had as many women as men working there and where the thought of her not being equal to her male colleagues or how she looked being a factor in her ability to do her job rarely crossed her mind. Between Paulson and her Met colleague Mealing, she was beginning to wish she'd never left.

21

Julien Ruiz was not remotely taken aback to find the police on his doorstep.

'I'm surprised it's taken you this long. I understand you've been in Saros since Friday evening.' He gave a shrug and aimed a smile in Maggie's direction. 'Not much gets missed in this place.' He stood aside to let them pass. 'Please, come in.'

Ruiz's circumstances had obviously moved on since 2009 and a smartly furnished one-bedroom apartment in a newly built block had replaced the hostel he'd bunked in back then. All that spoiled it was the pungent odour of cigarette smoke permeating every corner.

'I'm afraid I don't have long to chat,' he said. 'I have a plane to catch.'

'Where are you going, Mr Ruiz?' asked Maggie, eyeing the passport he'd left out on the table in the front room. Beside it was a leather weekend bag packed with clothes. Ruiz leaned over and zipped it up in one smooth action.

'Somewhere to escape the circus,' he said with a sigh. 'I know how people's minds work in this town and even though I was cleared of any involvement, fingers will still point.' He smiled again. 'I presume that is why you are here?'

Ruiz was one of those men that age adored. The past decade had honed his looks, vanquishing the plumpness of youth and giving him an even more alluring edge. His hair was darker and slicked back off his face with product, but Ruiz looked far more attractive now, at thirty-three, than he did in the photo of him and the mother and daughter he holiday-romanced.

'Why would we want to do that if, as you say, you've already been cleared?' asked Paulson without a trace of friendliness.

'Officer, we both know that mud sticks,' said Ruiz, his Spanish accent sliding off his tongue like liquid honey. 'Why else would British officers be at my door?'

'I'm Australian actually, mate,' said Paulson, like it mattered.

Irritated, Maggie shot him a look as she asked Ruiz again where he was going.

'London. I'm going to stay with some friends.'

'Heather and Bernice Cooper?' said Paulson with a chuckle. Maggie realized he was referring to the mother and daughter in the tabloid story and grew even more annoyed. If he carried on antagonizing Ruiz they might not get anything out of him.

Luckily for them, Ruiz had a sense of humour.

'Ah, the lovely Cooper ladies,' he grinned. 'I hope they got their money's worth selling their story.'

'We understand your parents weren't happy about it,' said Maggie. 'That must've been difficult.'

Ruiz fixed her with a look she couldn't quite decipher, then shrugged.

'My parents are hard people to please, so I gave up trying a long time ago. I see no reason in conforming to a life of domesticity just to make them happy. Why should I apologize for the company I keep? It's also why I stayed in Saros. People expected me to leave, but I liked it here and my friends were here. It was my home.'

Paulson gave him what Maggie took to be a sympathetic nod. Suddenly Ruiz the playboy was meeting his approval.

'How long will you be in London for?' asked Maggie.

'I don't know for sure. A few days at least,' said Ruiz.

'You haven't booked a return ticket?' asked Paulson.

Ruiz waved his hand airily. 'Next Saturday, I think that's when I'm back.'

Maggie's eyes narrowed. 'You do have a return ticket, don't you?'

'Of course,' he said, flashing her another smile, one that didn't quite meet his eyes. He reached into the side pocket of his holdall and pulled out a printed boarding pass that showed his return flight.

'It's a good thing we caught you before you left,' she said, handing it back.

Ruiz let out a long, strangled sigh.

'There is nothing new I can tell you. We met, we talked, that was it.'

'You're sticking to your statement that you never slept with her?'

Ruiz eyed Maggie suspiciously. 'I am. She was a nice girl, but I didn't take advantage of her.'

Maggie glanced at Paulson and gave him the briefest of nods. They had already agreed their interview strategy before arriving at Ruiz's apartment and she knew what was coming next now Ruiz had spouted his first denial.

'Here's the thing, Mr Ruiz. If you're so keen to escape the circus as you call it, you need to start telling us the truth,' said Paulson. 'Otherwise we might just have to haul you back to London ourselves on charges of perverting the course of justice. Don't mistake us for the idiots who investigated Katy's death the first time round and ballsed it up – we know what we're doing and we know when a witness is lying. Ten years is a long time to keep up the pretence, mate.'

Ruiz faltered. 'I haven't been pretending.'

'Ten years ago you shouted your conquests from the rooftops. The statements taken from the guys you shared a hostel room with confirmed it: you liked to brag about the many women you had sex with,' said Maggie. 'But Katy was different. Why? Was it non-consensual, is that it?'

It took Ruiz a moment to register what she was saying. Anger darkened his face, then his mouth twisted into a smile that made Maggie's skin crawl. He might be attractive but he was still a sleaze.

'I do not need to rape women to have sex with them.' He let out another sigh, then folded his arms. 'What is your real agenda here, officers? Why don't you get to the point?'

'The British couple who sold their story were adamant that you and Katy were flirting and that she'd asked them about the efficiency of Spanish condoms. Given your track record and reputation, we find it hard to believe you turned down sex with her,' said Maggie.

'Yeah, I'm not buying that age was a factor,' said Paulson. 'She was above the age of consent, you weren't breaking any law.'

'We think the only reason you lied about sleeping with her is because of how it looked after she was found murdered,' Maggie added. 'It would've put you right to the top of the list of prime suspects.'

'You're forgetting I had an alibi for the entire time she was missing,' said Ruiz, more amused than angry now. 'I swear to God I did not have sex with Katy Pope.'

Maggie regarded him for a moment as a thought suddenly crossed her mind. Why hadn't any of them considered this before?

'Sex doesn't just mean intercourse though, does it?'

Ruiz looked first at her, then at Paulson.

'Don't look at me,' said Paulson. 'She asked the question.'

Ruiz sank down onto the sofa and cupped his knees with his hands.

'Well? Did anything else happen that wasn't actual penetrative sex?' Maggie asked him.

Another sigh. 'Okay, we kissed.'

'Is that all?'

'Fine. We fooled around a bit, but then Katy said it was a bad idea and she wanted to leave. I promise you nothing else happened. I would *never* continue with a woman who had changed her mind.'

He sounded sincere.

'Why not tell everyone that?' asked Maggie.

'I thought it would make everyone think I was guilty of doing more. It was ten minutes of foreplay that could've landed me in prison for something I didn't do and frankly it wasn't worth it. Nor did I want to blacken the poor girl's name after her death by admitting she'd been unfaithful to her boyfriend.'

'It would've given Declan a motive,' Paulson said to Maggie, 'if he had known what she did. He could've killed her in a jealous rage.'

Ruiz shook his head. 'He never knew. He came to see me after that couple came forward and I told him what I told the police. The poor guy was grieving, why add to his misery?'

Maggie thought back to her earlier conversation with Johnnie.

'That evening in the bar, did Katy talk about Declan at all?'

'Yes, I was aware she had a boyfriend. She didn't seem bothered about cheating on him. In fact, it was because of him that we got chatting in the first place.'

'How's that?' asked Paulson.

'Her mum had said something about the boyfriend that upset Katy, so she stormed up to the bar to get another drink.'

'She had more than one drink?'

'By the time she left she'd had three cocktails.'

That was two more than Patricia claimed she'd had.

'Did she tell you what her mother had said?' Paulson asked.

Ruiz nodded. 'Her mum was talking about when he might propose. Katy thought it was ridiculous – she wasn't yet eighteen and she had her whole life ahead of her.' He stopped, abashed. 'You know what I mean.'

'There's nothing about this row in your statement,' said Paulson. 'Why didn't you tell the police this at the time?'

Ruiz shrugged again. 'They didn't ask. They were only concerned with whether we'd had sex, not what we spoke about.'

'We'd like you to make a new statement, clarifying what you've just told us,' said Maggie as Ruiz got to his feet.

'Now? But I have a flight to catch in two hours. I don't want to miss it.'

She looked to Paulson. 'Well?'

'We can arrange for you to give your statement to one of our colleagues at Belgravia police station while you're in London. Give me a contact number and I'll sort it out.'

Ruiz gave them his mobile number.

'Katy was a nice girl. She didn't deserve what happened to her,' he said. 'And I am sorry I wasn't more truthful back then. I thought I was doing her parents a favour by not sullying her memory.'

'You did yourself a favour too,' said Maggie matter-of-factly.

Ruiz turned on the full beam again.

'There's nothing wrong with a little bit of self-preservation, officer. Why should I destroy my life for a girl who was meaningless to me?'

22

Philip was so absorbed in his conversation with Johnnie that he didn't see Declan approaching them until it was too late.

'This is a surprise,' said Declan, before putting his hand out to Johnnie. 'I didn't know you were coming out here too.'

Johnnie ignored the handshake on offer and looked down at the table, his expression one of thinly disguised disgust. Declan gave an exaggerated sigh.

'Are we really still playing that game?'

Johnnie's head snapped up. 'Meaning?'

'Pretending I don't exist, the dirty looks, filling Katy's ears with poison.'

'I said nothing that wasn't true,' said Johnnie levelly.

'Course you did.'

The depth of animosity between the two men startled Philip. When George had first brought Declan home from uni, the two of them and Johnnie would go out for drinks and seemed to get along swimmingly. What on earth had gone on between them since to stir up such hostility?

Flustered, Philip asked Declan how his flight had been.

'It was fine, thanks. It was an early start though.'

'You must be in need of coffee. Do join us.'

Johnnie glowered with disapproval, which didn't go unnoticed by Declan.

'I don't think I'll bother. I know where I'm not wanted.'

Johnnie looked up and smiled at him sardonically. 'Shame you couldn't take the hint ten years ago.'

Declan's hands curled into fists at his sides as his face darkened.

'Please, the pair of you,' said Philip desperately. 'This is neither the time nor the place.'

'I'm sorry, Philip,' said Johnnie, clambering to his feet.

They looked such opposites, Johnnie in his scruffy shorts and vest, hair unkempt, Declan in smart, navy linen shorts and a white polo shirt, not a hair out of place.

'I can't be around this arsehole. Katy deserved so much better.'

'What, someone like you?' snarled Declan. 'Don't make me laugh. You still think you knew her better than me, don't you? You gave her such a hard time and she hated you for it. Did you know that?'

Philip stared up at them both, bewildered.

'A hard time for what?'

The anger that had propelled Johnnie to his feet was suddenly replaced by a look of anguish.

Declan let out a snort of laughter. 'What, you're surprised she told me? Katy couldn't help herself. You did everything you could to poison her against me but it didn't work.'

Johnnie seemed to recover then, the anger blasting back. 'We both know Katy had had enough of you and she couldn't wait to go to uni and leave you behind.'

'Haven't you got bored of saying that by now? Not a single one of our friends ever heard her say that. Where's your proof?'

Johnnie locked eyes with Philip and for a moment he appeared to be on the verge of saying something. Then he shook his head.

'Deny it all you like,' Johnnie spat, his voice tremulous, 'but deep down you know it's true. Katy had had enough, but you wouldn't let her go.'

23

Walker returned from Palma late afternoon and in the foulest of moods. The reception he'd received at the Dirección General de la Policía – the head of policing – in Palma had been perfectly pleasant but it was still a tricky meeting, as he was now explaining. He'd summoned Maggie and the others to his room for a debrief of the day's events, and the four of them were sitting outside on his balcony again nursing soft drinks.

'The only saving grace was the Vice-Consul from the British Consulate, a woman called Lyndsey Shepherd,' Walker was saying. 'She had to act as my translator *and* peacemaker. It's obvious the Spaniards don't want us back here poking around again, reminding everyone they've done jack-shit in the last decade to find the killer. It was made very clear to me that if we step on anyone's toes we'll be kicked off the island.' He took a swig of his Coke and managed to spray most of it down his front; using his hand, he patted the drops until they'd soaked into the navy fabric of his shirt.

'Can they do that? We've got Home Office clearance to be here,' said Shah.

'Just because the Home Office is happy for us to be here doesn't mean the Spanish have to treat us like VIPs,' said Walker with a sigh. 'They weren't going to say no to us coming because Patricia Pope would've gone running straight to the press to raise merry hell if they had, but that doesn't mean they have to like it.'

He turned to Maggie.

'Talking of ma'am, how did it go with her?' he asked. 'Did you manage to talk her round?'

He'd called Maggie at lunchtime to say the Director General of Police had requested his media team be involved in organizing the family's press conference – Walker suspected it was so they could try to muzzle Patricia Pope before she spewed forth her criticisms again. The family had wanted the press conference to take place immediately after the memorial service tomorrow, but the Director General of Police felt it was unnecessarily hasty and might cause too much of a media circus. For the sake of main- taining relations, Walker had agreed it would be better to create some breathing space between the two events but had decided to let it fall to Maggie to persuade the family – or rather Patricia – to fall into line. 'I don't care how you do it, just get her to agree,' he'd said.

'She was fine about it,' said Maggie, enjoying the looks of disbelief on her colleagues' faces as her response sank in.

'Really? She didn't kick off?' asked Walker sceptically.

'I simply pointed out that she might feel too drained to go through with it immediately after the memorial service, because while she's obviously experienced in these things even the most together person might find it tough. If she did get upset, which would be only natural, it might prevent her from getting across her message as planned at the press conference, and I could see how important that was to her.'

Walker laughed and raised his glass. 'Nicely played, pandering to her ego.'

Maggie shrugged as though nonchalant, but she was pleased by his comment.

'She clearly doesn't want people to think she's mawkish or can't control her emotions, so planting the idea she might be too upset to be her usual articulate self seemed the obvious thing to do,' she added. 'But even if she had been fine to do one straight after the other, I suspect her husband wouldn't be. He had to go back to bed after coming down with a migraine at breakfast. The anniversary is obviously getting to him.'

'I wouldn't have wanted to stay in the same place where my daughter's dismembered body was found, that's for sure,' said Paulson.

The four of them fell silent momentarily as they contemplated Philip Pope's private hell. It was obvious to all of them that Patricia called the shots in their marriage and that, for the most part, Philip accepted her way of doing things for the sake of a quiet life. Yet this was different: this was being cajoled into staying somewhere that must bring back the most horrendous memories. Had he even tried to argue against it? If he had, but Patricia still overruled him, what must he be feeling now? His potential suffering was, frankly, more than any of them could imagine.

Walker cleared his throat. 'So ma'am's agreed to wait until Wednesday?'

'Eventually, after I pointed that if everyone sees the

pictures from the memorial service, the level of interest in the press conference could be even greater,' said Maggie.

'You mean more press could attend?' asked Shah.

'Yeah. I said the papers and TV news stations might be spurred into sending more reporters to the island for it and suggested we reschedule for Wednesday evening so it gives them more time to get here. After that she was fine.'

Walker's expression showed how impressed he was. 'Fuck me, you've got the magic touch.'

'In family liaison we call it doing our job, sir,' said Maggie pointedly.

She was happy to be praised but also didn't want him to think it was a fluke. She might sound glib now, but her conversation with Patricia, which had taken place an hour ago after she nipped back to Orquídea to check the family were okay, had required every communicative skill she possessed. But while Patricia was not a woman easily persuaded, she was reasonable when presented with a reasonable argument, and that's what Maggie had focused on doing.

'We get results, but in a way that doesn't make the family feel like they're being pummelled into submission,' she added. 'It's what I'm trained to do.'

'Point taken,' said Walker, his smile indicating he didn't mind her not-so-subtle rebuke. 'You also did well getting Ruiz to admit he'd been lying about him and Katy too, and about her and her mum rowing. Clearly there was some tension there.'

'When should we ask Patricia about Annika's statement?' said Maggie. 'I did raise it with Philip like you said to, but predictably he took his wife's side.'

'You know what, leave it until after the memorial service. There's no point antagonizing the old dragon before her big moment in the sun.'

Maggie found the disparaging remark offensive and said so.

'Have you ever thought that she might be aware of what people say about her and that fuels her behaviour?' she snapped at Walker. 'Like, when you know people are being rude about you behind your back, why be nice to their faces? She's probably had a gutful of it throughout her career, just because she's a woman in a position of authority. No one would call her difficult or annoying if she was a man, they'd say she was assertive or confident.'

The three men stared at her as her words sank in. None of them knew how to respond, so Walker, his face flushed, swiftly changed the subject.

'Right, I don't know about you lot, but I'm starving. The manager here has recommended a great little restaurant in one of the back streets. It's off the beaten track and away from the tourist bit, so if you're a good girl and boys I might even let you have a beer.'

24

Tuesday

The heat was getting to Philip. The daytime high of thirty-three degrees had cooled to only twenty-four as the early hours set in, and Patricia didn't like to sleep with the air conditioning on, so it was impossibly muggy in their bedroom. So, as his wife slept soundly, he got up, gathered up the clothing he'd earlier left neatly folded on a chair, and slipped into the lounge, where he proceeded to get dressed.

As he did so he could hear faint snoring coming from the second bedroom and smiled. It felt good to have George under the same roof as them again. He'd never moved back home after university, preferring to spend all his earnings on renting a room in a house share in Camberwell with some fellow trainee barristers. He would often come home to visit, especially on Sundays when Philip would always make a roast, but never stayed over, because there was no point. In fact, the last time he'd stayed with them in Crystal Palace was ten years ago, after Katy's body was returned to England and the three of them had her funeral to plan.

Philip padded into the kitchen to make coffee, but then thought better of it: the machine might wake the others.

So he left a note on the kitchen counter explaining his whereabouts and slipped out of the apartment to go for a walk.

Nightfall and sparse lighting along the front had plunged the beach into darkness. Yet despite it being four in the morning, he wasn't the only person up and about. A couple had walked past him moments ago speaking in Dutch and further back towards the harbour he'd heard some Germans in loud conversation on the veranda of a second-floor apartment. Yet the resort had always been most popular with British visitors, which is why his friend Howard had bought a villa out here. The first time they came out to Saros, it was to join Howard and his family at their new villa and it had been the most wonderful, riotous time. The holiday from which Katy never returned was their third trip there, which made this their thirteenth stay in Saros. Thirteen meant unlucky for some and horrendous and heartbreaking for them.

He'd always known it would be difficult coming back for the memorial service but he hadn't realized quite what an ordeal it would be. It was impossible not to feel angry at seeing the smiling, happy faces of families sunning themselves around the pool beneath their balcony window, not to baulk at the sight of parents hugging their children. It hurt so much to know he could never hug his darling girl again.

He blamed himself for her murder and always had. If only he had been more proactive in the week when she was missing, he might have found her before the point of her death. He should've searched high and low himself rather than rely on the police to do it for him. He was her father and meant to be her protector, the man who'd held her in his arms moments after she was born, when she was still hot and sticky from her mother's womb, and whispered to her that he would love her forever and always keep her safe. Yet he hadn't.

Continuing his journey, his heart growing heavier with each step, Philip passed the hotel where Maggie, Walker and the other officers were staying, then ambled along to the marina where Johnnie's boat was moored. It was too dark to make out which was his among the many dozens, so Philip turned on his heel and headed back.

When he reached the security gate to Orquídea he took out his phone and pulled up the email that contained the pass code to get in. The gate buzzed louder than he had anticipated as it unlocked and he shut it quietly behind him.

There was a short cut to their apartment block through the ponds, but Philip couldn't bear to take it. It was bad enough that later today he would be forced to sit surrounded by them at the memorial service: he didn't need another reminder tonight of the vicious manner in which his daughter's body had been disposed of.

The entrance to their apartment was via a staircase at the front of the whitewashed building. There was a path alongside it that led to the swimming pool for their block; staring ahead, he could see the deep end, brilliant turquoise glowing in the darkness, illuminated by underwater lights.

He was about to climb the steps to the front door when the sound of the balcony door sliding open at the back cut through the silence. Curious to see who'd come outside, he went along the path a short distance and looked up to the first floor. It was George, in a T-shirt and his underpants, clutching a tumbler of something Philip suspected wasn't water, judging by the way he grimaced as he took a sip. Then he gripped the balcony rail with his other hand and downed the drink in one.

Philip was about to call up to him – quietly, so as not to disturb anyone sleeping nearby – when he realized his son's face was wet with tears. They were falling in steady streams and he did not move to wipe them away.

Oh, my poor boy.

Philip's heart ached for his son, who felt the loss of Katy as profoundly as they had and yet, through no fault of theirs, had been somewhat forgotten in the grieving process. At the beginning people would always ask after himself and Patricia and make kind offers of help, but George was almost an afterthought. Only occasionally would they think to enquire after him. Perhaps it was because he was the older brother that they assumed he could cope. But he was only twenty-one at the time, not quite the man he was now, and he needed people's sympathy and concern as much as his parents did.

It had been a while since he'd seen George cry though and the realization brought tears to his own eyes. Why did his son feel it necessary to cry in private and hide his tears? No one, least of all him, would think less of him for admitting he was finding this visit to Saros a struggle.

Then Philip was struck by a thought. Perhaps it was because of him that George felt unable to share his emotional state with anyone else. There were times when he hadn't been able to get out of bed because he was overwhelmed with grief and it had been left to George to support Patricia, to be the man of the house. Philip was the weak one, the father who had done nothing to save his daughter, the husband who couldn't be relied upon by his wife.

As he stood in the shadows and watched his son cry, his own heart splintering with every wracked sob, Philip vowed never to let his family down again.

25

Jade Reynolds was discovering that suntan lotion and glossy magazines did not mix.

'For crying out loud,' she seethed as her sticky fingers clumped the pages of *Brides* together for the umpteenth time.

'I don't know why you wasted your money buying that,' said her dad, Clive, peering at her over the top of his mirrored sunglasses from the sun lounger next to hers. 'It's not like we can afford anything that fancy.' He leaned across and poked the page she was reading with a sweaty finger. 'Three grand for a wedding cake that's no better than one your nan could make, it's bloody ridiculous.'

'I'm only looking,' said Jade defensively. 'For ideas.'

'Your dad's right,' her mum, Mandy, butted in. She was on the far lounger, next to her husband. 'Don't go getting ideas above your station, young lady. We told you the budget and you've got to stick to it.'

'I know, I know,' Jade snapped back. 'You've told me enough times.'

Her mood soured, she tossed the magazine onto the sand beneath her lounger and huffily rolled onto her front. She'd thought planning a wedding would be fun, but it was nothing of the sort thanks to her cheapskate parents. Okay, so they didn't have pots of money lying about the place, but she *was* their only daughter and she had hoped they might want to give her a wedding that was a bit more flash than a quickie service at the council offices and a stand-up buffet in the function room of the local rugby club. She couldn't even get the dress she'd set her heart on because they said they couldn't afford the two grand it cost, so now she was having to make do with a knock-off version run up by her Auntie Susan. Jade wasn't even sure the woman could sew properly.

At least she'd got the engagement ring of her dreams. Mason had done her proud by blowing two months' wages on a platinum-set, princess-cut diamond solitaire. She stretched her left hand out in front of her and waggled her fingers so the stone cast shards of light up into the underside of the umbrella that was protecting her from the sun's fierce rays.

'Are you sure you like it?' Mason piped up from the sun lounger next to hers. He looked groggy, having just woken from the nap that was necessary to sleep off the colossal hangover he'd woken with that morning. Him and her dad had got stuck into the cocktails at a bar last night like it was their last night on earth, rather than the last week of their holiday. Jade and Mandy were trying to lose weight before the big day so had only had two each.

Jade giggled. 'Will you stop asking me that, of course I do! It's perfect.'

'I wish I could've got a bigger one.'

It was the first thing he'd said to her after he'd popped

the question a month earlier. He'd been more worried about her not liking the ring than the proposal itself.

'Don't be daft. Any bigger and I'd be having the kids' eyes out with it.'

Jade was a childcare assistant at a nursery in Barnet, north London, working with the under-twos. She was permitted to wear her ring while working, but she had to be careful.

Mason groaned as he rolled onto his side so he was facing her. 'I feel terrible.'

'Serves you right.'

'It's not my fault the bar did two-for-one cocktails on Monday nights. It would've been rude not to.'

'Yeah, but now you've spent the best part of this morning trying not to puke. We go home in four days and you're wasting it being wasted all the time.'

'You know that nagging makes hangovers worse, right?'

'Tough,' she laughed.

'I know what'll sort me out. A can of Coke. Full fat though, not that diet crap. And crisps. Lots of crisps. I like those Ruffles ones they do here. Salt and vinegar flavour. I need the salt.'

Jade pointed towards the pedestrianized walkway that linked the hotels and restaurants to the beach, a few metres away from their heads.

'Shop's over there.'

Mason fixed her with a smile that melted her insides, then batted his eyelashes for maximum effect. 'Pretty please?'

She couldn't say no to him, she never could. From the minute she'd swiped right on his profile picture, Jade Reynolds had been smitten with Mason Embry. Halfway through their first date she knew he was the man she wanted to spend the rest of her life with. It took him six months to propose, helped by a bit of chiding on her part, but she knew it was meant to be, and so did he.

'Fine, I'll go. But we're getting cheese and onion.'

'I thought you were dieting?'

'I'll skip lunch.'

'Babe, you look amazing as you are.'

Mason winked appreciatively as Jade got to her feet and tied a sarong over her skimpy bikini bottoms. She tightened the halter-neck strap of the matching red top so her boobs looked perkier.

'I look fat,' she said, smoothing her hand over her tummy that, to her, felt bloated. 'Two weeks abroad eating nice food is too much – I said we should've only come for a week.'

'Don't be silly,' said her dad, who had been eavesdropping on their conversation. 'There's nothing of you.'

'That's what I keep telling her, Mr R,' replied Mason.

'Stop sucking up to the in-laws,' Jade hissed at him, but she was smiling. She loved that her mum and dad loved Mason as much as she did.

After taking orders from her parents for Pringles and beers – Clive Reynolds decided more booze was the only thing that would cure his hangover – Jade left the beach. Not wanting to take her bag, she tucked a twenty-euro note in her waistband and carried her phone in her hand.

The Eroski mini-mart looked pretty empty as she approached the entrance. She was just about to push through the waist-high swing gate when a hand suddenly grabbed her arm and she squealed in shock.

'I'm sorry, I didn't mean to startle you,' said the man whose hand it was. He was posh-sounding and highly agitated. 'Have you seen my little boy? He's about this tall,' he said, holding his hand level with Jade's waist, 'and he's wearing, um, patterned shorts – blue with yellow squares – and Crocs. Bright-green ones.'

'Sorry, I haven't,' said Jade.

The man, who wearing a baseball cap in the same red as his shorts, was close to tears. 'I can't find him anywhere. He's only six.'

Jade looked all around but couldn't see any child matching the boy's description.

'Where did you last see him?'

'I gave him money to get an ice cream in the shop. I was sitting over there waiting for him,' he said, pointing to the low wall that separated the beach from the pavement. 'I don't understand where he's gone. My wife is going to kill me.'

'I can help you look for him,' said Jade kindly. 'He's probably in one of the souvenir shops where they sell all those pool toys. Have you seen the size of some of them? I quite fancy one of the massive unicorns. They're as big as a dinghy.' She kept chatting away, partly to distract the dad and partly because talking non-stop was what she did when she was nervous. Even if she hadn't worked at a nursery she would've still appreciated that a kid going missing on holiday was every parent's worst nightmare and already her mind was dreading how the mum would be if they couldn't find the boy.

'There's one right up there,' said the dad, pointing up to the far end of the side street next to the mini-mart. Jade could see dolphins, crocodiles and sharks squeezed together in an enormous inflatable bouquet outside a shop that also had on display rolled-up wicker sun mats and rows of buckets and spades. 'Could you check that one while I do the next one along here?'

'Of course.'

Jade wasn't wearing any shoes and winced as the baking-hot pavement burned against the soles of her feet. She looked all around the shop but there was no sign of the boy. The dad hadn't told her the kid's name either, so she couldn't call out to him.

She went and stood outside the shop again and looked up and down the street. It was now empty of passers-by: the midday sun had reached its zenith and anyone with sense had retreated into the shade. Jade was about to do the same when something caught her eye. Across the street, on the doorstep of a disused cafe that had fallen into disrepair and was boarded up, was a bright-green child's shoe.

Her pulse racing, Jade hobbled across the street towards it. Oh God, she thought, it was a Croc just like the kid had been wearing.

She was reaching down to pick the shoe up when suddenly she was aware of someone right behind her. Before she could react, she felt a sharp prick in the side of her neck.

'What the—'

She tried to struggle but instantly her limbs went weak. With virtually no effort, the person pushed Jade towards the boarded-up door of the cafe and it swung open, already unlocked.

Her vision was becoming too blurred for her to take in her surroundings and the last thing she registered before falling unconscious was the boy's shoe being removed from her hand and the man she thought was his dad whispering in her ear.

'I'm sorry about this, but it's meant to be.'

26

The problem with them staying in an apartment, Philip had come to realize, was that it afforded him not an ounce of personal space. Had they been staying in a hotel, he could've escaped to the bar or, if he was exceptionally lucky, a designated library nook in which he could read. But in the apartment there was nowhere for him to hide without someone else being within speaking distance. He missed his garden.

Right now the apartment was full of people readying themselves for the memorial service at two. He felt invisible as they milled around him, his part in the production diminished from that of grieving father to bystander. Patricia was holding court in the middle of the room, barking her disappointment at the poor local florist who'd been commissioned online some weeks ago and had produced a wreath not to his wife's liking.

The door to the apartment was open to allow for all the frantic comings and goings and the next person to walk through it was their son, George. He was checking something on his phone, as was often the way, and Philip surmised he must be reading an email from the clerk of his chambers back in London. Earlier he had mentioned there was a problem brewing with his trial at the Old Bailey next week and he might have to cut his trip short and return to London before the press conference. Patricia was not at all happy and had insulted Philip by saying she needed George to be there to speak because 'you know what your father's like, he's useless at public speaking'. The atmosphere in the apartment was now strained to say the least.

George sat down and hooked his right ankle across his left knee. His legs were bare in shorts.

'You are changing into something else, aren't you?' asked Philip worriedly. 'I think your mother might have something to say about you wearing those.'

George grinned. 'Don't worry, I've got a suit to put on, as per the orders Mum emailed to me a month ago.'

'Orders? What else did she ask you to do?'

'Book the orchestra, arrange the champagne toast, send an invite to the King of Spain.' George burst out laughing as Philip recoiled in horror. 'Dad, I'm joking! The only thing required of me was to turn up on time and look smart. Although the bit about the King's invite is true.'

Philip found he couldn't stop trembling.

'The King of Spain? Oh, this is getting out of hand, George. Your mother –' Philip lowered his voice – 'she's obsessed.'

George's handsome features creased into a frown. 'Dad, she just wants to find the bastard who did this.'

'And I don't?'

'I never said that.'

Philip paused for a moment. For the past few days he'd been building up to asking his son an important question.

It wasn't something he felt able to raise in Patricia's presence and there had been little opportunity for any time on his own with his son. But now, with Patricia distracted, this might be the only chance he got.

'George, can I ask you something?'

'Sure, fire away.'

'Did you know Declan got Katy pregnant?'

The guilty look on his son's face told him he had known all along.

'She asked me not to say anything. She knew how you and Mum would react.'

'So it's definitely true? I had been hoping it might not be.'

'Why?'

Philip groped for the right words. 'No father likes to think of his little girl in that kind of situation.'

'Situation? Dad, you sound like a Victorian. She got pregnant. She chose how she wanted to deal with it. You knowing that doesn't change anything about her, or it shouldn't do.'

'I know, but—'

George reached over and gently took his dad's hand. 'Katy was nearly eighteen. She had a serious boyfriend. It can't really come as any surprise that they were sleeping together.'

Philip felt his cheeks colouring. His mind simply wouldn't allow him to entertain it.

'As I said, no father likes to think of his little girl in that situation.'

Shaking his head, George grinned and Philip seized the moment to change the subject.

'I wonder what those two are talking about.'

He nodded in the direction of Walker, who had just arrived and was now clearly losing whatever argument he was having with Patricia. His arms were tightly folded across his front, a classic defensive pose protecting him from the pointed finger that was getting perilously close to stabbing him in the chest.

'Look at his face,' chuckled George. 'He's dying to put Mum in her place. Maybe he's telling her about the email.'

'You mean the email sent to Declan? Has there been some news?'

George looked serious for a moment. 'They can't trace who sent it, but they've discovered that another email has been sent from the same address.'

'To who?'

'A woman in London. The police won't tell us all the details yet, but she was on holiday in Saros in April 2009 and was involved in an incident that could be related to Katy's case. That's all they're saying.'

Philip's brain scrambled to keep up.

'When did you find this out?'

'Just now. Walker was outside with Maggie when I came in and he told her it was okay to fill me in.'

'Is this woman someone we know?'

'No, she's not.'

'I don't understand then. How might it be related?'

George thought for a moment.

'Why don't I ask Maggie to explain it to you, like she did to me?'

There was something in the way George said Maggie's

name that made Philip stop. He was trying too hard to sound casual.

'Yes, that's a good idea,' he said, staring beadily at his son. 'I do like Maggie. She's a very nice young woman, very considerate.'

'She's great,' said George with enthusiasm.

Philip suppressed a smile. He knew his son well enough to know when he was keen on someone.

'Perhaps I should speak to her now, before the ceremony. Would you mind fetching her?'

From the way George shot out of his seat it was obvious he didn't mind at all.

27

As she surveyed the rows of chairs being set out next to the pond, Maggie was dogged by the uncomfortable thought that the backdrop to the service was beginning to look more bridal than *in memoriam*. Patricia had hired a company in Palma to provide slips to cover the chairs and the ones it had supplied were snow white and fastened at the back with elaborately fussy bows. Maggie debated whether to remove the bows to lessen their impact but decided she would wait to see what Patricia's reaction was to them – for all she knew she might want them like that.

Besides, it wasn't her job to oversee the decor, or the seating plan, or the after-service catering, even if Patricia did seem to think otherwise. She'd managed to escape outside on the pretext of needing to discuss something with Walker, which turned out to be prescient because he arrived saying he wanted the Popes briefed about the email sent to Lara Steadman at last, and that Maggie could start with George, who happened to be hanging around outside. Walker wanted to know if the family knew Lara in any way, but George said he'd never heard of the woman and Maggie believed him.

She was about to see what the others were up to when something moving in the pond caught her eye. Stepping closer, she saw it was a turtle, a tiny one, bobbing to the surface. Watching it disappear back into the depths she considered the lengths Katy's killer had gone to to conceal each body part beneath the lily pads, weighing them down with chains so they would stay under water. Whoever it was didn't want the parts to be found – had they stayed submerged much longer the enormous carp that lived along-side the turtles, frogs and minnows might've made a meal of them – but at the same time it was hardly the most inconspicuous dumping ground.

Waiting to see if the turtle re-emerged, Maggie fanned her face with her hand. The sun was at its peak and while the shade of the surrounding trees did lessen its glare some-what, the temperature remained high. She was finding it a struggle to stay feeling comfortable; there were only so many times she could lift her hair off the back of her sweaty neck to cool down.

'Is this really necessary?' said a voice behind her suddenly.

Maggie spun round to find herself face to face with an elderly gentleman with a bronzed, wizened face and eyes disappearing beneath drooping lids as they screwed up against the sun. His collar-length silver hair had receded to expose a pate covered in freckles and liver spots, a couple of which were crusted with scabs.

'Is there a problem, sir?' she asked politely.

'This ridiculous circus shouldn't be allowed,' he said haughtily, pointing to the chairs behind her.

With a start the man's identity came to her: he was Terry Evans, the ex-pat. He'd aged a lot since the pictures she'd previously seen in the case file but was still recognizable.

'It's Mr Evans, isn't it? I'm DC Maggie Neville, family liaison officer with Operation Pivot.' Evans shook her hand, albeit reluctantly; his fingertips barely brushed hers.

'I don't know why the management company has allowed this,' he frowned, casting another look at the neat formation of chairs. 'It's macabre.'

'It was very difficult for the Pope family to decide where to commemorate their daughter,' she said. 'Here made the most sense to them in the end because it's where she was found.'

'But why did it have to be the pond right outside my apartment?' Evans asked unhappily. 'There are five others they could've chosen. It feels like they're trying to make a point.'

Maggie looked at the apartments on the other side of the pond and guessed immediately which one belonged to Evans: the one with a garden awash with flowers and plants, including a trellis wall thick with greenery that would've taken more than a fortnight's holiday to cultivate. There were other little touches that also indicated there being a long-term occupant in situ – while every other garden apartment had a metal gate leading to the pool area, his was wooden and painted green. Just inside the gate, set up on the grass, were two traditional deck-chairs upholstered in bright-red fabric, holding court in place of sun loungers. It appeared as though Evans had created himself a home from home in his little corner of Spain.

'What point would that be, Mr Evans?' she asked.

He was a diminutive man, barely five foot five, but

indignation drew him to his full height and made him seem taller.

'The stigma never goes away, never. I will always be the ex-pat suspected of that poor girl's murder. Can you imagine what it's like to live with that every day for ten years?'

Maggie wasn't short of sympathy, but at the same time felt his tirade was ill judged given what was about to commence at that very spot in an hour's time.

'I'm sorry the memorial service is making you feel uncomfortable, Mr Evans, and I do understand why. I promise you the second it's over we'll clear away the seating and return the area to normal.'

Evans, still looking troubled, opened his mouth to retaliate but then tilted his head and smiled. The swift change in mood surprised Maggie, until she realized he was smiling not at her but at a young woman approaching them. In her mid to late twenties, she had long dark hair and was tanned, making her appear local, but when she spoke her accent was distinctly Mancunian.

'Hello, Terry, is everything okay?'

'It most certainly is now you're here, Ms Shepherd.'

The man was positively simpering, his earlier animosity evaporating like a mist of perfume.

'Hi, I'm Lyndsey Shepherd,' said the woman to Maggie. 'I'm a consular officer with the British Consulate in Palma.'

As Maggie understood it, a consular officer supported the Vice-Consul – an official a bit like an ambassador – in helping British nationals abroad when they found themselves in trouble. With the island's resort of Magaluf being the most popular destination in Europe for British youths holidaying without their parents for the first time, she imagined Lyndsey was kept pretty busy in her role.

Maggie introduced herself as they shook hands.

'DCI Walker said you were a big help at his meeting yesterday.'

Lyndsey smiled. 'Happy to do what I can for international relations. The local police are feeling very twitchy about today, with good reason. They wish as much as anyone that Katy Pope's killer wasn't still walking free. Now, Terry, I got the distinct impression as I was coming over that you were giving DC Neville a hard time about something, presumably the ceremony. We've talked about this, haven't we? It's only for a couple of hours and it's an extremely important occasion for the Pope family.'

Evans dropped his head like a child being chided.

'I've known Terry since I started working at the Consulate in 2015,' Lyndsey explained to Maggie, who imagined Evans was probably well known by everyone at the Consulate for bringing complaints to its door. 'We've been having a few discussions leading up to today, because Terry is concerned he'll be dragged into the investigation all over again.' She turned back to the elderly resident. 'I thought you decided to go to Palma for a couple of days to avoid all this?'

'I changed my mind. I don't see why I should be forced from my home again.'

'I agree, so let's get you back there before it starts,' said Lyndsey. She offered her arm to Evans and he took it eagerly. Then his expression fell just as quickly.

'Oh, please, let's get inside quickly. I don't want to talk to him.'

Someone else was approaching them. It was George.

'It's okay, Terry,' said Lyndsey soothingly. 'No one's going to cause a scene today.'

Maggie watched her curiously, noticing how her body language had noticeably shifted on seeing Katy's brother. Her face became sapped of any emotion and her posture stiffened, leaving Evans hanging awkwardly on the crook of her arm.

George ignored her, and Evans, as he fixed his gaze on Maggie.

'Can you spare us a minute, Maggie? I told Dad about our chat and he wants to talk to you about it.'

'Of course, I'll come now. It was nice to meet you,' she said to Lyndsey. The woman wasn't paying attention to her, though.

'When did you arrive on the island, Mr Pope?'

The question was as unexpected as its delivery was abrupt, yet George did not seem remotely ruffled by it.

'Is this an official line of questioning, Ms Shepherd?' he parried back.

'No, just making polite conversation.'

Maggie was baffled by the exchange. Lyndsey's sentence dripped with sarcasm and George's reply was equally brittle. What had caused such friction between them? George was the victim's brother and Evans once the accused, but to see Lyndsey interact with them was to think it was the other way round.

'I hope the memorial serves its purpose. It must be very hard for your parents,' said Lyndsey.

'It most certainly is when people seem to have conveniently glossed over what happened to my sister,' said George in a tight voice, his comment aimed firmly at Evans. 'People wouldn't be so quick to forget if it happened again.'

Evans looked disgruntled but said nothing.

'I shall bid you a polite farewell,' George went on. 'I'm sure Mr Evans has better things to do than watch my family suffer again over the death of my sister.'

'What's that supposed to mean?' Evans spluttered.

'Ignore him,' Lyndsey cautioned. 'Let's go indoors.'

The pair of them began walking away, then Lyndsey came to a halt and turned back to face Maggie and George.

'I hope the ceremony goes well for your parents, Mr Pope. It's about time they had closure, don't you think?'

28

Maggie waited until Lyndsey had led Evans back through the gate into his garden and shut it behind them. She turned to George.

'What was all that about?'

'I can't stand that man. All he's ever done is whinge and whine about what an inconvenience my sister's murder was for him. He's never expressed one iota of sympathy for my parents for what they've gone through.'

'He has had a pretty tough time of it,' Maggie pointed out. 'Being accused of murder takes its toll too.'

'I'll never be convinced that he had nothing to do with it,' said George grimly. 'I mean, how convenient that he pushes off to Palma just at the point the killer decides to drop Katy's body off outside his house.'

'What, you think he might have been an accomplice to the killer? There was nothing to suggest that, and his life was pretty much dissected to look for anything that could link him to Katy's abduction and death. Aside from the fact he was known to the police and lived here, there was nothing.'

'Please don't defend him,' said George hotly.

'I'm not,' she said hurriedly. 'I'm just saying I think your anger at him is a bit misplaced, although I agree he could be more sympathetic to you and your parents.'

'Good, because I don't want to think of you being on his side and not ours.'

The smile had returned to his face and Maggie found herself feeling flustered again. She really needed to get a grip around him.

'So, have you got a spare moment to talk to Dad now? He wants to ask you about the email sent to that Lara woman. I've told him everything you said, but he'd rather hear it from you.'

'Of course. Is he inside?'

'Yes.' George offered his arm for her to hold on to. 'Shall we?'

Maggie baulked; she really had to put a stop to this overt behaviour of his. It was crossing the line of what was acceptable.

'George, I'm your family liaison officer, okay? Please don't mistake my friendliness and willingness to help you for anything else. This is a purely professional arrangement.'

He grinned. 'If you say so.'

29

An hour past its proposed start time and the memorial service was still not underway. The guests who had already taken their seats by the pond were fidgeting and fanning themselves against the mid-afternoon heat, Maggie among them. Her thighs were welded together by sweat and she wished desperately she could nip back to her hotel room and change out of her dress into a pair of trousers.

The delay was, surprisingly, given her attention to detail, Patricia's doing. She had brought with her to Majorca a photograph of Katy blown up to A3 size and mounted on board that she planned to display during the service. It was the same image the family had given to the police to aid their search in the week before her body was found, and which was subsequently used time and time again in newspapers, online and on television.

Unfortunately, neither Patricia nor anyone else had given thought to how the board would be displayed and after she decided that propping it up on a chair simply would not do, George had been dispatched into the centre of Saros to see if any of the shops there selling artwork had an easel they wouldn't mind him borrowing. He'd been gone half an hour already and the police officer sitting next to Maggie, who'd earlier introduced himself as Inspector Jacob Jasso, told her to expect a long wait for him to return.

'They won't be open now,' Jasso had said with a chuckle. '*Es hora de la siesta.*'

'Time for siesta?' asked Maggie, who had a schoolgirl grasp of Spanish.

'For the next hour at least.'

Jasso was one of two Majorcan officers in attendance. He was from the local station in Saros while the other was a detective sent from Palma. From what DCI Walker had gleaned chatting to the pair of them beforehand, their presence at the memorial service was a box-ticking exercise for public relations. As far as the island's police were concerned, every avenue had been exhausted trying to find Katy's killer and the case was now as dead as she was.

Also present, however, was Chief Inspector Galen Martos, the detective who had led the initial investigation but was now retired from service. Martos, a short, stocky man in his sixties, said little on his arrival, keeping a respectful distance from the Popes, but when he took a seat in the back row Walker sat down next to him and the pair were now huddled in a whispered conversation.

Maggie was in the second row, directly behind Philip Pope and Declan Morris. It was after she and George had returned to the apartment to discuss the email development with Philip that Patricia had erupted about Katy's picture and everyone was scrabbling around trying to appease her. Not George though: calmly, he'd told his mother to stop making a fuss and that he'd sort something out. His words were all it took to tranquillize Patricia's hysteria and now she was seated quietly next to her husband on the front row, rereading the speech she planned to make. Maggie wondered if Philip had been given the option of saying a few words about his daughter and came to the conclusion he probably hadn't.

A handful of locals who wanted to pay their respects took up the other seats, including Annika, who'd swept her hair back into a bun and was also wearing a dress. She looked cool and possessed, as though sweaty legs weren't something she ever worried about.

Maggie surveyed the other attendees as she readjusted her sunglasses, which kept sliding down her nose. Lyndsey had left Terry Evans in his apartment to join the congregation and there were quite a few journalists seated as well. Johnnie Hickman-Ferguson had front-row status on the other side of Patricia, smartened up in a shirt and trousers with his hair greased back into a ponytail. Walker had gone down to the marina to follow up on his claims that Katy had wanted to dump Declan, but he hadn't been on his boat and now it was driving the DCI nuts that Johnnie didn't appear have a mobile he could contact him on.

'I'm all for quitting the rat race and living off-grid, but who the fuck manages without a phone in this day and age?' he kept saying.

Ten minutes later, at the point where Maggie thought she might pass out in the heat, George, in a navy suit, white shirt and black tie, returned brandishing a wooden easel, which he promptly set up by the pond. The picture of his sister in place, he slipped into the chair next to his father. Glancing over his shoulder, he caught Maggie's eye, smiled and winked.

Ignoring the frisson she felt, Maggie stared resolutely ahead. Patricia was on her feet now to say a short prayer and asked that everyone do the same. Paulson was sitting next to Maggie and complained in an undertone that he was an atheist, which she answered by jabbing him in the ribs with her elbow and telling him to shush.

Then she jumped out of her skin as Inspector Jasso's mobile began to ring right next to her. Patricia huffed loudly, furious at the interruption, and the officer apologized profusely as he scrabbled to silence the call. But even though he'd killed the volume, his phone wouldn't stop vibrating as the caller tried again.

'I do apologize,' he said again sheepishly.

He slid out of his seat and walked towards the path to leave. He was listening intently to the caller when he stopped abruptly. Maggie heard him ask '*¿Falta de dónde?*' after which he spluttered '*mierda*' – which she knew to be an expletive – then launched into a string of Spanish too rapid for her to follow. By now everyone else was watching him too.

'Anyone know what he's saying?' asked Paulson, looking around.

One of the reporters sitting two rows behind them raised his hand.

'He said, "Missing from where?" Then he asked which part of the beach and what time was she last seen and do they have a name for the woman yet?'

The reporter appeared smug that he was able to translate but as his sentence dwindled to an end, the shocked faces around him made him take stock of what he'd just repeated.

'Fucking hell,' he breathed.

Jasso became aware that all eyes were on him. Slowly, he

lowered the handset from his ear and covered the mouth-piece with his other hand. He was a visible confliction of emotions, shock wrestling with disquiet.

'A young woman has been reported missing from the beach,' he said, the graveness of his tone thickening his accent. 'They say she is British.'

'Like Katy?' gasped Philip, clutching George's hand for support.

Jasso nodded. 'Like your daughter.'

30

There was a moment's pause, then Walker jumped to his feet and gestured to Paulson, Shah and Maggie to do the same.

'You lot, come with me.' He turned to Jasso. 'Let us help you.'

The inspector nodded. He was ashen beneath his natural tan and Maggie could only speculate what else had been relayed to him by the person on the other end of the call. Even if it turned out to be a false alarm, a young British woman being reported missing in Saros on the anniversary of Katy Pope's disappearance was still going to thrust the local police back into an unwelcome spotlight.

But as they moved to leave, Patricia stepped forward. Unlike everyone else, she appeared not to be alarmed by the information Jasso had relayed, but instead was visibly aggrieved.

'You cannot leave before the end of the service. I will not have it,' she said.

'But, darling, didn't you hear what he said? A young woman's gone missing like Katy. They need to go and look for her,' implored Philip. He reached forward to take his wife's arm but she shrugged him off as though his touch was corrosive. Then she clapped her hands briskly.

'Can everyone retake their seats and I'll start the prayer again.'

'Mum, the police need to go,' said George, his voice strained.

Again, there was no acknowledgement from Patricia.

'Philip, George, do sit down,' she said. 'Come along everyone.'

Jasso peeled away from the crowd, muttering into his mobile. Walker stared after him, then turned to Maggie and mouthed, 'We need to go.'

She frowned. What did he expect her to do? Then she realized that what he expected was for her to appease Patricia rather than leaving him to do it himself. Cursing his cowardice, she took a deep breath and went to the front. For a moment it looked as though Patricia was going to ignore her, so Maggie moved forward until they were barely a hand width apart. She spoke softly, so only Patricia and Philip, who had joined her at the front, could hear her.

'We all understand how important the memorial service is, Mrs Pope, and the last thing any of us wants to do is disrupt it. But if a British national has gone missing from the beach then we should assist the local police in the search,' she said. 'You of all people must be able to appreciate that.'

The look of contempt on Patricia's face made Maggie's insides shrivel, but she held her nerve.

'It's up to you,' she went on, 'but you can either continue the service without us or postpone it for a couple of hours until we've had a chance to establish what's going on. With any luck, it will be a false alarm.'

'I think we should wait, darling,' said Philip weakly.

'Nonsense.' Patricia turned to Walker. 'Do you *all* need to go?'

That's me staying put, thought Maggie resignedly. She was their FLO – it made sense for her to remain behind. Besides, Paulson and Shah were already halfway along the path leading from the pond, hot on Jasso's heels.

'Yes, we should all go,' Walker said firmly. 'Come on, Maggie.'

'I'll come too,' said Lyndsey Shepherd, rising from her chair.

'This is ridiculous,' huffed Patricia. 'It's probably a fuss about nothing.'

There was no mistaking the sharp intake of breath behind her. Johnnie got to his feet, shaking his head.

'You've said and done some nasty things in your time, but I think you're about to surpass yourself,' he exclaimed. 'What would Katy think of you right now, ignoring some poor girl who might be in serious trouble?'

Declan, who until this point had remained passively seated, got to his feet. 'She just wants to remember her daughter,' he said.

'She's trying to stop the police from doing their job,' Johnnie hit back.

Patricia appeared to flounder for a moment, before gathering herself and retaliating with a scathing reply.

'Don't you dare tell me what Katy would've thought. As much as you like to think otherwise, you didn't know her like I did.'

Johnnie cocked an eyebrow at her. 'Oh, you have no idea, lady. No idea at all.'

Maggie didn't think it would be possible for the air to get any clammier, but it did in that moment as a heavy silence fell upon the group. Patricia looked as though she wanted to throttle Johnnie, while he stood there, hands on hips, wordlessly goading her to try.

'Please, stop this, the both of you,' cried Philip. 'This is not acceptable behaviour.'

'Dad's right,' said George, who looked as distressed as his father, his skin paled to a shade that almost matched his shirt. He turned to Maggie. 'You should go, we understand. We'll hold off the service until later – I don't think now's the time.' His voice cracked. 'Please let us know when you find her. I can't bear the thought that someone else—' He dissolved in tears and Johnnie put an arm around his shoulders.

'I'll call as soon as there's news, I promise,' Maggie said.

She went to move but George suddenly grabbed her hand. His touch sent a ripple through her body and she could feel her face scorch red.

'Thank you,' he said, his eyes boring into hers.

Flustered, she pulled her hand away and nodded, then scuttled over to where Walker and Lyndsey were waiting. Together the three of them headed down the path towards the exit, the reporters right behind them and the sound of Patricia Pope's ranting following them all.

31

It was a strange situation for the Operation Pivot team to be in – a major incident unfolding around them, but no obvious role for them to play in it. Walker in particular was becoming agitated by the four of them just standing on the sidelines, watching, as Jasso barked orders at his officers in Spanish but said nothing to them.

The next time Jasso went past, Walker forcibly grabbed his arm.

'Let us help, for crying out loud.'

Jasso looked annoyed at the interruption, but conceded.

'Fine. You can talk to any British holidaymakers on the beach. We've asked everyone to stay put until they've given their statements.' Then he stalked off again.

'Amit, Vince, you come with me,' he said. 'Maggie, I want you to see if you can find the parents. If I go steaming in there, Jasso's bound to kick off, but he might mind less if you talk to them, being a FLO. Call me when you've located them.'

'Sure, I will.'

She went over to the Eroski mini-mart where Jade was apparently headed to when she left her parents and fiancé on the beach. Jasso's officers had been darting in and out of the store for the half-hour that she and the others had been watching them. One of them had been pointing up at the CCTV outside. She wondered if Jade had been caught on camera and, if so, what she'd been doing.

There was a middle-aged woman standing outside the mini-mart who looked upset, so Maggie went up to her.

'Do you speak English?' she asked.

The woman said yes.

'Are you the manager? My name is Maggie and I'm with the British police.'

The woman baulked as Maggie held up her warrant card.

'Don't worry; I'm not here to talk to you. Inspector Jasso and his men will be taking your statement. I'm looking for the missing woman's parents. Someone said they were waiting inside your store?' She knew they wouldn't be, but she hoped that by asking the woman would send her in the right direction.

'I think they are at the Hotel Espléndido,' said the woman, pointing at the building next door.

'*Gracias*, thank you.' Maggie paused. 'Is she on the CCTV?'

The woman, close to tears now, shook her head. 'She never made it inside.'

Maggie thanked her again then crossed the paved walkway towards the hotel. She jumped out of her skin when Jasso suddenly appeared in front of her.

'Where are you going? I told Walker you could go on the beach, not anywhere else.'

She thought about lying, but decided to front it out.

'Inspector Jasso, I'm an experienced detective trained in

family liaison and all my previous cases have involved dealing with the relatives of victims in major incidents. I can help you here, if you just let me talk to Jade's parents—'

'No. My officers are dealing with them.'

'But—'

'I said no, Officer Neville.'

Just then, one of his uniforms came bolting along the pathway towards them, smiling jubilantly. On reaching Jasso he burst out with a torrent of Spanish that Maggie had no hope of translating. But, judging by the smile that spread across Jasso's face, it was good news.

'What's happened?' she interrupted. 'Has Jade been found?'

'There's been a sighting of her in the next town, in a car,' said the officer, clearly overjoyed to be the one delivering the news to his boss.

'I have to check this out,' Jasso said to Maggie. 'But I meant what I said – you are not to talk to her parents.' He walked off without waiting for her to acknowledge his order.

The young officer beamed at the inspector's retreating back, then turned to Maggie.

'This is good news, no? The girl is safe!'

'It's great there's been a sighting,' said Maggie cautiously. 'But I'll leave my celebrating to when she's actually found.'

The officer shrugged at her. 'You British, you are never happy.'

Maggie noticed he had something in his hand.

'What's that?'

'Oh, just a kid's shoe I picked up. It's nothing.'

With that, he dumped the small green Croc into the nearest bin.

32

What little alcohol Philip did drink was never consumed in daytime hours, but at that moment he was making an exception with the large gin and tonic Annika had served him. It was doing a good job of soothing his frayed nerves and he was also enjoying being able to drink it in peace because Patricia had, at George's urging, gone for a lie-down. She had grown hysterical when Walker disobeyed her order to remain at the service and took Maggie and the others with him, and by the time she'd finished her outburst she was exhausted. He would never admit it to anyone, but Philip was full of admiration for the way DCI Walker stood up to her, even if he did get Maggie to do it on his behalf.

He took another sip of his drink. George, Johnnie and Declan were on their second pints already and judging by what little was left in their glasses it looked as though a third might be imminent. Philip was concerned when George invited the other two to join them – particularly given Johnnie's flare-up at Patricia – but it was obvious their need for a drink outweighed any mutual loathing in this instance. They were in shock at the news a woman had gone missing from the beach and it was all they could talk about.

'It must be a coincidence,' Johnnie was saying. 'What else could it be?'

'What did Maggie say when you spoke to her?' Philip asked George. She had called him as they were ordering their second round.

'What I told you – a young woman in her twenties left the beach around eleven thirty to get some snacks and didn't come back. Her family didn't start looking for her until almost an hour later because they thought she might've nipped back to their villa for something.'

Feeling sick to his stomach, Philip gripped the table for support.

'It's exactly the same scenario,' he rasped. 'We were on the beach when Katy went off and she never came back.'

'But this girl apparently has her phone on her, and a bit of cash, Dad,' said George reassuringly. 'I agree with Johnnie. I bet it's a coincidence and there's been a misunderstanding about where she is, like she went off shopping or something and forgot to tell her family.'

'What if it's not a coincidence?' Declan blurted out. 'What if it was deliberately meant to happen today?'

The other three stared at him.

'It's exactly the same scenario. Even that police officer said it was just like when Katy disappeared.'

'I think that was a knee-jerk reaction,' said George, 'because of where he was. If he'd been at his station and the call had come in, I doubt he would've even considered a possible link. I'm telling you, it'll be a random crime, if it's even a crime at all.'

Philip could see his son was trying to convince himself there was no connection.

'Maybe that's the point,' said Declan cautiously. 'The police thought that Katy was chosen at random – well, apart from when they suspected me,' he added huffily.

'But why on earth would anyone want to copy what happened to Katy?' asked Philip, bewildered.

'Because it's the anniversary and they want to make a point?' suggested Declan.

Again, Philip struggled to understand. 'What point?'

'Unless it's not a copycat and it's the same person who's struck again to remind everyone they got away with it first time round,' said George sombrely.

He caught his father's horrified stare.

'But no one in their right mind would do that,' he added soothingly. 'The heightened media interest, the police over from the UK – you'd have to be crazed to attempt something so audacious.'

'Isn't that how the papers described Katy's killer – as being crazed?' pondered Declan. 'He did say in the email that he was going to come back.'

'What email?' asked Johnnie sharply.

Philip looked at George. Were they allowed to say anything? But Declan had no compunction about sharing the content of the email he'd been sent and Johnnie's face was ashen by the time he'd finished.

'Fucking hell. Why didn't you tell me sooner?' This wasn't to Declan, but to George.

'The police are investigating it and until they find out who sent it, the fewer people who know the better.' George gave his dad a sideways glance and Philip took it as a sign to not mention the other message sent to the woman in London. Declan still didn't know about that one.

'They can't really think it's the same killer who sent it,' said Johnnie, clearly rattled. 'It'll be someone mucking around, an online troll.'

'What if it's not?' said Declan. 'The killer's never been caught, so what's to stop them coming back for a new victim? They could've been biding their time, waiting for the right moment. The tenth anniversary could be it.'

'You're talking crap,' snapped Johnnie. 'Katy's murder was a one-off. The police said so.'

'To be fair, that's because they wanted it to be,' George pointed out. 'Better to portray it as a random attack than have tourists think a potential serial killer is at large in a popular holiday resort.'

Philip was lost for words. This was all too much for him to process.

'I'm telling you, there's no way it's the same person,' said Johnnie. 'It'll be a coincidence. Worst-case scenario, she's had an accident and the hospital can't ID her, so that's why it looks like she's missing.' He drained the dregs of his pint. 'I'm having another. Anyone else want one?'

George and Declan both raised their hands.

'What about you, Philip? Another G&T?' asked Johnnie.

Philip hesitated for a moment; the first was already making him feel a bit woozy and a second might tip him over the edge. Then he thought, to hell with it.

'Actually I would, thank you.'

Johnnie raised his hand to beckon Annika over.

'How are you gentlemen holding up?' she asked. 'I'm so very sorry about the service being cancelled.'

'Thank you,' said George. 'To be honest, we're more concerned with what's going on with the missing woman now.'

'A friend who lives down by the marina texted me to say the police are everywhere but there's still no sign of her,' said Annika. 'They're questioning everyone on the beach to see if they saw anything.'

'Did your friend say which bit of beach she was on?' asked Declan. Johnnie shot him a look.

'I think it was the stretch to the left of the marina, by the ice-cream stand,' said Annika. She checked her notebook. 'So, that's three pints of Estrella and a gin and tonic. Anything to eat with your drinks?' They all shook their heads. 'Okay, I'll be back in a minute.'

Philip could barely breathe. It was the same area of beach they had been on when Katy went missing.

'Dad, it's going to be okay,' said George, but his eyes betrayed his own shock. Even though he hadn't been with them that day, he was aware of the significance of the setting.

Declan cocked his head towards Johnnie.

'Your boat's moored in the marina, isn't it? You must've seen something, because you were there all morning. You didn't turn up here until the service was due to start.'

'I was sleeping. I didn't see a thing,' said Johnnie gruffly.

'Can you prove that?'

'Fuck off, Declan. We both know it'll be you the police will be rushing to question. Your first visit to Saros in ten years and another girl goes missing – you'll be top of their list, mate.'

'I was in my hotel room,' Declan spluttered. 'I slept in because I was knackered from my early start yesterday.'

'Can *you* prove that?' asked Johnnie bullishly.

'Guys, come on: stop winding each other up. We all know neither of you had anything to do with this,' said George.

'Today's meant to be about remembering Katy, not accusing each other of all sorts. Let's have a toast,' he added, as Annika returned with a tray of fresh drinks.

He took one of the pints and held it aloft.

'To my darling sister,' he said, his voice thick with emotion. 'Never forgotten, forever missed. To Katy.'

'To Katy,' chimed Philip and Johnnie, raising their glasses.

'To Katy,' said Declan at the same time. 'The girl we all loved to death.'

33

By the time they'd alerted the police to her disappearance, Jade's parents and fiancé had done everything Maggie would've done in their shoes.

When Jade hadn't returned from the shop after half an hour and hadn't answered her phone when he called it, Mason had sprinted back to the family's villa in nearby Soller to check if she was there, worried she had been suddenly taken ill. Meanwhile, Clive and Mandy Reynolds walked the streets closest to the beach to look for their daughter, ducking into shops and bars they thought she might have gone into, but no one had seen her.

The three of them met up again by the mini-mart another thirty minutes later and that's when they made the decision to call the police. On seeing their distress, a waiter serving diners in one of the hotel restaurants that lined the seafront had alerted his general manager, who then graciously gave the family use of a suite overlooking the paved walkway, somewhere private where they could talk to the police and also watch the search for Jade get underway on the beach and streets below.

The GM's generosity had a subtext though, as Maggie

was now realizing as he addressed her and Walker in the hotel foyer, their reflections staring up at them from the shiniest tiled floor she'd ever stood upon. He wanted to know everything in return.

'Is this the same scenario as the British girl ten years ago?' the manager asked. 'Has this one been kidnapped too?'

'There's nothing to suggest it's related,' said Walker briskly, unwilling to countenance any discussion. 'The circumstances are different.'

That wasn't a lie.

Inspector Jasso's officers had quickly established that Jade Reynolds had left the beach carrying both her phone and some money. Katy Pope had neither on her when she vanished. Jade had told her family exactly where she was going, but Katy had slipped away without a word – Declan was swimming in the sea at the time and both her parents were reading on their sun loungers. None of them saw her go.

Those distinguishable details were enough to make Walker heed caution about a possible link. That suited Inspector Jasso, who was over his initial panic at the thought of a second British woman going missing in the resort and was now proclaiming that Jade had gone off somewhere of her own volition based on the witness sighting and would turn up soon. However, as the search was now in its fifth hour he'd finally agreed that Walker and Maggie should speak directly to her parents, as the language barrier between them and the Spanish officers was beginning to grate on Clive Reynolds – he was complaining that he couldn't understand them and threatening to call the tabloids to say that not enough was being done to find her.

Before agreeing to introduce them to the Reynolds family, Jasso had made it clear that the Operation Pivot team had no jurisdiction in the case, but he conceded it would be good for them to provide support and reassurance to the family while they were on foreign soil, alongside Lyndsey Shepherd and her Consulate colleagues.

'Frankly, I'd rather you deal with him than I have to,' Jasso had remarked sourly. 'He's already insulted two of my officers using the c-word.'

The family's borrowed suite was on the top floor of the hotel. Walker rapped on the door and a short, stocky, middle-aged man with blond hair that looked anything but natural yanked it open. His face was tomato red, the product of either too much sun or dangerously high blood pressure.

'Have you found my daughter yet?' was his opening shot.

'Mr Reynolds, I'm DCI Gavin Walker and this is DC Maggie Neville. We're officers with the Met Police. I'm afraid there's no news yet, but we'd like to talk to you. Can we come in?'

Clive stood aside to let them pass.

'The Met? Blimey, you got here fast,' said Mandy Reynolds, getting to her feet. She was an attractive woman in her early fifties with – compared to her husband's – subtly bleached blonde hair that was set in waves. Her face was streaked with mascara and tears though, which she clumsily wiped away with the back of her hand. A good-looking young man, who Maggie presumed was Jade's fiancé, Mason Embry, was sitting on the sofa in the suite's lounge area looking wretched. He didn't get up to greet them.

'Actually, we were already in Saros, because of another case,' Walker replied.

Clive Reynolds's face turned even redder.

'Are you here because of that Pope girl? We've been reading about the anniversary, it's all over the papers.' To Walker's obvious discomfort, Clive reached over and grabbed his hand, clasping it between both of his plump, sweaty ones. 'You gotta be honest with me, Mr Walker – do you think my Jade's been had by the same person? Because they never caught him, did they?'

'The Majorcan police have told us they are treating your daughter's disappearance as unrelated,' said Walker. 'I know the anniversary must be giving you cause for concern, but they believe the timing is most likely an unfortunate coincidence. Inspector Jasso and his colleagues are doing everything they can to locate your daughter.'

Maggie noted how Walker was careful to make it clear this was Jasso's case and not theirs.

The DCI's answer seemed to calm Clive, but he still didn't let go of his hand.

'Can you not look for her, then? I don't trust them Spaniards – they got it wrong last time, that's for sure. That poor girl was missing for a week and then it was too late. Can't you take over?'

'I'm afraid we don't have the authority,' said Walker. 'But as I said, I can assure you that Inspector Jasso is doing everything by the book to find Jade. He and his team know what they're doing.'

'We are helping them, though,' said Maggie, coming to Walker's rescue as he tried to wrest his hand from Clive's grip. 'Inspector Jasso mentioned you were having some problems understanding his officers, so he's agreed we should interview you and pass any relevant information back to him. It would be really helpful to establish Jade's movements so far on your holiday, to see if anything's occurred that might help Inspector Jasso work out where she is.'

Clive finally let go of Walker's hand.

'What do you want to know?'

Maggie gestured to the sofa where Mason was still sitting. There were two matching easy chairs alongside it. 'Why don't we all sit down?'

They all did, except Walker. Maggie looked up at him expectantly, but he wouldn't meet her gaze as he instead addressed the family.

'DC Neville here is a trained family liaison officer, or what we call FLO for short,' he said. 'She knows how to help families in your situation and the right questions to ask. So I'm going to leave you in her very capable hands, because I'm needed elsewhere.'

Maggie reacted with surprise. This was the first she'd heard. Needed where, exactly?

'You can ask us anything,' said Mandy eagerly. 'We've no secrets, have we, Clive?'

Her husband slowly shook his head.

'Call me when you're done,' Walker said to Maggie in an aside.

She couldn't help herself.

'Where are you going?'

He looked at her blankly. 'I'm joining the search, of course. What else would I be doing?'

34

There was an awkward pause after the DCI left the room, the family obviously noting the tension his abrupt departure had created. Maggie punctured the uncomfortable silence by asking if they minded her taking notes as they chatted.

'This isn't a formal interview,' she said. 'All I want to do at this stage is establish a timeline of Jade's movements.' She neglected to add that Jasso had refused to extend their brief beyond that; he was insistent the British police did no more than the very basics, presumably so it didn't appear as though they were taking charge.

'Like retracing her steps?' asked Mason. His voice was reedy and hesitant and at odds with his masculinity. It was evident he put significant time and effort into maintaining his physique: his biceps were thicker than Maggie's thighs, the veins popping along them like electrical wires snaking down a wall.

'Exactly that,' she said, giving him a reassuring smile. 'So, let's start at the beginning: when did you fly out to Majorca?'

For the next twenty minutes Jade's parents gave Maggie chapter and verse on their holiday so far: how they'd set off at four a.m. from their home in Barnet to catch an early flight from Southend airport because it was the cheapest deal to Palma; how a hen party group on the flight had annoyed everyone with their lairy drinking games; how the car-hire concession at Palma airport had upgraded them to a bigger vehicle; how well Clive had taken to driving on the right; and so on. Both were entertaining talkers, furnishing their anecdotes with throwaway lines that made Maggie smile, and she could see that talking about their trip was doing a good job of distracting them from worrying about their daughter, but it didn't make her job easier. She needed to elicit details that were pertinent to the search for Jade and trying to get Mandy and Clive to focus on facts was a bit like trying to prise open a walnut with a pair of eyebrow tweezers.

Nor did it help that the heat was making them all listless. It seemed another reason the manager had been happy to let them use the suite was because the air con was broken and it couldn't be let to paying guests. The balcony doors were open and every now and then a gentle breeze lifted the bottom of the delicate voile curtains pulled across them, but for the most part it was baking hot inside.

After a few more minutes, Maggie proposed they take a break.

'Why don't I call down to reception and see if that nice manager will bring us some drinks?' suggested Mandy.

'And some grub,' said Clive, reaching for the room service menu.

While Maggie was declining their entreaties that she should order some food too 'because you may as well while it's free', Mason quietly rose from the sofa and slipped outside onto the balcony. Maggie left the parents to their ordering and went after him. She found him leaning against the metal railings, staring down at the walkway below.

'How are you holding up?' she asked.

The muscle in his cheek twitched as he ground his teeth together to stop himself from crying.

'I just need to know she's okay,' he eventually managed to say.

'I understand, I'd be feeling the same. But everything is being done to find her.' Maggie paused then, realizing that while at home she could say that with confidence, because she knew the protocol for a missing person's search in the UK, here it might be different.

'You didn't say much when I was asking about Jade's movements since you arrived in Saros. Is there anything you want to add, that her parents might have missed?'

His jaw clenched again.

'Mason? Is there anything you want to tell me?'

He shook his head, his reluctance weighing heavy on his face. Maggie couldn't let it slide though.

'Even if you think it might not be that important, it's still worth telling me,' she said. 'Just in case.'

'It's not just to do with Jade though. It was something that happened with both of us.'

'Since you got here?'

'Yeah. It was on our fourth night here, when we were out having a drink.'

Maggie did a quick calculation. 'You mean last Tuesday?'

He nodded. 'We'd all been out for dinner, then me and Jade decided to go for a drink on our own. It was still really warm, even though it was gone midnight, so we sat at a table outside this bar. That's when we saw this bloke.'

Maggie stilled. 'Go on.'

'There was another bar across the street and he was sat out the front, really knocking them back. He must've had about three pints in an hour. Jade finds it funny to make up stories about what strangers are up to – she likes to pretend they're spies and stuff – so we were coming up with all these mad reasons for why he'd hit the booze. He couldn't hear us,' Mason added hastily, 'so we weren't being rude. Anyhow, at one point Jade goes off to the toilet and then he comes over to me and starts saying stuff.'

'Such as?'

'That I should take care of Jade, because a girl like her was special. I laughed it off at first, thinking he was pissed but harmless, but then he started getting a bit ranty, if you know what I mean, saying I should take him seriously because jealousy makes people do nasty things and I wouldn't want anything nasty to happen to her.'

'He knew her name?' asked Maggie, scribbling fast in her notebook to keep up.

'No. He kept calling her the blushing bride-to-be. He must've clocked her engagement ring.'

'How did the conversation end?'

'That was the weird bit. I thought he was leaning over to nick my drink, but instead he puts something on the table next to my glass and tells me I might need it. I thought he was being a bit muggy when I saw what it was, like he was saying my breath was rank or something, so I told him to fuck off or else, and he went after that.'

'What did he give you?'

'A piece of chewing gum.'

'Gum?'

'Yeah. Like the stick kind, wrapped in paper. Cinnamon flavoured.'

'Did you see where he went after?'

'No, Jade came back then and I forgot all about it.' He gave Maggie a searching look. 'Do you think it's important?'

'I don't know. Do you think you'd recognize him again?'

'Maybe. He might've gone home by now though.'

Maggie frowned. 'What makes you say that?'

'He sounded British, like us.'

35

Declan and George decided to call it a day after their third pint and returned to their respective accommodation to doze off its effects. Johnnie pushed for a final drink so, out of politeness, Philip agreed to stay for one more to keep him company, but switched to sparkling water. There was no prospect of the memorial service going ahead now, given the creeping time, but he needed a clear head to cope with Patricia when he went back.

Heaven knew his thoughts were jumbled enough without them being lubricated by more alcohol, churning around his head so violently that he couldn't hear what Johnnie was saying, let alone pay attention to him.

Another young British woman was missing in Saros, just like his darling Katy. Was she the same age? Did she look the same? What was her name? He was also desperate to know how her poor parents were faring, because he knew exactly how they would be *feeling* – panicked, confused and terrified that their daughter had disappeared from right under their noses.

As Johnnie prattled on, Philip was transported back ten years to that heart-sinking moment when it dawned on him and Patricia that Katy hadn't gone for a stroll to clear her head and something was seriously amiss. At first he'd dismissed Patricia's concern that she'd been gone too long and could remember vividly his exasperation as his wife bullied him into packing up their bags so they could go and look for her. He'd been absorbed in a book he'd waited months to read and hadn't taken kindly to being forced to put it down. Now he couldn't remember the name of it, or what it was about. Everything before the moment they realized their daughter was missing now paled into insignificance.

The local police had been marvellous at first, offering assistance as soon as Patricia called them. Philip wondered afterwards whether it was because they'd mistakenly thought Katy was much younger – Patricia had used the phrase 'my child' during the emergency call to report her missing.

Certainly they seemed to give up looking for her far quicker than they might've done if she had been primary-school age. Only a few hours had passed before they'd started asking questions about whether she had gone off on her own before, did she like to party, did she take drugs recreationally? Philip found the questions highly offensive. Couldn't they see that a seventeen-year-old going missing during the daytime while wearing just a bikini top and shorts and having no other belongings upon her person was unlikely to be off on 'a bender'? (Philip had never heard that phrase until Declan had used it that day.)

Now he was worried this woman's parents were being subjected to the same treatment. He wished he could help them. Being abroad had exacerbated the terror and help-lessness he and Patricia felt and these parents had no idea what they were up against, the obstacles they'd have to navigate, the crushing blows they might face. Even being able to speak Spanish to a decent level hadn't helped him and Patricia as they fought to keep the police engaged in looking for their daughter.

Actually, he *could* help the parents, Philip thought with a start. He sat upright as the idea began to germinate in his mind. He could use his experience to guide them through theirs; who better to understand what they were going through than the father of the girl who went missing first?

Feeling a sense of purpose he hadn't felt for a long time, Philip looked across the table at Johnnie and was pleased to see he'd almost finished his pint.

'Why don't I walk you back to your boat?' he said. 'I could do with stretching my legs.'

''S'no bother,' said Johnnie, but as he tried to get to his feet it was patently clear he wasn't capable of walking unaided on a pavement, much less down a gangway onto a boat. Philip decided that once Johnnie was safely on board he would go in search of Maggie. From what she'd said to George during their earlier phone conversation, she, Walker and the other two chaps were helping with the search, so it was highly probable they were still on the front some-where, near the beach.

As he helped Johnnie along, he wondered if he should buzz up to Patricia in the apartment and let her know his plans. But in the same heartbeat he decided no, this was something he needed to do alone. For far too long he had taken a back seat with regards to Katy's murder, allowing others to relegate him to the position of passive observer in deference to his wife's leadership. Now it was his turn to take charge of matters – and in doing so he might save another family from the hell his was still in.

36

Maggie chose the moment Clive and Mandy's room service order arrived to go downstairs to reception to find a quiet corner in which she could call Walker and tell him about the man who'd approached Mason. He'd given her a fairly decent description: around six foot tall, somewhere in his early thirties, average build and wearing plain black shorts, a white T-shirt and a scruffy red baseball cap that, combined with how dark it was, unfortunately meant Mason hadn't seen what colour his hair was. He did sound British but he was so drunk and slurring his words so much that Mason couldn't say for certain which part he came from.

To Maggie's frustration, Walker didn't pick up. She was about to call Paulson's number, in case the boss was with him, when her phone began to ring. It was Umpire.

They'd spoken every day since she'd arrived in Majorca but she suspected the purpose of his call now, which he was making from his office, was not just to see how she was.

'Has the news broken then?' she asked upon answering.

'It's everywhere. Someone who was on the beach tweeted it and now it's snowballed because of the Pope anniversary.

Is there a connection though? Someone's also tweeted there's been a sighting of Jade in the next town.'

Maggie bristled. It was becoming harder and harder for police to stay ahead in investigations when social media users broke new leads before they had a chance to.

'What's Walker's take on it?' Umpire asked.

Not wanting their conversation to be overheard, Maggie left the hotel reception and crossed the walkway to sit on a bench next to the beach, hidden behind the spreading branches of a tree. Only a handful of families were on the beach compared to the usual hoard: news of Jade's disappearance must've sent the tourists running for the safety of their holiday lets.

'He's taking the same view, that until we have concrete proof of a link it should be treated as a separate incident. There are a few dissimilarities,' said Maggie, and she told Umpire about Jade having money and her phone on her.

She held back from mentioning the chewing-gum man, though. Much as she liked discussing cases with Umpire and thrashing out theories, and however much she trusted him never to impart information she shared, she felt it would be disloyal to DCI Walker to disclose it when she hadn't told him about it yet.

'I'm with the family at the moment,' she finished. 'We aren't officially involved, but the police here are happy to let me liaise for the time being. The parents don't understand a word of Spanish and it's causing friction.'

'They're lucky to have you. Is it still hot out there?'

'Boiling. What's it like where you are?'

'Damp. It's been drizzling all day.' Umpire paused. 'What do you reckon the chances are of you coming home on Friday?'

The Operation Pivot team was booked on a mid-evening flight back to the UK.

'If Jade Reynolds turns up safe and well, I'll be back no question. If she isn't found before then and we find out she hasn't disappeared of her own free will, I suppose we could be asked to stay on. It makes sense because we're already here, but even more so if –' she put emphasis on the word 'if' – 'it does turn out that there's a connection to Katy Pope's murder.' Suddenly she remembered the significance of the weekend. 'Shit, Lou and the kids are meant to be coming up on Saturday. Shall I put them off?'

'No, let's leave it. As you say, Jade could turn up before then and if we cancel we'll be disappointing the kids for nothing.'

'Maybe I should call Lou and warn her,' Maggie fretted. 'Then she can decide if she wants to make other plans. She might be cross if I don't give her the option.' Previously, when they'd both lived in Mansell, Lou had been used to Maggie's job interrupting their arrangements and put up with it, but Maggie wasn't confident she'd be the same now, not after things had been so rocky between them.

'Leave it another day,' Umpire counselled. 'Tomorrow's Wednesday so that would still give her time to make new plans.'

He was right. 'Okay,' Maggie agreed.

'How were the Pope family after the service was cancelled? A reporter who was there tweeted a picture of Katy's brother looking upset. You're in the picture too, by the way, but only from the back.'

Hearing Umpire mention George made Maggie feel edgy, as though he was testing her.

'I do love you, you know,' she blurted out.

'I love you too,' he reciprocated, sounding amused. 'I have to go; someone wants me. Call me later if you can.'

'I'll do my best.'

Maggie smiled as she hung up. She was being silly, reading too much into his comment about George. There was absolutely no reason for Umpire to doubt her.

So, *why*, a little voice rang in her head, *are you feeling guilty?*

37

Paula McCall couldn't control her giggles as her husband, Stephen, tried to manhandle the enormous inflatable unicorn they'd just bought along the pavement. The pool toy was three times the size of their daughter, Macy, who'd begged them to buy it after seeing it in the window of a charity shop. The assistant who'd served them said another tourist who didn't fancy deflating it and lugging it back to Britain had donated it, and as it was forty euros cheaper than the brand-new ones being sold on the seafront, it seemed silly not to buy it for the week they were in Saros, then donate it back again when it was their turn to go home.

'Honestly, Macy, I don't know how we're going to get this back to the apartment in one piece,' said Stephen, as he almost sent a male pedestrian flying off the pavement with the unicorn's massive wings. 'Sorry, mate, I didn't see you there,' he called out.

The man raised his hand in acknowledgement and smiled. He was trying to lift a suitcase into the boot of a hire car parked next to where Stephen had come to a halt.

'I know, it's big, isn't it! We must look so daft,' said Paula, as though the man had made a comment to that effect. She regarded him for a moment, head at a tilt. 'I don't suppose you could take our picture with it, just in case it doesn't survive the walk back?'

The man hesitated, then released his grip on the suitcase handle.

'Sure.'

Paula handed him her smartphone with the camera function set up ready to use. Naturally gregarious by nature, she noted how awkward he was being as she chattered away to him, and that she could barely see his face hidden beneath the peak of his red baseball cap. He must be shy, she decided.

Paula dashed back to where her husband and daughter and the unicorn were standing and struck a 'ta-da' pose, arms out to her sides.

'Say cheese,' the man instructed. He took a few images, then handed Paula's phone back to her.

'Ah, thank you,' she said.

She watched as he returned his attention to the suitcase. It was huge, one of the biggest she'd ever seen.

'Here, Stephen can help you with that.'

Before the man could decline her offer of help, she called her husband over. Stephen groaned as he lifted the case.

'Someone's going to get clobbered for excess baggage on the way home,' he grinned. 'This weighs a tonne.'

'Blame my wife,' said the man. 'It's all the stoneware she's bought.'

'You off to the airport now?' asked Paula.

'I'm afraid so.'

'We're here until Saturday.'

'You lucky things,' the man smiled.

Stephen had already gone on ahead with Macy, dragging the unicorn with him.

'I'd best catch them up,' said Paula. 'Have a safe trip home.'

The man slammed the boot down, the suitcase safely ensconced.

'Oh, don't worry, I shall.'

38

Philip decided he needed Maggie's help to introduce himself
to the family of the missing woman but he was unsuccessful
in his quest to locate her after he'd deposited Johnnie safely
onto his boat. He'd walked back and forth along the seafront
for half an hour but the only police he saw were two local
uniformed officers and he was reluctant to approach them,
wary of the reaction he might receive when they discovered
who he was.

Philip had never felt useful in any of his dealings with
the police. As the victim's father they had at first looked to
him to lead, until it became as clear to them as it had always
been to him that Patricia was in control of everything that
mattered. So, with a creeping sense of humiliation, he'd
found himself excused from the proceedings, with every
subsequent question directed at his wife, and if she was not
there, waiting until she was.

He lingered in front of a hotel restaurant. It puzzled him
there were so few police around – surely they should be
swarming the resort looking for clues – but then he overheard a waiter tell a table of diners there had been a sighting
of the woman in a car heading towards a neighbouring

town. It was, apparently, the talk of Saros. He edged closer to the table so he was better able to hear.

'Someone called 112, our emergency number,' Philip heard the waiter explain in broken English. 'It is a white Seat Leon, which is no good for the trace because it's Spain's most popular car in the most popular colour.'

It would be like looking for a needle in a haystack, thought Philip. Feeling defeated, he decided to stop for a coffee himself. When the waiter came over, he asked him to repeat what he'd said to the other diners, then asked if the police had said who'd called the emergency number. The waiter said he didn't know.

Two cups of strong coffee later, Philip felt his resolve returning. He would continue looking for Maggie and still offer his help to the family of the missing woman, presuming she hadn't yet been located. And even if she was found, he could still help them with tips on how to deal with the media.

Extracting a ten-euro note from his wallet, Philip deposited it on the table and got to his feet, ready to resume his search. He looked over at the beach. It wasn't as busy as usual and as he watched the few families who were there interact with one another, their expressions happy and their bodies relaxed, a chill ran through him. How could somewhere so beautiful and dazzling and full of life also appear so dark and malevolent?

Philip quickened his pace and kept his gaze resolutely forward as he passed the section of beach where he'd last seen his daughter. For a long time his mind had shuttered the memory of what happened that day, as though it was protecting him from the horror of it. Instead it came back to him in snatches, like a photo gallery scrolling on a computer screen: Patricia shouting at him to pack up the bags . . . him trying to locate Declan swimming in the sea, to tell him to get out . . .

He stopped suddenly, causing a young couple walking hand-in-hand towards him to yank apart to avoid a collision. The man muttered a rude word under his breath as they passed by him and reattached themselves.

Philip could feel his heart juddering against his ribcage as he forced himself to turn and look down at the spot where they had been that day. While Patricia had stuffed their belongings into their bags, scattering sand into every crevice in her haste, he'd gone down to the shore to look for Declan. When he hadn't spotted him, he'd gone back up the beach and, lo and behold, there was Declan, towel in hand, looking bewildered as Patricia barked orders at him to get dressed and pack up.

Philip had thought nothing of it at the time, assuming Declan must've got out of the water and gone past without him noticing. Afterwards they had been so focused on finding Katy that he hadn't dwelled on it.

But being at the scene of her disappearance had brought it back into sharp focus and he was now certain that when Declan had returned to their sunbeds after saying he'd been in the sea swimming, he had in fact been bone dry.

So if he hadn't been in the water like he claimed, where had he been?

39

Maggie got up from the bench and walked across to the hotel, pushing thoughts of Umpire and George to the recesses of her mind as she focused on what else she needed to ask Jade's family. Experience had taught her that relatives never quite knew what information was helpful, and either held back crucial details thinking they were irrelevant, or instead dumped a tsunami of trivia at her feet for her to wade through, as Clive and Mandy had earlier. But time was of the essence now and, after Mason's revelation about the man in the bar, she needed to hone in on other incidents that might be related.

She was about to cross the threshold into the hotel's reception when a hand suddenly grabbed her arm and she twirled round to find a breathless Philip Pope beside her.

'I'm so sorry, I didn't mean to make you jump,' he said. 'I've been looking for you for ages, and then I tried to call your name when I saw you, but I couldn't do that and run at the same time.' He peered through the double glass doors. 'Is this where the missing woman's family is staying?'

'No, they aren't staying here but the hotel is kindly letting them wait inside for news.'

'Where are they staying?'

'I'm not entirely sure,' she hedged. She did know, but she didn't want word getting out and the family being besieged there.

'Is it a villa, out of town?'

'What makes you ask that?' She was curious that he'd landed on the correct answer so quickly.

'The one where we stayed ten years ago was up in the hills,' said Philip worriedly. 'We had to drive to get to the beach. What if it's the same place?'

Maggie knew it couldn't be: the villa where the Reynolds and Mason were staying was only a ten-minute walk across the main road at the back of Saros. There were no hills between there and the beach.

'It's not, I promise,' she said, before swiftly changing the subject. 'Are you heading back to Orquídea now? Me and the others won't be free until later, so if you do want to go ahead with the memorial service today I'm afraid it'll have to be without us.'

'It's on hold for now,' said Philip with a solemn shake of his head. 'It would be wrong to proceed while history is repeating itself.'

'The police in Saros don't believe today's incident is connected,' she said gently, hoping the assurance would calm him down. 'There's been a sighting of Jade in the next town.'

'Yes, a waiter in a cafe just told me. But the person who reported it could be mistaken,' he said firmly. 'You know as well as I do that there are more similarities with this case and my daughter's than there are differences. The location, the time of day, the fact she was wearing her beach attire

– she's even a brunette like Katy, or so I've been told. It's the reason I've come to find you. Actually, one of two reasons.'

His eyes were lit up with emotion. It was the most animated Maggie had seen him since they had been introduced. He was usually so docile, the tortoise to Patricia's hare.

'Okay, what's the first reason?'

'I've remembered something. About the day Katy went missing.' He exhaled deeply before his words poured out in a long gush. 'I don't think Declan went swimming like he said he did. I went looking for him on the shoreline when Patricia and I realized Katy had been gone too long but I couldn't spot him anywhere,' he said. 'Yet when I returned to where we'd been sitting, he was already there. He said I must've missed him as he walked up the beach a minute or so earlier, but I am now positive, absolutely positive, that he was completely dry when I found him by our sun loungers.' He paused for another deep breath. 'Maggie, I am now certain he hadn't been anywhere near the water.'

It took her a moment for the implication of what Philip was saying to sink in. By doubting Declan's whereabouts that day, Philip was effectively withdrawing his alibi for him.

'Well?' Philip prompted.

She knew what he wanted to hear, but she couldn't bring herself to say it. She should speak to Walker first, so he could decide what action should be taken – if any. Maggie didn't doubt that Philip was being sincere now, and he didn't strike her as someone who would make something up for the sake of it, but what if his memory was now being muddied by what was going on with Jade?

'Has Declan said something to make you question what you remembered?' she asked.

'No, I haven't spoken to him about it. I think it was because I was down at that part of the beach. I've always avoided it, you see. But something about being there, seeing the spot where I last saw Katy, made me go over it again.' He looked troubled. 'I always accepted at face value that Declan had been in the water because he said he had. Now I think he was lying.'

'There is another possibility,' said Maggie cautiously. 'If he only went for a paddle, that would account for him not being fully wet.'

'No, no, I would've seen him. I went down to the shore-line and walked back and forth. If he'd been standing there with only his feet getting wet I would've come across him.'

Maggie was struck by a thought.

'Was Katy still with you on the beach when Declan said he was going for a swim?'

Philip's brow furrowed. 'Yes, I'm sure she was. In fact, she was going to go in with him, but he stopped her—'

'What are you two conspiring about?'

George Pope suddenly swooped over them like an eagle defending her chicks with her wingspan. He was almost as tall as Umpire, and fair-haired like him too. Maybe that's why I'm drawn to him, Maggie thought, because he reminds me a bit of Will. But when his hand brushed against her bare arm she experienced another involuntary shiver.

'Oh, it was nothing,' said Philip quickly.

Maggie was surprised. Why wouldn't Philip want his son to know his suspicions about Declan?

'I thought you were napping,' Philip added.

'That was ages ago, Dad. Do you realize you've been gone for hours? Mum's doing her nut wondering where you are. She sent me to track you down,' said George.

'Have I really? I should get back.'

Maggie held a hand up to stop him. 'You said there was another reason you wanted to see me?'

'Ah, yes.' He paused. 'I was hoping you could introduce me to the missing woman's family. I believe I can be of some assistance, because I understand their position. I want to help,' he added eagerly.

Maggie floundered for a response and looked to George, who gave her a quick nod as he put his arm around Philip's shoulders.

'Dad, that's such a lovely idea, but, really, you can't possibly meet them, not at the moment anyway.'

Philip looked upset. 'Why ever not?'

'How do you think they'd feel if you of all people knock on their door? They must be worried sick about their daughter and hoping – no, *praying* – that her going missing is just a coincidence. The last thing they'll want is Katy Pope's father offering to sit down and share his thoughts with them on the subject.'

'I wasn't going to make it about me,' said Philip forlornly.

'But it would be. It'd be about you and Katy.' George looked at Maggie. 'I'm right, aren't I?'

She nodded. 'You are. Now wouldn't be the right time.'

Philip nodded morosely.

'Will you at least tell me her name?' he asked.

'It's Jade, Jade Reynolds,' said George. He caught Maggie's frown. 'It's everywhere online,' he clarified.

'Jade is a lovely name,' said Philip. 'Does she look like Katy? They have the same colour hair, don't they?'

George squeezed his dad's shoulders tighter. 'Come on, let's get you back to the apartment.' He mouthed 'thank you' to Maggie, then asked if they would be seeing her later.

'Yes, I'll come by as soon as I can,' she said. 'Please tell your mother she can call me if she needs to.'

'Are you mad?' George laughed. 'You'll never get her off the phone if I tell her that. Best I say nothing and let her store it all up until you get there.'

'Thanks,' she said, matching his grin and trying to ignore the fluttery sensation in her stomach as their eyes locked.

'See you later,' he smiled.

She felt tense as she watched them head along the seafront. Even if she were single there would be no question of her acting on her attraction to George – any FLO who became intimately involved with a member of a family they were assigned to would end up on a disciplinary charge, and rightly so. FLOs arrived in people's lives at a time when they were at their most vulnerable as they grieved for a loved one. Even though George was a decade along that path compared to some, to pursue an attraction, however strong, would still be seen as her exploiting his vulnerability.

Nor did it change matters if it was the other way round and the relative was pursuing the officer. Maggie knew of a male FLO who had to be reassigned after a victim's girlfriend propositioned him because she'd misread his attention as being something more. It meant she had to deal with two men disappearing from her life: first her dead lover, then the FLO she had convinced herself should take his place.

But even if the rules were different, no way would she risk ruining what she had with Umpire for someone she'd only known for a few days. It was crazy even thinking about it.

40

Maggie hadn't got more than two steps towards the hotel again when someone else called her name.

She turned to see Lyndsey Shepherd, the consular officer, bearing down on her.

'How's it going with the family?' Lyndsey asked.

'Good. I'm getting a lot of info from them – now it's a case of deciding what's relevant and what isn't. What brings you here?'

'I wanted to see how they're bearing up and to discuss rearranging their return flights and accommodation in case Jade doesn't turn up by the time they're due to go home. It's not going to be the easiest of conversations, so it would be good if you were there while I had it.'

'Agreed. Let's go up together.'

They walked into the reception and Maggie revelled in its air-conditioned coolness after the heat of outdoors.

'I passed George Pope and his dad a moment ago,' said Lyndsey. 'The dad looked upset.'

Maggie felt her cheeks warm and cursed herself for reacting to the mere mention of George's name.

'That's my fault. He wanted me to introduce him to Clive

and Mandy so he could offer his support. I told him it wasn't a good idea. George was walking him back to his apartment.' She caught the look of disquiet on Lyndsey's face. 'Philip meant well.'

'I'm sure he did. It's a shame the same can't be said of his son.'

'You really don't like George Pope, do you? What's up with that?'

Lyndsey pulled a face. 'Is it that obvious?'

'Blindingly,' Maggie laughed.

'I know I should be kinder because of his sister, but I find him obnoxious. The way he talks down to people really grates on me.'

'I can't say I've noticed myself.'

'He's on his best behaviour for the anniversary. But George is a regular visitor to Majorca and he's not a nice person to deal with, trust me. The last time he was in Palma the police had to be called when he threatened a jeweller at his store – the same one your boss tracked down over Katy's missing ring. I was called in to smooth things over and the way he spoke to me was so awful I should've let the police arrest him.'

Maggie felt a spike of alarm.

'Why was he there?'

'He said he wanted to see if the jeweller could remember anything else about the man who came in asking about the value of a ring like Katy's.'

It sounded like a plausible reason for him being there, Maggie thought.

'He wants his sister's killer to be caught. There's nothing wrong with that,' she said.

'He called me a stupid bitch for doing my job,' said Lyndsey.

Maggie was shocked: she couldn't imagine George calling anyone by that name, let alone a consular officer.

'No, you're right, that's indefensible.'

The lift pinged to announce it was on the ground floor and the doors slid open for them to board.

'Exactly. He's got a nasty streak, so watch yourself with him.'

'What's that supposed to mean?' asked Maggie abruptly.

Lyndsey shot her a look. 'George Pope is all charm when he wants something, that's all I'm saying.'

Maggie squirmed under the woman's hard stare. 'How regularly does he come over here?' she asked, wanting to deflect it.

'Once or twice in the spring usually but this year it's been four times since April. Each time he's stayed in Orquídea.'

The lift rose smoothly, taking them towards the top floor.

Maggie was shocked. George hated the place so much, why would he stay there on a regular basis? 'How do you know all this anyway?'

Lyndsey gazed up at her reflection in the lift's mirrored ceiling as though she was mulling something over, then looked back at Maggie. 'I've been keeping tabs on him. There's something about him I don't trust.'

'Is that based on anything specific besides how he was at the jewellery shop?'

'No, it's just a gut feeling I have.'

Maggie knew all about trusting gut feelings – normally hers never let her down. But right now it wasn't sharing Lyndsey's concern about George; nothing he'd done so far had alarmed her, other than being too attractive for his own good. She decided to deflect the conversation.

'What happens if Jade isn't found in the next few days? Do you think we'll be asked to stay on?'

'If the police here put in a request to the Home Office asking for that, then yes. But they might not want outside help.'

The lift glided to a halt and the two women got out.

'Why wouldn't they?' Maggie asked.

'People have long memories and they haven't forgotten the kicking that the British press gave the police here over their handling of the original investigation. It still smarts. Plus Brexit being dragged out hasn't helped. Police from non-member states can ask for cooperation on investigations involving nationals in EU countries but it's not as easy when you're one yourself.' Lyndsey explained. 'I suspect Inspector Jasso will bide his time before any invitation is issued. That doesn't mean you can't stay on though – whether you do is up to you, as long as DCI Walker remembers that it's not in any official capacity.'

As though aware he was being talked about, Walker chose that moment to text Maggie demanding she return to the team's hotel as a matter of urgency.

'I'm being summoned,' said Maggie, closing the text. 'Can you let Clive and Mandy know I've been called away? They can ring my mobile if they need anything. I know I'm not officially their FLO, but I'm here to help them for whatever reason. It's bad enough being the victim of a crime at home, but it must be bewildering when it happens abroad.'

'It really is,' said Lyndsey. 'I've never dealt with a missing person's case involving a British national before, but I've had my fair share of sexual assaults, robberies and fatal car accidents to deal with. Magaluf alone is a nightmare for incidents involving tourists. People say to me it must be lovely working on an island where there's pretty much sunshine all year round but I get to see the darker side of life on Majorca and, believe me, it's no holiday.'

41

The atmosphere in Walker's room was tense when Maggie arrived there ten minutes later. Paulson and Shah were sitting on the bed with what appeared to be most of the case files strewn next to them. The rest were on the floor. Standing over them both was retired Chief Inspector Martos.

'We haven't met,' he said, leaning across to shake Maggie's hand. 'I am—'

'I know who you are, sir,' she said politely.

The presence of the officer in charge of the initial investigation into Katy's murder came as a shock and Maggie's expression must've registered as such, because Walker blustered an explanation as to why he was there.

'Mr Martos has information that might assist us in the search for Jade,' said the DCI.

Maggie's eyes narrowed. 'But we're not leading the search, boss. Inspector Jasso is.'

Walker looked away shiftily, so Maggie turned to Shah and Paulson. Neither would meet her gaze.

'What's going on?' she asked, already sensing she wasn't going to like the answer.

'Perhaps I can explain, DC Neville,' said Martos, his accent even thicker than Jasso's. 'The inspector was part of my team who looked into Katy Pope's murder; he was a lower rank then. I believe his involvement then presents a problem now.'

Maggie's brow furrowed deeper.

'Why is that of any concern to you?' she asked, unable to mask her scepticism and sounding rude with it.

'Maggie—' Walker cautioned.

'I made many mistakes investigating Katy's murder,' said Martos. 'I hold my hands up to that.' And he did, literally, raising them in a position of surrender. 'I let too many things slip down the crack until it became a gaping chasm. I don't want the same to happen with Jade Reynolds.'

'Shouldn't this be a discussion for Jasso? We don't have jurisdiction here,' Maggie said to Walker.

Martos made a dismissive 'pfft' sound.

'He doesn't want my help. To the police here I am *El hombre que dejó morir a una niña*.'

'It means the man who let a girl die,' Shah translated quietly.

Maggie regarded Martos for a moment. He didn't seem too troubled by the description, returning her stare with a defiant one of his own. He was a short man, but powerfully built, his rounded tummy solid rather than flabby and his forearms, exposed by the short-sleeve shirt he wore, thick and sinewy. He had a shock of white hair that was vivid against his dark tan and deep-brown eyes that blazed with something she couldn't quite put her finger on. Arrogance? Disdain? It was definitely one of the two.

'I'm all for making amends, but hasn't there been a sighting of Jade now?'

'This might be a good point to fill her in, Amit,' said Walker, nodding to Shah.

Shah began cautiously. 'Ten years ago a witness claimed to have seen Katy being bundled into a car on one of the back streets behind the beach and driven off, but the police were never able to trace the vehicle, and –' he side-eyed Martos – 'because of that it was ruled out as a false alarm. Half an hour ago, a call was made to the emergency services reporting a sighting of Jade in a car at a junction on the outskirts of the marina. It's another similarity.'

'Plus the killer did warn us he was coming back in the emails he sent.'

Maggie was unnerved to hear Walker mention the messages to Declan and Lara in front of Martos.

'Aren't we meant to be keeping those under wraps, boss?' she said warily.

Martos handed her a piece of paper she hadn't noticed him holding.

'I was sent one too,' he said quietly. 'About a week ago. It was written in Spanish, but this is the translation.'

Maggie's eyes widened as she read it.

Dear Chief Inspector Martos

I do hope you are enjoying your retirement, but you may be spending less time in La Taberna in the coming weeks. I am coming back to Saros. You and I both know why. Katy was never going to be my swansong.

Be seeing you soon . . .

'At first I dismissed it, but now . . .' Martos's voice trailed off as he took the printout back. 'I told Jasso about the email but he dismissed it as nonsense.'

'I got the same reaction from him when I told him about the ones sent to Declan Morris and Lara Steadman,' said Walker. 'He thinks someone's just trolling them.'

'You've told him about Lara?'

'Yes, and he did acknowledge that it was strange she was sent a message from the same email address and he is going to have someone contact her. But he's still not convinced there is any link between what she says happened to her and what happened to Katy and now Jade, especially since the sighting.'

'Can I call Lara and warn her?' asked Maggie. 'I'm worried how she'll react if the Spanish police ring her out of the blue.'

'Yes, do it. I don't think Jasso will make it a priority, so you should have time to contact her before they do.'

'Is he really unwilling to consider the cases might be linked?' asked Paulson.

'He's pursuing the line Jade went off willingly with someone based on the fact she took her phone and a bit of cash with her, because it gave her the means to arrange to leave Saros. But I think he's wrong and so do you, don't you?' Walker looked to Martos, who nodded, then turned to Maggie. 'That's why I'm happy for the Chief Inspector to help us – because he knows what was missed the first time round.'

'We think Jasso is wrong too,' said Paulson, nodding inclusively at Shah.

'Did Jade's parents tell you anything that might be useful?' Walker asked her.

'Actually, Mason did. A few nights ago a man approached him outside a bar while Jade had gone to the toilet,' she said. 'He'd been sitting across from them and must've been watching them. He warned Mason to keep an eye on Jade and said that young women like her attract the wrong attention. Then he made this weird show of giving Mason a piece of chewing gum.'

Shah sucked in a breath.

'Are you absolutely sure about that?' he asked, looking even more serious than usual.

'Yes.' She retrieved her notebook from her bag and read aloud from her notes. 'Mason said it was a piece of cinnamon-flavoured chewing gum, the old-fashioned stick kind wrapped in foil and paper. He also gave me a description of the bloke and said he thinks he had a British accent.'

Shah dropped to the floor and began rifling through the files there as the others watched him keenly. Maggie stayed quiet too, knowing it would slow the process to interrupt him.

After a minute, Shah got to his feet, two photographs clutched in his hand. He passed the first one to Walker.

'These were taken by the crime scene investigators when Katy's body was recovered at Orquídea. This one was found by the pond where her right leg was dumped and this –' he handed the second image to Maggie – 'was next to where her torso was submerged.'

The photographs were almost identical. Both depicted the same foil and cherry-red chewing-gum wrappers, screwed up and discarded on the grass by the edge of the ponds – and both were clearly labelled as cinnamon flavour.

'I remember the CSI flagging them up but I never lent

much significance to them,' said Martos, an edge of defensiveness to his tone. 'They weren't the only bits of rubbish found at the scenes.'

'They're significant now,' said Walker grimly. 'Did the man actually give the chewing gum to Mason or did he just toss the wrapper down like he was discarding it?' he asked Maggie.

'The piece was still wrapped and by the sounds of it he made a point of putting it down on the table. Mason said he thought the man was saying his breath smelled and was narked. I think that's why it's stayed in his mind,' said Maggie. 'He didn't keep it, before you ask. It's probably in a bin now.'

Walker stared down at the photos.

'That's annoying, because I think the killer's left us his first new clue.'

42

Maggie shivered; it felt like the temperature in the room had inexplicably dropped. She was swinging between excitement at being involved in what could now be an even bigger case and a sense of foreboding that they were barking up the wrong tree and about to make massive fools of themselves if it turned out Jade had gone off with someone else.

Walker turned to Martos.

'I'm afraid I'll have to ask you to leave now. In the light of this –' he gestured at the photographs of the chewing-gum wrappers – 'the email makes you a witness.'

Martos nodded solemnly.

'I understand. You have my number if you wish to ask me further questions.'

Walker shook his hand.

'We'll be in touch.'

Martos left without saying goodbye to the others. Maggie was relieved to see him go.

'Right, let's go over everything again, from the top,' said Walker, once it was the four of them. 'Maggie, is Mason sure the man who spoke to him had a British accent?'

'As sure as he could be. The man was drunk and slurring

his words.' She took a deep breath, not quite believing how events were gathering pace. 'There's something else. I ran into Philip Pope near the hotel where Jade's family is waiting for news. He's now disputing Declan's statement about what he was doing when Katy went missing off the beach.'

There was a collective intake of breath as Maggie parroted what Philip had told her.

'Even though the obvious explanation is that Declan didn't fully submerge himself in the sea and that's why his hair was still dry, Philip is now adamant he would've noticed him paddling in the surf,' she finished.

'The alibi that the Popes gave Declan Morris is what ruled him out as a suspect,' said Paulson. 'Does Philip get what he's saying now?'

'I don't know,' Maggie answered honestly. 'He's very het up at the moment – with reason – and it may be clouding his judgement. I don't doubt that he believes he's now remembering correctly, but his mind could be playing tricks on him, if that makes sense.' She turned to Shah. 'On what grounds was Declan considered a suspect, other than the fact he was Katy's boyfriend?'

'The savings pot she had. It was money left to her when her granny died and not an inconsiderable sum. The police here thought he was after the money.'

'How much was it?'

'Twenty-five thousand,' said Walker. 'It was a lot of money for a girl her age but killing her wouldn't have made it any easier for Morris to get his hands on it – it wasn't like they were married and he'd automatically inherit it, or that she'd written a will naming him, plus Patricia had put it in a trust fund until Katy was older. I think the Spanish police fixated on the money because they hadn't done enough to establish other credible leads; making Declan the prime suspect because she had some money tucked away was lazy and convenient.'

'Which leaves us with Johnnie Hickman-Ferguson's theory that Katy was going to leave Declan because he was controlling,' said Paulson. 'Good enough reason to kill her?'

'Even if he did, I don't believe he would've disposed of her body the way it was,' said Shah. 'The way she was carved up and dumped was ritualistic and designed to grab attention. Murders that are crimes of passion are usually sloppy and the body left at the scene where it was committed. Our killer kept Katy hidden for a week then dumped her with fanfare. It was the work of a psychopath and Morris doesn't fit the profile.'

'I still want him looked at again, especially if his alibi is bollocks now,' said Walker.

'How much do we want to trust Johnnie's word that Katy was going to dump him though?' asked Maggie. 'Him suddenly coming forward after all this time doesn't sit right with me. It's like he's trying to force our attention back onto Declan.'

'I agree: me and Amit have gone back over everything and Johnnie doesn't get so much as a PS anywhere in the case file,' said Paulson. 'If you knew something that damning about someone you didn't like, you'd have said something at the time. So why didn't Johnnie?'

'I've an idea – why don't I talk to Katy's brother to see if he'll corroborate or deny what Johnnie's saying,' said Maggie. 'He was best friends with Declan and close to his sister – if anyone's going to have an idea of the state of their relationship, it'll be him.'

'Good idea,' said Walker approvingly. 'While you're doing that, I haven't given up wanting a chat with Hickson-Ferguson myself.'

'He's still dodging our attempts to speak to him,' said Paulson.

'I'll go down to his boat again after this and wait until he sodding well turns up,' said Walker. 'We can't threaten him with arrest for not talking to us, but we can make it clear it's in his best interests to cooperate.'

Maggie thought for a moment. 'Johnnie said he'd gone to stay at his parents' place in Ibiza while the Popes were using their villa in Saros. It might be worth us checking out if that's true. He said he was with his girlfriend at the time. Her name was Camila.'

'Amit, find out what you can about his family's place in Ibiza and see if you can track down the girlfriend.'

Shah nodded. 'By the way, the alibis for the two known sex offenders check out,' he added. 'The Spanish police at least got that right. But here's something interesting – one of them is now living in Palma only two streets away from the jeweller you tracked down, boss.'

Mention of the jeweller reminded Maggie of what Lyndsey had said about George. Should she mention the incident to Walker? She hesitated for a moment, then decided no; she'd ask him herself about it first.

'Which one?' Walker was asking Shah.

'Araya, the one who was done for raping a minor.'

'Have we got a picture of him?' Walker asked.

Shah nodded.

'Good. I'll go to Palma tomorrow to show it to the owner. I know you said his alibi still checked out, but it's worth a punt to see if he was the person asking about Katy's ring. We've always assumed her murder was the work of one person, but maybe Araya was involved somehow.'

'Boss, we agreed with Jasso that I would brief him after talking to Jade's parents,' said Maggie. 'Do I tell him what Mason said about the chewing gum?'

'We can't withhold evidence,' said Walker. 'Tell him everything Mason said and mention that we are aware similar chewing-gum wrappers were found near the ponds at Orquídea. It's up to him to join the rest of the dots.' Walker looked pensive as he appraised his team. 'I don't need to tell you how carefully we need to tread. Jasso's telling the world that Jade's waltzed off of her own accord, and if word gets out we're looking into the opposite, it's going to cause a shit storm. So if anyone has a problem with what we're doing, now is the time to speak up.'

Paulson was resolute. 'I'm in. Jade's life might depend on it. If it is the same killer and he sticks to the script again, we've only got a week to find her.'

'Amit?'

'Yep, I'm in.'

'Maggie?'

All eyes were on her as doubt clawed at her throat, robbing her of what to say. This could be career-ending if it backfired. But what would happen to Jade if they left it to Jasso to find her? If he stuck to the line of inquiry that she'd gone off willingly with someone, it could be a fatal error. Maggie swallowed the doubt down.

'Whatever you need me to do, boss.'

43

The table was exquisitely set. The glassware had been rinsed in lemon juice so it sparkled and the cutlery polished to within an inch of its life. At the centre of the table was a small arrangement of gerbera daisies. Less romantic than roses, granted, but in floristry they were a recommended choice to give your love interest in a new relationship, or when you were hoping a friendship might develop into something more. The message they gave were, according to one online expert, 'I'm getting to know you. Accept these flowers as a token of my growing affection for you.' The flowers were the pink variety as well, which symbolized adoration.

There were more of them stuffed into vases on the sideboard and in the front room next door, on the coffee table beside the sofa – but Jade Reynolds paid no notice on her way past.

She was still unconscious and had been since she reached her destination, curled up like an infant in the confines of the suitcase. The effects of the opiate injected into her neck meant she was oblivious to the hire vehicle pulling up the long driveway and being parked as close to the villa as it possibly could without leaving tyre marks on the lawn out the front, and she felt nothing as the boot was opened, the suitcase unzipped and she was lifted out.

Her head lolled against her abductor's chest as she was carried into the bedroom that was to be hers for the next week. It had already been set up for her arrival: the room had been stripped of everything except a made-up bed and a chamber pot. Not the most dignified way for her to relieve herself, but it wasn't as though she could be left to stew in her own urine and faeces. On the opposite side of the room was a cool box filled with food and water to keep her going for the time being. With the police now actively searching for her, only so many trips could be made here from the resort without arousing suspicion.

Still, there was little chance of her being discovered while she remained there. From the veranda at the front of the building it was just possible to make out the roof of a neighbouring property in the distance. It was why the place was so perfect – not overlooked by anyone and too far away for any screams to be heard. As far as the locals were concerned, it was disused and had been for many years, so there was no danger of unexpected callers or delivery drivers turning up and discovering who was being kept there.

Jade didn't stir as she was laid down on the bed next to a pile of fresh clothes in her size. All basic: some T-shirts, shorts, jogging bottoms and underwear. The fancy stuff would come later. Also arranged for her use was a packet of fragrance-free baby wipes, a toothbrush and toothpaste.

She was left alone then, the door locked and the wooden shutters bolted firmly across the windows. A few minutes later, there was the sound of a tap running somewhere else in the building and the clink of a glass being placed on a granite worktop. Then a beer can cracking open and a mouth sucking noisily on the foam that exploded from the opening.

But Jade heard nothing.

44

George had deposited his father back at the apartment then disappeared, saying he had an errand to run. Patricia was waiting for Philip in the kitchen, arms folded, boot-faced, expecting an explanation, but he chose not to offer one and instead silently took himself off for a bath that he managed to make last for more than an hour. By the time he surfaced, his skin even more prune-like than usual, she had gone out herself. He let out an enormous sigh of relief and spent the next hour alternating between reading a book and plotting how he could make contact with the Reynolds family without alerting Maggie.

It was almost seven when Patricia returned, with George, bearing salad vegetables, cold cuts and a freshly baked loaf. She didn't ask him whether he was hungry, but proceeded to make him a prosciutto salad and plonked the plate down on the table in front of him.

'I'm not hungry,' he said.

'Oh, so you're talking to me now, are you?'

Philip stared up at his wife as resentment flooded through him. How dare she speak to him as though he was one of her underlings?

'I think you owe me an explanation for this afternoon,' she added.

There was, as far as he was concerned, nothing to explain: he had had a couple of drinks with his son and the other two, had taken Johnnie back to his boat because he was in no fit state to take himself, and then he had enjoyed a quiet coffee on his own. Where was the harm in that?

Of course, there was more to it, but he was certainly not inclined to tell Patricia about him wanting to help Jade's family. He smarted, however, as he recalled Maggie's reaction to his request. On the one hand he could appreciate her reluctance to introduce him to Jade's parents when only a few hours had passed, but on the other he feared waiting any longer was foolish. There was so much he could do to help them *now*, because those first few hours were also the most crucial. It felt short-sighted and, well, a bit cruel of Maggie to deny him the opportunity.

Thankfully, he could be confident that George, currently observing both of his parents from his position on the sofa, would not tell Patricia about the conversation with Maggie because Philip had asked him not to on their way back to Orquídea. George had agreed because he recognized how incendiary it would be for his mother.

George was sitting with his arms folded across his chest. Philip adjusted his own posture to mirror it. There was something defiant about the pose that made him feel bolder facing down the heat of his wife's stare.

Had she always dominated him? It pained him to think that she had, and yet Philip could recall the early days of their relationship when he was the one who led the discussions and made the decisions on behalf of his family. It was he, in fact, who decided they should set up home in Crystal Palace after they married in 1971. He had got to know the area well when he had been lodging in nearby Sydenham while studying for his degree in Art History at the Courtauld Institute of Art on the Strand. Patricia was from north of the river, born and raised in Whetstone, but she never questioned his choice for them to move south.

It was only after she'd joined the police that the balance of power between them began to shift. It did not happen overnight, but rather by stealth, until the disagreements between them became so bad it was easier for him to give in to her demands than continue to butt heads. He also wanted to protect the children, who were becoming distressed by their rowing; George's teacher at primary school called them in to say he'd begun picking on younger boys as a means of venting his frustration and he was falling behind with his learning.

Philip was less able to pinpoint when Patricia's assertiveness began to make him feel emasculated. Was it when his friends started to mock him for allowing her to nag him as she did? When she banned him from playing golf at the weekends because she found his absence irritating? He couldn't remember when it stopped bothering him though. It simply became the norm.

A few more minutes ticked by in silence. Philip could see Patricia's lips begin to twitch, her burning desire to say something overriding her determination to wait for him to reply. He began counting in his head: he'd reached nine when she cracked.

'So, where were you?'

Philip crossed his arms tighter across his chest before responding.

'I escorted Johnnie back to his boat because he was too drunk to walk unaccompanied. Then I stopped for coffee to clear my head,' he said evenly.

'You should've called to let me know where you were.'

'Why?'

'I beg your pardon?'

'I said, why?'

'Dad . . .' Such was the caution in George's tone that it came out as 'Daaaaad'.

Philip smiled benignly at his son.

'George, I'm asking a simple question of your mother, it's fine.'

'You're asking me why you should've called me? Because it's courtesy,' Patricia spluttered. 'I'm your wife.'

'Yes, you are, but I am not answerable to you, any more than you are to me. If I decide to have a coffee on my own, I do not need to seek your permission to do so.'

'I never said that you did.'

He had expected her to be furious but her reaction was one of bewilderment, as though she couldn't understand why he was daring to talk back to her. He uncrossed his arms and got to his feet.

'Good, that's settled then.'

'Why are you being like this?' she asked him, her voice quivering.

'Because I'm tired, Pat,' he said, without a trace of rancour. 'I'm tired of being nagged and berated and forced to please everyone but myself. I toe the line because I feel I have no other choice.' He took a deep breath. 'Katy was the same.'

Patricia went ghostly pale.

'Dad—' George cautioned again, this time more abruptly.

'No, I shan't shut up, George, not this time. I should have said this many years before now. Patricia, I should never have allowed you to bully our daughter like you did and I deeply regret that. She wasn't happy, we both knew that, but instead of giving her our blessing to go to Durham, you attached conditions to it because it didn't suit you for her to leave London. You shouldn't have withheld my mother's inheritance from her.'

'She would've just frittered it away if I hadn't,' said Patricia.

'Your preoccupation with the money running out made Katy think she should stay with Declan because he could give her a financially secure future, even though we all knew the relationship had run its course. Our darling girl was so conflicted and you ignored it.'

'No I didn't,' his wife protested. 'I don't believe the relationship was on its last legs either. She jumped at the chance to bring Declan on holiday with us.'

'Because you told her the holiday wouldn't happen otherwise! She was seventeen and far too young to settle down,' said Philip exasperatedly. 'She'd made up her mind to call things off, which would've been the sensible thing to do at her age, but you bullied her into changing it. Then we lost her for good.'

Patricia jolted in her chair as if it had electrocuted her.

'There is nothing I can do to change that now, no matter how desperately I wish I could. But I can change us, how we are,' continued Philip. From the corner of his eye he could see George staring at him in shock; his son had never witnessed him speaking like this before. 'No longer do you get to tell me what to do, Patricia. I won't put up with it.'

He walked out of the apartment, slamming the door behind him, his stunned family rooted to their seats in his wake.

45

Inspector Jasso was apparently too busy to talk to Maggie himself and instead had one of his officers call her back to take notes of what she'd gleaned from Jade's family. It was hard to contain her temper as she relayed the details: it felt as though she was doing Clive and Mandy a disservice not to be talking to Jasso himself and she wasn't used to being this removed in an investigation.

Yet she and the others could only pursue matters so far in any case. They couldn't arrest any suspects themselves on foreign soil and would need to apply for a European Arrest Warrant before the Spanish police could detain any person or persons on their behalf. However, applying for an EAW would mean them admitting what they'd been doing – and the fallout would be far too great if they did.

She wasn't a rule breaker by nature, although she definitely pushed boundaries when she felt it necessary. On a previous case as a FLO she'd gone against an explicit order from the SIO – Umpire in fact, and the first time they'd worked together – because she believed it was in the best interests of the parents of their victim, an eight-year-old girl called Megan Fowler. The child had been murdered and her killer cut off her long hair to keep as a trophy. Umpire wanted the detail withheld so it could be used as leverage, but that meant delaying Megan's mum and dad from viewing their daughter's body because he didn't trust them to see her shorn hair and not tell others about it.

Maggie argued against his decision, saying it was cruel to deny the parents the opportunity to see their child and there must surely be a way around it, like shrouding Megan's scalp to hide what was left of her hair. When Umpire rejected the suggestion, she privately told the girl's parents why they couldn't see her and swore them to secrecy, which they did abide by until after an arrest was made. Umpire went ballistic when he found out Maggie had disobeyed him, however, and had her suspended from family liaison duties; the four months she was sidelined was enough of a scare to ensure she acted more cautiously going forward. But the situation Walker had corralled her into now was a different league to the Megan Fowler case – she wouldn't only lose her specialism if they were found out, she might well lose her entire career.

She knew Umpire would try to talk her into catching the next flight back to London if he found out what Walker was asking of them – so she'd made up her mind not to tell him.

After passing on her notes about Jade Reynolds, Maggie stayed at the hotel going through the case files again. She trusted that Shah knew them inside out but she wanted to read the statements again for her own satisfaction. The 'three dates' angle was niggling away at her. She was certain it must mean something to the killer, because it was so specific. If they were to believe Shah's Google search and think it applied to how many times a couple should date before sleeping together, then it might suggest the killer was old-fashioned in his values, thinking it was good to wait. But then his treatment of Katy's corpse after murdering her proved there was nothing remotely gentlemanly about him.

She called it a day just after seven, packing away the files neatly in Shah and Paulson's room. The two of them and Walker had gone off to grab some food but she wanted to check in with the Popes first. As she walked along the front to Orquídea, she questioned how much of Jasso's experience on the first investigation into Katy's death was driving his handling of this one. Did he feel the same as Martos did, that mistakes were made which prevented them from catching the killer? Or was he confident they did all they could and he had nothing to prove now?

She was so deep in thought that she almost overshot the gate into Orquídea: it was only the sound of it slamming shut that alerted her to it. Turning round, she saw Philip striding in the direction of the seafront and she could tell from his expression that he wasn't happy. She called out to him, but even though she was certain he must've heard her, he continued on.

The gate clanged again as George came rushing through it.

'Have you seen my dad?'

'Yes, he went that way.' She pointed towards the seafront. 'I called to him but he ignored me. Is he okay?'

George stared in the direction his father had gone, his manner tense and troubled.

'Do you want to go after him?' she asked. 'Or I could?'

He was obviously thinking about it, but shook his head. 'I think it's best we leave him to it.'

'Has something happened?'

George's shoulders dropped.

'Mum and Dad had a row, a really nasty one. Dad said . . . um, I probably shouldn't say for Mum's sake, but it wasn't nice.' He looked close to tears. 'I don't know how they'll come back from it. I seriously think coming out here again has pushed them to breaking point.'

'Where's your mum now?'

'Indoors. She's very distressed. I should probably get back to her.' He went to open the gate, then gave Maggie a puzzled look, as though he'd only just noticed she was there. 'Were you on your way to see us?'

'You, actually, but it can wait. Go and see to your mum.'

George was torn. 'Is it something to do with the investigation though?'

'Yes, but—'

'Give me half an hour. I'll check on Mum and then I'll meet you next door in the restaurant.'

'Are you sure?'

'Yes, if it's about the investigation then it's important.' He grimaced. 'I could also do with being distracted from worrying about how my parents' marriage is imploding.'

46

Twenty minutes later, Philip arrived at the hotel. Thinking on his feet, he pretended he was from the British Consulate in Palma and, luckily for him, the receptionist didn't question it. Perhaps because, in his smart stone-coloured trousers and crisp white shirt, his Panama hat in hand, Philip looked as though he could be someone official, someone with gravitas. The receptionist told him the room number and directed him to the lift with a lipsticked smile.

Clive Reynolds was stunned when Philip explained who he was, while his wife, Mandy, burst into tears.

'But Spanish police told us they don't think Jade's been taken like your daughter,' said Clive. 'They're saying she got into some bloke's car willingly.' He paused for a moment and looked deep into Philip's eyes. 'You think she has been taken, don't you.' He said it as a statement, not a question. 'You wouldn't be here otherwise.'

'I am fearful for your daughter's safety, yes.'

Mandy choked down another sob.

'I'm so sorry, Mrs Reynolds, I don't mean to upset you. But when I look back at that period of time when Katy was first missing, there is so much I would have done differently. I allowed myself to become redundant in the process and let the police do my job for me.'

The young man who'd been introduced to him as Jade's fiancé piped up. 'Your job?'

'My job as her father – I should've done more to find Katy myself and I will never forgive myself for not.' He looked at Clive and was buoyed to see in his expression the realization that he should be doing the same now, for Jade. This was what fathers did: they rescued their children when they were in trouble. They didn't sit on the sidelines watching other men take charge or letting their wives tell them what to do. 'I'm here to help you. Please, let me help you.'

'But you're not the police, what can you do?' asked Mandy doubtfully.

'Plenty, actually. If this is a repeat of what happened to Katy, we can retrace the steps of what happened in the week between her going missing from the beach and –' his voice caught in his throat – 'her body being found. I know who the police questioned back then – some of them still live in the resort, so we can talk to them.'

'The police won't like that,' said the fiancé.

'They can't stop you looking for Jade yourself – you don't need to sit here doing nothing if you don't want to,' said Philip insistently. 'You simply need a plan of action first.' His eyes locked on Clive's again. 'So many times since Katy died I've thought about what more I could've done to find her. I was her father, the one who was meant to protect her, and I let her down. I wish with all my heart I could go back and change things.'

DEAD GUILTY

Clive Reynolds squared his shoulders, his expression blazing with determination.

'Talk me through this plan of yours.'

47

Maggie swirled the ice cubes in the sparkling water before lifting the glass to her mouth to take another sip in the hope it would quell the rumbling in her stomach. She hadn't eaten all day and it was now ten past eight. She thought about asking Annika to bring her some olives and bread to keep her going and hoped George wouldn't mind if she ate as they talked.

It was now a good half an hour after he'd said he'd meet her. Part of her thought she should text him to say he should stay with his mum if Patricia was upset, but she really needed to hear his take on his sister's relationship with Declan in the light of Philip throwing doubt on his alibi.

Maggie pondered again what had caused Philip to storm off as he had and whether the row could be smoothed over before the press conference tomorrow evening. If Patricia and Philip weren't able to present a united front, the press would most likely focus on that rather than any plea for new information. She was certain Patricia could be persuaded to put up appearances, but would Philip?

Still waiting for George to arrive, she checked her phone again for the umpteenth time. Jade's disappearance was big news both there in Majorca and back home in the UK. Jasso was sticking firmly to the line that the evidence so far pointed to her going off willingly – there had been another sighting of her, this time in Palma, again in the white car. The press were speculating wildly about the man she'd apparently gone off with and had already dredged her Instagram account for pictures of her posing with men who weren't Mason.

She could only imagine how he, Clive and Mandy were reacting to Jade's reputation being trashed and it bothered her that Walker wasn't able to tell them what the British police suspected because of how Jasso would react. Then again, was it not better for them to think Jade might be okay for now, rather than fill their heads with horrifying thoughts of what might be happening to her? Perhaps, in this instance, ignorance was best.

Maggie checked the time again and debated whether to put in a quick call to Umpire. She was feeling a bit twitchy about being alone with George and she wanted to hear her boyfriend's voice for reassurance. But before she could call, Annika strolled up to her table.

'Can I get you an appetizer while you wait?'

'You read my mind. Some olives would be great, thanks. And some bread.'

'Drink?'

Maggie faltered. She could kill for an ice-cold beer but Walker's warning about being caught drinking on the job rang in her ears.

'Best not. Another sparkling water, please.'

Annika scribbled her order down.

'Any news on the girl?' she asked.

'Not yet I'm afraid.'

'Do you think she's gone off with someone else like they're saying?'

'That's what the police here think.'

'But you're not sure, I can tell by your face.' Annika pulled out a chair and sat down uninvited. 'The people of Saros are scared,' she said, keeping her voice low so the family tucking into paella on the next table couldn't overhear. 'They think it's the same killer who's come back, the one who killed Katy Pope.'

'I can understand why they're thinking that, but there's nothing to suggest Jade's disappearance is linked to Katy's murder,' said Maggie. She felt guilty lying to Annika, but she couldn't possibly tell her what she and the others really suspected and were investigating when they shouldn't be.

'I hope not, because the town won't recover from this a second time. It's creating such an atmosphere of tension. People are worried Julien is going to be blamed again.'

'Julien Ruiz? Do you know him?'

Annika nodded. 'I've known him since he was a young boy. His grandparents lived in Saros so he would visit them regularly. They're dead but his great-aunt lives here still and she's very upset.'

'Is he popular, then?'

'What?'

'You said people are worried he's going to be blamed again.'

'Well, he's left, hasn't he?'

'That was his choice. It was not because of anything we said to him.'

Annika stared intensely at her.

'Are you sure?'

'I am.'

'Hey, why the serious faces, you two?'

Maggie hadn't noticed Declan Morris approaching the table.

'Oh, it's nothing,' said Annika airily.

'It didn't look like nothing,' he said, easing into the chair opposite. Maggie was annoyed – he was the person she wanted to discuss with George and now she'd have to find a way to get shot of him.

Declan turned to Annika.

'Don't tell me you're obsessing over my girlfriend's murder again.'

Maggie was surprised by his comment but Annika regarded him coolly.

'I don't know what you mean.'

'I've heard you can't stop discussing it with your customers.' He glanced around the restaurant, where every table was occupied. 'It looks like you're doing a roaring trade off the back of it.'

'I am doing no such thing,' said Annika haughtily, rising to her feet.

'But you're the waitress who had the lucky escape from the killer – you're famous! The customers must lap that up.' Declan caught Maggie's eye and clocked her confusion. 'Didn't you know? A few weeks before Katy was abducted, a man tried to lure Annika into a car parked close to the marina but she managed to escape. She gave the police a description of the man, which was a bit unfortunate for me because it happened to match mine.' Declan was trying to make a joke of it but Maggie could see the resentment simmering in his eyes.

'I don't remember hearing about a previous incident,' she said.

Annika flushed. 'I – I changed my statement. I realized I was mistaken, that the man was just being overly friendly.'

'Shame the police didn't disregard it completely, though,' Declan addressed Maggie. 'As I said, it was extraordinarily bad luck for me that I looked exactly like the man who'd manhandled her.'

Annika was backing away from the table now, clearly rattled.

'How could I have possibly known they would use my description to go after you? I just did what I thought was right by reporting it to the police.'

Maggie tried to ease the tension.

'Any incidents of assault should always be reported,' she said.

'Besides,' said Annika, ploughing on as though she hadn't heard Maggie, 'I'd never even met you then, so it's hardly my fault you looked the same as the person I thought was trying to grab me.'

Declan nodded thoughtfully.

'True, you hadn't met me. Silly me, I must've got that wrong.'

George chose that moment to arrive and Maggie was so grateful for the interruption that she couldn't stop herself grinning at him. The smile he returned stripped the worry and fatigue from his features.

'I thought it was only going to be me and you,' he said.

'It is. Declan's just leaving.'

'Am I?' Declan didn't look too happy at being dismissed.

'I'm sorry, but I have a few police matters I need to discuss with George in private.'

Declan got to his feet. 'Fine. Meet me for a beer later?' he asked his friend.

'Maybe. It depends how tired I am.'

'Well, text me if you fancy it. I'll be at my hotel.'

As he walked away, George made a grab for the menu. 'I'm hungry. Shall we order?'

Maggie was suddenly floored with nerves now it was just the two of them. *This is crazy*, she told herself. *Just do your bloody job.*

Steadying her voice, she told George about the exchange between Declan and Annika. He expressed surprise – neither he nor his parents had been made aware of any previous incident either.

'Annika said she changed her statement because she'd been mistaken about the man's intentions,' said Maggie. 'I think there is more to it though.'

George smiled. 'Do you always suspect there's more to every situation than meets the eye?'

'I do question a lot, yes,' she said wryly.

'I'd love to know what you think of me.'

Maggie's throat caught as she struggled for a reply that couldn't be misconstrued as anything but professional. Luckily, George let her off the hook while she floundered.

'Actually, don't answer that. I think I'd rather not know.'

A waiter came over to take their order; Annika was now nowhere to be seen. Maggie was just deciding between the chorizo salad and a tortilla omelette when her phone rang.

'Where are you? I need you!'

Patricia Pope sounded nothing like her usual self: she was panic-stricken and breathless. Maggie knocked her chair over in her haste to stand up. 'It's your mum,' she mouthed to George. 'I'm in the restaurant next door, Mrs Pope. What's happened?'

'You need to come . . . I think he's going to kill him.'

48

Clive Reynolds was inches away from attacking Terry Evans and all that was stopping him was Philip's desperate attempt to hold him back. He could feel his grip slipping from Clive's shoulders, though, his fingers straining to the limits of their flexibility as they tried to cling on, but he knew he couldn't let the man loose, not when his blood was up like this.

Clive was also yelling as he aimed punches in Evans's direction and Philip's proximity meant his hearing was bearing the brunt of both the man's volume and coarseness. The swear words spewing from Clive's mouth were unbelievably explicit – one word Philip had never heard spoken aloud before, much less said himself – and it was making his task of holding the man back much harder, because his abhorrence was making him want to let go.

Evans, unsurprisingly, was cowering in fear. That he hadn't run off when Clive went for him was a surprise but, then again, where was there for him to run to? Clive's rage had him pinned up against the exterior wall of his apartment and to flee would mean having to push past the incensed man. One of those punches was sure to meet its target if he tried.

Perhaps if Evans hadn't provoked Clive he wouldn't be

in this position, thought Philip uncharitably as he desperately clutched the dad's shoulders and pleaded again for him to calm down. When they'd called at Evans's apartment, entering Orquídea through the back way to avoid being seen, he had reacted with surprise – to have Katy Pope and Jade Reynolds's fathers at his door was most unexpected. But when he realized they wanted him to account for his whereabouts when Jade went missing, Evans grew belligerent, telling them they had no right to treat him as a suspect and he would enjoy instructing his solicitor to pursue them for a harassment claim if they didn't leave him alone. That had proved the last straw for Clive who, with a bellow of anguish, launched himself at the man.

In that split-second moment Philip realized he had woefully underestimated the depth of Clive's distress. Far from being in control of his emotions – the conclusion Philip had reached as they'd calmly hatched out their plan of action at the hotel – the man was a simmering pot of fear and torment, waiting to explode.

'Clive, please, he's not worth it,' Philip implored, tightening his grip. 'Don't give him the satisfaction.'

'My daughter's missing and he thinks he can fucking stand there taking the piss out of me,' Clive howled.

Suddenly there were footsteps behind them and a voice calling out. Philip saw hands reach for Clive's shoulders besides his own and glanced round to see Declan and Johnnie behind him. Philip was relieved at the additional show of strength and together they pulled the distraught man away from Evans, who bolted back inside his apartment and locked the door the moment there was enough distance between them.

Realizing he was beaten, Clive collapsed to the floor and began sobbing. Before Philip could offer any comfort, Patricia appeared from behind them. She dropped to her knees and wrapped her arm around Clive's shoulders. To Philip's disbelief, she was crying too. He looked over at Declan, who appeared equally flummoxed. Patricia crying was a sight neither of them was used to.

'I know, I know,' she whispered to Clive as she gently cradled him. 'I understand.'

Maggie and George came bowling round the corner then, panting from running. Maggie went straight over to Philip.

'What's going on? Why were you and Mr Reynolds confronting Mr Evans?'

Philip couldn't find the words to answer her. He was shaking from head to foot.

'Okay, let me ask you another question,' she said, and he quailed at the firmness of her voice. 'Why did you ignore what I said about introducing yourself to Jade's dad?'

'I wanted to help,' he said lamely. 'I thought I could.'

'I'd say you've achieved quite the opposite, Dad,' said George, but not unkindly.

Philip looked down at Clive, a man utterly broken by fear and loss, being comforted by his wife, who knew exactly what he was feeling but could say nothing that would take away his pain – and in doing so exposed her own. It was heartbreaking to watch them and Philip felt tears begin to wet his own cheeks. Johnnie squeezed his arm.

'It's okay, we know you were only trying to help,' he murmured.

Philip frowned at him. 'You've recovered quickly. You were very drunk when I left you.'

Johnnie didn't reply.

Maggie crouched down beside Patricia and Clive.

'Mrs Pope, why don't I take Mr Reynolds back to his hotel?' she said quietly.

Patricia gulped down another sob and shook her head.

'Upstairs,' she managed.

'I don't think that's a good idea,' said Maggie warily.

'Look at the poor man,' Patricia cried. 'I can't send him back to his wife like this. He needs to stay strong for her sake. One of them has got to hold it together. If he goes to pieces, what will the rest of them do? They won't be able to manage!'

In a flash Philip knew she was talking about herself.

'Oh, Patricia,' he breathed. 'You didn't have to shoulder it all on your own. I never expected you to or asked you to.'

His wife's face crumpled again as she looked up at him, her eyes misty and bloodshot from crying. 'I did, for you. Katy was such a daddy's girl and you were destroyed by what happened and it wouldn't have done us any good to have me falling apart too.' Then, as though it had suddenly occurred to her she had an audience, Patricia hastily snapped to. 'Help me get him to his feet,' she ordered her husband. 'Don't just stand there like a lemon.'

Philip did as he was told, then followed behind as his wife led Clive and the rest of them up the exterior stairs to their apartment.

As he ascended the steps, Philip was assailed by an indescribable sadness. In that fleeting moment Patricia had allowed him a glimpse of her vulnerability. He wondered if he would ever get to see it again.

49

Clive didn't stay long inside the Popes' apartment. In fact, almost as soon as he'd crossed the threshold he became visibly uncomfortable in both the surroundings and company. Despite Patricia's insistence that he stay for a drink at least, he said he needed to get back to Mandy and Mason, and left. Maggie got the impression he was embarrassed to have been seen crying and was the type of man who would rather extract his own teeth with pliers than admit to having feelings. Johnnie went with him, saying he should get back to his boat and adding in an aside to the others that he'd make sure Clive returned safely to his hotel as it was on the way.

Almost immediately Philip withdrew into himself, a monosyllabic husk of the man he was. George told Maggie they'd have to leave their chat until tomorrow now, because his parents needed him, but Patricia refused to let him stay.

'Your father and I need to talk alone,' she said.

George reluctantly stepped outside with Maggie and Declan.

'I thought you'd gone back to your hotel,' George said to Declan.

'I left something in your parents' apartment after the memorial service, so I popped back to get it. Then I heard your dad's voice and lots of shouting, so I went to see what was going on.' Declan shook his head. 'That Reynolds bloke is a right thug.'

Maggie shot him a disapproving look. 'Why, because he's got a few tattoos and swears a bit? Give him a break, his daughter's missing and he's in a state.' She glanced at George. 'I don't know what your dad was thinking, taking him to see Terry Evans,' she said, shaking her head.

'Dad meant well,' he replied tightly.

'I know, but you saw the state of Clive. He doesn't need your dad spurring him on to conduct his own investigation.'

Now it was George's turn to shake his head.

'You have no idea what it feels like to be in Clive's position, but my father does. He's actually the best person to help him deal with what he's going through.'

'I disagree. Thanks to your dad's intervention, Clive's even more of an emotional wreck now.'

George regarded her for a moment.

'How long have you been a family liaison officer?'

The question wrong-footed her.

'What?'

'How long have you been a family liaison officer?' he repeated.

'Um, I guess nearly seven years now. But what's that got to do with anything?'

'I'm curious how long it's been because I'm not sure you're very good at it.'

Maggie stared at him, speechless.

'You seem to have little appreciation for how my parents

are feeling right now. Can you imagine what this is doing to them? They came here to remember their daughter and now they're plunged into this horrible, nightmarish situation where they don't get to hold the memorial Mum's spent months planning, the press conference might have to be cancelled and now you're telling Dad off for showing some compassion to someone who's going through the same thing. You're acting as though my parents are meaningless in all this. You should be supporting them, but you haven't been around for most of the afternoon.'

Maggie could feel her cheeks burning.

'I'm so sorry if that's the impression I've given you. Of course they're not meaningless.'

'Really? It doesn't seem like it.'

Declan stepped between them.

'Look, everyone's a bit upset. I think you two should postpone whatever it was you were going to do until tomorrow, when you've calmed down, mate,' he said to George.

'I think that's a good idea,' said Maggie stiffly. She could feel tears clumping behind her eyes and she wanted to get out of there before George saw. Never before had anyone said she wasn't a good FLO and she was upset that he of all people was the one who had.

'I'll walk you out,' Declan offered.

She nodded.

'I'll see you tomorrow,' she addressed George. 'I am sorry.'

He said nothing and slammed the door shut as they left.

50

Once they were outside, Declan asked Maggie if she was hungry still.

'I haven't eaten and I know you haven't. Let's get something quick next door.'

'I don't think I should,' she said, still struggling not to cry. The only thing that had persuaded her throughout the past six months that Mealing was wrong to question her competence was knowing what a good FLO she was and how many families she'd helped over the years. Now it felt like George had ripped the rug out from under her.

'He didn't mean what he said,' said Declan shrewdly. 'He's lashing out because he's upset and you're an easy target. What you need to know about George,' he went on, as Maggie trailed him down the stairs to the pathway, 'is that he's a textbook example of what happens when you're raised to never say what you really mean. Katy was the same, completely repressed. So when he does let rip, it can be pretty harsh. That doesn't mean he thinks you're terrible at your job,' he added hastily, catching the look on Maggie's face, 'it means he's gone for the one thing he thinks will hurt you the most. Which, judging by your face, it has.'

Maggie knew she should be more bullish about the criticism, knowing it was part and parcel of being a police officer, but it had upset her. She'd never had her actions called into question so stridently by a relative and part of the reason she was upset by it was that she feared George had a point. Thanks to Walker's directive that they surreptitiously investigate Jade's disappearance, she *was* less available to the Popes, mentally at least. That didn't sit well with her either, because the last time she'd been forced to step away from being a FLO and assume more responsibility on a case, it had resulted in her colleague's death. She couldn't handle something else like that happening because she was being diverted from the job she had been brought out to Majorca to do.

'He'll be fine in the morning. It'll all be forgotten about.'

Maggie hoped he was right. As they left Orquídea through the guest gate, she realized that going to the restaurant with Declan would give her the chance to question his version of events on the day Katy went missing. As long as she was careful not to say Philip had cast doubt on his story, she might be able to get the truth out of him.

'Thanks, I appreciate you saying that,' she said. 'You know what, you're right – some food would be good now.'

Annika had held her table. Maggie settled on the chorizo salad, but rejected Declan's suggestion they order some wine.

'I'm technically on duty,' she said.

'Really, this late?'

To her surprise she saw it was nearly nine thirty.

'One glass of wine won't hurt, will it?'

Maggie wavered, then caved.

'Okay, but I'll only have a small glass of dry white. Don't go ordering a bottle.'

A trio of guitarists had set up in the corner of the restaurant and were playing some lively acoustic tunes that jarred her nerves. But at least it created enough background noise that she and Declan could talk freely without fear of people at the other tables listening in.

'Are you okay now?' he asked.

'I am, thanks. I do understand why George was being so being protective of his dad. He was, what, twenty-one when Katy died? He's spent his entire adult life so far watching his parents grieve for his sister. It must be really hard.'

'He was very protective of Katy too,' said Declan. 'He wasn't happy when I asked her out and we had a big bust-up over it. He didn't talk to me for weeks.' He took a glug of the pint the waiter had brought over to him, while Maggie savoured a sip of her perfectly chilled wine. 'I'm not sure anyone would've been good enough for her in his eyes.'

He'd given her the perfect opening to ask him about Johnnie's comments.

'Johnnie Hickman-Ferguson didn't rate you as her boyfriend either.'

Declan rolled his eyes. 'He was even more protective of her than George was. He was a pain in the backside throughout our relationship.'

'He seems to think Katy was going to dump you, but was killed before she could.'

'If she was, it was only because he kept filling her head with poison about me. He couldn't stand that we were happy.'

'So it's jealousy making him say those comments?'

Declan shifted in his seat. 'I guess.'

'Had anything ever happened between him and Katy to your knowledge?'

'What, you mean were they ever boyfriend and girlfriend when they were kids? No, I don't think so. She would've said, or George would've.'

Maggie regarded him for a moment. 'You're in a relationship with her best friend now, aren't you?'

He nodded.

'Sorry, what's her name again?'

'Tamara.'

'How long have you been together now?'

Declan flushed beet red. 'Nearly ten years.'

'Oh.' Maggie's eyebrows shot up. 'Quite soon after Katy—'

'Nine months, and before you say anything, I'm well aware of how it looks. But we weren't serious at first; it was just a physical thing. Comfort, even,' he said earnestly. 'It was another six months before we realized we really liked each other and started properly dating.'

George might not think much of her FLO skills, but Maggie was a good detective and knew when someone was lying to her. So she came right out with it.

'Were you sleeping with Tamara behind Katy's back?'

Declan made a big show of denying any impropriety, but the more he blustered, the more Maggie was convinced.

'Lying to a police officer about something that could have a bearing on an ongoing investigation is a serious offence,' she said.

Declan had another swig of beer, buying himself some time.

247

'Well?' Maggie prompted.

'Look, it only happened twice before Katy died, both times when we were far too pissed to think about the consequences. It wasn't some full-blown affair that involved us sneaking off for the night behind her back.' He looked sheepish. 'The first time we had sex was in a pub car park and the second time was on Tamara's parents' sofa while Katy was asleep upstairs. Both times I felt really guilty afterwards. I told Tam that it was wrong and we shouldn't do it again and she agreed.'

'But you liked her enough to start seeing her after Katy was murdered.'

'I wouldn't have slept with Tam if I hadn't fancied her. So yes, the attraction was always there. But I never planned to do anything about it. I wasn't going to end things with Katy and Tam knew that. But after Katy died, it felt right for us to be together. But if she hadn't . . .' He stared into space. 'I know that must sound awful and I love Tam, I really do.' His eyes refocused and he smiled. 'Did I mention she's pregnant?'

'You didn't. Congratulations, when's the baby due?'

'End of December. I'm excited, we both are, but I'm also terrified I'm going to be a rubbish dad.'

'I think lots of men think like that. I have a friend, Belmar, who said the same. His little boy, Stanley, is a month old now and not only does he love being a dad, but he's good at it too.'

'Tamara's going to be an amazing mum.'

'But she's not Katy,' said Maggie sagely.

He shook his head forlornly.

'Katy was something else. I wish you could've met her.

She was –' he searched for the right word – 'luminous, like she had this glow around her that drew everyone to her. We were all moths to her flame.'

The waiter came over with their food then, salad for her and a stacked burger and fries for Declan. The smell of freshly griddled chorizo made her stomach gurgle appreciatively, her appetite revived, but Maggie ignored her plate, keen to continue her questioning.

'Do you think anyone else knew that you'd slept with Tamara and had told Katy? It could explain why Johnnie believed she was going to leave you.'

Declan's expression darkened and he stabbed the chip he was holding into the small pot of ketchup balanced on the side of his plate.

'Anything Johnnie says is pure spite. There's no way he or anyone else knew about me and Tam.'

'So you definitely weren't planning to leave Katy for Tamara and she got wind of it?'

'Christ, no. I told you, Katy never knew. It's the one thing I'm grateful for – that she died not knowing how I'd betrayed her.' His skin mottled and he looked down quickly to hide the tears forming. 'I really did love her. We went through a lot together.'

'You mean with the termination?'

He nodded, his head still bent low, and Maggie suddenly remembered the row that Katy and Patricia supposedly had the day before her disappearance and Annika's comment that it might've been about a boy Katy met during the holiday.

'How were things between you on the holiday?'

He raised his head and shrugged. 'Pretty good.'

'Is there a chance Katy could've met someone else while you were in Saros?'

Declan's eyes widened with surprise.

'Another bloke? No, absolutely not. We were together the entire time, apart from that one night she went to the bar with Patricia and met that waiter – and he swore to me nothing happened between them. Why would you ask me that?'

She shrugged. 'I'm just throwing theories out there,' she said.

Declan looked shaken, so Maggie gave him time to compose himself, forking up mouthfuls of salad in the interim. She was inclined to believe him when he said his affair with Tamara hadn't meant anything prior to Katy being murdered, but there was still the matter of him being dry on the beach.

She waited until he was calm again before steering the conversation on to it.

'The day Katy disappeared, when you were on the beach with her and her parents, how far out did you swim?'

His surprise at the question registered on his face but he did not ask why she wanted to know, instead giving a cautiously worded reply.

'I'm a strong swimmer and the sea here is really calm, so you can venture quite far out. You just have to keep an eye out for jet skis and pedalos.'

'How far is quite far? Enough that you couldn't see your sun lounger clearly from that distance?'

'Yeah, it looked pretty far away.'

'I'm guessing you didn't notice Katy leave the beach then?'

He shook his head morosely. 'No.'

His honesty in telling her about Tamara meant Maggie knew for certain he was now lying about this.

'It's lucky for you that you were swimming. The police in Saros seemed convinced you had something to do with Katy's murder but being in the water was a good alibi.'

Declan went still.

'But if you hadn't been swimming and were in fact bone dry when the search for Katy began, that's a different story,' said Maggie, watching him carefully.

Declan's features twisted. 'I don't know what you mean.'

'I think you do. Where were you really when you told Patricia, Philip and Katy that you'd gone swimming?'

She sat back, waiting for him to do one of two things: bluster an answer that would be a lie, or tell the truth. Because, judging by his reaction again, Philip's recollection of him being dry was indeed correct.

The seconds ticked by. Maggie forked in another mouthful of salad, savouring the smoky spiciness of the chorizo sausage, all the while keeping her eyes trained on Declan's face. When she finished chewing and swallowing, she raised her eyebrows.

'Well?'

He exhaled. 'I'd gone to phone someone.'

'Who?'

'It doesn't matter.'

'Oh, I think it does. For ten years you've lied about being in the sea when Katy went missing. Do you realize how serious that is?'

Another deep breath sucked in and released.

'Okay, I went to call Tamara.'

Maggie slowly put her fork down.

'You interrupted your holiday to call the girl you'd cheated with?'

'She was threatening to tell Katy we'd slept together. She'd texted me the night before, but the villa where we were staying had rubbish phone coverage, so I didn't receive the message until we'd driven down to the beach. I panicked, because I knew she'd be upset I hadn't responded. So I pretended I was going for a swim, then I went to call her.'

'I find it very surprising that Katy and her parents didn't see you sneak past.'

'I went down to the shore, waited a bit, then came up a different side of the beach from them. I doubt they would've spotted me, the beach was busy that day.'

'Why did you keep up the lie? All you had to do was tell the police you called Tamara and they'd have checked with her and you'd have had an alibi that way.'

'We both felt so guilty afterwards. We couldn't bear for Katy's parents to know what we'd been getting up to. I know it sounds crazy, but it was more preferable to lie to the police than to Patricia.'

'Patricia was a serving police officer back then,' Maggie pointed out.

'But it wasn't her case.'

'I'm surprised the police didn't pick up on the call in your phone records.'

'Maybe they did and ignored it. I think it suited them to have me as a suspect and that call would've ruled me out completely.'

Maggie shook her head. 'That's what I don't get: you

could've cleared yourself in a heartbeat but you chose not to.'

'When Tamara and I decided to cover up the phone call it was because we both assumed Katy would be found, and neither of us could bear what her reaction would be to finding out about us. It would've been awful for her.'

'Hang on, a minute ago you were telling me Tamara *wanted* to tell her.'

'She did at first, mostly because she was sick of lying to her. She was her best friend and she couldn't cope with seeing her knowing what she'd done and because she had feelings for me. But after Katy went missing, she agreed with me that it would be awful for her to come back to the news that her boyfriend and best friend had been having sex behind her back, so we agreed to keep the call a secret between us and I stuck to the line that I'd been swimming. Once Katy's body was found it was too late to go back on it, because I'd been lying for a week by then, plus I still didn't want Patricia and Philip to know I'd cheated on their daughter.' He paused, his face a picture of utter misery. 'Are you going to tell everyone I lied?'

'I'll have to inform my senior officer, yes. But if your phone records do prove you were on the phone to Tamara when you say you were, then it's another alibi.'

Declan looked wretched. 'I know I've fucked up – I was just trying to protect the woman I loved.'

Maggie levelled her stare at him. 'Yes, but which one?'

51

Jade Reynolds prided herself on having a good memory. She could recite lyrics having only heard a song a couple of times, knew the first and last names of every child who attended the nursery, even the ones she didn't look after, and what she didn't know about Kim Kardashian West could be written on the back of a stamp.

But right now she couldn't recall a single thing about the man who'd abducted her.

It must've been the stuff he'd injected into her neck that was muddling her mind – ever since she'd regained consciousness she'd had a banging headache and could barely see straight. But she knew she was far from Saros now, because wherever she was there was no noise. All that surrounded her was deathly quiet and she was alone.

She tried to focus on what her abductor looked like and was wearing so she could tell the police, but nothing was coming back to her – not his hair colour, how old he was, whether he was wearing shorts or not . . . it was as though he'd become this featureless, generic non-entity in her mind and it was driving her mad that she couldn't remember.

She tried to flip herself over in the bed but the binds

were making it difficult. Her wrists were tied behind her back with some kind of plastic fastening and the skin beneath them was already raw and bleeding from repeated attempts to pull her hands free. Her feet appeared similarly tied, but she couldn't see because of the blindfold. She began to cry again, hot, angry rivers of frustration that coursed down her cheeks and over the piece of tape gagging her mouth.

But being tied up wasn't what had bothered her most when she came round: it was the fact that he'd removed her bikini and dressed her. She could sense she was now wearing a T-shirt and loose leggings and the sensation of them against her skin made it crawl, while the thought of him seeing her naked made her want to throw up.

After a minute or so of crying, Jade forced herself to stop and gave herself a good talking to. Crying wasn't going to get her out of there: she needed a clear head, and a plan. The man who'd abducted her had taken a massive risk doing it in broad daylight, so she knew she had to be really careful. If he was brazen enough to do that, God knows what else he might do. Her best chance of escaping was to be cleverer than him and she could be pretty smart when she wanted to be.

She had her dad to thank for that. Clive Reynolds had been a bit of a local name when he was younger, known for fencing goods that fell off the backs of lorries and on occasion being the driver of said lorries. It was a sideline to his day job on the bins and it gave the family extras they might otherwise have had to do without, like holidays. Clive liked to describe himself as being on the 'nice side of shady' and never knowingly got involved in anything nasty or violent. That said, he knew how to handle himself – and he'd raised Jade to do the same. If anyone tried to bully her at school, she stood up for herself.

She might be trussed up like a Christmas turkey right now, but she wasn't giving up without a fight—

Suddenly she heard a noise, a door opening and shutting somewhere in the building.

Jade began to tremble as the footsteps neared the room and the door swung open. She braced herself, terrified of what was going to happen to her.

Then he was there, right by the bed.

'Hey, sweetheart, how are you?'

She could feel him stroking her hair. She tried to move away, pulling herself out of his reach. Her chest heaved because she could barely breathe in the gag.

'Hey, there's no need for that.' He sounded wounded. 'I'm not going to hurt you. Here, let me take this off or you'll choke.'

His fingertips were gentle against her cheeks as he pulled off the tape masking her mouth. Jade let out a gasp, then gulped in huge mouthfuls of air.

'Oh dear, you have got yourself in a state. I was going to suggest that tonight we have our first dinner together but, frankly, you're a mess. I don't want to sit opposite you looking like this.'

'Please let me go,' Jade begged. 'I want to go home.'

His answer chilled her to the core.

'But, darling, you are home.'

52

Thursday

Maggie awoke early after a decent night's sleep but she still felt tired as she dragged herself into the shower and turned on the water full blast. After the drama of Tuesday and Declan's confession over dinner, yesterday had been another mentally punishing day. Patricia had requested that the press conference due to take place early evening be postponed, until she and Philip were better able to face it, but the Director General of Police, whose press team was now involved, wanted to push ahead to get it out of the way. From what Maggie could ascertain, the police in Majorca had decided the subject of Jade's disappearance would inevitably be raised during the press conference, but questions could easily be dealt with if they stuck to the line that she'd left willingly. If they waited any longer, more British media would arrive on the island and the press conference would become a bun fight for information. It was couched as concern for the Pope family, but Maggie could see it for what it was: them protecting themselves.

Patricia, true to form, dug her heels in and refused point blank to participate, so Maggie had spent the day relaying messages between the two camps and imploring the Spanish police to dismantle the press conference area they'd set up on the seafront by the beach because the Pope family weren't coming. It was only with half an hour to go that they finally believed her and the press conference was called off. Now relations between the Spanish and British police were tense to say the least.

Maggie lathered a second application of shampoo into her hair. At least the debacle had given her the opportunity to show George she wasn't treating his parents as meaningless. Their conversations yesterday had been perfunctory and confined only to the press conference, but he hadn't seemed as angry with her and, when the event was finally cancelled, had expressed his gratitude for her tenacity in making the Spanish concede to his parents' wishes.

The problem now was the press conference had been rescheduled for tomorrow afternoon – only a few hours before the team had flights booked back to the UK. Any delay would mean her potentially missing her flight and not being at Umpire's house when Lou and the kids arrived for their stay. She hadn't had the chance to warn him that might happen as he'd been working late on a case. Nor had she rung Lou: she was hoping it wouldn't have to come to them postponing as well.

Her shower finished, Maggie stepped out of the cubicle and towelled herself dry. She was due to meet Walker, Shah and Paulson in forty-five minutes to catch up on what they'd been doing yesterday: beyond a brief exchange with Walker when she'd filled him in on her illuminating conversation with Declan, she hadn't spoken to them all day. While she was dealing with the press conference, Walker had gone to Palma again to speak to the jeweller and Shah and Paulson were chasing up the other leads – including asking if any locals could remember seeing Declan on his phone to Tamara near the beach. Walker wanted them to now investigate the possibility he had called Tamara but was interrupted by Katy and had done away with her. His admission that he'd lied for ten years and had been sleeping with his girlfriend's best friend behind her back had put him back in the frame for her murder.

Meanwhile, Lyndsey Shepherd had been in touch to inform them Terry Evans wanted Clive Reynolds and Philip Pope prosecuted for assault, even though neither had actually laid a finger on him. It was taking all of her diplomatic intervention to make Evans realize why it might be callous to report them given what both men were going through.

Shah was the only one already seated when Maggie arrived in the hotel dining area. Breakfast was an all-you-can-eat buffet, but her colleague's plate was empty.

'I daren't get up or I'd have lost the table,' he grinned. 'It's dog eat dog in here this morning.'

Maggie could see what he meant: the room was busy with guests piling their plates high and tempers were straining as elbows grazed in the rush to serve themselves.

'I'll hold the table while you get something,' she said. 'I'm not that hungry.'

Paulson and Walker appeared soon afterwards and made beelines straight for the large aluminium dishes bearing sausage, bacon and eggs. The thought of eating a cooked breakfast in thirty-degree heat turned Maggie's stomach so when Shah relieved her of table-hogging duty she got herself a bowl of fruit and a pastry.

The four of them seated, Walker dropped his voice to a

hush and eyed the people at the table next to them, who were busy tucking into their own fry-ups.

'I know this isn't the best place to talk, but we need to get a clip on today, there's a lot to chase up. My trip to see the jeweller proved interesting: he didn't recognize the ex-con who's moved nearby but he did mention a visit from someone else connected to the case: George Pope.'

Maggie almost choked on the piece of grapefruit she was chewing. Shit, she should've informed him about George almost being arrested at the shop, instead of storing the information away until she'd spoken to him herself.

'Apparently there was an incident a few months ago – George went to speak to the shop owner after the papers reported on me tracking him down and there was a bit of a row. So George apparently went back this week to apologize and while he was there he asked how difficult it would be to make a replica of Katy's ring.'

Paulson frowned. 'Isn't that what the suspect asked the jeweller ten years ago?'

'No, the suspect wanted to know about the value of the ring. Besides, the jeweller says the man who went into the shop after Katy's murder definitely wasn't Katy's brother. I'm just curious to know why he's asking about a replica now.'

'Why don't I talk to him about it?' Maggie interjected hurriedly. 'I'll be seeing him and his parents in a bit.'

Walker nodded as he speared a piece of sausage on his plate with his fork and shovelled it in.

'So, anyone got anything else interesting to share?' he asked.

Paulson said he'd drawn a blank trying to find witnesses

who might have seen Declan calling Tamara, then Maggie told them about Annika from the restaurant reporting the incident of a man trying to drag her into his car.

'She later decided she was mistaken and withdrew the allegation,' Maggie finished. 'But it might be worth following up.'

'It does sound weird,' said Paulson.

'Any mention in the case file about it?' Walker asked Shah.

'No, boss, but I'll see what I can find out. I've made a couple of decent contacts here now.'

'Good lad. How did you get on finding out about Johnnie's stay in Ibiza?' he asked through another mouthful.

Shah paused for a moment, then leaned into the centre of the table. The others did the same.

'There was no stay. Johnnie wasn't there when he said he was.'

53

'What the fuck,' exclaimed Paulson, loud enough to make people turn and stare.

'Keep your voice down,' said Walker furiously. 'Are you sure?' he asked Shah.

'The family still own the house in Es Cana. I called the company that manages the property for them and they put me in touch with a woman called Marta Hernandez who was their housekeeper ten years ago. She is adamant Johnnie was never at the house during June 2009. In fact, she insisted the property was empty throughout that entire summer.'

'So where the fuck was he?' said Paulson, his voice lowered.

'Well, I thought he might've stayed on his boat, but Marta said she would've known he was in Es Cana because the villa has a private jetty and that's where he always moored. But that's not the only reason.'

The three of them leaned in even closer.

'The girlfriend Johnnie was supposedly with? That was her daughter, Camila. They were in a relationship in 2009 – but they broke up two months before Katy was murdered.

Camila was so upset she told him to sod off and stay away from Es Cana.'

'So he lied back then and he's lying to us now,' said Walker.

'He's also British, like the man who accosted Jade and Mason at the bar,' Maggie pointed out. 'We should see if Mason is able to identify him.'

'Hang on, let's not get carried away. Why would Johnnie want to kill Katy in the first place?' asked Paulson. 'We need a motive.'

Maggie spoke first. 'If I had to choose any, it would be jealousy. The way he speaks about Katy, it's clear he really cared about her. Maybe it went beyond a brotherly kind of love. Maybe he couldn't bear that she was with someone else and wanted her for himself. He could've dumped Camila because he was hoping Katy would give him a shot, but when she turned him down he lost it. He said he knew she wanted to dump Declan so maybe he thought his chance had come at last.'

'That's a good enough motive for me,' said Walker, putting down his knife and fork with a clatter. 'But we're on very dodgy ground if we show Mason a photo of him. See if you can get a better description for now. Then it might be worth asking Lara Steadman to see if she remembers seeing a man in the club who matches the same profile.'

'She said she never saw who abducted her,' said Maggie.

'It's worth a punt,' said Paulson. 'Try to get a better description of the flat from her too. If we can find out where it was, there might be a link to Johnnie. His parents have owned a lot of property over the years.'

Maggie nodded. 'I'll call her.'

'The one person who knows Johnnie better than anyone is George Pope,' Walker mused.

'I was going to talk to him on Tuesday about Declan, but then Clive Reynolds went after Terry Evans and since then I've not really seen him other than to discuss the press conference,' said Maggie. 'I can ask him about both of his friends today.'

'Tread carefully. We don't know how loyal he is to them and we can't risk anything getting back to them,' said Walker.

'Boss, I've had a thought,' said Shah. 'We're pretty certain that because of the email she was sent Lara Steadman was an early victim of the killer and had a lucky escape. What if there were more like her, but not in Saros?'

Walker's eyes narrowed. 'Meaning?'

'What's to say the killer hasn't used the same MO on other women in other places? I think we should be looking into finding similar crimes in Ibiza and the other two places where Hickman-Ferguson's parents owned property.'

Maggie's breath caught in her mouth. The Popes were long-time friends of Johnnie and his family: it would devastate them to think he might have been involved in Katy's death and now with Jade's disappearance.

'Excellent suggestion, Amit,' Walker was saying. 'Where are the other gaffs?'

'There was a house in Menorca they had for about a year when Johnnie was at school, but they sold it to buy the villa here. They also rented an apartment in Palma for a time too. I've got the addresses though.'

'Get on it, and you help him, Vince.'

'We could always catch ferries across to those islands if

we need to,' Paulson said. 'I think the one from here to Ibiza takes a couple of hours.'

Walker thought for a moment. 'Find out if one's leaving for Ibiza today and get yourselves on it. I want the girlfriend tracked down – see if she had any concerns over the way Johnnie spoke about Katy. If he's our man, I want every stone turned to prove it.'

54

George wasn't at the apartment when Maggie arrived. In fact, he wasn't even on the island.

'He's had to fly back to London for work,' Patricia informed her. 'I can't imagine he'll come back now. His trial is due to start on Monday.'

It shocked Maggie how disappointed she was and she knew it wasn't only because she'd missed the opportunity to quiz him about his two friends. She minded because she didn't like how they had left things.

'What about the memorial service, though? Don't you want to still do something?'

'There seems little point now,' said Patricia resignedly. 'After Tuesday's debacle, it feels like the moment has passed.'

Maggie could see she was upset and felt a huge surge of sympathy for the woman. 'How about you and Mr Pope do something privately, just the two of you? I could arrange for some flowers for you to place by the pond, if you want?'

Philip had been listening to their conversation. 'That sounds like a lovely idea.'

'The whole point was to make it a public event so people would remember Katy and be reminded of the fact her killer has never been caught,' Patricia retorted.

'I thought it was for us to remember her,' said Philip quietly.

Keen to avert another row, Maggie thought on her feet.

'Why can't it be both still? We could ask the reporter from the Press Association to attend on his own to take one picture that he can then circulate to all the other media.'

Philip looked to his wife to answer first. Maggie thought Patricia was going to shoot down the idea, but to her surprise she nodded.

'That would be perfect. Thank you.'

'Shall I arrange some flowers, then?'

'Actually, just one would be enough. A yellow rose, if they have it. Yellow signifies missing someone.'

Maggie could see it was taking all of Patricia's willpower not to lose her composure. The events of the last couple of days had cut deep.

'I'll call the florist now,' she said, reaching into her bag for her phone.

'The signal isn't great in here,' said Patricia. 'You're better off standing out on the balcony. The door is unlocked.'

Maggie thanked her and went outside. She was expecting it to be busy down by the pool but there was only one person using it, an elderly woman slowly breast-stroking from side to side. It was still early, not quite ten.

As she looked up the number for the florist and dialled it, she stood at the railing and watched the woman swim. The call went unanswered but didn't go to voicemail so Maggie tried again and as she did so something in the pond closest to the apartment block caught her eye. It was pale and long and at first she assumed it was one of the huge carp that populated the murky depths. Then she realized it wasn't moving, but was lying prone just below the surface.

'Oh my God,' she breathed. 'It can't be.'

Dropping her phone and bag on the floor, she pelted back inside the apartment and ran for the door.

'What on earth!' Patricia exclaimed.

'Call DCI Walker. Tell him to get here now,' Maggie yelled, already out of the front door and halfway down the stairs. She ran along the pathway alongside the building and skidded to a halt as she reached the pond.

Now, staring down at it, there was no mistaking what she'd seen from the balcony.

Suddenly she heard a voice behind her.

'Is that . . . oh my God . . . is that someone's *hand*?'

Eyes wide with shock, Terry Evans clamped his own hand to his mouth to muffle the low moan coming from it.

Swallowing hard, Maggie inched closer to the pond. She could see fingers, ghostly pale, reaching from the depths to graze the surface, then a slim hand and wrist and then—

She stood bolt upright and exhaled, her body trembling with the release.

'It's not real.'

Terry unclamped his hand.

'What?'

'It's not a real hand. I think it's from a shop dummy. Look, it's got a join at the end.'

Terry scrabbled closer to the pond, Maggie moving aside so he could see.

'Oh, you're right. Thank goodness. But who would do

such a thing, knowing the Pope girl's hand was dumped here? What a terrible, awful joke to play.'

Maggie, still trembling from the initial shock, looked around. 'We need something to fish it out with.'

'Wait a minute,' Terry interrupted. 'What's that on its finger?'

She peered into the pond and saw he was right: there was something on the fourth finger. She knelt down, wincing as the sharp stone edging cut into her flesh, and reached out her own hand. The water rippled as she delicately took hold of the littlest finger and pulled.

As the dummy hand broke through the surface of the water, they both gasped. There, on the fourth finger, was a diamond solitaire ring.

Maggie looked up at Terry, who was ashen with shock.

'Isn't that an engagement ring?' he asked.

She didn't answer him, fearing that if she did Evans would take her words and spread them around Saros and beyond. Because it *was* an engagement ring – and she was pretty certain it was Jade Reynolds's.

55

Were it not that she didn't agree with a single word of his hypothesis, Maggie might have conceded that Inspector Jacob Jasso was doing a good job of arguing against the inarguable link between the cases of Jade Reynolds and Katy Pope. It was four hours since she'd found Jade's engagement ring submerged in the pond on a severed shop dummy's hand, and the team from Operation Pivot had been invited by Jasso to attend a briefing at the station in the centre of Saros old town.

'We have now had four reported sightings of Jade in the same car with the same man at different places on the island, the most recent being first thing this morning, before the discovery of Jade's ring in the pond. The last caller said she and the man she was with were embracing and appeared happy. Based on this call and the others, I believe that Jade either threw her ring away when she decided to leave Saros to be with this gentleman and someone picked it up and decided to play a joke on the rest of us by dumping it in the pond because of all the press interest in the anniversary of Katy Pope's murder, or Jade did it herself, to distract from her leaving.'

From the corner of her eye, Maggie could see Walker chewing the inside of his mouth. He was probably dying to proclaim the theory as 'bollocks', as she was too, but they still had to tread carefully. The discovery of the ring had done nothing to convince Jasso there was a need for British officers to take on a greater role in the search for Jade, even though their Commander had authorized them to delay their return to the UK if necessary. Walker had at least persuaded Jasso to have the ring thoroughly examined: the dummy limb and the ring were currently on their way to the Spanish mainland to be tested for forensics, although their submergence in the pond meant there was no hope of finding fingerprints.

The Commander and Walker had discussed whether additional officers might be needed to join the Operation Pivot team if they stayed on but had decided for the moment to keep it to the four of them. Until they received an official invite to participate in Jasso's investigation, it would be hard to justify to the budget crunchers.

As Jasso droned on, Maggie was finding it difficult to concentrate. An extended stay in Saros would mean her missing Lou and the children's visit on Saturday. She thought about asking them to rearrange for another weekend, but it wasn't fair on Jude and Flora, who, judging by the texts her nephew had sent her, were both really excited.

Her mind strayed to the Popes. She hated having to leave them to come to the station now George wasn't there. The discovery of Jade's ring had triggered a wave of grief that had floored them both: as Patricia put it, they knew Katy was dead and never coming back, but the loss of her amethyst ring had hung over them like a dark cloud for ten years. Someone copying their daughter's mutilation and using another ring to do it felt like salt being poured into their wounds.

Before she left, Maggie had broached the idea that they should get an earlier flight home, as their return trip was booked for the following Tuesday morning. But Philip had been the one to say no, they should stay, because the entire point of their visit was to hold the memorial service and that still hadn't happened. They shouldn't go home without it taking place.

Maggie stifled a yawn and forced herself to concentrate. Jasso was once again citing the witness reports of seeing Jade happily wrapped around another man as proof she wasn't dead or had been abducted.

'Even your newspapers are saying it.'

Walker and Maggie exchanged looks. They were acutely aware how skewed the coverage had been so far and for Jasso to cite it as proof was troubling.

'See for yourself.' Jasso beckoned to one of his officers at the back of the room who had a couple of newspapers draped over his arm like a towel. 'Show them.'

The officer held them up. The *Sun*'s splash was an interview with an ex-boyfriend of Jade's who was claiming she'd cheated on him too. The other newspaper was *The Times*, which had a story less prominently displayed on its front page with the headline SIGHTINGS RULE OUT KATY POPE LINK IN MISSING WOMAN HUNT.

'I wonder where they got that angle from,' said Walker darkly.

Jasso ignored him.

'We have finite resources and cannot waste time looking for someone who doesn't want to be found,' he addressed the room at large. 'It has therefore been decided that we shall scale down the search.'

'I think you're making a terrible mistake,' said Walker, visibly seething.

Jasso mirrored the DCI's anger. 'You sit there and tell me I'm wrong, but what proof do you have that she's been taken? I'll tell you – none. No witnesses, no forensics, nothing.'

Walker didn't contradict him, because Jasso was right. They hadn't produced any concrete proof beyond the chewing-gum wrappers and Jasso wasn't convinced there was anything sinister about Mason being handed a stick of gum by the man at the bar. All Walker was going on was Martos's theory. Looking at the two men glowering at each other across the room, it struck Maggie that this was becoming a battle of egos as much as experience.

Walker rose to his feet and motioned at her to do the same.

'Thank you for allowing us to attend your briefing,' he said tightly, as though it was a battle to force the words through his lips.

They went outside and congregated in the shade of one of the flat-topped trees that seemed to line every street, which – from asking Annika – Maggie had learned was called a holm oak.

'There must be something we can do to make him see sense,' she said peevishly. 'He's scaling back the search while God knows what is happening to Jade.'

'I know, but I don't know what else we can do right now,

other than keep digging away ourselves to find out what's happened to her. Jasso has his own agenda he's sticking to, and that's to prove history isn't being repeated in Saros. You know what it's like when someone questions a case you've worked on – it makes you defensive. I think that's what's happening here with Jasso. He won't consider any other possibility because that means facing up to the fact that the police investigation he personally worked on ten years ago was such an abysmal cock-up the killer's swanned back to Saros to have another crack.'

'All the more reason for him to want to stop history repeating itself, surely?'

'You'd think,' said Walker wearily, wiping the sweat beads that had broken out on his forehead. 'This bloody heat is doing me in. I can't think straight.'

'Do you want me to drive back?' she asked.

'No, I'll be fine. There is something else I want you to do, though.'

'What's that?'

'Retrace Jade's footsteps from when she left the beach to the first sighting at the roundabout near the marina. I don't think Jasso's lot have done it properly, so I want to make sure we do.'

'Sure. What are you going to do?'

'I think I should go to see Jade's parents. I want them to know we're considering staying in Saros for the time being,' he said, wiping his forehead again. 'They need to know they're not alone here.'

56

'Ouch.'

The splinter of wood Jade had managed to pick off the edge of the bedside table scratched the delicate skin of her wrist as she tucked it up her sleeve. She wasn't sure if it was sturdy or long enough to stab through skin, but it should do some damage to an eyeball, which was her intended target even though the thought of it made her feel a bit squeamish. It was something her dad had taught her and his voice had rung in her ears during the many hours it had taken her to pick at the wood.

If all else fails, go for the eyeballs, love. Jab them with your thumbs, fingers, keys – whatever you can get your hands on. Trust me, that'll make whoever attacks you wish they'd never bothered.

She had never yearned for her dad as much as she had these past two days. Even her desire to see Mason was trumped by a certainty that, if Clive Reynolds knew where she was, he'd be getting her out of there and taking care of her. It was what he'd always done, since she was little. He was the one who'd taught her to stand up to bullies, encouraged her to play football and climb trees and do anything just as well as boys, and it was he who'd pushed her to do well at school because *qualifications are important, love. I didn't get any, so I know what I'm talking about.* The slew of GCSEs she'd achieved was the reason she was able to get on the Nursery Nursing diploma course; Clive said the day she graduated was the proudest of his life.

Jade tried not to dwell on why he hadn't come for her. She had to believe he was trying everything he could to find her, but that it wasn't easy being in a foreign country where you don't know the language. She'd even managed to make herself laugh thinking about it – as much as she loved her dad, he was no Liam Neeson. Clive Reynolds was so short he could probably fit in Liam's pocket.

She pushed herself up into a sitting position. Her skin was clammy and she didn't feel well, but it was probably because she was starving hungry, the last thing she'd had to eat now a distant memory. The bottle of water on the bedside table she'd finished as well. Before he'd left her alone again last night her captor had removed her wrist binds and handcuffed her left hand to the metal frame of the bed, so she could use her right one to drink and to also reach for the chamber pot to bring it closer to the bed. She'd almost wet herself in the time it had taken to shuffle off the mattress, pull down the pyjama bottoms and knickers and angle her body near enough to use it. It helped that she'd been able to remove her blindfold though – he'd said she could, as long as she waited until he'd left the room first. She'd been too scared to disobey.

Then she realized he'd removed her engagement

ring and that had set her off again. She'd cried so much in the past two days she was amazed she had any tears left.

An hour later, she heard him return.

Jade, lying on her side, tucked her right hand up her left sleeve and curled her fingers around the piece of wood, ready.

It was a few moments before he came to her room, however. She could hear him walking through the villa – she'd made the assumption that's what the building was because the shutters obscuring the windows were the same as the ones they had in their villa – opening and closing doors. She had managed to keep track of the days and knew it was Thursday and she wondered who he was that he wouldn't be missed. Round her way, Thursday was the start of the weekend, when everyone went out. The thought of not seeing her friends made her want to cry again.

He was humming a tune to himself, an upbeat little number that made her angry. How could he be so cheerful when she was like this? She was going to enjoy sticking the splinter in his eye. She hoped it hurt like hell.

As he came into the room, she went through the pretence of rousing from a supposed sleep, eyelids flickering open slowly. Immediately he commanded her to shut them again, and when she did he came over and told her to sit up so he could release her from the bed frame and put the blindfold over her face. He was so close she could smell coffee on his breath.

Jade tensed as she felt her wrist be freed and the blindfold go on. He was behind her now, about to fasten it. She didn't know exactly where his eyeballs were in relation to her position, but she was going to have a damn good guess.

With a cry, Jade thrust the piece of wood over her shoulder in the direction of what she hoped was his face. Her hand slammed against something and an agonized, high-pitched scream ripped through the room. Jade spun round, sending the unsecured blindfold flying, to see her abductor on his hands and knees, back to her, clutching his bloodied scalp as he sobbed in pain. She might've missed his eye but the wood was sticking out at a ninety-degree angle and wasn't going to come out easily.

Now she had to move fast. Legs still shackled, she half staggered, half crawled for the door. If she could just make it outside, she could lock him in and go and get help.

She was almost at the threshold, heart pounding from the effort, when she felt two hands grasp her ankles and pull her back.

'You're not going anywhere!' he roared.

Jade fought as hard as she could but he was far stronger and managed to drag her across the floor on her stomach towards the bed. Then he roughly rolled her over so she was on her back – and that's when she finally saw her abductor's face again. He was better looking than she remembered and to her surprise he was wearing one of those fancy black suits that celebrities wore on the red carpet. Then, before she could say anything, he jabbed another needle in her neck.

57

The stretch of beach where Jade was last seen was right in front of the hotel where her parents were now permanently based. The new arrangement had been organized by Lyndsey Shepherd, who appreciated why they wanted to be close to the last place they'd seen their daughter and had persuaded the hotel's manager likewise.

Maggie slipped off her shoes as she reached the sand and revelled in the warmth beneath her bare soles as she crossed to the sun loungers the Reynolds family and Mason had occupied two days ago. Walker wanted her to retrace Jade's steps, so here she was, at the start of them. Another family, with two small children, were using the loungers now, so Maggie went as close as she could without attracting attention, then turned her back on the sea and stared in the direction of the walkway and the Eroski mini-mart Jade had left the beach to visit.

Her stride purposeful, Maggie walked back up the beach and went to the store. Its manager had given a statement to Jasso's team to confirm Jade never made it inside, which was backed up by CCTV. Maggie stood in front of the entrance for a moment as she contemplated where Jade might've gone next.

The first supposed sighting of her was at a junction past the marina and the most direct way for Jade to have got there would've been by walking along the front. But, supposing the sighting was false and she had been snatched, it would surely have been somewhere far more secluded, where the abductor wouldn't be seen or disturbed. There was a long, narrow street that ran up the side of the mini-mart, so Maggie set off along it.

She took her time, drinking in her surroundings and scouring every building facade. Most of them appeared to be residential properties, their balconies adorned with the paraphernalia of everyday life. On one she saw three adult-size bicycles stacked together; on another what looked like a week's worth of washing was drying.

Further along, the sun's reach diminished as the buildings grew taller and Maggie was grateful for the coolness that enveloped her. She wasn't suited to a hot climate and she knew what Walker meant when he said the heat made it impossible to think straight.

She could see the main road up ahead and the buildings began to morph in anticipation, with shops replacing the apartments again. Most of them were derelict apart from one store selling tourist trappings, its front hidden from view by a vast array of inflatables. Had Jasso's team spoken to whoever worked here? The door was locked, however, and a sign stuck to it declared that it would reopen in an hour's time.

Frustrated, Maggie cleared a path back through the beach toys and looked up the street. The main road was about ten metres away, and parked cars lined the kerbside. Any one of them could be used as a getaway vehicle if someone wanted to make a quick exit. She looked around again and her gaze fell upon the building opposite, a former cafe that had been boarded up. Crossing the street to it, Maggie peered through a narrow gap where the boards didn't quite meet. There was light coming from a window at the back of the cafe so the inside was illuminated; judging by the dust motes circulating, it didn't look as though it had been open for some time.

Hang on, she thought. If the cafe wasn't being used, why had the dust been disturbed?

She gave the door a shove but it wouldn't budge, locked tight by an old, rusting padlock. But when she examined it more closely she could see it wasn't as old as it appeared, but had been roughed up to look that way. Her pulse quickening, she decided there had to be a back way in, an entrance where deliveries could've been made, perhaps. She walked up the street to the main road, examining every doorway but rejecting them all as a possible means in. Then she rounded the corner and saw it – a wooden louvre door adorned with a sign that erroneously stated there was an electricity sub-station behind it. The hazard symbol stamped next to the words was probably enough to stop curious types venturing further, but not Maggie.

Kicking as hard as she could, she managed to cave the lock in and the door swung open. She moved slowly along the narrow passageway that led into the back of the cafe. There was a door right ahead and whoever had been there last hadn't been bothered with security, because it was unlocked.

Inside, the first thing she noticed were the drag marks on the floor. Something heavy had been pulled along, creating tracks in the dust and grease that lined the tiles. Cautiously she ventured onwards, passing through a storage area that still held catering-size tins of tomatoes and olives. There was another door ahead that led into the kitchen area and, as she crept forward, her heart suddenly skipped a beat. Peeking out from under one of the industrial-sized stoves was a bundle of diaphanous pink fabric that, unless she was very much mistaken, matched the sarong Jade had been wearing when she went missing.

Maggie scrabbled in her bag for her phone. Walker picked up on the first ring.

'What's up?'

'Boss, you need to come. I think I've found where Jade was being held.'

58

It was seven in the evening before Maggie finally found a window of time in which she had a minute to herself. Walker had done the sensible thing and called Jasso as soon as he saw the sarong for himself. The inspector wasn't happy at being summoned and, determined to stick to the line that nothing untoward had happened to Jade, had tried to argue that it might not actually be hers, or that she could've dropped the sarong in the street and someone else picked it up. Walker came back at him with both barrels, demanding he explain its presence in a disused cafe that, according to the owner of the store opposite, hadn't been opened in three years. Backed into a corner, Jasso agreed to have the cafe forensically examined and allowed Maggie to take a picture of the sarong on her phone to show Jade's family.

Clive and Mandy were predictably distraught after confirming it did match their daughter's sarong. Maggie had taken a close-up of the label and Mandy had explained that she had been with Jade when she'd bought it in the Brent Cross branch of Accessorize. Maggie then spent the rest of the afternoon with them going back over the timeline of the morning Jade went missing. What struck her most was how quiet Clive was being, the talkative man she'd first met a few days ago now a subdued shell. They had Philip Pope to thank for that, according to Mandy, who was clearly peeved at her husband being led on a wild goose chase and getting all worked up in the process. 'Make sure you keep telling him to stay away,' she said.

Maggie also spoke to Mason to see if he could remember anything more about the man who'd given him the chewing gum but, disappointingly, he had nothing to add to his original description.

Afterwards, she'd returned to her own hotel, where she'd caught up briefly with Walker. There was no update from Shah or Paulson other than to say that Marta had put them in touch with her daughter, Camila, and they were due to be meeting with her later that evening. Marta had confirmed again in person that Johnnie had not been in Es Cana when he'd said he was and she had made a statement to that effect.

Now, back in her room, Maggie stretched out on the bed, her tired body propped up on pillows and grateful for the cool, clean sheets. She needed to call Umpire to let him know it was looking increasingly likely she wouldn't be home tomorrow, but first there was someone else she needed to speak to.

'Lara's phone,' answered the male voice.

'Oh,' said Maggie, taken by surprise. 'Is Lara available?'

'No, this is her husband. Who is this?'

Maggie was very aware Lara hadn't told anyone, least of all her husband, what had happened to her in Saros and she must choose her words carefully.

'I'm DC Maggie Neville with the Metropoli—'

'Oh God, have you found her?'

There was no mistaking the anguish in his voice. Maggie swung her legs off the bed, her pulse racing.

'Mr Steadman, I'm ringing because I spoke to your wife about a matter last week and I have some more questions for her. Are you saying she's gone missing?'

'Yes. Well, no. She's taken herself off and she won't tell me where.' He paused. 'What matter?'

'I'm afraid I can't discuss that with you.'

'Is she in trouble? Is that why she's gone off and left me to cope with the kids? They're so upset because I can't tell them where she is or when she'll be back.'

'Your wife isn't in trouble, no. Are you sure you don't know where she is?'

His response was icy. 'Do you not think I would've found her if I knew where she was?'

'Yes, of course, it was a silly thing to say,' said Maggie, feeling foolish. 'Do you have any means of getting in touch with her?'

'She has her work phone on her. The number you've called is for her personal one.'

'Can I please have her work number?'

He paused. 'How do I know if you're who you say you are?'

It was a good point. 'If you call this number, my colleagues will vouch for me.' She gave him the number of her department in Islington. 'There might not be anyone there at the moment though.'

Ten minutes passed before he called her back.

'What has my wife got to do with why you're in Saros?' he demanded to know. 'I just spoke to a DS Mealing who

285

confirmed you're who you say you are, but he also told me you're in Saros because of the Katy Pope case. I know my wife went there on holiday once, and it wasn't long before that murder, so you'd better start telling me what's going on.'

If Mealing had been in the room right then, Maggie would quite cheerfully have murdered him too. Damn him for picking up the phone.

'I'm so sorry, Mr Steadman. It's true that I'm in Saros, but I can't tell you anything else because your wife asked me not to. I don't want to betray her trust, but I can assure you she's not in any kind of trouble,' said Maggie, hoping that would be enough to appease him. 'I do need to speak to her urgently though. Please, can I have that other number?'

His voice crumpled. 'If I give it to you and she tells you where she is, will you let me know?'

Maggie hesitated. She couldn't make that promise – if Lara didn't want her husband to know where she was, that was up to her.

'I'll let you know your wife is safe.'

Lara's husband read out the number, which Maggie scribbled down in her notebook.

'Please tell her we love her and want her to come home.'

That she could promise.

'I will.'

59

It took Jade a moment to realize she was sitting up in a chair. As her vision came into focus, she looked around groggily and all she could see were daisies. In vases, on the table – so many bunches. Except they weren't the kind of daisies you picked off the lawn and threaded into a chain, they were much bigger than that. And these ones were pink, not white. There were so many of them they made the room seem lurid.

'Hey, you're awake!'

It was his voice, coming from somewhere behind her.

'I'll be with you in a minute.'

She could hear the sound of pots and pans being moved about on a hob and tried to shift in her chair to see what he was doing, but it was as though she was glued to the spot. Looking down, she realized she was tethered to the chair by a rope tightly fastened around her waist and her head swam as she stared down. Then her gaze fell upon the table and she was bemused to see it had been laid out for dinner like they do in fancy restaurants, with a white tablecloth and at least three forks and knives on each side of the plate. Two glass tumblers had already been filled to the brim with water and Jade licked her dry, cracked lips in anticipation. Next to them were empty champagne flutes.

She tried to stay focused but her head lolled forward and her eyes closed again. She felt so, so tired, as though she could lie down and sleep for a week. But then she jerked her head up and forced her eyes open. *Stay awake*, she begged herself. *You need to get out of here.*

'Are you happy with the dress?'

He was standing beside her now and was smiling. He was still wearing the posh suit but there were a few drops of blood on his white shirt. He followed her gaze and looked down.

'Oh, it's nothing. I know you only did it because you were confused about where you were, so I'll let you off this once.' Then his smile slipped and Jade cowered as he glared at her. 'Try anything like that again and I won't be as forgiving.' His voice brightened again. 'So, the dress?'

'What dress?' Jade's voice sounded weird to her own ears, like she was speaking to him from a distance.

'The one you're wearing, silly!'

She looked down at herself in surprise. He was right. The jogging bottoms and T-shirt had been replaced with a black dress that clung to her hips. Tears pricked her eyes and she began to shake. He'd undressed her again.

'You look so beautiful, my darling. Here, let me show you.'

Jade almost dry-heaved as he bent down to loosen the rope around her waist. The stale coffee she had smelled on his breath earlier had been replaced by a scent that, inexplicably, reminded her of Christmas. It was almost spicy, but sweet. It suddenly came to her – cinnamon, that's what it was.

The rope discarded on the floor, he helped her to her feet. She shuddered as his fingers closed around her bare arms; she couldn't stand him touching her. There was a mirror on the wall by the fireplace and as he walked her towards it she hated that she needed to lean on him for support, but her legs felt as though they might give way if she didn't.

Seeing her reflection came as a shock.

'What have you done to my hair?'

'I removed those dreadful extensions. It looks much nicer natural.'

Her hair hung limp around her face and she realized he must've straightened it too. Then she noticed the large, gold hoop earrings she always wore were missing, like her ring.

'You'll have to forgive the make-up. I'm not very good with a mascara wand,' he laughed, helping her back to the chair. 'I'm sure you'll do it better next time.'

'Next time?' she echoed. 'What do you mean?'

He stared at her blankly. 'For our second date.'

Fear mounting, Jade shook her head. 'This is mad. You need to let me go.'

He acted as though he hadn't heard her.

'I was going to do seafood for the starter, but then I thought you might not like it or you might even be allergic. So I hope gazpacho is okay.'

'I'm not hungry,' she said as tears began to fall. 'Please let me go.'

She could see the muscles in his jaw tense.

'I've spent all afternoon preparing this special meal for you,' he said, teeth gritted. 'The least you can do is try some, darling.'

'I'm not your darling!' she cried. 'I'm engaged to someone.'

His face suddenly shifted and where his smile had been there was now a monstrous, twisted look of anger.

'Don't you dare say that!' he bellowed.

Jade shrank away from him, terrified.

'You are mine, do you hear me? Mine!'

His palm came crashing down on the table, sending glasses and cutlery flying. Jade screamed and tried to push away from the table but he grabbed her by the wrist.

'Let me go, you're hurting me! Please, don't hurt me!'

He hauled her out of the chair and onto her feet. Cringing with fear, Jade closed her eyes and braced for the blow she was sure was to follow.

Instead, to her surprise, he let go. She opened her eyes and looked into his face expecting to see the monster staring back but the ugliness had vanished and he was back to being him again, handsome and full of concern.

'I'm sorry! Oh, sweetheart, please forgive me,' he cried. He gently wrapped his arms around her in a hug. 'I didn't mean to spoil our first proper evening together.'

He's not right in the head, Jade thought in a panic. She tried to wriggle away.

'It's fine if you're not hungry, Katy. We can just have some wine.'

Jade froze.

Katy.

He's talking about the girl in the paper, the one from ten years ago.

'I'm not Katy,' she whispered.

He pulled away from her and let out a bark of laughter. 'Silly me, of course you're not. You're my beautiful Jade.'

She trembled as he reached forward and ran his finger gently down her cheek. Terrified that he might attempt to kiss her, she took a step back. He laughed again.

'Am I coming on too strong for a first date? I do apologize. As much as I'm desperate to have sex with you, darling, we must wait until our third. That's the rule. Any sooner and we risk ruining this amazing thing we have, because a relationship built on lust never lasts.'

Jade thought she might throw up. This whole charade was insane.

'I will never sleep with you, you sick bastard.'

There was a long pause and she could see the monster creeping back, tugging at the edges of his smile and darkening his eyes. She began to tremble again.

'We'll see,' he sneered.

Suddenly, she knew. 'Katy said no, didn't she? That's why you killed her.'

'Katy was a disappointment, yes.'

Jade began to cry. 'I don't want to die.'

'Then don't disappoint me, it's as simple as that.' There was no menace in how he said it, but that did nothing to calm Jade. As she sobbed uncontrollably, he looked down at the mess of glass and cutlery on the floor and sighed. 'I think we should call it a night. It's disappointing we didn't get to eat and talk more, but don't worry, we can have our second date tomorrow.'

60

Lara Steadman called Maggie back within thirty seconds of her leaving a voicemail message saying they needed to talk urgently. Exactly why Lara had been so quick to return the call was immediately clear.

'Have you caught him?'

The hysteria in Lara's voice was alarming and Maggie spoke haltingly as she answered.

'Well, the thing is, that's not why I called you.'

'It's him, isn't it, the one who's taken Jade Reynolds. I know the Spanish police are saying she's gone off with someone, but I don't believe a word of it.'

As much as she wanted to confirm Lara's suspicions, Maggie knew she couldn't. Paramount was keeping their under-the-radar investigation from being exposed.

'Where are you, Lara?' she asked.

Silence.

'I spoke to your husband. He's very worried about you, as are your children.'

Lara's voice cracked. 'I'm doing this to protect them. What if he comes after me again once he's finished with Jade? He emailed me!'

'Whoever sent you that message made it very clear he was going to be in Saros this week, and you're hundreds of miles away in the UK,' said Maggie. 'However, there are things that can be done to make you feel safer, like installing a panic button or giving you a direct line to the nearest station – but we can only do that if you're at home. We can't help you if you're hiding in a hotel on your own.'

More silence.

'Lara, your husband seems like a really nice man who loves you very much. He's worked out that you going off now is something to do with your holiday in Saros, so why don't you tell him the truth.'

'I can't!'

'You did nothing wrong, Lara – there's nothing to be ashamed of. Someone took advantage of you and almost certainly spiked your drink to enable them to lock you up in the apartment. Then you got yourself out of there, which was really brave. Your husband isn't going to be angry with you – he's going to be thankful you had a lucky escape. Please, Lara, go home, talk to him.'

'I lied.'

'Sorry?'

'I lied about not talking to any men in the club. There was one.'

Maggie scrabbled across the bed to get her notebook and pen.

'Tell me what he was like.'

She heard Lara take a deep breath to steady herself.

'Tall, well-spoken, blondish hair, I think, but it was dark in the club and the lights made everything look funny.'

'What nationality was he?'

'Spanish, I think. He spoke with an accent.'

That stopped Maggie short. Mason had said the man who accosted him with the chewing gum was British.

'How did you get chatting?'

'He came over while I was at the bar and asked to buy me a drink. I said no, and flashed my ring at him to put him off, but he was really charming and kept paying me compliments. I was flattered, I suppose. He was really good-looking.'

Johnnie's face filled Maggie's mind. Could he be considered good-looking? With shorter, groomed hair, perhaps. But Johnnie was also British.

'Did he buy you a drink in the end?'

'Yes. We shared a bottle of champagne, which he paid for. It wasn't a cheap one, either. The next thing I remember I'm in the toilet feeling ill, then I woke up on the sofa like I said.'

'Why didn't you tell me this when you came into the station?' Maggie asked gently, aware how fragile Lara sounded and not wanting to tip her over the edge.

'Because I thought it made me look bad. I shouldn't have been flirting with him like that. I was getting married.'

'Is there anything else you can remember?'

Silence again.

'Lara? Is there something else? You must tell me everything.'

'There's nothing else.'

Maggie didn't believe her.

'Was it when you were inside the apartment? Did something more happen there?'

Lara let out a sob. 'I'm sorry, Maggie. I can't help you.'

There was a click and the line went dead.

61

Maggie found Walker in the downstairs courtyard bar, nursing a beer. Breathlessly, she told him what Lara had said.

'She's holding something back, I know it,' she finished. 'If I had been talking to her face to face I could've got it out of her. Boss, if I could go back to London overnight, I could—'

'But you don't know where she is and nor does her husband,' said Walker. 'She could be anywhere.'

'I could get a trace on her mobile,' said Maggie. 'Please, boss.'

He shook his head. 'The budget crunchers won't swing for extra flights.'

'Speak to the Commander then, get him to okay it. If Lara has remembered more details about the apartment where she was held, we need to know. For all we know, the killer might still be using it. Boss, Jade's life might depend on it.'

Walker paused for a moment, then picked up his phone and went online. After a few moments he looked up from the website he'd been checking.

'Flights back to London look pretty booked up,' he said. 'But you can wait at the airport for a standby, or fly some-where else like Birmingham and catch a train to London. Are you sure this is the only way she'll talk to you, though?'

'Yes. What's happened to Jade has scared Lara so much that she's walked out on her husband and her kids to keep them safe,' said Maggie. 'Whatever she's not telling us, we need to know and I think she'll only tell me in person.'

Walker looked at his phone again. 'According to this website, if you already have a valid ticket you can be put on standby for no extra cost.'

'Why don't I go to the airport, show them my ticket for tomorrow evening and say I need to fly back earlier and see what the airline can sort out? I can find Lara in the morning then be back on a flight here by tomorrow evening.'

'All right, do it,' Walker agreed. 'It looks like we're going to have to reschedule our flights anyway. Go and find her and see what she has to say.'

Three hours later, Maggie was no closer to getting back to London. The airline representative at Palma airport had put her on standby but wasn't hopeful of a seat becoming free.

'It's a Thursday night in June, one of the busiest times of the year,' she'd said. 'The chances of you getting home tonight are pretty much on a par with Ryan Gosling asking me to marry him.'

Maggie had asked at the other airline desks but it was the same story – there were no spare seats on any flights and she'd have to wait on standby.

Now, sitting on a hard plastic seat nursing her third coffee of the night on the wrong side of passport control, Maggie was wishing she hadn't excitedly called Umpire on her way to the airport to say she was coming back. Her plan had been to get a hire car at whatever airport she landed in, drive to his house in Trenton to spend the night with him, then head into London first thing to track down Lara. She had a feeling the woman wouldn't have ventured too far from home and that she was probably in a hotel in central London. Somewhere large and anonymous, where she could hide in a crowd.

She'd also texted Mike Steadman to say she was heading back and asked him to ring in the meantime if he had any update about his wife's whereabouts.

Maggie yawned and stretched her legs out in front of her. It was gone midnight and she was shattered. Flights ran until the early hours though, so she had to stay put, just in case a seat came up. She closed her eyelids for a moment and wondered if she could get away with taking a nap.

'Keeping you up, are we?'

Her eyes snapped open to find George Pope standing over her, grinning. He was in a suit, his shirt collar undone beneath it, and had a leather overnight bag slung over his shoulder.

Maggie scrambled to her feet, embarrassed at being caught resting her eyes but grateful she hadn't reached that point of a snooze where she was slack-mouthed and dribbling.

'What are you doing here?' she asked.

'I could ask you the same question. But seeing as you

got yours in first, I'll tell you. I've just landed from London. I had to go back today for work.'

'Your mum said you probably weren't coming back.'

'My trial has been postponed. Would you have minded if I hadn't?' he asked, staring at her intently.

She didn't reply.

'I'm sorry for what I said to you the other day about you not being a good FLO. It was awful of me. You've been amazing with Mum and Dad, but especially Mum. I know she's not the easiest person to deal with. I was upset that day and I shouldn't have taken it out on you.'

'Thank you for the apology. I'm sorry too, for upsetting you.'

As George already knew about Lara because of the email, she wasn't breaking any confidences by telling him the reason she was waiting for a flight home.

'I think it's great you're going back to find her, but I don't rate your chances of flying tonight,' he said. 'Why don't you come back first thing and get an early flight out?'

'There's no point. I haven't got anywhere to stay in Palma overnight and our budget won't stretch to a hotel.'

'Can you pay for yourself? There must be somewhere nearby where you can get a cheap room. Look, I could do with a drink and I know a great late-night bar we could get a taxi to from here, then we can look online for some-where for you to stay. If you wait here all night, you'll be too exhausted to do your job, and it sounds like this Lara needs you on it.'

He had a point.

'Shouldn't you be getting back to Saros though?'

'I will, after I've had a drink and sorted you out.'

Maggie laughed. 'I don't need looking after.'

'I know. But I want to make sure you've got somewhere safe to crash. Come on, what say we get that drink?'

Doubt twisted her stomach into a tight knot. Deep down she knew that going for a drink with him was a bad idea and that she should walk away now.

'It's only a drink, Maggie. You won't get into trouble with Walker.'

As their eyes locked, she knew that wasn't the kind of trouble she was worried about.

62

Friday

Philip slipped out of bed as quietly as he could so as not to disturb his still-sleeping wife. It was early, before six, but he hadn't been able to conjure up nearly enough sheep to count, so gave up trying and got up.

He decided to go for a walk along the beach. The shutters were still down at Annika's restaurant as he walked past, as was to be expected at such an ungodly hour, but he hoped that by the time he reached the marina one of the cafes would be open for him to buy a coffee. Right now he was fatigued down to his bones and needed a strong shot of caffeine to bolster his energy levels.

He was used to feeling tired, a symptom of the insidious creep of old age. Not that he was *old* old: he would be turning sixty-one in the coming November. In his mind, however, he felt a decade further along and he knew he looked it too. Grief had done that to him – it had robbed his body of its vitality and gouged out deep lines to leave its mark on his face.

Early retirement had also played a part in his physical decline. He hadn't wanted to give up working when he turned sixty but Patricia had begged him to. His job as a

Curatorial Fellow at the National Gallery had given him purpose, and walking between its vast rooms and up and down its wide staircases had kept him fit. The gallery had offered him a part-time associate position when he had tendered his resignation but Patricia had dismissed the idea. They didn't need the money, so why on earth should he continue? But gainful employment had meant so much more than the salary it provided, especially after Katy died. Getting lost amongst his 'beauties' – how he referred to the paintings in his care – was his escape. The worst moment of his day was at five minutes past five in the afternoon, when he would step outside the gallery into Trafalgar Square to venture home and the grief would again hit him as hard as if Nelson himself had toppled off his column and landed on his head.

A woman walking a small dog that looked more rat-like than canine smiled as she passed. Philip smiled back. The interaction made him aware of his surroundings again and he realized he was at the point in the promenade where a semi-circular jetty jutted out into the sea. He walked up to the edge of it and spent a few moments watching shoals of small silver fish darting through the shallows, marvelling at the uniformity of their movement. When he finally looked up, he saw something in the bay ahead that made him stop and stare.

It was Johnnie, in a small, motorized dinghy.

Philip's first inclination was to laugh – in all the years he'd known Johnnie, never once had he known him to rouse from his bed before eight in the morning, even on a school day. He was famously sloth-like, which is why it had come as no surprise to anyone, least of all Johnnie's parents, that he resisted pursuing a career that would require him to present himself at a reasonable hour and instead had chosen to roam the world, picking up odd jobs along the way to fund himself.

As the dinghy bobbed across the harbour, Philip frowned. It was travelling back towards the mooring where Johnnie's boat was, not away from it. Which meant Johnnie had been up even earlier than this to venture somewhere.

Curiosity mounting, Philip hurried the quarter of a mile to reach the jetty Johnnie's boat was moored closest to. By the time he got there the dinghy was tied up next to it and Johnnie, ponytailed hair tucked beneath a red baseball cap, was busy at work on the deck, sluicing it down with water. Philip didn't want to shout across in case people were sleeping in the neighbouring crafts, so he called Johnnie's name as loudly as he felt respectable, which wasn't very loud at all, and it took four or five goes before Johnnie heard him and looked up.

For a second he looked confused to see Philip standing there, but then a wide smile split his face. He went round the other side of the boat and unfolded the gangway so Philip could come aboard.

'What are you doing up so early?' he asked.

'I could ask you the same thing,' Philip chuckled. 'It's so unusual to see you awake at this hour that I had to check I wasn't seeing things.'

Johnnie casually motioned to a vast cool box on the deck. 'Oh, I've been fishing. I'm not paying the mark-up these restaurants charge when I can catch it for myself.'

'Does that mean we're invited to lunch?'

Johnnie looked uncomfortable. 'Um—'

'I'm sorry, how rude of me to impose ourselves.'

'It's not that,' said Johnnie hurriedly. 'It's just that I have plans already.'

'Oh?'

'An old friend; you don't know them. But we could do dinner tonight instead?'

Now it was Philip's turn to falter.

'Actually, Patricia and I are going ahead with the memorial at sunset. You're invited, of course. It's going to be just us, you, George and Declan. After everything else that's happened, we feel it best to keep it exclusive this time.'

Johnnie's expression darkened. 'I still don't get why you're letting Morris be involved.'

'Please don't start. I know you two don't see eye to eye, but he was Katy's boyfriend—'

'—who was screwing around behind her back with her best friend. Oh, come on, Philip, don't give me that look. You'd guessed what he was up to with Tamara but you chose to look the other way.'

'I did no such thing.'

'Well, Patricia definitely did. She was more into Declan than Katy was.'

Philip felt obliged to defend his wife.

'Patricia always acted in what she thought were Katy's best interests.'

Johnnie shook his head peevishly.

'For crying out loud, why can't you be honest for once, Philip? I know you said the other day you now regret encouraging Katy to keep their relationship going. George told me.'

Philip bristled at his son for sharing what he thought was a private conversation.

'Where was this concern for Katy when she was alive?' he retaliated. 'I don't recall you battering down our door to convince us she was unhappy, but suddenly it's all you can talk about.'

Johnnie looked pained. 'You're right, I should've said at the time. Maybe if I'd spoken some sense into Patricia back then she might have let Katy alone.' He paused. 'I told Katy I loved her.'

Philip was agog. 'When?'

'The Christmas before she died.' Johnnie's eyes brimmed with tears. 'I loved her so fucking much. She was the most perfect, most beautiful, most amazing girl I've ever met. It killed me that Morris couldn't see how lucky he was. So I decided to tell her. I said she should be with me, because I loved her and always had.'

He shook his head sadly, which Philip interpreted as disappointment. Katy must've turned him down. He gave Johnnie's shoulder a tender squeeze.

'For what it's worth, I would've been very happy if she'd reciprocated. There was a time when I did think you might end up together.'

There was the longest pause as Johnnie stared out to sea. When he turned to face Philip again, tears were streaking down his cheeks, wetting his blond stubble.

'We were together. The baby was mine.'

Philip sank down heavily onto the moulded plastic bench that edged the deck. Johnnie was the one who got Katy pregnant? It was unthinkable, and yet one look at Johnnie's face told him it was true. In all the years he'd known him,

Johnnie had never given him any reason to disbelieve him, so why would he now.

'Do you remember that Christmas? Mum and Dad had come here, to Saros, so I spent it with you. Declan had gone home to see his family and that's when Katy and me got together. I told her I loved her and she said she felt the same. We carried on in secret for a couple of months and she was going to finish it with Declan, but then she got pregnant.'

'How can you be sure it was yours?' Philip could barely get the words out.

'The dates added up. I said she should get rid of it because we were both too young, she had university to look forward to, and a baby would change everything. Katy agreed, but because she was terrified Patricia might find out we'd been sleeping together and be furious, she decided to say it was Declan's,' said Johnnie desolately. 'I hated him thinking it was his.'

'He still thinks that.'

Johnnie nodded. 'The other day at the restaurant, when he said Katy told him everything, I thought he knew then. But he didn't.' He let out a tremulous sigh. 'After the baby was gone, Katy couldn't bear to be around me. Making her have the termination was the worst mistake I've ever made. We should've had our baby and made a go of it, because afterwards she hated me.'

Johnnie dropped to his knees and cried like an anguished animal, howling his grief around the marina, but still Philip couldn't move to comfort him. He was pinned to the spot. He couldn't believe that Johnnie, who he loved like a son, had forced poor Katy into aborting her child. It was unforgivable.

His anger mounting, Philip rose to his feet and stumbled across the deck to the gangway. In his haste he knocked into the cool box and sent it flying. The box landed on its side and the lid burst open, sending a cascade of ice skidding across the deck – along with a pair of large, gold hoop earrings and some scrunched-up chewing-gum wrappers.

Bewildered, Philip turned to Johnnie.

'Where are all the fish you caught?'

63

Her eyelids flickering open, Maggie became aware of a noise and wondered vaguely what the sound was and where it was coming from. It was an unwelcome accompaniment to the banging in her head that was heralding the start of what she could tell was going to be an epic hangover. Gin-laced, mostly, but with at least three shots of tequila thrown in.

Groaning, she flopped onto her back and stared up at the ceiling – and that's when it hit her.

The sound was George Pope whistling as he showered in the en-suite bathroom.

Maggie sat bolt upright, pulling the sheet up to cover herself. Her clothes and underwear were strewn across the floor where George had removed and dropped them.

She drew her knees up and buried her face into them as guilt burned through her and tears pricked her eyes. She was a horrible, despicable person for cheating on Umpire and, worse, for wanting to.

She and George had both known what was going to happen. The cocktails, the flirting, the air between them crackling with electricity – it was all foreplay. When he offered to walk her to the hotel they'd found online, she didn't decline. When he offered to see her to her room, she didn't decline. And when they went inside the room and he pushed her up against the wall to begin kissing her, she'd kissed him back. She had wanted him as much as he'd wanted her.

Now, in the cold light of day, she felt terrible. She checked the time and jolted when she saw it was nearly nine. She should've been back at the airport hours ago, checking for a flight home.

She jumped out of bed and looked around for her bag and, more importantly, her phone. Damn it, where was it? She was on all fours, scrabbling beneath the bed for her bag, when she heard a voice behind her.

'Now there's a sight.'

Maggie spun round to see George standing in the doorway to the bathroom, naked except for the smallest towel imaginable wrapped around his waist. Despite how she was feeling, she found herself laughing.

'You're wearing the bathmat,' she said.

He looked down at himself, grinning. 'I thought it was a bit small.' To her shock, he whipped it off and used it to rough dry his hair. She didn't know where to look.

'I need to go,' she stammered. 'I'm running late.'

'Really?'

She clawed her bra and knickers across the floor towards her. 'I need to get dressed.'

George said nothing and she was relieved when he reached for his own clothes. When they were both fully dressed, he crossed the room and gently held her shoulders. She could feel the warmth coming off him after his hot shower.

'Hey, it's okay.'

Her eyes swam with tears.

'No, it's not. I have a boyfriend who I love very much.'

'I'm sorry. I shouldn't have come on to you like I did.'

She shook her head. 'No, it's not your fault. I wanted it to happen as much as you did.' She rested her forehead against his chest. 'I'm sorry too.'

George wrapped his arms around her and stroked her hair as she cried.

'It's okay. No one ever needs to know. It can be our secret.' He kissed the top of her head. 'I won't deny I'm sorry there won't be a repeat, though, because I do think you're lovely and beautiful and sexy—'

She pulled away from him. 'Please don't, it's not fair.'

'If there wasn't someone else, would you be keen?'

A flashback came to her, of warm lips and tongues intertwining, a hand in her hair, pulling her closer – and a feeling that she never wanted it to stop. Choking back tears, she managed a smile. 'I wouldn't be standing here with my clothes on, let's put it that way.'

'And there's me hoping you liked me for my intellect,' he joked. 'Look, the last thing I want is to cause you trouble. I promise you it shall remain our secret. Consider it forgotten.'

But Maggie couldn't forget. She'd slept with another man and while George might be able to file it away, it crushed her to think how upset Umpire would be if he ever found out. Her betrayal was unforgivable. Lou would have a field day too knowing Maggie had been disloyal again.

'I promise you I won't tell a soul,' he reiterated.

'Thank you.' She had no alternative but to trust him at his word. 'I should call for a taxi.'

'We can share one. I'll drop you off, then I'll carry on back to Saros.'

'I don't need chaperoning.'

'How about I stalk you then and follow in the taxi behind?'

As her eyes widened with shock, George laughed.

'I'm joking. That's Johnnie's MO, not mine, don't forget.'

Maggie continued to stare at him.

'Don't you remember us talking about it last night? You asked me about my sister being close with Johnnie—'

Shit, thought Maggie. Please tell me I didn't reveal anything about Johnnie's alibi in Ibiza being false. Walker might forgive me getting hammered when I'm meant to be on my best behaviour, but he'd never forgive me shouting my mouth off.

'—and I told you how he would chase after Katy like a heat-seeking missile, to the point where she asked me to tell him to back off because it was getting creepy. Then you asked me if I thought he could have hurt her, to which I replied he wasn't even on Majorca when she was murdered, and then you went a bit weird and so we ordered another drink.'

Maggie was mortified beyond words, for being drunk, for being indiscreet, for throwing herself at another man. When did she become this awful person?

'Why *were* you asking me about Johnnie? Do you know something we don't?'

'No.' She paused. 'I also asked you about the jeweller's, didn't I?'

George nodded. 'I told you the truth – I was clutching at straws when I went there. I had this mad idea that the owner might remember something if *I* asked him rather than the police. I didn't mean to cause a row. There was nothing sinister about me going: I only asked about the cost of making a replica because I was thinking it might be nice for Mum and Dad to have a copy of it.'

Only half listening, Maggie began looking for her phone again and found it slid between the mattress and the bed frame. Pulling it out, she saw she had a missed call from Lara's personal mobile. It must be her husband.

'I need to make a call in private,' she said. 'You should head back to Saros now. I may be here for a while.'

'Sure.'

He picked up his overnight bag and headed for the door. Then, on the verge of opening it, he doubled back, wrapped his arm around Maggie's waist and pulled her close until his lips found hers. Maggie sank into the kiss, seeing it for what it was – a goodbye.

As he let go, she noticed a flash of red in his hair.

'Wait, your head is bleeding.'

George's hand flew to his scalp. Blood was visible in his blond hair.

He withdrew his fingers and examined the tips, now stained red.

'Oh, so it is. I caught it on the doorway as we left the bar last night. I'm surprised you don't remember. It bled a bit then stopped. I must've knocked the scab drying my hair.'

Maggie didn't remember it happening. She peered closely at the wound. 'It looks nasty. Here, hold this against it.'

She grabbed the bathmat off the floor and held it gently against the cut, trying to force from her mind thoughts of kissing, and anything else, as they stood toe to toe.

'You should get it checked out,' she said briskly.

'Maggie—'

'There's a walk-in medical centre near the marina in Saros,' she continued. 'You should go there when you get back. It might need glueing.'

His mouth opened to say something but he thought twice.

'I'll see you later,' he said.

She nodded. When the door closed behind him she breathed a sigh of relief.

64

It wasn't Mike Steadman who answered Maggie's call but Lara herself.

'Oh, I wasn't expecting it to be you,' she said.

'I came home last night. You were right: it wasn't fair on Mike and the kids, freaking them out like that. I told him everything and he's been amazing.' Maggie could tell from Lara's voice that the impact of unburdening herself to her husband had been positive – she sounded lighter, happier. 'So you don't need to come back to see me. I'm fine, I really am.'

'That's great to hear,' said Maggie, relieved that it meant she could get back to Saros instead of waiting for hours again at Palma airport. 'Does that mean you can tell me what else you remembered? I got the distinct impression yesterday that there was something you weren't telling me.'

'There was. I told Mike and he said I needed to tell you, however upsetting it might be, because it might be important.' Lara paused for a moment and Maggie hoped she wasn't changing her mind again. 'When I woke up on the sofa, I wasn't wearing the clothes I'd gone out in. I was in a black strapless gown, the kind of dress you'd wear to a black-tie function. I didn't check the label but I could tell it was expensive.' Lara let out a hollow laugh. 'It was actually one of the nicest dresses I've ever worn.'

'Whoever took you to the apartment got you undressed?'

'Yes, which is why I couldn't tell you. I feel violated just thinking about it. But Mike was right, I had to say something.'

'I wonder what the significance was,' Maggie mused. 'Why put you in an expensive dress you'd wear to a function and then lock you in the apartment?'

'Last night, after I told him everything, Mike suggested I close my eyes and really think about what I saw in the apartment after I came round . . . and there was something I'd forgotten. When I went past the dining room into the kitchen to escape, I remember seeing that the table was laid out like a restaurant setting. Like, all the cutlery, plates and glasses were in place. There were flowers everywhere too. I don't know what kind, but they were pink.'

'This is brilliant, Lara,' said Maggie. 'This should really help us. I don't suppose you remembered anything about where the apartment was?'

'A bit. It was in a street filled with apartment blocks and I don't think it was far from the seafront: a street or two away at most.'

After ending the call, Maggie rang Walker to pass on what Lara had said. He was intrigued by what she'd recalled about the apartment and its location and was also pleased that Maggie no longer had to go back to London. He didn't ask where she'd spent the night and nor did she volunteer it.

Thankful she no longer had to dash to the airport, Maggie stripped off again and jumped in the shower, scrubbing herself furiously as though trying to eradicate any lingering trace of George on her skin, all the while cursing herself for getting so drunk that she'd slept with someone else.

It scared her how attracted to George she was, though, and her priority now had to be keeping her distance. Professionally, she had crossed a line – getting involved with a family member she was liaison to could result in her removal from Operation Pivot, and she wasn't about to ruin her career over a silly mistake.

She was leaning down to slip her shoes on when she spotted the wallet on the floor, half tucked beneath the bedside table. She checked inside and the credit cards confirmed it was George's. Shit. Now she'd have to speak to him to give it back.

She was about to close it when the logo on a business card tucked into one of the pouches made her stop. Easing the card out, she saw it was for the jewellery store in Palma where George was almost arrested for causing a scene. She turned the card over in her hand and saw there was writing on the back:

Replica, 255 euros.

Maggie sank down onto the bed. Was it really for a present that he'd asked about copying the ring? Surely it would've been easier for him to have one made in London? Maybe he felt he needed to appear as though he was going to buy something from the jeweller, however mawkish.

She went to slip the card back into George's wallet, but after a moment's hesitation decided to have a quick rifle through it. Amongst the credit cards, driving licence and euro notes in tens and twenties were three more business cards. Laying them out on the bed in front of her, she saw they were each for villa sales companies, which struck her as odd, because Lyndsey said every time George had visited Saros he stayed at Orquídea. Why would he want a villa here, in a place he professed to hate?

She picked up the first one, for a company called Saros Villas, and dialled the number. The card was for a sales rep called Valeria and it was she who answered. Maggie was about to announce herself as a police officer, but changed her mind at the last second and decided to take a punt.

'My name is Lucy and I'm calling from London. My colleague George Pope recommended your firm,' she said amiably. 'I'm looking to buy a villa similar to the one you found for him.'

'Just one moment.'

Maggie heard the faint sound of fingers clacking on a keyboard.

'I'm sorry, but you've been misinformed. We have no client of that name.'

'Oh, I'm sure he said it was your company that found him one in Saros.'

'All our properties are out of town, in the hills around Saros rather than in the town itself. I'm sure we can find something perfect for your requirements though—'

'Lucy' didn't bother with goodbye before she hung up. Moments later, George was back at the door. Maggie hastily stuck the cards back in.

'I forgot my wallet!' he grinned.

She handed it over. 'I'm afraid some of the cards fell out where you dropped it, and I might've put them back in the wrong order. So, thinking of buying a place over here?' she asked breezily.

'Eh?'

'I saw there was a card for a company selling villas.'

George remained impassive. 'Oh, Johnnie gave me that. He was trying to get me to invest in some property. Frankly, I can't think of anything worse than buying somewhere here, where my sister died. Right, I'd better go, my taxi's waiting.' He hesitated then gave her a peck on the cheek. 'Bye then.'

Her phone went as she was closing the door behind him. It was Lou.

'Hey, how's it going?' she answered brightly, pleased to hear from her sister. 'I was going to call you. I don't know if we'll be flying back this evening now, with this missing person case still—'

'What the fuck have you done, Maggie?'

She was used to Lou swearing at her, but it was usually done in anger. This time though, she sounded concerned, and that worried Maggie far more.

'Me? Nothing.'

'Will's just called me. He's in pieces.'

Maggie's heartbeat accelerated in panic. What was wrong with Umpire?

'Why? What's happened? Is he okay?'

'He heard what you did last night. You must've accidentally called his phone and it went to voicemail. He's just played the message back.'

The air squeezed from Maggie's lungs and she couldn't breathe. *Oh God, no.*

'Maggie, he heard you and whoever you were having sex with.'

65

Philip looked down at the deck and then again at Johnnie.

'I thought you said you'd gone fishing.'

Johnnie stood very still, his face pale and expressionless.

'I think you should go now, Philip,' he said, his voice a monotone to match.

But Philip was not going to be intimidated off the boat without an answer.

'You lied about the fish. Why?'

'Please, you need to go.'

'Johnnie, why is there blood on that ice? And whose earrings are those?'

He could see it was a struggle for his friend's son to stay calm and while he was not frightened of him, equally he did not want to antagonize him.

'What have you done, dear boy?' he asked as softly as one could ask.

'I haven't done anything!'

Johnnie grew agitated, yanking off the baseball cap he was wearing and raking his hand through his hair. That's when Philip saw it was streaked with red.

'You have blood in your hair,' he stated matter-of-factly.

'I tripped on the deck when it was dark and caught myself on a winch.' Johnnie advanced towards him. 'You need to leave now. I want you to go.'

Philip looked deeply into the eyes of the man he'd known since boyhood and saw the desperation there.

'Whatever it is you've done, I can help,' he said. 'Talk to me, and we can work through it together.'

Johnnie shook his head and shoved the cap back on.

'There's nothing to work through. Trust me, you're barking up the wrong tree. Now go,' he said, even more forcibly.

Philip stood his ground.

'No, not like this.' He reached forward and grabbed him by the shoulders. He felt Johnnie's muscles tense beneath his grip but he did not relinquish his hold.

'If you loved Katy like you said you did, then you'll tell me for her sake.'

He felt Johnnie's shoulders give slightly.

'Please, talk to me—'

'Philip?'

The voice startled them both and Philip spun round to see Clive Reynolds standing on the jetty. Such was his surprise that he instantly let get of Johnnie, who took advantage of the moment to bundle Philip forcibly towards the walkway.

'Go and talk to your friend and leave me be,' he hissed.

'Is everything okay?' asked Clive, apparently sensing he'd interrupted a tense moment between the two men.

'Yes, all fine,' said Philip, trying to hide how shaken up he was at being manhandled off the boat. 'You're up and about early.'

'I came looking for you. I went to the apartment and your wife said you'd gone for a walk along the front.' Clive paused. 'I need to show you something. It's urgent.'

Philip's curiosity as to why Clive had tracked him down overrode his wanting to force the truth from Johnnie. With a brief backward glance, he climbed onto the walkway, accepting the offer of a helping hand from Clive to step safely onto the jetty. Johnnie looked relieved to see him go.

'Show me what?' he asked Clive.

Jade's dad shook his head. 'Not here. Let's grab a drink. You're going to need to sit down for this.'

For the second time in ten minutes Philip experienced a spike of anxiety. What could Clive possibly want to share with him? But the man's face was giving nothing away, its impassiveness an unfathomable mask. Philip was heartened, however, to see that Clive looked in better shape than the last time he'd seen him, sobbing in Patricia's arms. His posture was upright, his manner resolute. He had purpose again.

'A coffee would be good,' Philip agreed.

He took a last look at Johnnie on the deck of his boat as they walked down the jetty towards the cafes and restaurants of the Pine Walk. He'd replaced the baseball cap and was chucking the scattered ice overboard where the tepid water of the marina swallowed it up.

Clive ordered a beer. The waitress didn't bat an eyelid, seemingly resigned to British customers wanting alcohol at all hours. Philip couldn't help himself though, pointing out that it was not even eight o'clock yet.

'Hair of the dog,' said Clive gruffly. 'Don't be so quick

to judge either – you might be needing one yourself in a minute.'

Philip couldn't think what could be so bad that it would make him want a drink at breakfast.

'I'll have a latte, please,' he said to the waitress.

'Anything to eat with that?'

'Toasted cheese sandwich on white bread, with chips,' said Clive. 'But not two bits of toast with a slice of hard cheese in: I want it properly melted. Can you do that?' She nodded and he handed the menu back to her. 'Thanks.'

'What about you, sir?'

'Just a croissant, if you have any.'

'Plain or with chocolate?'

'Plain, please.'

'You're a man of simple tastes,' Clive commented as the waitress peeled away from their table to process their order.

He made it sound like a criticism and Philip was stung. They might not be alike by any stretch of the imagination but he wanted Clive to like him. He wanted them to be friends. They shared a special kinship, two fathers united in grief over the loss of their daughters, and he would be dreadfully upset if he thought Clive didn't gift it the same importance he did, or was dismissive of its uniqueness. But rather than confront the issue head on, he sidestepped, like he always did.

'What do you want to show me, then?'

Clive leaned back in his chair.

'Last night, the missus and me went for a drink in the hotel bar. Not for a big knees-up, though: we were getting cabin fever from being stuck in our room and needed to get out for half an hour. Mandy was worried people would point fingers at us – like, what are they doing having a nice time when their daughter's missing – but actually everyone was decent. People came up and said how sorry they were and how they hoped Jade would turn up soon.' Clive paused for a beat, swallowing hard before continuing. 'Then this chap comes over called Stephen, lovely fella from Scotland, staying at the next-door apartments with his wife and daughter. He said he'd heard the police had found Jade's sarong in an old cafe on a side street and, well, it might be nothing, but something had stuck in his mind and he'd reported it to the Majorcan police, but no one had been to talk to him about it yet.'

Philip was on tenterhooks, his body tense with anticipation as Clive's account continued.

'Him and his family were walking back from shopping the other day when they saw a man with a suitcase coming out of the gate that leads to the rear of that cafe. Stephen remembered it because they'd asked the fella to take their picture and in return he'd lugged the man's suitcase into the boot of his car and it was really heavy, like he had bricks in it or something. Stephen even makes a joke—'

To Philip's frustration, the waitress chose that moment to interrupt them with their order. He nearly told her to leave them alone as she went through a checklist of supplementary questions: did Clive want ketchup for his chips and would Philip like some butter with his croissant, or perhaps jam? Eventually she took the hint and went away, but both ignored the food and drinks in front of them as Clive resumed his tale.

'So, Stephen makes a joke about excess baggage and that's that. They walk off, but a little bit further down the road

Stephen and his family stop again, because their kid wants another picture taken – they'd bought her this massive unicorn inflatable,' Clive added, as though that was important. 'Anyhow, when Stephen hears about Jade, and the sarong, he starts thinking about the bloke they saw coming out of the back entrance, and how shifty he was. He calls the police and they say they'll follow it up, but that was two days ago.' Clive fixed Philip with a grim smile. 'Then last night, while we're talking, Mandy asks Paula – that's Stephen's wife – if they checked the pictures they took that day, because you never know, the car might be in the background when they took the second picture. So Paula goes through her phone and, well, blow me, they didn't just get the car, they got a shot of the man too.'

Philip's mind raced.

'Are you saying this man might be connected to Jade's disappearance?'

'They're certain he was coming out from behind the cafe where they found Jade's sarong, opposite the shop where she was last seen, lugging a massive suitcase that weighed a tonne. What do you think?'

Philip's eyes widened in shock as the nub of Clive's theory hit home.

'You think Jade was in the suitcase,' he said breathlessly.

Clive pushed his untouched plate out of the way and leaned over the table, resting on his forearms.

'I think she could've been.'

'What have the police said?'

'That's the thing, Philip. I haven't told them yet. Not until I give you the courtesy of showing you the picture first.'

Philip faltered. 'I don't understand.'

'I know you've had a rough time of things, with what happened to your girl. I get that,' Clive looked pained for a moment, 'because I'm going through it too. I don't want to cause you and your missus more upset, but I will be, when I hand this picture to the police. Call me soft, but I thought you should have a heads-up first, before the shit hits the fan.' He slowly pulled his phone from his pocket and laid it on the tablecloth. 'Paula kindly forwarded me a copy.' Clive slid the phone across the table with his finger. 'It's him, isn't it?'

Philip peered closely at the picture.

'It can't be. That's not possible.'

'I think it is.'

Philip stared at the photo, which was taken at a distance. The man was standing at an angle so only part of his face was visible and the red baseball cap pulled down low.

'No, it's not him,' he stated, but there was uncertainty in his tone.

Clive jabbed the phone screen with his finger, the white-hot anger he'd obviously been fighting to contain finally erupting.

'That's because you don't want it to be,' he snarled. 'But unless I'm very much mistaken, that's a picture of your fucking godson.'

66

Maggie burst into tears. It was bad enough that Umpire now knew that she'd slept with someone else, but forcing him to listen to it, inadvertently or not, was the most terrible thing she could ever have done to him.

'I'll call him now,' she cried.

'He doesn't want to talk to you, sis. He's distraught.'

Lou didn't say it with rancour though and Maggie knew why. Nothing her sister could say to insult or berate Maggie would be any worse than what she was thinking herself.

'Who is he?' Lou asked.

'Someone I met in a bar,' Maggie lied. 'It was a stupid, drunken mistake.'

She couldn't tell her sister that George was the son of the family she was liaison to in Saros. Umpire might get even angrier if he knew and could report her, and she couldn't lose her career as well as him.

'God, I need to talk to Will. I need to explain.'

'He doesn't want to talk to you,' Lou repeated. 'He asked me to call to say he knows what you've done and that's all.'

'He must've said more than that,' said Maggie desperately. 'Will he forgive me?'

'It's far too early to be asking him that,' said Lou. 'Look, give it a few hours for him to calm down a bit, then I'll see if he's changed his mind about talking to you. If you push him before he's ready to, you might make things worse.'

Maggie wasn't sure it could get any worse.

'Does this mean the weekend is cancelled?' she asked, suddenly remembering that Lou and the children were due at Umpire's in the morning. 'Oh God, Flora and Jack will hate me when they find out what I've done.'

'I don't think Will is going to say anything yet,' said Lou. 'I haven't said anything to Jude either, but yes, the weekend is cancelled.'

'Jude's going to be so upset with me too,' said Maggie tearfully.

'He's a kid. He'll get over it.'

But would Umpire? thought Maggie. How could she have done this to him? She would hate herself forever.

'If you speak to Will again,' she sobbed, 'tell him I love him.'

'I don't think he wants to hear that right now—'

'Please, Lou.'

'Okay, I'll tell him.'

'Thank you. I don't deserve you being nice to me.'

Now it was Lou's turn to sound upset.

'I'm not going to lie – I'm still bloody angry with you for what you and Jerome did and I can't believe you've done the same to Will, but I don't like the thought of you being in Majorca on your own right now when you're this upset.'

'Don't worry about me, just look after Will,' said Maggie. 'He's the one who deserves your sympathy, not me.'

'You're not a bad person, sis – but I really don't get why you do stupid, hurtful things to the people who love you the most. It's almost as if you don't believe we care about you, so you test our affection to the limit, then wonder why we're struggling to forgive you afterwards. I've just about managed it, but I honestly don't know if Will can.'

The fifty-minute taxi ride from Palma to Saros passed in a blur. Maggie managed to pull herself together long enough to stop crying, but she felt increasingly desolate as she imagined the horror Umpire must've felt as he listened to the voicemail of her and George. She checked the timing of the call on her phone and was appalled that it had lasted for more than a minute before cutting off. She knew she should stick to what Lou said and not call him yet, but she couldn't not do anything so she instead sent him a brief text:

I'm so sorry. I never meant to hurt you like that.

When her phone began to ring a few moments later she felt elated, thinking it was him calling her back, but it was Philip, wanting to know where she was.

'I can't talk now,' she said wretchedly, and put the phone down on him. She felt awful for doing so, but the last thing she wanted right now was to talk to George's father. Whatever he wanted to discuss with her would have to wait until she was back in Saros.

After the taxi dropped her off she went in search of Walker but he wasn't in their hotel and neither were Paulson or Shah, who she presumed were back from Ibiza.

She tried the DCI's number but he didn't answer, so next she tried Shah, who picked up after a few rings.

'Are you in Saros?' she asked.

'Yes, we got back first thing this morning. We've left the police there checking their records for any similar abduction attempts that might tally with Johnnie being there.'

'Is the boss with you?'

'He is. We're at Annika's restaurant.'

'Oh. How come?'

'The place was trashed last night. Jasso called Walker about half an hour ago. We've just got here.'

'Shit. Is she okay?'

'She's shaken up but she's fine. She wasn't here when it happened.'

Maggie tried to think straight, which wasn't easy now her hangover was operating a jackhammer on the inside of her skull and with her mind preoccupied with Umpire.

'The restaurant was trashed? You mean burgled?'

'No, I mean trashed. Whoever did it wasn't there to steal anything, they were making a point.'

67

Jade had done everything she could in the past twenty-four hours not to rile her captor. She'd force herself to smile when he entered the room and asked him how he was, thanked him for the meagre rations he gave her and even offered to clear out the chamber pot so he didn't have to. That one had amused him the most: 'Oh, but I don't mind doing it, my love,' he'd said. 'When you love someone you take the rough with the smooth.' It took every ounce of concentration she had to make sure her smile hadn't slipped at that.

Now, however, her good behaviour was being rewarded. He'd agreed to let her dress herself for the dinner he'd planned for that evening and had even granted her request to have a shower, taking her to the bathroom in the handcuffs but staying outside in the hallway while she washed. To her disappointment, there was no window in the bathroom, and therefore no means of escape, which is probably why he'd been happy for her to use it.

There was a lock on the inside of the door, though, and she was tempted to bolt it shut and refuse to come out, but she knew that he'd go mad if she did and it terrified her that he seemed to become a completely different person when he was angry, the monster that took him over making him ugly inside and out. The rest of the time, it pained her to admit, he was actually nice.

Aside from the drugging-you-and-locking-you-up bit, she reminded herself.

She slipped back into her T-shirt and jogging bottoms, unlocked the door and opened it. He greeted her with a smile.

'You're done? Good.'

She touched her wet hair. 'Do you have a dryer I can use?'

'Everything you need is in here,' he said, leading her down the hallway to another door, which he pushed wide open. From behind him she could see it was a bedroom with a double bed pushed up against the far wall. Her step faltered: she did not want to go any further.

'Hey, it's fine,' he said, sensing her reluctance. 'This is the spare room. I don't want you to see the master bedroom until the time is right, otherwise it will spoil the surprise.' His expression flickered, hardening for a moment. 'That time is coming, make no mistake. I won't be denied again.'

Jade's stomach churned as she forced herself to nod at him. She was starting to feel unwell: she was stiflingly hot because there appeared to be no windows open anywhere in the villa and she felt faint from the lack of food. Part of the reason she needed to go through with the dinner was because it would at least mean she'd get something to eat.

He led her across the room to where there was a dressing table. Laid out across the glass top was an array of make-up and brushes and a hairdryer and a comb.

'The light in here is good for doing make-up,' he said.

He helped Jade to sit down on the stool – she tried not to cringe at his touch.

'Are you okay?' he asked, peering closely at her. 'You don't look quite right.' He raised a hand to her forehead. 'You're very hot. Is it the heat?'

Jade nodded.

'I'm sorry this place doesn't have air conditioning, darling. Let me get you a glass of iced water.'

He left the room without locking it. Jade swivelled round on the stool, eyes wide with surprise that he'd been so lax in leaving her unattended. Should she make a run for it? But what if the front door was locked and she couldn't get out? What would he do to her if he caught her? She shuddered in fright, turned back to the mirror, and began combing her hair, tears rolling silently down her face. He'd trapped her there without even having to lock her in.

He returned and set the glass down next to her. On seeing her crying, he crouched down so his face was level with hers.

'Oh sweetheart, what's the matter?'

'I don't feel well,' she admitted.

He stared at her anxiously. 'Maybe you're coming down with something. Perhaps we should rethink our dinner—'

She reacted too quickly, her nod too vigorous. In an instant his face changed and he rose to standing.

'Oh, I get it. You're just pretending so I'll postpone it,' he said coldly.

'I'm not, I promise. I feel terrible.'

'I don't believe you. Do you know what happens to liars,

Jade? They are punished. Katy lied to me and she paid with her life.'

'Please don't hurt me,' Jade begged, tears coming faster.

Anger and spite had twisted his face beyond recognition.

'That's what she said too,' he mocked. '"Please don't hurt me, I'll do anything you want",' he mimicked in a young girl's voice. 'You should've seen how she reacted when I told her it was too late,' he added in a chilling voice that rocked Jade to her core. 'So young, and yet so willing to please.'

Desperately she tried to clamber off the stool but he towered over her. He raised his hand as though he was going to grab her throat, but was stopped in his tracks by his mobile going off in his trouser pocket.

Jade was stunned when he answered the call in rapid, smooth, uninterrupted Spanish. The way he spoke it was as though he'd been speaking the language his entire life.

He ended the call and looked down at her.

'I have to go out for a short while.' Then his expression softened. 'Why don't you have a nice lie-down, darling, then you might feel better by the time we eat.'

His sudden niceness terrified her as much as his anger.

'What about my hair?' Jade stammered, the comb still in her hand.

'We can fix it later,' he said, helping her to her feet. 'But if you're still not feeling better later, we can postpone for a few days.'

Jade's heart sank at the thought of being held there a few more days. 'I thought you wanted to get to the third date,' she said.

It sickened her to have to ask about the stage where he

expected sex to be on the menu, even more so when he smirked.

'Aren't you keen! But there's no rush. Neither of us is going anywhere. You and me have all the time in the world, my love.'

68

Maggie hoped her hangover wasn't as obvious to everyone else as it felt to her as she hurried along the seafront to the restaurant. She ducked into a mini-mart on the way to grab a banana to line her queasy stomach and some chewing gum, mint flavoured, to mask any lingering fumes from last night's alcohol consumption. The gum also helped rid her of the sense that she could still taste George's mouth on hers.

Approaching Annika's restaurant, she could see the shutters were still down but the seating area outside was a hive of activity, with local police officers steering members of the public out of the way as they tried to rubberneck. She could hear voices echoing around the inside of the cafe, Walker's among them, and went to join them after informing the officer guarding it that she was a member of the British police team.

The scene presenting itself was exactly as Shah described it – tables and chairs on their side, food spilled from containers and produce pulled off shelves. More unexpected, however, was the sight of Walker and Jasso sitting together at the one table that remained righted: between them lay a sheet of paper with lines of type on it, which they were both closely examining.

'What's that?' she murmured to Paulson, who was closest to her.

'It's a note left at the scene. It's from our friend @three-dates.com.'

Maggie's blood ran cold.

'You're kidding.'

Walker must've heard her and looked up.

'Come and have a read, Maggie.'

Pushing aside her relief that he hadn't made a dig about her tardiness or her appearance, she went over to read the note.

Dear Annika
This is all your fault.
me@threedates.com

Maggie shared a look of concern with Walker.

'He's being so blatant now, it's like he wants us to find him,' she observed. 'Does Annika know what he's referring to?'

'She hasn't said anything so far, she's too upset to talk,' said Jasso.

The inspector appeared worn out and dispirited, the toll of the past few days catching up with him.

'Where is she now?'

'A friend has taken her back to their apartment in town.'

Walker cleared his throat.

'Inspector Jasso has had time to reflect since your discovery of the sarong,' said Walker. 'He now shares our belief Jade Reynolds has been abducted and that it ties into the Katy Pope case.'

'I shouldn't have been so quick to rule it out,' said Jasso quietly.

Maggie admired him for admitting it in front of a room full of people. Now they had to hope his change of heart wasn't too late for Jade.

'We need to get Annika to talk,' said Maggie. 'Can I try?'

Jasso looked sceptical.

'We get on well and if she's really shaken up she might respond better to a woman.'

'We should let her,' Walker said to Jasso. 'She's good at getting people to open up. And if it wasn't for her, we'd never have known about the cafe.'

Maggie's stomach chose that moment to force the banana she'd quickly eaten back up her throat.

'Excuse me,' she said, and bolted outside, where she took refuge under the nearest holm oak, gulping in deep breaths to stop herself being sick.

'Are you ill?'

Maggie looked up to see Julien Ruiz standing in front of her.

'I'm fine,' she said.

'You don't look it. Would you like some water?'

He proffered a small bottle of water in her direction and her stomach lurched in protest. Right now it didn't want to keep anything down.

'I'm okay, thank you.'

His expression darkened as he gazed at the restaurant entrance.

'Poor Annika. What a horrible thing to happen.'

'Do you know her well?'

'Kind of, in the way lots of people in Saros know each other. Annika's one of the good ones.'

'Can you think of anyone who might have a grudge against her?'

Ruiz was contemplative for a moment.

'Perhaps a disgruntled girlfriend or wife?'

'What does that mean?'

'There is a reason Annika is single. She likes to play the field, always has done.'

'You mean she's had lots of boyfriends? Were you ever one of them?'

He shook his head. 'No, I was never her type. In my teens I had a crush on her, I thought she was a stunning older woman, but –' he swirled his index finger at his temple – 'she can be crazy. She threw a brick through one guy's window once when he traded her in for a younger model. Ask Johnnie if you don't believe me.'

Maggie was surprised. 'Johnnie Hickman-Ferguson dated Annika?'

'Many years ago. He was barely out of his teens. She likes her lovers to be young and fit,' Ruiz smiled.

'So you know Johnnie too?'

'Again, kind of. He spent every summer in Saros with his family, as did I with mine. I'm sorry, officer, I must excuse myself now. I have to get ready for work.'

Maggie wasn't finished though.

'When did you get back from London?'

'Last night.'

'I thought you were staying until tomorrow?'

'I changed my mind.'

'Another young woman has gone missing. You must've heard.'

A flash of anger crossed Ruiz's face, rendering his handsome features ugly, but then he caught himself.

'I did hear the unfortunate news. If it's really necessary, I can provide details of my flights,' he said, forcing a smile.

'If we need to we'll be in touch,' she said. 'Do you have any other trips planned?'

The smile was genuine now. 'I'm afraid not. Back to work for me.'

He said goodbye, then walked away. He was a short distance off when she watched him toss some rubbish to the floor from his pocket. Litter bug, she thought.

Feeling marginally better after some fresh air, Maggie was about to head back inside the restaurant when an ashen-faced Philip Pope appeared at her side, as if from nowhere, and grabbed her by the arm.

'I need your help,' he whispered. 'I don't know who else to turn to.'

69

Philip trusted the police more than any other authority in the land. It was only natural, given his wife's stellar career as a serving officer. So he had no doubt that turning to Maggie for help now was the correct course of action. No other option made as much sense: Maggie was more empathetic than Walker in her approach and she would understand why it was imperative that he cleared up the misunderstanding about Johnnie being in the photograph before Clive took it to the local police. This was his godson and he needed to protect him.

Maggie would also, he'd decided on his way to find her, understand why he'd chosen not to tell Patricia about the picture. He wanted to be able to sort it out himself, like any husband would, before involving her.

Unfortunately, Maggie was not complying with the version of events he'd mapped out in his mind, which involved her rushing off with him to prove Johnnie's innocence.

'You need to tell me what's going on. I can't just leave without letting DCI Walker know,' she protested as Philip tried to steer her away from the restaurant.

'I have something important to talk to you about, but I can't do it here,' he said, his voice still lowered to a fierce whisper. 'It's about Johnnie.'

Her manner changed abruptly then, her expression shuttering at the mention of his godson's name. With a firm nod, she followed him across the road and back onto the seafront where Philip quickened his pace. The sooner they sorted this out, the better.

'What's the rush?' Maggie asked, walking fast to keep up.

'We need to find him before it's too late.'

'Meaning?'

Philip didn't answer and kept walking, but Maggie ground to a halt.

'Mr Pope, I won't come with you unless you tell me what you mean,' she called after him.

Exasperated, Philip stopped and waited for her to catch up.

'What is going on with Johnnie?' she asked.

'Someone took a photograph of him near to where the Reynolds girl's sarong was found and now Clive Reynolds has put two and two together and has come up with six. He's saying it looks like Johnnie is involved and I know he isn't and we should talk to him, you and me, to prove that he isn't before the photograph causes terrible trouble for him.'

'Whoa, slow down! I'm sorry, you said that so fast I didn't get any of it. Start at the beginning . . .'

Philip heard voices and saw a large group approaching them: a young couple, two children in buggies, three older children trailing behind carrying an assortment of beach equipment, and a couple of elderly people, presumably grandparents, bringing up the rear. Philip gestured at Maggie to sit down on the sea wall, out of their way.

'Right, tell me again about this photograph,' she prompted him.

In a low voice, Philip recounted Clive's evening in the hotel bar with Stephen and Paula from Scotland and the discovery of the photograph that showed Johnnie with the hire car moments after loading it with a heavy suitcase. By the time he'd finished, Maggie looked shell-shocked.

'Stephen believes he saw Johnnie near the gate that leads to the back of the disused cafe?'

'That's what Clive said he said. But it's a mistake, it has to be.'

Maggie gazed past his shoulder out to sea, her brow furrowing as she became lost in thought. Philip felt a stab of relief: she was obviously trying to make sense of it all so she could help him clear up the misunderstanding. After a few moments she returned her focus to him.

'Did Johnnie hire a car when he arrived on Majorca last week?'

'I don't think he can even drive.'

'But you don't know for sure.'

'Well, no,' Philip blustered, 'but he'd have said if he had hired one.'

'Did you know Johnnie's been making enquiries about buying a villa in the hills?'

Philip was baffled. 'Whatever for?'

'That's something he will need to explain.'

'Wait, are you suggesting you should question him about this? But that's preposterous, Maggie. He hasn't done anything wrong.'

To his horror, she got to her feet.

'I need to bring this to the attention of DCI Walker and Inspector Jasso.'

Philip was close to tears.

'I came to you for help, not to get my godson into trouble.'

'I'm so sorry, but I have to tell them.'

'Patricia will be furious with me,' he whimpered.

'I think your wife will understand more than anyone. She knows we can't ignore a suspect, even if it's someone she cares about.'

70

Philip did not wait for Patricia to shut the apartment door behind him before spilling the entire story about Johnnie and the photograph and how Maggie at that very moment was probably telling Walker and Jasso that their godson was involved in the disappearance of Jade Reynolds.

Then he stood back and braced for his wife's reaction, his expectation being that she would be either furious or disgusted that he'd made matters worse. What he hadn't anticipated was the calmness that seemed to wash over her as she let his confession sink in. She walked into the kitchen, him trailing behind, and flicked the kettle on.

'Would you like a cup of tea?' she asked.

He was confused by her response, and frightened.

'I know I've made matters worse by going to Maggie instead of coming straight to you,' he said as he hovered in the doorway.

'You did the right thing,' she said matter-of-factly, as though they were discussing a matter as innocuous as the weather forecast and not something that could see their best friend's son jailed for a long time. 'The police needed to know.'

'Aren't you concerned what will happen to him? Kidnapping, or worse – he'll go to prison.'

She plopped two teabags into mugs and fetched the milk from the fridge.

'Patricia?'

She fixed her lovely eyes on him.

'Johnnie has done nothing wrong and the police will see that.'

Her calmness was unsettling.

'These are the same police who have made mistake after mistake in their search to find Katy's killer. How can you trust them to do the right thing now?'

'Because, despite what impression I might otherwise give, I trust DCI Walker and Maggie to thoroughly investigate this supposed sighting of our godson and find him innocent. To say Johnnie is involved is to imply he also killed Katy and that's nonsense. We all know how much he adored her.'

Her assertion instantly made Philip feel better. Patricia was right – Johnnie had no motive for abducting Jade and certainly no motive for murdering and butchering their daughter. As he watched his wife busy herself making the tea, he realized there was a reason he should always let Patricia take control – it was because she was so much better at it.

They were about to take their tea out onto the balcony when there was a knock at the door. To his surprise it was Johnnie and he was clutching the gold hoop earrings and chewing-gum wrappers that had been in the ice box on his boat.

'Is Patricia here?'

'Um, yes, she's in the next room. Is everything all right?'

Johnnie shook his head. His skin was wan and he was trembling.

'I need her help.'

'What is it?' asked Patricia, who had come to the door too.

Johnnie held out the hoops and wrappers.

'I think someone's trying to frame me.'

71

Maggie didn't go straight to Walker to tell him about the photograph of Johnnie. She should've done, but she wanted to be sure herself. So, after texting the DCI to say she wasn't feeling well and was nipping to a chemist to get something to settle her stomach, she headed for the hotel where Clive, Mandy and Mason were staying.

Clive wasn't surprised to see her at the door.

'You've come for the picture, haven't you?'

She nodded and he gestured to her to come inside their suite.

'I didn't give a copy to Philip because I didn't trust him with it,' he said over his shoulder as he crossed the room, where Maggie could see a mobile plugged into a charger. 'He would have shown his godson and he'd have come up with some cock-and-bull story about why he was there. That's what I would've done if I was him,' he added grimly. 'Here you go.'

Maggie peered closely at the image on the screen. The man did look like Johnnie, but the image wasn't clear enough to say for sure, his face obscured by the baseball cap. When she tried to zoom in, the image became pixelated because of the distance it had been taken at.

'It's him, isn't it?'

'We need to get this enhanced properly before we can say for sure,' she said, grateful she could stall for time. Clive nodded approvingly. 'Can you forward me a copy to my phone so I can send it back to our tech team in London?'

Clive duly did as she asked.

'You'll let us know how you get on, won't you?' he wanted to know.

'Of course. It may take a day or so for us to get the image enhanced.'

Mandy was most upset by this.

'Jade might not have a day to wait,' she responded shrilly. 'Why can't you just arrest him?'

'It'll be up to the Spanish police to do that, but they're going to want solid proof first or he could walk free on a technicality. So we need to do this properly. But we can watch him closely in the meantime – see where he goes and who he's with. *If* he is holding Jade somewhere, he might lead us to her.'

Outside the hotel, Maggie called Walker and told him about the picture. She didn't say she had just come from speaking to Clive and Mandy – the boss thought she was at the chemist, after all – but instead explained Clive had forwarded on the picture and she was now sending it to him.

'I'll ask for it to be pushed up the queue to be processed,' he said. 'Shah's on the phone now to the cops in Ibiza – they've got an update for us.'

'There's something else. Julien Ruiz was at the restaurant a minute ago and he said Annika and Johnnie had a fling at some point, so there's history there.'

'You need to talk to Annika and ask her if Johnnie is me@threedates.com. I'll text you the address of where she is.' He cleared his throat. 'Inspector Jasso will meet you there.'

'Oh.'

'He's happy for you to interview her still, but he wants to sit in.'

Maggie wasn't thrilled at the prospect but knew she couldn't exactly refuse.

'Fine, I'll see him shortly.'

'Oh, and Maggie?'

'Yes, boss?'

'Try not to drink so much next time.'

72

The apartment block Annika's friend lived in was almost as luxurious as Orquídea, but fell short because it overlooked the main road that cut through the back of Saros and not ornamental ponds and swimming pools. A steady flow of traffic rumbled beneath the balcony where Maggie, Jasso and Annika now sat nursing cups of mint tea. Annika's friend had retreated inside so they could talk in private.

'This is the first time in ten years that I haven't opened up the restaurant,' said Annika. Her eyes were puffy and rimmed red and her hair scraped back into an unflattering bun that made her look older than she was. 'The last time was after Katy Pope was found. The restaurant stayed shut out of respect.'

Maggie cut to the chase. 'Who's behind @threedates. com?'

'I've never heard of that name until now.'

'Are you sure?'

Annika said nothing and averted her gaze. Jasso raised an eyebrow at Maggie. She'd met him outside the building and they'd agreed that they wouldn't ask her about Johnnie straight away, in case Annika clammed up. If there was history between them, there might be loyalty too, however misguided. So the plan was for Maggie to build up to it.

'Can you think why someone might target you in this way?' she asked. 'The message he or she left said it was all your fault – any idea what they're referring to?'

Annika remained silent and stayed that way as the minutes ticked past, and all the while Maggie grew more frustrated.

Jasso finally spoke. 'Ms Lindström, if you do not cooperate I can have you arrested for obstructing my investigation.' Annika reacted with alarm, clamping her hand to her chest. 'But I don't want to do that,' he continued. 'So please, answer DC Neville's questions.'

'I will, I'm sorry. This is very hard for me,' she said.

'I want to rewind a bit first, if that's okay, sir,' said Maggie. Jasso nodded. 'I've been thinking about that incident you reported in 2009, Annika. Do you ever regret withdrawing your allegation?'

The restaurateur frowned, clearly wondering where Maggie was going with this.

'No. Never.'

'Not even after Katy's body was found? It must've crossed your mind that the same person could've been responsible. I'm not sure I could've lived with the "what if".'

There was a subtle shift in Annika's body language. She was wary now, on her guard.

'Only two things would've made me withdraw my statement in the light of another woman's murder,' Maggie went on. 'That either I knew the person and didn't want to get them in trouble because I thought they were innocent, or they'd threatened me to make me withdraw it.'

'You're forgetting there is a third reason,' said Annika

abruptly. 'Mistaking the man's intentions in the first place, which is what happened.'

'I'm not sure how you can mistake a man trying to force you into his car.'

'It – it wasn't like that. He came on too strong, I backed away. I realized in hindsight he wasn't going to hurt me, so I went back to the police and set them straight.'

Maggie's mind came to rest on the memory of George the previous evening. Was the way he'd cajoled her into leaving the airport and going to the bar with him his way of coming on strong? The nausea she'd experienced earlier threatened a comeback and she had to force herself to refocus on Jasso, who was staring at her as though something was amiss.

'You only retracted your story after Katy's body was found, didn't you? It was a bit late for Declan Morris. Your description made him a suspect.'

'I don't understand why you're bringing this up now,' said Annika. 'What does this have to do with my restaurant being looted?'

'I think it has everything to do with it. Declan Morris was sent an email from someone claiming to be Katy's killer about a week ago saying they were coming back to Saros this week. Another woman, who we believe was the killer's first intended victim but who fortunately managed to escape, also received an email. Do you know what address they were sent from?'

The way Annika's face fell told them that she did, but Maggie said it out loud anyway.

'Me@threedates.com. So I'm going to ask you again, do you know who is behind it? Because that's almost certainly our killer and now he's coming after you.'

Annika began to weep.

'I never meant for any of this to happen.'

Maggie cast a wary look at Jasso, who looked equally uneasy.

'Meant what to happen?' he asked.

Annika faltered.

'It *is* my fault – I unleashed the monster.'

73

Patricia broke the stunned silence that followed Johnnie's outburst.

'I'll make another cup.'

Minutes later the three of them took seats in the lounge area.

'I think the police are coming for me, so we haven't got much time,' Johnnie said. 'But I need to tell you this myself, so you hear my truth and not someone else's version of it.' He dragged in a deep, heavy breath then exhaled loudly. 'I wasn't in Ibiza when Katy was taken and murdered. I was here, in Saros.'

Patricia shared a bewildered look with her husband.

'Dear boy, that can't be possible,' said Philip.

'It is. I lied. I'd sailed across from Ibiza two days before because I wanted one last shot at persuading her to dump Declan for me. Katy knew I was coming.'

Philip and his wife sat in stunned silence, until Patricia spoke.

'That day on the beach, she left purposely to meet you, didn't she? She engineered a row with me so she could flounce off.'

Johnnie nodded.

'Yes, but she never turned up where we arranged to meet. I waited and waited but there was no sign of her. I assumed she'd changed her mind about seeing me.'

'Why on earth didn't you tell us?' asked Patricia, her voice quavering with rage. 'That was vital information that could've helped the police track her movements. Where were you planning to meet?'

'On the boat I had back then,' said Johnnie, shamefaced. 'I was moored on the far side of the marina, where I wouldn't be noticed.'

'Where *we* wouldn't have noticed you,' she said icily. 'That's almost half a mile from the beach – Katy could've gone missing at any point between there and the marina. But instead by saying nothing you let the police search in the wrong place. I will *never* forgive you for this, Johnnie.'

'I don't blame you, but in my defence I just panicked. I never thought we wouldn't ever see Katy again, I thought she'd turn up safe. I knew she wouldn't want to risk your wrath by admitting she was seeing me, so I kept quiet, for her sake.'

Patricia erupted. 'Don't you DARE try to blame me for your actions—'

'I'm not trying to! I was being selfish too. I knew what the police would make of our secret meeting – they'd assume I was the one who must've killed her.'

Philip couldn't help himself.

'Did you kill Katy?'

Their godson's face drained of colour.

'How can you ask me that?'

'Because you've lied about everything else! And now there

is another girl missing. Are we to assume those are Jade's earrings and they just happened to turn up on your boat?'

'Someone put them there!'

'But that's not the only evidence against you.'

'Philip!' Patricia admonished. 'You mustn't say anything.'

But her warning was not enough to stop him.

'We've also seen the photograph of you with the hire car, and we know about the suitcase. Is that where you put Jade, before you hid her someplace else?'

'What hire car?' asked Johnnie, flabbergasted. 'What suitcase? What are you talking about?'

'You were seen,' said Philip, ignoring his seething wife.

'I've never had a hire car in Saros.'

'What about the earrings then? Where did you get those?'

'I told you, someone planted them in the ice box.'

'Poppycock! You lied about going fishing. Where had you been on that dinghy? To dispose of Jade's body somewhere?'

Johnnie looked to Patricia in desperation.

'I never hurt Katy, I swear. I loved her.'

Her expression wavered. 'I know you did. But people kill all the time in the name of love.'

'But not me! I wouldn't have harmed a hair on her head. Nor Jade – it's not me who's got her.' Johnnie raked a hand through his hair, desperation coming off him in waves. 'Look, this morning I was out on my dinghy because I had to deliver something to my friend's yacht, which is in the next bay. I said I'd been fishing because what I was doing was illegal. I swear to God I've never seen these earrings until you knocked the ice box over and they fell out. Someone came on board my boat and put them there.'

Philip didn't know what to believe.

'What were you delivering?' he asked.

Patricia answered for their godson. 'It was drugs, wasn't it? I always wondered how exactly you funded your lifestyle. I should have guessed.'

As Johnnie hung his head, Patricia turned to her husband. 'I believe him—'

A volley of bangs on the apartment front door suddenly interrupted them. Philip jumped in fright and Johnnie reared out of his seat in obvious panic.

'It's the police,' he said.

'Let me deal with them,' said Patricia, rising quickly to her feet.

But nothing she said could dissuade the Spanish officers from doing what they were there to do. DCI Walker, DC Paulson and DS Shah had accompanied them.

'Johnnie Hickman-Ferguson, we are arresting you on suspicion of the abduction and homicide of Katy Pope, the abduction of Jade Reynolds and the attempted abduction of Lara Steadman,' said one of the Spanish officers in broken English. 'You are also wanted for questioning in connection with the attempted abductions of three women in Es Cana . . .'

Johnnie drowned out the rest of it by letting out a high-pitched wail.

'It wasn't me; I didn't kill Katy! Tell them, Patricia, please.'

But it was too late. The officer restrained Johnnie's arms behind his back while a colleague applied handcuffs.

Horrified to see their godson arrested, Philip grabbed Walker by the sleeve.

'You can't possibly think it's him,' he implored.

'I'm sorry, Mr Pope. We need to let them do their job.'

'I'll call George,' Patricia told Johnnie. 'He'll know what to do. Where is he?' she asked Philip, as Jasso's men bundled a now-crying Johnnie out of the apartment.

'I don't know. I haven't seen him since he got back from the airport.'

74

Jade had vomited twice in the last hour and now lay listlessly on the bed, her skin glistening with sweat. She was napping fitfully when the door to the bedroom burst open and he came in. She barely had the energy to turn her head to look at him but when she did it made her quail: he looked furious. She had no idea what about, though, as he was muttering in Spanish.

He came over to the bed and retched.

'Oh God, you've been sick everywhere.'

The stench of her vomit made him cover his mouth and nose with his hand and he backed away from the bed.

'You need to get up,' he ordered.

'I can't,' moaned Jade. 'I'm too sick.'

He went across to the window and opened the shutters to let in some air. Jade winced and snapped her eyelids shut as bright white daylight flooded into the room, her eyes too accustomed to darkness to adjust properly.

'You need to get up,' he said. 'I need to move you.'

'To where?'

He wouldn't meet her eyes. Jade felt her terror rising.

'What about our second date tonight?' she said desperately.

The sequence of three dates was the only guarantee she had that he was going to keep her alive.

'I don't want to do it any more,' he said dismissively.

Jade grew hysterical and tried to sit up.

'You said I was the most beautiful woman. You said you wanted me.'

'Well, now I don't.'

'Please don't kill me.'

Suddenly he snapped. 'Why are you women all the same? Don't do that, do what I say – it's never-ending.'

Summoning her last bit of energy, Jade managed to swing her legs off the bed, but couldn't raise herself up and her upper body lolled backward onto the pillows, where she promptly threw up again. There was nothing in her stomach, however, and all that splashed on the pillows was bile and hot breath.

'Just leave me here and go,' she whimpered. 'I won't tell anyone. I don't even know who you are.'

'Do you think I'm stupid?' he breathed malevolently, thrusting his face towards hers so their noses were almost touching. 'You've seen what I look like. And because of that I'm afraid it's your turn to follow Katy into the pond.' Then he pulled back, disgusted. 'You reek of vomit.'

Jade knew that reasoning with him was pointless. The person he was had disappeared and all that was left was the monster who was going to kill her and cut up her body. With an almighty effort, she sat up.

'Please don't kill me,' she repeated.

He grinned maliciously as he advanced towards the bed.

Then, screaming as loudly as she could, Jade rammed the comb's plastic spike handle into his left eye socket. Blood began to spurt as he yowled in terror and she ran for the door, her legs pumping quickly. The sound of his screaming followed her into the hallway and downstairs, but to her horror there was no way out – every exit was locked and she couldn't find keys for them. Running back upstairs, she hurled herself into the bathroom and locked the door. She would rather die in here, alone, than be murdered by that madman. She dragged herself over to the sink and gratefully lapped cold water straight from the tap, ignoring the hammering on the door that had started up.

Pretending to be ill was a genius move her dad would be proud of. She'd had to force herself to throw up on the bed to make it look realistic, which wasn't easy when she had barely anything in her stomach, but it had worked. Her abductor had been too distracted to know she was faking it, just as he'd been too distracted to see her sneak the comb into the waistband of her jogging trousers when she was in the other bedroom. This time she'd made sure she didn't miss.

'Open this now,' he shouted, 'or I'll break it down.'

But he sounded weak, like he was in pain.

'Do your worst, you arsehole,' she screamed back.

More hammering, then he must've decided the conciliatory approach was going to have more effect. 'Jade, my love, I'm sorry. I didn't mean it. Come out here and we can talk about it.' Then she heard him let out a low moan, followed by a string of angry Spanish.

'Jade,' he faltered. 'I need a doctor. My eye—'

Suddenly there was a loud thump, then silence. Had he passed out?

Jade took the heavy ceramic lid off the cistern and sat

down with her back against the bath, cradling it in her lap, ready to use it as a weapon if she needed to. She had seen enough horror films to know that there was always a final scene when the victim was lulled into thinking everything was okay and they were safe, then the killer jumped out again to finish them off. Her dad had taught her to never be so stupid, so she sat on the floor behind the locked door and waited.

75

Maggie leaned forward in her chair, fixing her gaze unflinchingly on Annika's face.

'Who is the monster, Annika?'

'Before I tell you, I want you to know that I never encouraged him. It was the opposite, in fact. I never liked him – and that's why he's done all this. He punished those women because he couldn't bring himself to punish me instead.' She paused then, clearly upset.

'Go on,' said Jasso gruffly. 'We don't have the luxury of time right now.'

Annika nodded quickly. 'I understand. But I think it's important you know what caused this.' Her gaze landed back on Maggie. 'He had a crush on me. It was sweet at first and even though he was younger I found myself drawn to him. I thought he had a good soul. But I was wrong.'

She sucked in a deep breath while Maggie held hers in anticipation.

'He asked me on a date. I humoured him and said yes. It was a drink, nothing else.'

'When was this?' Jasso interrupted.

'A few weeks before Katy was murdered. During the drink he was being very forward, aggressively so. He kept saying I was the most beautiful woman he'd ever met and that we were going to have an amazing life together. He started talking about us having children and that we should start trying straight away, that evening. I felt very uncomfortable and scared.' Annika fought back tears. 'I knew he wouldn't listen to me saying no and I needed to make him slow down, so I told him that I always abided by the three-date rule – I never took things further with a man until we'd had three dates. But he knew it was a lie, because he knew I'd had other flings, some lasting only one night. That's the trouble with living in Saros, everyone finds out your business.'

'How did he react to you lying?' asked Maggie.

'Oh, he got so angry. It was like he became this different person. He dragged me outside the bar and tried to force me into his car. I knew that if I didn't fight back, he would take me somewhere and rape me. I discovered a strength I didn't know I possessed and managed to get away.' Annika choked back a sob. 'He was so strong, a young girl like Katy didn't stand a chance against him.'

'So he was the person who you reported?' Jasso was asking, as Maggie's phone suddenly pinged with a text. For a split-second she thought it might be from Umpire, saying he was willing to hear her out, and her stomach somersaulted in hope, but it was from Walker.

The Ibiza cops say someone matching Johnnie's ID tried to abduct 3 women in Es Cana over 4-year period, ending June 2009 – Katy murder date. We've got him.

'Yes. But when he found out what I'd done, he threatened to kill me,' said Annika. 'I was terrified.'

'You let Katy Pope's killer walk free,' said Jasso accusingly.

'So did you,' Annika shot back. 'You had him in your palm and you let him go.'

Maggie froze. 'How can that be? The police never brought Johnnie in for questioning.'

'Johnnie?' Annika reacted with surprise. 'You mean Johnnie Hickman-Ferguson? That's not who I'm talking about. Johnnie and I did sleep together once but we both knew it was just a one-night thing, nothing more, and we became friends afterwards. He's a lovely, kind man. No, the person I'm talking about is Julien Ruiz.'

76

Fifteen minutes later, Jasso stumbled out of the apartment ahead of Maggie, his face ashen after hearing the rest of Annika's account. Annika watched them leave, tears streaking her face, her grief raw.

'I was the one who checked his alibi,' Jasso said as they clattered down the staircase to the apartment block's car park, where his vehicle was. 'I spoke to the friends at the hostel who vouched for him.'

'You heard what Annika said he was like – I expect he either threatened them into covering for him or paid them to.'

'I took them at their word, Maggie – I never double-checked what they said. Martos was so convinced the killer was Declan Morris that he told me not to spend any more time on Ruiz, so I didn't. I filed my report and forgot about it.'

'You did what you were told to do,' she said. 'The blame lies with Martos.'

She was being kinder than she needed to be. Even acting under orders, it was still a monumental error on Jasso's part, who back then was an experienced officer and should've known better than to take the word of Ruiz's friends without verifying it, especially in the light of the statement given by the couple from Penge who claimed Ruiz had slept with Katy.

Less understandable was why Annika had never come forward with her suspicions about Ruiz. She claimed she was too scared of what he might do to point the finger directly, so she made up the story about seeing Katy crying on the seafront the day before she died in the hope it would plant the idea in the police's minds that there had been another male involved. But because the police – presumably under Martos's orders – had been so determined to implicate Declan, his name had been inserted into her statement and all thoughts of a second boy were forgotten.

Outside in the street, Maggie called Walker, who sounded jubilant.

'We've got the bastard. He was arrested at the Popes' apartment ten minutes ago. He was only sitting there holding Jade's fucking earrings.'

'It's not Johnnie, boss.'

'Don't be ridiculous. He's banged to rights.'

'He's being framed by Julien Ruiz. Annika has identified Ruiz as me@threedates.com and it all adds up. We need to find him before he kills Jade and before he lets an innocent man go to prison for what he's done.'

She heard Walker gasp.

'Start at the beginning and this had better be good,' he said, his voice hoarse.

Jasso got into his car and began revving the engine impatiently. Maggie jumped in beside him, explaining to Walker what Annika had told them about Ruiz attacking her and how she was now certain he'd killed Katy weeks later in a fit of retaliation.

'Why Katy though?'

'I'm only guessing here, but I think it's because she knew Johnnie and he might've introduced her to Ruiz while she was in Saros. It turns out Johnnie and Ruiz were as thick as thieves when they were younger. Both of them used to spend their summers in Saros visiting their grandparents and Annika said they started hanging around together and became friends. Ruiz was obsessed with her and was furious she picked Johnnie over him.'

The tyres of Jasso's car squealed against the concrete as it peeled out of the car park.

'Where to first?' he asked her.

'The restaurant.'

'What was that?' Walker wanted to know.

'Sorry, I was talking to Inspector Jasso. We're heading for Annika's restaurant.'

'Why?'

'When Ruiz was there earlier he dropped something on the ground. I think I know what it is, but I want to check. Can you meet us there?'

'Yep.'

'But can you find George Pope and bring him with you? Tell him to bring his wallet.'

Even though they were up against the clock and adrenaline was running high, Walker couldn't resist cracking a joke.

'Now's not the time to be asking him to shout us lunch,' he said.

'I'm hoping he'll do more than that, boss – I want him to shout us a house.'

77

Maggie had the passenger door open even before Jasso had applied the handbrake. She ran down the street and rounded the corner to the restaurant. Walker was already waiting, with Shah, Paulson and George. But Maggie ignored them, and went across to the holm oak she'd been standing beneath earlier, when she was feeling unwell.

'What is she doing?' she heard Paulson ask.

'Quiet,' Walker ordered him.

It took her five paces to find it. There, screwed up on the floor where Ruiz had tossed it earlier, was a chewing-gum wrapper. Cinnamon flavour.

The bastard. He'd dropped it right under their noses.

'Hey, you got a bag?' she called out to Shah. He hurried over, pulling a plastic evidence bag out of his pocket, Walker and Paulson in close pursuit.

'Ruiz dropped this when he was here earlier. It's like he wants to be caught.'

'I don't know how we didn't notice how similar he and Johnnie are,' said Paulson.

'When they were younger perhaps, but Johnnie's long hair makes it harder now,' said Shah.

'Yeah, but all it took was a red baseball cap and a false ponytail and Ruiz was the spit of his old friend again. I bet that's who's really on that photo with the hire car,' said Maggie. 'I bet it's also him who attacked those women in Es Cana – Annika said he and Johnnie regularly went clubbing in Ibiza together. Johnnie's been the gift of a patsy for him – not only do they look alike, but Ruiz knew Johnnie had lied to the police about being in Saros in 2009. Thanks to Johnnie's own stupidity, it hasn't taken much effort for Ruiz to point the finger at him. I'll bet you anything there's a paper trail for the lease of the disused cafe that leads right to Johnnie's door, because Ruiz will have set it up that way.'

Jasso, who'd joined the group, grimaced. 'I suspect she's right.'

'So where the fuck is Ruiz now?' asked Paulson.

Maggie stood up. 'George can help us with that.'

The group went over to where George stood. She had no time to dwell on the look he gave her, or the shiver she felt from standing so close to him.

'Have you still got that card from that villa company?' she asked him.

He fished it out of his wallet and handed it to her. She pulled out her phone and began dialling Valeria the sales rep's number.

'You said Johnnie gave you this.'

George nodded. 'Yes, he said someone he knew in Saros had been talking about investing in property out here and Johnnie thought we should look into it. The friend recommended this company.'

'I bet that someone was Ruiz,' said Maggie. 'It'll be another part of his paper trail.'

As the call was about to connect, she handed her mobile to Jasso.

'My Spanish is terrible, so you should do this. If I'm right, Ruiz will have bought the villa in Johnnie's name.'

The rest of them stood silently while Jasso addressed Valeria in rapid Spanish. They all exchanged looks as he said 'Johnnie Hickman-Ferguson', then he abruptly motioned the action of scribbling in the air.

'Someone needs to write this down,' he hissed. Shah obliged, pulling out his notebook and pen.

'Can you repeat that please?' Jasso said in English. '*Villa Concorde, 2818 Camí de la Ladera*. Right, got it. *Gracias*.'

He hung up.

'You were right,' he said, passing back the phone. 'It is in Johnnie's name. I need to arrange tactical support. Julien Ruiz is a very dangerous individual and may be armed.'

'How long will that take?' Walker demanded.

'Thirty minutes, maybe more.'

'We can't wait that long,' said Maggie. 'If Jade's not already dead, she could be soon.'

Jasso hesitated.

'You know, she's right,' said Walker. 'I don't want a dead girl on my conscience just because we waited for the cavalry. We've got this.'

'Okay, but I'm in charge and I decide how we do this,' said Jasso firmly. 'I'll have some uniform officers join us. You can go with them,' he ordered Walker, Shah and Paulson. 'Maggie, you come with me.'

As they went to leave, George grabbed her arm. She glanced at the others, fearful they might notice, but they were already walking ahead.

'Be careful, Maggie,' said George. 'This Ruiz bloke sounds really scary.'

She nodded. 'I will.'

His next words tumbled out in a rush. 'I know I said we could forget about last night, but I don't want to. I want to see you again. I don't know where things stand with your boyfriend, but if there's a chance for us . . .'

'I have to go,' she said. 'I can't talk about this now.'

She felt like she was betraying Umpire all over again even talking to George. But as she walked away, she knew it wouldn't be the last conversation they had.

78

The temperature in the hills was far hotter than anything they'd experienced by the coast and Maggie could feel her skin already reddening beneath the blazing sun as she silently trailed Jasso round the side of Villa Concorde. She could see why it was the perfect hiding place for Ruiz to keep Jade captive – from the outside it appeared derelict, with the windows shuttered and the overgrown garden resembling scrubland. Anyone passing along the remote road would never suspect for a minute it was being occupied.

Jasso had his regulation pistol held out in front of him at arm's length, left hand supporting the weapon held in his right. It rattled her to think that he might be forced to use it if Ruiz was armed and that Jade could get caught up in the crossfire. Walker had begged Jasso to bring Ruiz in alive and let the courts deliver justice for Katy, but the inspector could give no such guarantee. They had to hope they could get to Jade before it was too late.

Walker, Shah and Paulson were quietly circling the other side of the villa in the wake of two of Jasso's officers, who were also armed. Two more were staking out the perimeter of the property's land, in case Ruiz decided to make a run for it.

As the two parties met at the rear of the villa, Jasso issued instructions to his officers in a low voice.

'Say it in English!' Walker hissed.

Jasso glared at him, but complied.

'I shall go in through the front entrance while my officers will enter through the kitchen door you just passed. You must all stay here, where it is safe – that is an order. When it's all clear, I will call for you.'

Jasso slunk off in one direction, while his officers went in the other.

'Fuck this,' said Walker. 'Let's go back round the front.'

'Shouldn't we do as he said?' asked Shah in a fierce whisper.

'Nah, the boss is right,' said Paulson. 'Let's go where we can see what's happening.'

Because of where she was standing, Maggie was first to lead the way. Moving slowly and as silently as she could, she inched round the side of the villa, her baton drawn. Suddenly, there was an almighty crash and Jasso fell head-first through the glass of an upstairs window. There were gunshots, then the front door burst open and Julien Ruiz sprinted through the garden and vaulted over the fence into the scrubland that surrounded the villa. He was covered in blood and where his left eye should have been there was a livid scarlet mess of tissue.

Without thinking, Maggie took off after him. She heard Walker calling her name but she ignored him and ploughed on, her eyes trained on the blue of Ruiz's T-shirt as he dived through bushes and darted round trees.

Despite his injury, Ruiz kept going. He was about half a mile ahead, but he was slower than she was, his pace and agility impeded by the flimsy deck shoes he was wearing. Gaining on him, Maggie saw his ankle turn as he swerved to avoid a tree and she knew this was her chance. He was hobbling now, barely able to jog. With a final burst of speed she caught up with him and threw herself at his back, sending them both flying to the ground. Ruiz yelled in pain, but managed to roll out from under, sending her crashing into a bush with spiky leaves that clawed at the flesh of her bare arms. Panting, she got to her feet and saw Ruiz had done the same. They stood a few feet apart, his one good eye boring into hers. The injury was sickening to look at and very new, but it filled her with hope – Jade must've done it, which meant she must still be alive.

'It's over,' she said. 'You need to give yourself up.'

'I am not going to prison for that bitch,' Ruiz snarled.

'Jade's alive?'

'Not her,' he spat. 'Annika.'

'You really did all of this just because she rejected you?'

Ruiz panted heavily as he spoke; he looked like he'd lost a lot of blood.

'She told us everything, Julien. She didn't fancy you and you didn't like it, so you decided to get your revenge by going after other women. You're not much of a man though, are you, Ruiz? You could only get them by hurting them? No wonder Annika thought you'd be a crap lover.'

Everything she said was designed to provoke a reaction and it worked.

'Have you ever loved someone so much you'd do anything to be with them?' he yelled at her. 'I wanted to make Annika my wife and the mother of my children. She was everything I wanted in a partner. But no, she said I was sexually impulsive and had no control when it came to women and that I wasn't capable of being in a committed relationship.'

'You think snatching Katy off the street and killing her was the way to show Annika she was wrong about you?' Maggie asked him scathingly.

'You don't understand. I did it to prove I could wait until after we'd had three dates to consummate the relationship, like Annika said she wanted. So I practised being patient on other women.'

Maggie gasped. 'You mean that Katy was an *experiment*?'

'If you're asking was she a means to an end, yes.'

Maggie was reeling. 'All those women you tried to abduct – Lara Steadman, the victims in Es Cana . . . you wanted to practise being the perfect boyfriend on them?'

'Yes. Most of the women I meet are sluts,' Ruiz said matter-of-factly. 'They will have sex with me within half an hour of meeting. It's so easy. I needed girls who already had partners, who wouldn't succumb too soon.'

'Your accent – Jade's fiancé said you were British.'

Maggie recoiled as a rictus grin spread across his face, morphing him into someone she didn't recognize and wanted to recoil from.

'Oh, but I can be anyone I want to be, officer,' he said in a perfect British accent that betrayed no hint of his Spanish roots. 'I have an aptitude for languages,' he added, now with a German twang. 'My tutors at school said I was most gifted.' Finally, French. 'I have travelled Europe and, wherever I have visited, the people there have presumed I am a native.'

With growing horror, Maggie suddenly realized Ruiz's victims could number far more than the few they knew about. How many other women had he lured into his experiment with flattery and compliments who were now too ashamed to come forward and admit what he'd done to them?

Maggie could hear footsteps crackling in the scrubland behind her and felt a pang of relief that help was coming, but didn't turn round.

'Why did you kill Katy?'

'I had to: she was willing to have sex with me after only the first night. She begged me, in fact. I was very angry, because it meant I was back to square one. So I had to get rid of her.'

Maggie boiled with fury. 'She was probably terrified you were going to kill her and thought the only way to not get hurt was to let you rape her, you bastard.'

Ruiz's one good eye widened.

'Really? I hadn't thought of that.'

Maggie clenched her fists at her side. She could quite happily rip his other eye out with her bare fingers.

'Why did you dispose of her body like that?'

'It was fun,' he shrugged. 'The excitement of almost getting caught near the ponds was thrilling.'

The man's a psychopath, she thought with a shudder.

'So why stop now? The emails you sent, the chewing-gum wrapper you dropped this morning, trashing the restaurant – you *wanted* us to catch you.'

His shoulders sagged. 'I am tired of making all the effort. I want to settle down now and have my children.'

Maggie laughed incredulously at his crazed notion that he could just move on from this as if nothing had happened.

'I don't think Annika has been swayed by your experiment,' she said.

Suddenly he turned on her, teeth bared.

'What about you, DC Neville? Do you always wait for the third date? No, I bet you're a slut, just like all the others.'

As he suddenly lunged for her, a shot rang out. Ruiz slumped to the floor and blood began to blossom from the wound in his shoulder. Paulson and one of Jarso's armed officers scrambled past her to check his pulse.

'He's still alive,' said Paulson. 'We need an ambulance.'

'There's already one on the way,' said Walker, coming towards them.

He took Maggie by the arm, concern etched deep on his features. 'You okay?'

'A bit shaken up, but I'm fine.'

'You did great, Maggie,' said Paulson. 'We heard everything.' He had his fists pressed against Ruiz's chest to stem the bleeding. 'I'm not letting the fucker die – there's a prison cell waiting for him where he can rot for the rest of his life.'

'What about Jade?' Maggie asked Walker.

'She's alive and unharmed. She'd managed to lock herself in the bathroom after stabbing him in the eye. She's a very brave and very lucky young lady.'

'And Jasso?'

'Multiple fractures but he'll live. Shah's with him.'

Maggie stared down at Ruiz's prone body.

'There are more victims out there, boss. I don't believe Ruiz has sat twiddling his thumbs for the past ten years, waiting for Katy's anniversary before staging another abduction. He's been practising, honing his craft. This goes way beyond wanting to win Annika over; it's about the control he can exert over women.'

'I agree. I think that when we look at the places he's visited in the last decade we'll find others. The number of victims could run into the hundreds.'

79

Patricia was on the balcony, a glass tumbler in one hand and a bottle of vodka in the other. She'd drunk quite a volume already but Philip saw no point in pulling her up on it. Instead, he went to the kitchen and fetched a glass for himself.

'May I?' he asked, holding the glass up.

She poured a healthy measure, which to both their surprise he knocked back in one gulp.

'Another?' she asked.

'Why not? It feels like we should be celebrating, doesn't it, finally knowing what happened to Katy and with the person who did it in custody, but instead all I want to do is drown my sorrows.'

Her smile was tinged with sadness. 'I agree. It's bittersweet. I'm very thankful the Reynolds girl survived, though, and we should drink to that. Here's to Jade.'

She raised her glass and, as he did the same, Philip's thoughts turned again to Clive Reynolds, as they had many times during the past few hours. He must be overjoyed to be reunited with his daughter and overwhelmed with relief she was safe. At some point, when it was appropriate, he would write to him. Even though the photograph hadn't been as it appeared and Johnnie was innocent, Clive was respectful in showing him first and he should thank him for that.

'When will Ruiz appear in court?' Philip asked, knowing his wife would be up to date on everything that was happening.

'It depends on his injuries.'

Ruiz was now in hospital in Palma, under armed guard.

'Do you want to stay until the hearing?'

Patricia shook her head. 'I'm ready to go home now.'

They had decided, together, not to have any kind of ceremony, private or otherwise, for Katy in Saros. Instead, they were going to plant a tree at home in her memory. One that was beautiful and delicate, like she was.

After Ruiz's trial they would never return to Saros again.

George poked his head out of the door.

'Mind if we join you?'

'Of course not,' said Patricia.

He and Declan came out onto the balcony, each with a bottle of beer in hand.

'What a day,' said Declan. He looked haggard and Philip guessed why. Jade's description of her incarceration, fed back to them by the police, had left none of them in doubt about what poor Katy went through.

'Have you spoken to Johnnie?' Philip asked George.

His son nodded. 'I tried to convince him to come over, but he's in a pretty bad way. He blames himself for introducing Ruiz to Katy. I wouldn't be at all surprised if we went down to the marina tomorrow and he'd already set sail.'

Philip felt nothing but sorrow for his and Patricia's godson. None of this was his fault. He hoped Johnnie wouldn't become a stranger to them after this.

Patricia set the bottle of vodka down on the ground. 'I've been thinking, Declan. When we get back to London, you and Tamara should come for dinner.'

'Are you sure?' Philip blurted out, taken aback. His wife hadn't had a kind word to say about Tamara in almost ten years. Declan looked equally sceptical.

She nodded. 'I've always blamed Tamara for stealing Katy's happiness and I was too caught up in my own grief to think how she must have felt losing her best friend like that. The thing is, I know Katy would have wanted her to be happy and she would've wanted you to be happy too, Declan. I think, in her own way, she would have approved of your relationship. You found solace and stability – isn't that all any of us are looking for, really?'

She raised a hand and gently stroked Philip's cheek. George fought back tears as he watched his parents.

'I know I'm bloody impossible to live with and the way I am makes you feel inconsequential at times, but you do know there is still no man I would rather have at my side in life than you, don't you? I'm so very sorry I don't show it enough.'

Philip was so moved he couldn't speak. Patricia set down her glass next to the bottle and, for the first time in a long time, they held each other as they cried.

The fussing was starting to get to Jade, everyone clucking around her like she was a fragile ornament that needed careful handling. Her dad was the worst: he wouldn't stop crying, kept saying he blamed himself for not coming to rescue her. But she hadn't needed rescuing, she told him – she took care of herself and that *was* down to him. He'd taught her self-reliance and instilled her with an iron will to survive that she hadn't even known she possessed until the last few days.

'Don't be angry with yourself, Dad. You might not have found me, but you really did get me out of there, if you get my meaning.'

That set him off again.

They were at the hotel where her parents and Mason had been staying. She'd refused to stay in hospital and had discharged herself after being checked over. Bar dehydration, she was in pretty good health.

'Are you sure I can't get you anything?' Mandy asked her again, hovering anxiously next to the sofa where Jade and Mason were sitting together.

'Mum, that's the millionth time you've asked me. I've told you, I'm fine, I don't want anything.'

Mandy flushed. 'I'm only trying to help.'

'I know you are, and it's lovely. But it's all a bit much right now.'

Her mum nodded. 'It'll be better once we're home. Dad's on the phone next door to the travel company, trying to get some flights for first thing tomorrow. The police said as long as they can keep in touch with you by phone, it's fine if we leave.'

Jade shook her head.

'I don't want to go home tomorrow.'

'Babe, it's better if we do,' said Mason. 'We need to get back to normal.'

'I'm not bloody going home until I've had the rest of my holiday,' she retorted. 'I'm not letting that arsehole rob me of a decent tan.'

Clive heard the commotion and came through from the bedroom, his phone still pressed against his ear.

'What's going on?'

'Jade doesn't want to go home yet,' said Mandy.

'Why can't we stay until next Saturday? Come on, Dad,' Jade pleaded. 'Let's enjoy ourselves. I had a lucky escape and I'm fine – we should celebrate that.'

At some point she would have to process what had happened in that villa and face up to the horror of it. There would be the court case to come back for as well. But, for now, she didn't want to think about it.

Clive's eyes brimmed with tears. 'She's right. We should stay on and have the holiday we were meant to have. I'll ring down to the manager, see if we can keep the room a bit longer.'

'I don't know if we can afford it,' said Mandy worriedly.

'Don't worry, Mum, we'll get one of those newspapers that keep pestering you and Dad to pick up the bill,' grinned Jade. 'If they want an interview with me that much, it'll cost them.'

Clive laughed. 'That's my girl.'

Galen Martos had dined alone every evening since his wife left him seven years previously. He never blamed her for going, or for their children drifting away from him after the divorce was finalized. For too long they had to compete for his attention with the ghost of Katy Pope.

As he wiped up the last traces of sauce and rice from his dish of *arròs brut* with a piece of bread, he pondered what headlines tomorrow's papers would bring. No doubt his incompetency and failure to solve the case would be raked over again. There was a time when the criticism cut him deep but now he had toughened his skin enough to let it settle like a fine film of dust that did not penetrate. Who knows, perhaps Walker would mention his contribution, small that it was.

Meal finished, he left his apartment and crossed the road to the bar across the street, as he did every evening. Its tiny opening and location off the beaten track meant locals were the only patrons to frequent it and that was why Martos liked it. At the height of the original investigation it was his only place of solace, where he could escape from the pressure mounting on him and where no one gave him the time of day, much less badgered him for a progress update or a quote justifying why the killer hadn't been caught yet.

The mistakes he'd made back then were many. He had been absolutely certain Declan Morris was the person they should be focusing on and had too readily dismissed Julien Ruiz as a suspect. He wondered how Jasso must be feeling now, knowing he'd let the killer slip through his fingers by not checking his alibi properly. At some point they should meet and talk.

Stepping through the narrow doorway into the bar, Martos sensed immediately that something was different. Heads stayed resolutely lowered, no greetings rang out, and his usual drink, a shot of Grappa, wasn't on the bar waiting for him.

'What's going on?' he asked the barman in a low voice.

The young lad gestured to the small television perched on a ledge high up in the farthest corner of the bar. It was a news programme, proclaiming the killer of Katy Pope had been arrested.

Martos looked around at the regulars who had previously been so supportive. They all ignored him, bar one.

'You could've saved her,' he said. 'You let the bastard go.'

Martos had taught himself over the years to never let his emotions show in his expression, but in that moment he couldn't help himself as his face crumpled. The Katy Pope case had cost him his marriage, his children, his reputation. He would never escape it.

'I know,' he nodded, blinking back tears. '*Soy el hombre que dejó morir a una niña.*'

I am the man who left a girl to die.

Paula and Stephen McCall, the couple from Scotland, returned home as minor celebrities for the part they'd played in identifying Julien Ruiz as the man behind Jade's abduction. They were considerably richer too, with newspapers and magazines all over the world paying to publish their picture of Ruiz standing beside the hire car that everyone now knew Jade was hidden inside.

They used some of the money to pay for another holiday in Saros, because despite everything, they did love the resort. But this time they splashed out and booked to stay in one of the luxury apartments at Orquídea.

Two days in, their daughter Macy's brand-new dolphin inflatable developed a puncture after they left it overnight by the pool. Terry Evans swore blind it wasn't him this time.

80

Tuesday

The flight back to Gatwick was both excruciatingly long and also too short. On the one hand Maggie couldn't wait to be back on familiar soil; on the other she didn't want the plane to land, fearful of what she must face up to.

Umpire hadn't acknowledged any of the texts or voice-mails she'd left him in the past few days. Maggie spoke to Lou and all her sister could tell her was that he was devastated still and he wouldn't discuss with her whether he and Maggie had a future. He told Lou that he couldn't get the sound of the voicemail out of his mind: it was playing on a loop he couldn't switch off, no matter how much he tried.

Maggie's final message to him had been a text to say when her flight was due to land. It killed her that he still wouldn't talk to her, but she was hoping that, knowing the kind of person he was, he was waiting until they could discuss in person what she'd done. Then, hopefully, he would see how sorry she was.

She was grateful that she was seated away from Walker and the other two – they were all dotted around the plane, less of a priority to be seated together than the families returning from their holidays. The chatter of children excited to be flying echoed around her and she tuned in to it, allowing the sound to distract her from her own jumbled thoughts.

By the time she reached baggage reclaim she was churning with nerves. Only a few more doors to pass through . . .

Walker caught up with her as she hauled her suitcase from the carousel.

'The other two have already got theirs and gone,' he said. 'Mine's still not come round.'

She was disappointed Paulson and Shah hadn't said goodbye, but she knew they were both desperate to get home. It had been a long, tiring and emotionally draining eleven days and they were all shattered.

'I'll need you at Belgravia on Thursday to be debriefed, but we'll stay in touch anyway ahead of the trial,' he said. 'Operation Pivot might be over, but there's still work to do.'

Jasso had informed the team before they left Saros that they were all likely to be called to give evidence for the prosecution. Maggie would continue to be the Popes' FLO in the meantime.

'That doesn't mean you've got tomorrow off, though – your DCI wants you back at Islington as usual.'

The churning in Maggie's stomach shot up a gear as she thought about having to work alongside Mealing again, but she hid her anguish behind a brisk smile.

'Thank you for asking me to be a part of Operation Pivot, boss,' she said.

'It's been a pleasure.' He paused. 'Actually, once we've tied up all the loose ends on this case, the Commander's saying there's another cold case he wants us to have a crack at, this time going back twenty-five years. There's a place for you on the team if you want it,' he said.

'Seriously?'

'Seriously.'

The thought of never working with Mealing again made her grin. 'I would love to take you up on that, boss.'

'I was hoping you'd say that,' Walker smiled. 'Let's chat more on Thursday.'

After saying goodbye, Maggie rolled her suitcase along the 'Nothing to Declare' channel then went through the automated double doors into the arrivals lounge. Her heart pounding, she scanned the faces of the people standing there, a few holding up signs proclaiming the names of those they were waiting to greet, but Umpire wasn't among them.

Fighting back tears of disappointment, she walked on a bit then heard her name being called. Spinning round, she was stunned to see Lou emerging from the crowd. As her sister wrapped her arms around her, Maggie began to sob. She knew why Lou was there.

Umpire wasn't coming.

Lou steered Maggie and her suitcase over to a coffee concession.

'Wait here,' she ordered.

Maggie slumped down at an empty table and used her fingertips to mop her tears. Then she counselled herself. Had she honestly thought Umpire would come to the airport for their first confrontation? Of course he wouldn't. There's no way he'd risk unleashing his anger at her in a public place.

But it was worse than that.

Lou set a cup of steaming hot tea in front of her then took the seat opposite.

'Who's looking after Mae?' Maggie asked.

'Mum is. The boys are going to hers after school as well, so I can stay overnight with you. I've already bought the wine. Two bottles, in fact,' she said. 'They're in the car.'

Maggie blinked back fresh tears as she tried to make a joke.

'It must be bad if it's a two-bottle job.'

Lou nodded, her face full of sadness.

'Will called me last night.'

Maggie held her breath.

'I'm so sorry, sis. He doesn't want to see you.'

She felt a physical pain tighten her chest as she struggled to get her next words out. 'Not ever?'

'I don't know about that, but certainly not for the fore-seeable future. He's asked that you give him some space, then he'll contact you when he's ready.'

In that dark, grim corner of her mind where she filed away the uncomfortable truths she didn't want to confront, Maggie had known this was coming. What she had done was so hurtful and so unforgivable that she knew deep down there might be no coming back from it.

'I know it's easy for me to say this, but you will be okay, eventually,' said Lou, leaning over and clasping her hand. 'You'll get through this.'

Maggie shook her head.

'You will,' Lou insisted. 'This is the worst of it, I promise you. You won't feel like this forever.'

'It's not just that.'

'What?'

'I'm late.'

It took Lou a few moments to catch up and when she did she gasped.

'Your period is late? You mean you could be—?'

'Well, you know how like clockwork I usually am.'

'If you are, it'll be Will's, surely?'

'Of course it would be Will's. But me and –' Maggie couldn't bring herself to say George's name out loud – 'the other one, in Saros, we didn't use anything. We were too drunk.'

'Christ almighty, sis, you really don't do things by halves, do you!' Lou exclaimed. 'What will you do if you are? I mean, I know you've always wanted kids and you're not getting any younger, but . . .'

Maggie flashed her a wry smile. 'Thanks.'

'You know what I mean.' Lou squeezed her hand tighter. 'You know from what I've been through that it's really tough being a single mother.'

'You've managed,' said Maggie. 'You're a great mum and the kids have turned out brilliantly.'

Lou's eyes widened. 'Does that mean if you were pregnant you'd keep it, regardless of who's the dad or whether they wanted to be involved?'

Maggie stared at her sister for the longest time before she answered.

'Yes, I think I might.'

Acknowledgements

This novel was written in memory of two very special women. Firstly Lyndsey Shepherd, whose sister Tyler bid for her name to be given to a character in my series in the Authors for Grenfell auction, which raised £150,000 for the victims of the 2017 fire and their families. Lyndsey died from sarcoma in 2012, but in life she was an avid crime-fiction fan and always wanted to publish her own novel. I am thrilled to have named a character after her and I hope Tyler and the rest of their family take great delight in seeing her name in print.

The second woman whose memory powered me through writing this is Ruth Bond. Ruth was one of my earliest and most enthusiastic readers and I was always touched to hear how much she was enjoying the series. Ruth died unexpectedly last year and is missed by everyone associated with George Carey Primary School in Barking, where she was a much-loved member of staff.

As always, I must thank Vicki Mellor and everyone involved at Pan Macmillan for their support and hard work in getting this book to publication, in particular Grace Harrison. Enormous gratitude is also extended to my agent

Michelle Davies

Jane Gregory and the brilliant team at David Higham, and, of course, to Rory and Sophie, my reasons for everything.

But lastly I want to thank you, dear readers, for your enthusiasm and support for the books I write. You have taken DC Maggie Neville to your hearts and to your bookshelves and for that I am endlessly grateful.